Two of a Kind

Two of a Kind

Mina Ford

W F HOWES LTD

This large print edition published in 2006 by
W F Howes Ltd
Unit 4, Rearsby Business Park, Gaddesby Lane,
Rearsby, Leicester LE7 4YH

1 3 5 7 9 10 8 6 4 2

First published in the United Kingdom in 2006
by Headline Review

A CIP catalogue record for this book is available
from the British Library

ISBN 1 84632 624 9

Typeset by Palimpsest Book Production Limited,
Grangemouth, Stirlingshire
Printed and bound in Great Britain
by Antony Rowe Ltd, Chippenham, Wilts.

For Rob

A huge thank you to:
Rob Brock, my real-life happy ending, for your unwavering faith, patience and rock-like support, especially during those stiff gin and cranberry times – you are my strength; Rick Brock, for responding most unselfishly to those last-minute laptop emergencies and Sue for trying hard not to ask 'Is it finished yet?' too often. As always, a big thankyou to Judith Murray for everything – those teeny sandwiches and cakes were cracking; Marion Donaldson, for being very, very patient among other things too numerous to mention. Also, enormous thanks and love to Gerald and Sandra Ford – quite simply the very best sort of parents a girl could wish for and, of course, to Ginny Augustin, for bringing a new dimension to my life with the boy Reuben and for providing the inspiration for the theme of this book – I'm sorry I always used to cheat you out of your sweets.

RUBY

Cornwall, 1970

The new swimming pool, a flawless sunken kidney, sparkled Hockney-blue at the bottom of the garden. The sun glowed, white-hot, in a perfect powder-blue sky. Somewhere, Isaac was working. The sound of his circular saw, slicing through slabs of cool white marble, whined like a hoverfly on the hot, soupy air. Still full of breakfast egg, eighteen-year-old Ruby Gladstone flipped over onto her back like a beetle and stared at the fat moon of her stomach, silver-white and traced with fine raspberry lines, ballooning up at her from under her red polka-dot bikini top.

Isaac had built the pool to keep her away from the sea. Away from the waves that crashed onto the pale scoop of sand below the house, churning up chips of translucent pink shell that scoured the skin on her elbows and knees as, over and over again, she and her precious surfboard were washed up on the beach. In all his thirty-six years, Isaac had never forgiven the moiling monster that had

1

claimed the life of his fisherman father. He wasn't going to lose Ruby and the baby as well.

Ruby clambered out of the pool and slipped her feet into her favourite raffia wedges, intent on spending the rest of the beautiful day on the candy-striped sun lounger up by the herbaceous border. Earlier, she had heaped it with everything she might need for a serious day's baking in the sun. Oil. Grape-flavoured lip gloss. A tube of Spangles. Big sunglasses. Juice. A floppy sunhat and – last but not least – a battered copy of her favourite Agatha Christie novel, corrugated like a shed roof from an accidental dunk in the bath water and smudged with melon-coconut finger-prints.

She wasn't going to think about the baby. Not today. Moths flapped giant fuzzy-felt wings under the great cathedral arches of her ribcage whenever her thoughts drifted to the box room at the top of the stairs, freshly painted primrose and filled with snowy blankets, neatly folded and awaiting the tiny alien, curled like a butterbean inside her.

It all seemed to happen in slow motion, as accidents are wont to do. One moment, Ruby was happily trooping past the jumble of purple petunias, ox-eye daisies and jam tart flowers by the fence. The next, her heel caught on something and she was arcing through the air, crashing onto the crazy paving below. Dazed, she watched a drop of bright blood seep from a gash on her knee and trickle down the smooth biscuit of her shin as Isaac, alerted by her shriek of surprise, came running around the side of the house.

'HELL'S BELLS.'

'Language!' The midwife lifted the paper gown and prodded Ruby's privates with icy, unforgiving fingers. 'You've a long way to go yet, my girl. Baby was quite happy in there until you saw fit to go throwing yourself about like a rag doll. What were you thinking?'

Ruby gritted her teeth as another ring of white-hot pain gripped her middle. She didn't know about 'Baby' but if this agony went on for much longer, she was surely going to split in two. Burst, like the papaya Isaac had bought in the Indian market and left to ooze sticky amber liquid and glossy black seeds all over the tiled kitchen windowsill. This had definitely not been part of any plan. Her dreams for the future had been so much larger than this. Blowsy sugar-spun visions of herself, wrapped, like some morsel of marvellous confectionery, in fluffy layers of tulle. Bobbing in a curtsey to a round of thunderous applause. Bouquets as big as fruit bats, raining down at her feet. She'd always been going to be a Somebody.

But then she'd gone and fallen for Isaac. Isaac Harker, with his lopsided smile and a voice like golden syrup. And now she was going to be Somebody's Mum.

It was a girl. A fat little girl, Ruby saw as they lifted her up; a feisty Buddha bellowing gustily at the top of her lungs. Piglet-pink and squealing, she was a carbon copy of her father. Isaac's sloe-black eyes, starred with sooty lashes, stared intently from the crumpled face. The head was a mass of silky hair that stood up like a Chinese fan. The pain forgotten already, Ruby watched, surprised by the fierce protective impulse that swelled in her breast as the midwife bundled her daughter into a crocheted blanket and placed her in her arms.

She gazed down at her little one, drinking in every delicate feature. Cellophane eyelids. A dainty button mushroom nose. A tiny starfish hand, the fingers curling instinctively around her own as she traced their outline with a glossy lacquered fingernail.

'Hello,' she said in wonder. 'So that's you.'

Pain hit her like a punch.

'Something's wrong.'

Isaac snatched up his new daughter and ran out into the brightly lit corridor for help. Suddenly, the room was filled with people in masks and gowns. Poking. Prodding. Hurting her. High on a blast of gas and air, Ruby looked down at the livid splotches of strawberry splattering the sheets. Blood. Her own. Was she dying?

At long last, somebody spoke.

'Here we are. Tucked right behind her big sister, she was. Playing hide and seek with us, weren't you, little one? Nobody knew you were in there.'

There was a burst of jubilant whooping. Isaac? The nurses? Ruby wasn't sure. She was exhausted. Hovering on the smudgy fringes of delirium. She was vaguely aware that something important was going on but, after the searing agony of the past minutes, all she wanted to do was sleep.

Voices wafted through a green pethidine fog.

'Is she going to be OK?'

'Too early to say.'

'She is awfully small.'

'Looks as though the other twin was somehow able to absorb the lion's share of the nutrients.'

Ruby struggled to sit up. The doctor was holding something small and shrivelled in his arms. She could just make out a wisp of hair, curled into a lemon meringue peak.

'Did you say twin?'

The doctor nodded.

'Can I see her?'

The doctor and nurse exchanged glances.

'I'm sorry. We're going to have to take her straight to the special care unit.'

'You'll save her though?' Ruby's mouth had gone dry.

'Miss Gladstone . . .'

'Ruby!' Ruby said firmly. 'I'm Ruby.'

'Ruby. Your daughter is very poorly.'

'But she's my daughter,' Ruby told him.

She hadn't been expecting two babies. Hadn't even really been looking forward to having one. But now they were here, the idea of going home without both of them was unthinkable. They'd spent nearly nine months curled like coffee spoons in her womb together. It wouldn't be fair to part them now.

The doctor's voice was grave. 'We'll do everything we can.'

RUBY

Margate, 1976

The Garden of England was in the suffocating grip of a heat wave. Eighty-five in the shade, it was, and rising. A hosepipe ban was in full force. Ruby's parents' back lawn, once lush and peppermint-striped, was a parched and rusty scrub. A plague of biting ladybirds had invaded. They lay in tomato-soup drifts on the front steps and no amount of sweeping would get rid of the blighters. They were driving Len Gladstone mad.

'They can't get on the beach at Eastbourne.' Grace rolled up the *Daily Express* and fanned her face with it. 'Too hot. I'll be glad to see the back of this weather and no mistake.'

Ruby poured more tea. It was just like her mother to see the negative side of things. Her glass was always half empty. She lived her life according to a 'something might happen' maxim. Always expecting the worst. If the prospect of something good hovered, a silver hope bubble on the horizon, Grace's sharp tongue would always manage to pop it.

'That sort of thing's not for the likes of us,' she'd said, when Ruby's dancing teacher suggested twelve-year-old Ruby audition for a place at the Royal Ballet School. Ruby had hopped from foot to foot, her initial euphoria dissolving like a bath cube. Did her mother really imagine that a job packing Bourbon creams in a factory was preferable to spending one's life twirling across the hallowed boards of Sadler's Wells?

Apparently so.

Grace had never approved of Isaac, of course. For one thing, he was almost twice Ruby's age. And he lived in Cornwall. The other side of the country. They would never see her. But Ruby had stuck to her guns. She hadn't known Isaac long. But he felt like home. His house, on the cliffs above the higgledy-piggledy streets of St Ives, was about as far away from the tawdry glitter of Margate as you could get. Unlike her mother, Isaac didn't care if the washing-up never got done or if she never made the bed. In Cornwall, Ruby's life was her own.

She hadn't meant to fall pregnant so soon. Which wasn't to say she'd actively done anything to prevent it. Isaac had been delighted. Grace, needless to say, had been horrified.

Ruby's own feelings had verged on the terrified. But that was more to do with the prospect of giving birth than anything else.

Grace and Ruby hadn't spoken for over a year. Grace had learned of her granddaughters' birth from her husband. She missed their first steps. Their first words. Contact was resumed only when, shortly after the twins' second birthday, Ruby and Isaac decided it was about time they got married. Grace, encouraged by Len, had reluctantly agreed to attend the wedding. She was in all the photos, clutching a square leather handbag in front of her like a shield, her lips crimped like a Cornish pasty with disapproval.

'They'll have those runners off if they're not careful.' Grace nodded towards Len's careful wigwams of beans, dark green pyramids jewelled with scarlet blooms, through which, amid much hilarity, Harriet and Hermione were dodging their father in a convoluted game of chase. Hermione, always the ringleader, kept stopping the proceedings to issue Isaac with ever more complicated rules. Watching him try to keep up was a treat in itself.

Ruby cut another piece of church window cake and stretched out her legs. The hot sun had dusted her knees the sheer pink of freshly cut Turkish Delight. She knew it would be futile to point out that the two small figures, dressed in their current favourite summer attire of gypsy skirts and T-shirts scattered with rosy apples, were obviously having the time of their lives. Grace wouldn't understand. In her book, life was something to be endured. You got on with it. You didn't expect to *enjoy* it.

The girls, oblivious to Grace's pinch-lipped disapproval, were wrapped up in their game. They were both brown as conkers. Grace might not be enjoying the heat wave, but there was no denying that the twins were thriving on it. The endless procession of sunny days meant they could spend every waking moment outside. It had been a very Swallows and Amazons summer.

Isaac, stopping to catch his breath for a minute, caught her eye and winked. Grace couldn't have been more wrong about him. Really, Ruby thought, her heart swelling with love, he was smashing. She was a lucky girl.

She watched Harriet squat down to rescue a ladybird from the pond. That was her youngest daughter all over. She was such a sensitive plant. The other day, a baby bird, blue-grey and opaque-eyed, had fallen to its death from a nest up in the eaves. Harriet, finding it on her grandmother's garden path, had been inconsolable. Hermione's pragmatic 'It doesn't even know it's dead' had done nothing to comfort her. But then that was Hermione for you. Matter-of-fact to the last. Her girls were so different. Hermione was bolder. More optimistic. Harriet could be a bit of an Eeyore at times.

It was such a privilege to be allowed to play a part in shaping two young lives. Watching their different personalities develop was fascinating. Her early doubts seemed inconceivable now that the girls were here. She couldn't imagine life without these two bright sparks in it. The thought that she could have considered, even for a second, the possibility of not going through with the pregnancy coddled her insides.

But then, she'd never known before now what motherhood was like. A gummy smile lighting up a room. Fat thighs splashing joyfully in the bath. That first fistful of crushed primroses on Mother's Day. A pair of eyes waiting anxiously for approval as she examined a tissue paper lantern, stiff with flour and water glue. She'd never sat in a school hall that smelt of chalk dust and gravy browning before and felt unseen hands squeeze her heart like a bath sponge upon spotting a king with a wonky tinfoil crown and a small potato sack donkey shuffling onto the stage amid a host of tinsel angels and teacloth shepherds.

They'd almost lost Harriet. Two days after she was born, she developed a lung infection. Ruby and Isaac, shell-shocked and red-eyed as tree frogs, were told to prepare for the worst. Their daughter was slipping away. With tears coursing down her face, Ruby, still sore from the birth and already producing rivers of milk with which to feed her, had begged to be allowed to put Hermione in the incubator with her sister. If her smallest girl was going to have to do something as utterly momentous as dying, she didn't want her to have to do it alone.

The doctors had relented. An alert and bright-eyed Hermione was placed next to her sister. Instantly, instinctively, she'd curled round her like a coffee spoon and somehow, as though fortified by the protective cocoon her big sister provided, Harriet began to rally. Within days, she was over the worst. Five weeks later; she came home.

But they hadn't been in the clear yet. Harriet was smaller than her sister. She was delicate. She caught every bug going. At twenty-one months, she caught whooping cough. She was rushed to hospital, where Ruby and Isaac were told that things couldn't be worse. A more robust child might just have found the strength to fight. But their little girl was so fragile.

That time, Ruby and Isaac had deliberated over the wisdom of allowing Hermione to see her sister in such a state. Tubes snaked, Medusa like, from Harriet's thin, white body. From time to time, she was rocked by spasms. Nothing would keep her temperature down. It was a terrifying enough sight for them. What would it do to a baby?

In the end, they'd decided it couldn't do any harm. Hermione was dandled on the end of her sister's bed and, for the first time in days, Harriet opened her eyes. In that instant, Ruby, who had long believed the twins had some secret connection nobody else could see, was absolutely certain of it.

In the garden, Grace got to her feet. 'This is too much. I can't stand it any more.'

She made it seem as though she thought the sun had shone deliberately to spite her. The pointed look at Ruby, stretched out on the grass with her skirt rolled up to let the sun prickle the tops of

12

her knees, was meant to suggest that, if Grace couldn't stand the heat, then nobody else ought to like it either. It got Ruby's back up.

'For God's sake, Mum,' she said. 'If you don't like it, go indoors where it's cool. Weather like this is rare enough without you casting a flipping black cloud over it.'

Grace made her way towards the house, her shoulders sloping in a defeated fashion that made Ruby feel momentarily guilty. She shouldn't have snapped. But it was difficult to comprehend how anybody could complain about this beautiful sunshine.

She closed her eyes and relished the warmth leaching into her bones. A moment or two later, a shadow fell over her and she opened her eyes to see her father squinting against the sunlight. She smiled. Even in this hot weather, he was still wearing his cloth cap. His trousers were held up over his paunch by a pair of jaunty red braces and his vest was clearly visible under the cotton of his formal shirt.

'Hello, love.'

'Dad.' She grinned. 'Aren't you boiling in all that? You ought to find a pair of shorts. You'd be so much cooler.'

'I'm all right.' He nodded at the space beside her on the tartan picnic rug. 'Mind if I join you?'

'Course not.' It wasn't often she got to spend time alone with her father.

'Lovely little family you've got there.' He nodded

13

at Isaac and the girls, still playing their game among the beanpoles.

Ruby smiled. 'I know.'

She got the impression that there was something else he wanted to say. Like many men of his generation, he found it difficult to express his feelings.

'Is there something on your mind?'

'I was watching you with your mother.'

'*Dad!*' Ruby groaned. 'You *know* what she's like. She's so negative. Always bringing everybody down.'

'You mustn't be too hard on her.' Her father's eyes clouded with sadness. 'She wasn't always like that, you know.'

'Really?' Ruby sounded doubtful.

'She was a darling girl once. So full of life.' He brightened at the memory. 'Did you know we met in a dance hall?'

She smiled, surprised. 'I never knew that, no.'

Her father's purple eyes, faded now to a washed lavender, misted over at the memory. 'I saw her straight away. All dark curls and big brown eyes. I thought she was the loveliest creature I'd ever seen.'

'Did you ask her to dance?'

'Not right away.' He winked. 'I had a couple of gin and its first. Had to work up the courage, didn't I?'

'And then?'

'I went right up to her,' her father said proudly. He closed his eyes as if to let the good memory wash over him.

'Go on,' Ruby prompted. 'What happened?'

14

'She smiled at me. And I knew. Knew she was the girl for me.'

'What did you say to her?'

He smiled. 'I was that nervous, I just said the first thing that came into my head. I said, "Well, aren't you just gorgeous?"'

'So what went wrong?' Ruby asked him. 'When did she change?'

'You had a sister,' her father said awkwardly. 'A twin.'

'What?'

'Lovely little thing she was,' he said sadly. 'Like a little doll. She had these big china-blue eyes. Emerald, we called her. Born two minutes after you were.'

Shock seeped through Ruby like damp. She was a twin? Why had she never known? She'd never even suspected.

'What happened to her?'

'There were complications.' Her father's face worked. 'She . . . she lived for just twenty minutes.'

A cold, hard lump filled Ruby's throat.

'Was she . . .' She paused. 'Were we identical?'

Her father shook his head. 'No. Born from two different eggs, you were. Just like your two.' He nodded towards the girls, who had finished their game and were now sucking lurid ice lollies while they egged each other on to annoy Simon, next door's malevolent marmalade cat, who was curled like a bagel on the pink brick wall at the end of the garden. 'Must run in the family.'

'Was that . . . Was it why Mum didn't want to see the girls when they were born?'

'I think it brought it all back for her,' he said. 'She never really got over losing Emerald.'

'I thought it was because she didn't approve.'

'It was easier for her to let you think that. I reckon she might have been better if she'd had some of this, what d'you call it?'

'Counselling?'

'That's it. Course, you didn't hear of it then. It was only for loonies. But she might have done better to talk about it. I did try. I was upset too, you see. I needed to talk about it. But she wouldn't have it. Wouldn't hear the poor little mite's name mentioned. It was as though we'd never had another baby.'

Ruby wiped away a tear. 'But never to acknowledge she'd existed. All this time . . .'

'I didn't want your mother upset.'

'I know.' Ruby put her arm round her father's shoulders. They felt thin. Brittle. It suddenly occurred to her that he was getting old. 'It wasn't your fault, Dad.'

Together, father and daughter watched Harriet and Hermione collapse, panting, on the spiky brown grass by the shed. For the first time, Ruby understood her mother. She could empathise totally with the pain Grace had suffered, because she'd been there too. Of course, Harriet had survived. But Ruby would never forget what it had felt like to be on the verge of losing her.

16

Her father picked up his cap and replaced it on his thinning sand-coloured hair.

'I wouldn't . . .' he began awkwardly. 'I wouldn't mention this conversation to your mother.'

'I do understand,' Ruby said.

'I always wondered,' he said, 'if you felt it.'

'What do you mean?'

He shrugged. 'Well, they say, don't they, that if you lose a twin, you always feel as though there's something missing. Even if you've never been told.'

'I'm not sure,' Ruby told him. 'I always wished I had a sister. But I think it was more because I was lonely rather than out of a sense that something was actually missing. It *did* get lonely, you know, being an only child. Especially when Mum's nerves got really bad.'

A shriek, swiftly followed by a squeal of highpitched laughter, pierced the air. Harriet, egged on by her sister, had poked Simon with a piece of willow and he was hissing at them both, his back arched with indignation.

'No need to worry about those two.' Len fumbled for his pipe and started to stuff the end with cherry tobacco. 'They won't ever be lonely. Little minx, that Hermione, isn't she? Just like her mother.'

Ruby smiled. She'd always wondered what it might be like to have shared a womb with somebody. To be so close that nothing could ever come between you. It was strange to think that she had and that she couldn't remember anything about it.

She watched the girls squat simultaneously as they spotted something in the soil of the vegetable patch. There was no end to the things that fascinated them. Worms. Caterpillars. Oddly shaped stones. Most of the time they inhabited a strange, private world filled with sherbet and secrets. They even seemed to have their own language.

It was comforting to know that they would always have each other.

Her father struggled to his feet. 'I'd best get on with sorting those potatoes.'

Ruby watched him potter down the garden towards his beloved vegetable patch, then turned to look at the house she'd called home for the first eighteen years of her life. It looked just the same as always. A jubilee-striped fly curtain fluttered in the open doorway. Several plastic pots, filled with African violets and geraniums, lined the kitchen windowsills. Exactly the same. But different. Different because Ruby herself was different now. She wasn't an only child after all. She was somebody's sister.

As she looked up at the house, oblivious for once of Harriet's squeal of dismay as she brushed her hand against a stinging nettle, she was surprised to see a shadowy figure watching her from the bedroom window, a rueful smile on her lips. From the way she was standing, it seemed likely that her mother had watched the whole exchange between Ruby and her father. As Ruby caught her eye, the smile became wider and her mother waved at her. Actually waved.

A lump wedged itself in her throat.

'You should have told me,' she said quietly. 'I would have understood.'

A piercing scream, from the bottom of the garden, sliced through her thoughts like a sashimi knife through dolcelatte.

'She *pinched* me.'

'Only ' 'cos she pinched me first.'

Ruby stood up and brushed down her skirt.

'Come on, girls,' she said to them. 'What do we say about little birds in their nest?'

'They agree,' they chorused solemnly.

'Good,' Ruby told them. 'You two are very lucky, you know. You should be looking out for each other, not knocking each other's blocks off.'

'It was only a pinch,' Hermione, always the one to answer back, began. 'She started it.'

'I don't care who started it,' Ruby told them firmly. '*I'm* finishing it. Now then. If you can leave each other alone for five minutes, I'm going to go inside and make your Grandma a nice cup of tea.'

HERMIONE

Greece, 1988

Hermione had been lying low in the hammock between the olive trees on the edge of the beach for so long she'd given herself pins and needles. Judging from the position of the sun, it was midday. Which probably explained why her favourite stretch of sand was dotted with mad dogs and Englishmen, all disturbing the peace of this lovely little bay and stopping her from getting on with writing her journal.

She shifted position and lifted up a long, slender leg to admire her tan. She'd gone a couple of shades darker in the last day or so. The dusty toffee hue she'd built up as a base had finally deepened to a rich mahogany. The contrast made her fingernails, already bleached from all the salt water, look white as bones and the silver ring she always wore on her second longest toe seemed sparklier than ever.

There was actually only one mad dog on the beach. A scruffy brown one that, in keeping with

20

the rest of the livestock here, was rope-skinny and decidedly doddery on its feet. And the Englishman was in fact female. Her friend Lisa was over by the brightly painted fishing boats, talking animatedly to one of the men mending nets. As she threw back her head and laughed exaggeratedly at something he'd just said, Hermione slunk further into her hammock, hoping to remain hidden from view. She wanted to be left in peace with Gigi, which was what she'd called her diary ever since she was about thirteen. It was rather like confiding all her secrets to a French can-can dancer with a naughty glint in her eye.

When Lisa had invited her to come island-hopping for the summer, it had seemed like a great idea. She'd had nothing better to do. And she could definitely do with some sun after all the stress of exams. At least, that was what she'd told Harriet, holed up in her unnaturally tidy bedroom, surrounded by brushes and tubes of gouache for the summer.

Hermione didn't know much about art. But she was a great lover of words. She particularly loved learning new ones. Meeting a person with a name she'd never heard before was always a source of fascination. She would roll the word around her tongue like a gobstopper until she'd got the feel of it before she used it. Harriet's paints held the same sort of allure. The colours had amazing names. Rose Madder. Burnt Sienna. Havannah Lake. Raw Umber. Zinc White. She just had to remember to put them back in their correct order after she'd looked at them. If Harriet found them all jumbled up when she came to use them, she would be mad as snakes.

Hermione squeezed a worm of Banana Boat lotion into the palm of her hand and started to rub it into the tops of her feet, inhaling the sweet, holiday scent. She was damn sure that, unlike her sister, who was hoping to study for a degree in fine art, she wouldn't be going anywhere near a university in September. She'd applied to study English. It was her favourite subject. She'd loved all her set texts. Shakespeare. Chaucer. Austen. Atwood. Unlike Harriet, she tended to leave everything to the last minute. She never intended to. She started each school year with a bagful of pristine exercise books and a whole bunch of good intentions, only to discover in late May that if she didn't get a wriggle on, she was going to cock things up spectacularly. Usually, she managed to pull her finger out just in time and got through by the skin of her teeth. This year, however, something had happened in the last couple of months that had impinged rather heavily on her studies.

She'd discovered sex.

Actually, she decided, flipping to the relevant page in her diary to relive it all in glorious, sordid detail, it wasn't so much that she'd discovered sex. Sex, in all its deliciously naughty splendour, had discovered *her*.

May the twenty-second. The date was etched

indelibly on her brain, like the last split second of a firework on the night sky. She'd made an appointment to see Mr Sinclair, the English teacher. Ostensibly, it had been about Hamlet's first soliloquy. But it wasn't exactly a hardship to have to sit in Mr Sinclair's office for an hour on a sunshiny Monday lunchtime, even when it had become apparent from the aroma wafting from the dining hall over the rose garden that she was missing out on chocolate toothpaste pudding.

Mr Sinclair was what was commonly known among her contemporaries in the Lower Sixth as a bit of a fox. As perfectly sculpted as Michelangelo's David, he oozed an appeal that had very little to do with pastoral care and a lot to do with the mysterious delights Hermione and her friends giggled over in the advice pages of *Just Seventeen*. The mere sight of him reaching up to write something on the blackboard, which almost always resulted in his shirt rising to reveal a delicious caramel-coloured slice of back, had half the class drooling in their seats. It was pretty difficult to concentrate on T.S. Eliot's use of imagery in *The Love Song of J. Alfred Prufrock* with such a honed and toned example of manhood staring you in the face.

In honour of her visit to Mr Sinclair's office, Hermione had bunked off the last lesson before lunch. European history. Grimmer than grim. The foreign policy of Ferdinand and Isabella of Spain and the shenanigans of Richelieu and Mazarin

23

seemed to her to have very little to do with real life. Instead, she spent half an hour in the common room, winding a red liquorice bootlace round her finger as she pored over the make-up tips in somebody's glossy magazine before slap-slapping in her black ballerina slippers to the toilets to rim her eyelids with thick, black kohl and douse herself liberally in Paris. When she was satisfied, she undid her ponytail, sending chestnut curls tumbling down her back, and rolled up the waistband of her regulation skirt to reveal a generous expanse of sun-blushed thigh.

Even with her careful preparations, she'd never actually intended anything to happen. Mr Sinclair was *ancient*. Thirty, at least. *And* he was married. He wore a gold wedding ring on the appropriate finger. His office, Hermione noted with pleasure, was a complete mess, just like her own room at home. There were piles of papers everywhere. It might explain why he'd had so much trouble returning her essay on the portrayal of hopelessness in Marlowe's *Dr Faustus*. She perched herself on the leather chair by the fireplace, folding her long legs beneath her like a zip.

To her delight, Mr Sinclair offered her a cigarette, a sure sign that he regarded her as the grown-up sixth-former she was, rather than one of the little brats in the first year. She accepted the Benson and Hedges and leant forward, only a little self-consciously, to accept the light.

As they smoked and talked, Mr Sinclair told her

she displayed an understanding of Shakespeare that was mature beyond her years. With his battered copy of the play in one hand, he started to explain the inner turmoil Hamlet must have been feeling when he came out with all this stuff.

When he got to the bit about flesh melting, his eyes came to rest on Hermione's thigh and he shuddered. Actually shuddered. After all the effort she'd been to in the toilets, this made her skin prickle with indignation. Did the stupid sod not realise how lucky he was to have a seventeen-year-old sitting here in his office? OK, so she wasn't as pretty as some of the girls in her year. She wasn't an English rose like Melissa Danson. Or a dusky beauty like Priya Patel. But she wasn't that bloody bad-looking. How dare he recoil from her?

As usual, she spoke before she'd actually had time to think about the consequences.

'Do you find me repulsive?' she whip-cracked.

Mr Sinclair jumped as though he'd been stung. 'I'm sorry?'

'You shuddered.' Hermione blew hula hoops of smoke towards the ceiling. 'When you looked at me just then you actually *shuddered*. I found it offensive.' She ground her cigarette out and made as though to leave. But Mr Sinclair got there first, pushing his weight against the door and barring her exit.

'You really have no idea, have you?'

'About what?' Hermione's heart was beating wildly. There was an odd sort of glint in Mr Sinclair's

25

eyes that made her feel scared and excited all at the same time. Something told her that the sensible thing to do would be to demand that he move aside and get the hell out of there. But she didn't feel very sensible. Besides, this was a bit of an adventure. She wanted to see what was going to happen next.

'About what little girls like you do to men like us.'

'What?' Hermione hoped she sounded braver than she felt.

Mr Sinclair swallowed hard and reached out to brush her thigh with his fingertips. When she didn't move, he reached out his other hand. Brushed the other one. Sliding both hands up towards her hips, he took her weight and lifted her up, carrying her over to his desk and sitting her on the edge of it. Shocked, Hermione was dimly aware that she ought to try and stop him. But she couldn't. She knew this was all wrong, yet she wanted it. For the past few months, she'd been carrying her virginity around like a lead weight. And wouldn't it be something to say she'd lost it to Mr Sinclair? They'd all be jealous as cats in the common room later.

She watched him unbutton her blouse.

'You come into my office,' he said thickly, 'with your lacy little bra showing through your shirt and I'm supposed to just ignore it? Pretend I haven't seen it?'

'Well, not exactly . . .' Hermione began. 'I don't mind if you . . . *Oh!*'

Mr Sinclair had expertly worked her breast free from the confines of her Marks and Sparks A cup and fallen upon it with a strangled sort of cry.

'You wanted this all along, didn't you?' He fumbled with his zipper.

'Well . . .' Hermione flinched as she felt his thing spring out and slap the back of her hand. It was the first time she'd seen a live penis in its erect state and it was a bit of a shock. Even so, she was determined to go through with this if possible.

Mr Sinclair was easing her school skirt up her thighs. He hooked his fingers into the sides of her knickers and pulled them down, discarding them with a flick of his wrist. Then he separated her thighs with his knee and, with a grunt of satisfaction, buried himself inside her.

It was over very quickly. Afterwards, he'd pulled out of her and, without meeting her eye, straightened to tuck away his now lolling penis. Hermione, still spreadeagled on the desk, a staple gun digging uncomfortably into her coccyx and a glut of pearly semen making a bid for freedom down the inside of her thigh, had been quite taken aback. Had she been that bad? So bad that he couldn't even look at her?

'Here.' Mr Sinclair fished her pants from the top of his anglepoise lamp, where they sat in a little lacy heap, like the top of some extravagant Knickerbocker Glory. 'You'd better take these.'

'Right.' Hermione's cheeks flashed with shame as she caught sight of the innocent little Marks and Spencer label sewn into the back of her knickers. She forgot all thoughts of boasting in the common room later. She wasn't quite sure what she'd expected might happen afterwards but she certainly hadn't anticipated this. This . . . *indifference*. As Mr Sinclair, apparently unaware of her continued presence, briskly went about his business, stuffing a pile of essays into his bulging leather bag and embarking on a mad hunt for a battered copy of *Coriolanus*, Hermione scrunched her pants into a sweaty ball and backed hastily out of the room.

She squinted against the lemon-bright sunlight and watched as Lisa waved farewell to the fisherman and started to hobble over the hot sand, her striped beach towel streaming behind her like a flag as she looked for a good place to sit and fry herself in the sun. The blue chambray shirt, knotted under her breasts, gave her already considerable cleavage a boost. Her round bottom, constrained by the tight pink cotton of her miniskirt, looked like two bouncy Andrex puppies fighting in a pillowcase. Her crunchy curls were in a stupid pineapple ponytail on top of her head and there were broad strips of lobster-pink down the backs of her moony calves. She'd insisted on lying out by the pocket handkerchief-sized pool at their apartment yesterday afternoon, even though Hermione had warned her she was burning. Privately, Hermione had thought Lisa was making herself look a bit pathetic. If it had been her with the porcelain skin, she would've made a big song and dance about preferring to stay pale and interesting, rather than try and compete. Lisa had a lot to learn.

Hermione picked up her journal and started to flip through it. Her encounter with Mr Sinclair was all there, described in vivid detail in peacock-blue ink. It was just as well she'd packed it. She couldn't risk leaving this sort of thing lying around.

She flipped four pages to the twelfth of August, ringed in bright red for her birthday. She was still in two minds about going back for it. There were the exam results to consider. She was fairly sure she'd failed everything. Here in Greece, it didn't seem to matter. The pine-fringed roads and pretty sugar cube villas seemed far, far away from the biscuity streets of Bath. And she and Lisa were having a ball, soaking up sunshine by day and downing noxious concoctions, coloured lurid lime-green and swimming-pool blue, by night. The weather here was fantastic. It was wonderful to wake up to the certainty of another sparkly blue day. Who wouldn't want to live here forever?

Lisa had said she could get them jobs handing out flyers at Coco Loco in the old part of town by the harbour. Nico, the bartender she'd snogged the face off the night before, had said he could swing it with his uncle. It would mean they could stay on the island for the rest of the summer. What could be better?

Yesterday, Hermione had been tempted. Today, she wasn't so sure. Lisa had started to grate on her nerves a bit. It was probably just the strain of being cooped up together in the tiny apartment they were renting. But there were things about her friend that had started to drive Hermione quietly bonkers. She never stopped fiddling with her hair. The air in the apartment was thick with lacquer, which seemed to pile up in the back of Hermione's throat like sand. Lisa left her bras hanging, like exquisite lace desserts, all over the balcony. Her nose sounded like a penny whistle when she ate. Hermione knew she couldn't help that but it didn't stop her from tensing her shoulders every time Lisa came anywhere near her with a plate of food. Which was often. Lisa liked to eat a lot. Hot dogs, slathered in ketchup and mustard and piled with fried onions from the man up the beach. Crisps the size of waffle irons. She never refused food. If Hermione offered her one of her barbecue flavour chips, she would accept immediately, only saying, 'Sorry, is that really piggy?' once the morsel was safely gobbled up. And she never offered her own back.

Hermione stared at her journal and her heart gave a little blip. There, in the space for 12 August, Harriet had written PARTY in her careful, neat handwriting. With a twinge of sadness, Hermione realised it wouldn't even cross her sister's mind that she might not come home for their big day. Every birthday, for as long as Hermione could remember, had started out exactly the same. Ruby made chocolate spread sandwiches for breakfast and then, when everybody had eaten so much they were fit to burst, Isaac would gleefully produce two large pink envelopes, each containing a set of clues to the whereabouts of their respective presents and they would spend the rest of the morning on an elaborate treasure hunt. Last year, it had crossed Hermione's mind that they were getting a bit old for all these silly traditions. She would have preferred to be given money, so she and Lisa could get the train to London and go shopping in the big Top Shop by Oxford Circus. Not that she'd said anything. Harriet was clearly delighting in the childish ritual and she hadn't wanted to hurt her feelings.

She glanced along the beach and saw that Lisa had found a good spot and was unhooking her bikini top to avoid getting strap marks. She had weird nipples. Big and brown and kind of floppy-looking. Very different from Hermione's own, which were small and petal-pink. She watched as Lisa oiled herself up like a salad and took a trashy paperback novel from her citrus-yellow beach bag. Hermione knew from experience that she wouldn't manage a page of it before she got bored. The only reading material that held Lisa's attention for longer than five minutes at a time came in the form of glossy magazines, filled with photographs of lipstick and eye shadow. Hermione wasn't averse to such delights herself. But she did like to balance things out. She enjoyed something a little meatier from time to time. She'd lent Lisa her copy of *Emma*. It still lay, unopened, on her bedside table.

She was tired, she realised suddenly. Tired of blue drinks in bars. Tired of living off beer and chips, because they were the cheapest things on the restaurant menus. Tired of the sewagey stench in the apartment's cramped bathroom. She was even tired of this weather. It would be nice to be able to get to sleep at night again.

Slowly, so as not to alert Lisa's attention, Hermione folded down the all-important page in her journal and shimmied out of the hammock. Not to go back for their birthday would be unthinkable. She could never willingly hurt Harriet. It was all very well wishing she could be a bit sassier sometimes. It had got kind of annoying recently, not being able to talk about the things she got up to these days. Especially the Mr Sinclair business. Having secrets from her own sister was unfamiliar territory. As children, they'd told each other everything. But perhaps that was something she was just going to have to accept. They'd grown into very different people now.

Harriet had said she didn't mind Hermione going off with Lisa for so long. But she hadn't really meant it. It was there in her eyes. She was struggling with herself because she knew she *shouldn't* mind. And, instead of saying she wouldn't go, Hermione had pretended to believe her, just so she could come on this holiday.

She knew she wouldn't enjoy the rest of her time here. Not if it meant missing the birthday traditions that meant so much to her sister.

She made her way through the dusty olive groves back to the apartment. There, she picked her way through the clutter, cursing as the ball of her foot came into contact with the plug of the enormous space-age hairdryer Lisa used for scrunching her hair into those brittle, lacquered curls. The cheap plywood coffee table was littered with stuff. Glossy magazines. Mascara wands. Tubes of lipstick, worn right down to the last millimetre. A giant can of hair mousse. She started throwing the things that belonged to her into her make-up bag. That done, she yanked jeans, dresses, flip-flops and little vests out of her half of the wardrobe and chucked them into her case. Her packing accomplished, she went downstairs to the lobby to wait in the queue for the public phone. Her flight from Athens was due to leave at eight tomorrow morning. If she got a move on, she could still make the ferry in time.

Now that she'd made the decision, she couldn't wait. It was funny. A month ago, she'd been dying to get away from Bath and its stupid smalltown attitude. But she'd missed her family more than she'd ever thought she would. She missed Isaac's stupid 'Dad' jokes at breakfast. She missed Ruby's weird experimental cooking. She missed the mod cons of home. Clean washing, appearing, as if by magic, in a neat pile on the end of her bed. Tea with proper milk, instead of the foul UHT stuff they served here. The bathroom with the huge roll-top bath that she and Harriet shared between them.

She missed Harriet!

Going home wouldn't be all plain sailing. There were still the exam results to consider. It wasn't going to be much fun having to explain to Ruby that the sum total of her efforts in the literary criticism exam had been an A4 drawing of Boy George in his Karma Chameleon phase. And there was Chris to deal with. The guy she'd slept with the week before she and Lisa had flown out here. He'd turned up at the airport, just as they were about to board their flight to Athens, to tell her he was going to wait for her. What a complete spoon! Shaking him off was going to be pretty tricky . . .

Even so. It would be good to be home.

She dialled her parents' number. It would be about ten in the morning at home. Isaac would be in his workshop along the street, his black hair grizzled with marble dust as he turned blocks of glittering white stone into carved angels and scrolls. Ruby would probably be in the sunny basement kitchen, listening to the radio and making something for lunch. Harriet would be in her room on the second floor, her salmon-pink tongue poking out with concentration as she worked at her painting.

Hermione imagined the phone ringing in the hall. Ruby stopping whatever she was doing and unclipping her earrings to come and answer the phone. It was reassuring, somehow, to think of everything carrying on as normal.

The phone was answered after a couple of rings.

'Hello?'

'Harry? Thatchoo?'

'Yes.' The voice, if anything, sounded disappointed. Hermione's heart flopped. She'd been away too long.

'It's me.'

'I know.'

'Did you miss me?'

'Sure.' Harriet's brittle voice, suggested otherwise. 'Did you want Mum? She's making syllabub.'

'It's OK,' Hermione said, crushed. 'You'll do.'

She shook herself. What had she expected? A street party, with bunting and beef burgers, like they'd had for the Queen's silver jubilee? The full-on fatted calf?

But then, perhaps something was wrong. Perhaps one of them was sick and Harriet wasn't supposed to tell her because it would only worry her.

'Is everything OK?' she asked.

'What do you mean?'

'Ruby. Isaac. Are they all right?'

'Oh, they're fine,' Harriet said. 'You want them?'

'No.' Hermione took a deep breath.

'Any message then?'

'Just tell them . . . tell them I'm coming home tomorrow as planned. The flight lands at half eleven your time. They said they'd pick me up.'

'OK.'

'What about you?' Hermione blurted suddenly, before her sister could put the phone down. 'Everything cool?'

'Sure,' Harriet said breezily. 'Everything's cool. Look. I have to go. I'm expecting a call. See you later.'

'But—'

The buzz of the dialling tone cut her dead.

HARRIET

Bath, 1988

Harriet stood just inside the flap of the marquee and watched Hermione show off her tan. She was the colour of finely polished mahogany.

This evening, sashaying down the back stairs in a pink cloud of Paris, Hermione had managed to eclipse Harriet's own party outfit completely. The flippy black skirt and scoop neck vest she'd chosen so hopefully had seemed gauche and awkward in comparison to Hermione's charcoal chiffon confection, which plunged in a deep V almost to her belly button, showing off the burnished knobs of her elegant collarbones and falling away at the back to reveal shoulder blades curved like sea-gulls' wings. Her long brown feet were bare, the toenails painted a delectable shade of metallic Calpol pink. Her eyebrows were perfect arches, her lips were glossed and her cheeks were like polished Beauty of Bath apples.

Harriet had been so looking forward to tonight. Their birthday was the one thing that had kept her focused while Hermione was living it up with Lisa in Greece. She and Ruby had spent the whole of August preparing for her return. They'd whiled away whole evenings poring over cookery books, finding the perfect food to mop up all the champagne Isaac was providing. They'd spent days stocking the freezer with hearty fare. Spicy Mexican dip. Chilli con carne. Saffron-coloured dhal. Slabs of garlic bread, oozing butter and fresh herbs. The marquee that had mushroomed in the back garden yesterday afternoon looked fantastic. Hundreds of tiny white fairy lights twinkled behind backdrops of fondant-pink voile. Vases of fat blowsy peonies stood on all the tables and pink helium balloons, shaped like stars, bobbed in the corners.

Over by the dance floor, where the DJ was playing the latest hits, Vince Greenwood and Tim Luttrell had untied several shiny clusters and inhaled the contents amid much hilarity. Harriet found their squeaky Mickey Mouse voices irritating.

It was funny how you could so look forward to something only to find that, when it actually arrived, you couldn't summon an ounce of enthusiasm. As the fat beat of Salt'n'Pepa's 'Push It' filled the slightly fusty air in the tent, Harriet felt a great blueness engulf her like a prison blanket.

Salt'n'Pepa segued into Yazz and the Plastic Population and the floor filled with sweaty bodies, writhing and popping in time to the music. Harriet checked her watch. Nine o'clock. If he was coming, he would surely be here soon.

Will.

She'd met him the day after Hermione, laden with suntan lotion and a dozen rainbow bikinis, had waved her goodbye at Gatwick. Since then, he'd been all she could think about. Dark of hair and chiselled of jaw, he was a teenage girl's wet dream. To Harriet, he was an opportunity to shake off the ball and chain of her virginity and gain a foothold in Hermione's brave new world. Lately, she'd felt distanced from her sister. This way, when Hermione got back from Greece, they would finally be able to share secrets again.

She'd lost her virginity all right. That bit, at least, had gone according to plan. Will had been only too pleased to relieve her of it in the back of his peppermint-blue Ford Cortina. Thereafter, they'd done it as often as possible. Two weeks ago, Will's parents, Keith and Sheila, had gone to their apartment in Marbella and Will and Harriet had taken up residence in their large four-bedroom detached, complete with feature fireplace and serving hatch. They'd gone to the pub every night and brought back a noisy crowd, who stubbed out their cigarettes in the cheese plant and bugged Will's sister by playing U2 at all hours of the night. Though she didn't really get off on all the drinking and smoking, Harriet had joined in, secretly longing for the moment when Will's kooky friend Edith would stop swigging from the Cointreau bottle and

Spooner and Jim would cease trawling through Will's pile of vinyl and they would all just go home. Because, when they went home, she and Will would go upstairs again and have sex.

When they weren't having sex, they were talking about having sex. Harriet would sit, the squiggly telephone cord wrapped around her wrist as they whispered to each other for hours on end. More than once, Isaac had come in from the garden to say, 'Come on, you two lovebirds. Time to call it a night. I hope that isn't my phone bill.'

Six days ago, Will had simply stopped returning her calls. One morning he was making her toast and marmalade at Shirley's pine kitchen table and borrowing a pound from his sister so he could put enough petrol in the Cortina to run her home. The next, it was as though he'd simply stepped off the planet. It had been the day Hermione phoned from Greece to say she was coming home. He was supposed to call her that afternoon to arrange a trip to the cinema. Shirley and Keith would be back from Spain, toting litre bottles of Bacardi and a bottle of Jazz, so there would be no more sleeping in their chintz-covered bed. It was a shame. But she'd been looking forward to the cinema anyhow. Not the film, particularly. It was an action thing, full of guns and shouting. But it would mean time alone, cuddled up in the dark with Will.

She'd spent the whole morning getting ready, shaving her legs in the shower and slathering baby lotion all over herself until she was as soft as a peach. Two o'clock, the agreed time of his telephone call, came and went. Three. Four. At half past four, the phone had finally shrilled in the hall and she'd thundered downstairs, two at a time, to answer it. But it hadn't been Will. It had been Hermione. It struck her as ironic that the voice she'd been waiting to hear since Hermione had boarded the plane at Gatwick now filled her with disappointment. She hadn't meant to sound so flat. She'd just so wanted Hermione to be Will.

Will didn't phone that night. Or the next. On the third night, she'd swallowed her pride and called him at home, where Alison, his sister, told her he'd gone out. No. She didn't know where. She didn't know when he'd be back either. Yes. She would pass on a message.

After two more days, Harriet had started to think that reading of Will's tragic demise in the local paper would be preferable to the alternative.

In the days leading up to the party, her heart had shrivelled like a windfall apple. What had she done, in those brief minutes between making the arrangement and being driven home, to make him change his mind? Had her mouth dropped open while she was eating her toast, revealing an unappealing bolus of food inside? Had she been disgustingly noisy? Greedy? Had she farted during her sleep?

Hermione caught her eye across the smoky dance floor. The DJ was playing a Soul to Soul classic. It was one of their favourites.

41

'Dance?'

'In a minute,' Harriet mouthed back.

She'd never felt less like dancing. Her tummy was flippering like a fish. The alcohol, wafting up from the plastic cup she cradled in her hand, was making her feel icky. All she could think about was Will. Every delicious inch of him was stamped on her mind. The muscles in his stomach, as defined as the squares on a bar of chocolate. The white teeth and very red lips that made his smile so acutely disarming. His feet, lightly tanned and spangled with fine blond hairs, nestling next to her own in the bed.

She'd thought she was safe. Stupidly, she'd imagined that giving herself to Will sexually meant there was a bond between them. A connection that couldn't be broken.

The pain of rejection was like the shock of cold water on a blisteringly hot day.

She took her wine and picked her way up the alyssum-frothed steps to the house. In the hall, she bumped into Isaac, who was clutching a pottery bowl laden with Ruby's honey sesame-dipped sausages.

'Wotcher, Shortcake.' He winked at her. 'Having fun?'

'Sure.' A cello string of guilt twanged in the pit of her stomach. Her dad had put so much effort into this celebration. How sad he would be if he knew she wasn't enjoying it one little bit.

She knew what she had to do. When Isaac was

out of earshot, she picked up the phone and, heart snapping like a click beetle, dialled Will's number. She imagined the phone purring from the wall above the cork board in Sheila Cartwright's kitchen.

'Answer,' she pleaded silently. 'Please answer.'

She counted the rings. Twenty. Twenty-one.

She was about to admit defeat when, suddenly, the phone was snatched up and she heard a breathless voice on the other end.

'Hello?'

'Hi,' Harriet said awkwardly. 'It's Harriet.'

'Hi, sweet,' Alison said annoyingly. 'Did you want Will?'

'Yes.' Harriet was embarrassed. She wondered if Alison was aware that she hadn't actually seen Will in between all these phone calls she'd been making of late. Perhaps she had no idea of her brother's movements. Perhaps it didn't matter that Harriet had called – what – four, maybe five times now.

'I'm sorry.' Alison sounded sympathetic. 'He went to a party, I think. Somewhere in town. Belvedere, was it?'

'Belmont?' Harriet butted in hopefully.

'That's the one,' Alison said. 'Mum was going to drop him in town on her way to bridge.'

Harriet's heart soared like a seagull. He was coming after all. There'd been a misunderstanding about the cinema. He'd got the day wrong. Or he'd forgotten completely. Anyway, it didn't matter. At this very moment, she could forgive him anything.

It was all going to be OK.

She picked up her wine and trooped happily outside again to find Hermione. They would have that dance after all. And then, in a minute, Will would be here. She would introduce him to everyone. They'd all be impressed.

At the top of the steps, she stopped and looked across the tops of the heads in the garden for Hermione. Now that she'd cheered up, she'd be able to talk to her properly again. She could hear all about the Greek holiday without that awful plumb line of dread swinging like a pendulum in her stomach. She'd neglected her a bit since she came back from Greece. Now she could put it right.

There she was, over by the little wooden gate in the garden wall. She would recognise her sister anywhere. Slender figure, still encased in that gasp of grey chiffon. Chestnut curls tumbling down her back. Hands groping that same back. Hands that weren't Hermione's.

Harriet grinned. Her sister had made quick work of finding someone to snog.

She started down the steps to go and break up the passion. Hermione wouldn't mind. It was their eighteenth birthday, after all. Hermione would want to have a bop with her. It was traditional.

She was almost upon them when her sister broke away from whoever it was she was kissing so

44

passionately. Hermione had her back to her, which meant that Harriet could see the man's face quite clearly.

He saw her the second she saw him. Their eyes locked, Harriet had to stifle a gasp as her dreams of introducing Will to Hermione came crashing down around her like a house of cards.

Clearly, they'd already met.

HARRIET

Bath, 2003

Harriet and Dan's marriage ended over the washing-up.

'This isn't working.' Dan dried the sky-blue mug covered in love hearts that had been a wedding present. A soap bubble, caught in the handle, wobbled and shimmered briefly before vanishing. Harriet saw her own hands, clad in seaside-yellow Marigolds, stop swishing about in the soapy water.

'Did you add salt?' She nodded towards the Finnish cooking pot, containing a pasta sauce for their supper later, bubbling happily on the stove. If she simply refused to acknowledge what she thought he was saying, then it wouldn't be true.

'I wasn't talking about the sauce,' Dan said flatly. 'I meant us.'

Harriet's heart spun like a bead on an abacus.

'We're OK,' she said hopefully. 'Aren't we?' Even as she said the words, she knew they sounded hollow. Things hadn't been OK for a long time. Not since they'd decided to try for a baby.

46

She watched Dan replace the wedding present mug on its hook. It was hard to believe they'd been trying for two long years. Twenty-four months of waiting and hoping. Once or twice, it had seemed as though fate was on their side. Every missed period had seen her locked in the bathroom, the little white paddle of the pregnancy test balanced precariously on the side of the pink alabaster sink as she waited for the longed-for blue line to appear.

She'd tried everything. Ovulation prediction kits. Taking her temperature every five minutes. Lying on her back with her legs in the air for hours at a time. And then, three months ago, the hospital for tests.

The results had been inconclusive. But due to an infection she'd had a long time ago, it seemed likely that Harriet might well be infertile. They would need more tests to be sure. But they had to consider the possibility.

The news had sounded a death knell for their sex life. They'd gone from being at it like rabbits to lying curled away from one another, back to back in the big bed. A flesh and blood fleur-de-lys. Instead of making them stronger, the bad news had precipitated the slow dissolution of what they had together. For weeks now, Harriet had watched through a gauze, helpless to intervene as their relationship drained away like sand in an egg timer. With every day, Dan seemed further away than ever. She wanted to reach out to him. But she couldn't.

'You blame me,' she said, as Dan removed a wooden spoon from the pan of Bolognese sauce and turned off the gas. 'For us not being able to conceive. That's it, isn't it?'

'Don't be silly.' Dan came over and took her slippery, yellow-gloved hands in his big strong ones. 'Of course I don't blame you.'

'So why does it feel like you do?'

Dan shrugged. 'I don't really know. I suppose I just . . . don't want to go on feeling like this. You're so out of reach. So distant. I'm lonely, Harry.'

'I know,' Harriet said sadly. 'So am I.'

She looked around at the kitchen. The gleaming SMEG cooker, its green dial glowing like the control panel on an aeroplane. The sleek granite-topped units, cleverly arranged in ergonomically friendly fashion, with the cooker, sink and fridge in a perfect triangle. The walls, carefully eggshelled the pure, perfect blue of a robin's egg. The slabs of slate underfoot. She'd spent so much time on the flat, decorating it in a classic palette of soft sage greens, dove greys and chalky blues. Dan sometimes teased her over how precise everything had to be. Surely, he said, it didn't really matter if a pink had a smidge too much yellow in it or if the funky Jocelyn Warner paper she'd chosen for one wall of the bathroom didn't quite tone with the skirting board. But then, when Dan had moved in with her during her third year at university, he'd thought it was OK to store the bottles of ketchup and hamburger mustard they didn't have room for in the kitchen in a box under the bathroom sink. What did he know?

She'd met Dan during Freshers' Week. A medical student from Queen's College, he was visiting his sister, Gabby, Harriet's flatmate. In Dan, Harriet, emerging from the most difficult, painful phase of her life, had seen a place of safety. He was older than her. Four years older. He was kind. Thoughtful. He always thought to ask if she was warm enough. He walked on the outside of the pavement to protect her from splashes. He covered her in cola bottle kisses that made her feel warm and secure. And he never pushed for anything more than kisses. He was content to wait until she was ready.

She wasn't supposed to have ended up in London at all. Her parents had been pushing for her to go. She was a talented artist. And St Martin's was the best. She really ought to make the most of her potential.

Ruby had known all about making the most of your potential. Or rather, not making the most of it. She'd been going to be a dancer once. Although Harriet had never actually seen her dance, she'd always known that she was dazzling. There had been photographs all over the walls at home. Ruby, sheathed in white satin, fringed with clouds of tulle, in an amateur production of *Swan Lake*. Ruby, mid-arabesque, in the sparkling pink and violet-tinged tutu she'd worn to dance the role of the Sugarplum Fairy. Ruby in black leotard and slouchy legwarmers, warming up at the barre. Ruby in a pale body stocking that showed off every sinewy contour. According to her, she'd been good enough to go professional. But then Harriet's Grandma Gladstone's refusal to acknowledge anything outside her own frame of reference had put the lid on it all. As a result, Ruby had been acutely conscious of her own role in shaping her daughters' futures. She'd always taught them they could do anything they wanted if they put their minds to it. Anything at all.

Harriet hadn't wanted to go to London. Unlike her sister, who'd been drawn to bright lights and glitter like a magpie to gold, she'd always been overwhelmed by big cities. She'd applied for a place at the art college in Bath where, she hoped, she would feel more at home. But, at the beginning of September, with three A grades under her belt, she'd changed her mind and applied to St Martin's through clearing. Three months before, the idea of living in London would have been unthinkable. But that was before the terrible events of the summer had changed everything.

Pip, Isaac's sister, had helped her find a room in a flat in Battersea. It had been a far cry from the rambling Georgian town house she'd shared with her family in Bath. Part of a crumbling tenement block, the flat itself was up four flights of stairs. The hallway had had a distinct whiff of ginger biscuits about it. But the flat itself had been bright and clean. Even better, it had come complete with a new, ready-made family in the form of Lizzy and Gabby. On the first night, when she was all completely at sea, they'd sat her down and made her hot chocolate with bobbing marshmallows as they told her about themselves. Dreams. Aspirations. The courses they were doing. The boys they fancied. At the end of the first week, Gabby, who liked to think of herself as slightly more sophisticated than your average student, had held a dinner party, complete with wine and candles. Dan had come to make up the numbers. And that was that.

'I'm wondering if we don't need some sort of break.' Dan put the lid on the Bolognese pot and wiped his hands on one of the fuchsia tea towels Harriet had chosen to offset the delicate blue of the walls.

Harriet panicked. 'Split up, you mean?'

'Of course not,' Dan said. 'I'm not going to just walk out on ten years of marriage. I just think we need time to take stock. We've both been a bit . . . distracted lately.'

To Harriet's horror, a fat tear oozed from the corner of her eye and plopped onto the sleeve of her sweatshirt.

'Hey.' Dan's big, earnest face crumpled and he came over to pull her towards his chest as she gulped back hot tears. 'Hey. Please don't cry.'

'I'm sorry,' Harriet said. 'I can't help it. I don't want you to go.'

'I don't want to go either.' Dan took her hand

and led her into the sitting room to curl up on the sofa. The same sofa on which they'd sat, scooped together like Pringles, on countless occasions to drink bottles of wine and watch DVDs.

'I just think that, if I don't go, this gulf between us will only get bigger. We'll start to resent each other. And you're busy, aren't you? You've got a lot on your plate.'

Harriet nodded, in as much as her achy, breaky throat would allow her to. Work-wise, she was manic, designing the interior of Blue Ginger, Bath's newest laid-back drinking establishment. It belonged to Jesse, who lived in the basement. He'd inherited some money – enough to buy the lease on a place in the city centre – and he'd asked Harriet to get involved. Thus far into her new business venture, it was her biggest challenge yet. She'd found it really rewarding, trawling markets and paint shops for scraps of material and samples and putting together a whole concept board. Fortunately, Jesse had loved all her ideas. Now there were only a few weeks to opening and there was still so much to do. She probably wouldn't be at home very much over the next few weeks. But, even so, that didn't mean she didn't want Dan around.

'Where will you go?'

'I'll stay with Scott,' Dan told her. 'He won't mind me kipping on his sofa. Milo and Midge are running them ragged at the moment. They could probably do with a babysitter on site. Give them both a break.'

'It's because of the baby, isn't it?' Harriet blurted. 'You don't want me any more because I can't give you children.'

'No.' Dan looked sadly at his feet. Such great big feet. Size fourteen, or thereabouts. But then he was an enormous bear of a person. It was one of the things she'd liked most about him. His great size seemed to her to represent safety. And safety was why she'd married him, at the tender age of twenty-two, when Lizzy and Gabby and the others were all out playing the field.

Gabby had been pleased to be gaining a sister-in-law. She'd designed Harriet a beautiful wedding dress. A column of Thai silk in the faintest blush pink. But she still thought she was loopy to be getting married so young. Everybody did.

Now, looking at Dan's big, squashy face, she wondered if perhaps they hadn't all been right. At the time, it had seemed so simple. She loved Dan and Dan loved her. Only four years before, when the unthinkable had happened, she'd thought she might never feel part of a family again. And now here was someone who wanted to make a new one with her. It had all been a bit of a relief. For years now, Dan had provided her with the security of knowing she was loved.

And now he wanted to leave.

'I don't *want* to leave you,' Dan said. 'I love you.'

'I love you too.' Harriet stared fixedly at a piece of lint on her jeans. There was a 'But' coming. She could smell it a mile off.

'I'm not happy,' Dan said at last. 'I haven't been for a while.'

Harriet felt a lump roll, like a lottery ball, up her windpipe and lodge itself against her epiglottis.

'Is it the baby thing?'

Dan shook his head. 'I'm not sure having a baby would make any difference. I mean, I know all this waiting and hoping hasn't made things easy. And it's upset you. I know it has.' He touched her cheek. 'I've tried to help you . . .' He hesitated.

'Help me?' Harriet said. 'Help me with what?'

'The accident,' Dan said frankly. 'Losing your parents. Your own twin. I know it hasn't been easy for you.'

Hearing Dan say it out loud made Harriet's stomach ululate like a wobble board. 'You have helped me.'

Dan jerked his head towards the photograph, in its silver frame, propped above the fireplace. Harriet and Hermione at their parents' wedding. Two little dots in identical smocked dresses the colour of the strawberry juice moustaches that stained their mouths. Hermione's hair, wild and enormous from the day she was born, mushroomed out around her head, so she resembled some exotic feather duster. Beside her, Harriet, with her pale brown locks, looked small and transparent. But she was smiling. They both were. Something the photographer was doing had quite clearly tickled them pink.

'I sometimes worry that you never had time to deal with it all.'

'I'm OK.'

'Look at this,' Dan continued as though she hadn't spoken, waving his hand at the sitting room Harriet had redecorated in bitter chocolate and mocha hues, with just a flash of orchid purple a month or two ago.

'Don't you like it?'

'It's not that,' Dan said. 'I just think you spend too much time worrying about it. It's as though, if everything looks perfect on the outside, you won't have to worry about what's inside.'

'You're leaving me because I want the flat to look nice!' Harriet couldn't quite believe what she was hearing. She loved this flat and all the things in it. The big roll-top bath at the end of her bed. Her dining room, sparkly white and carefully accessorised with an eclectic jumble of old and new furniture. Church pews. A French armoire. Two perspex Ghost chairs. This living room, complete with worn brown leather sofa and pink silk and cashmere cushions . . .

'No!' Dan protested. 'And I'm *not* leaving you. I'm just going to Scott's for a bit. I need to sort my head out.'

Harriet hesitated. 'What about me?'

'You'll be OK.' Dan smoothed a noodle of hair away from her forehead. 'I promise.'

'How do you know?' she croaked.

'I'll phone you.' Dan said.

'When?'

'Perhaps not right away. But I will call. When the time's right.'

She watched him pack through a veil of tears. Part of her wanted to run over and yank the brown leather bag clean out of his hands. It would be so easy to beg him to stay. But the words wouldn't come. Instead, she was silent as he kissed the top of her head and told her he still loved her, no matter what. She watched as he let himself out and, with the big bag slung over his back, like a snail shell, sloped off, a familiar lolloping figure, in the direction of his brother's house.

Afterwards, she raced upstairs to their bedroom and flung herself onto the deep blue velvet throw on their bed to breathe in lungfuls of Dan's smell. She cried until there were literally no tears left. After an hour and a half, when her face resembled a bulbous mushroom and her arm had gone all fizzy where the blood had drained out of it, she surfaced and went to look in the mirror.

Her own face stared back at her. Apart from being all puffy, she looked much the same as she always had. There was the dip in her chin that Hermione had always said made her face look like an upside down heart. The three freckles, arranged in a perfect isosceles triangle on her cheek. Mustardy brown eyes, almond-shaped and set slightly too far apart. Skin as pale as spring blossom. She'd always longed for skin like

Hermione's. Golden delicious skin, with a ripe olive-oil hue. In summer, Hermione turned the same shade as the iced coffee their mother drank by the gallon, while she, Harriet, had stayed junket-pale for days on end before her skin finally relented and took on the brownish tinge of an old pillow.

She glanced at the photograph on the mantelpiece again and wondered if Dan had been right. Was she really harbouring the sort of feelings that prevented her from getting on with life? Did she love changing her environment every five minutes only because it meant she could avoid what was occurring on a deeper level, somewhere in the nooks and crannies of her psyche?

She didn't think so. Her love of design went much further back than the accident. The roots of it lay somewhere in her childhood. Ruby had had a wonderful knack with interiors. She'd turned every house they'd lived in into something special. The pile of granite, crumbling away on the Cornish cliffs. The skinny town house in Bath. Her sitting room had been filled with piles of interiors magazines, which Harriet had loved flipping through. She liked to think she'd worked a bit of Ruby's magic on that first flat in Battersea she'd shared with Lizzy and Gabby. She'd transformed it from a porridge-coloured apartment, with lumpy tapioca carpets, into a bright and breezy place where everyone loved to come and flop after lectures.

But it wasn't just the design. Almost as soon as she'd asked herself Dan's question, she knew the answer. There were things about 1988 that even Dan didn't know. He knew about the tragic accident that had killed both her parents. He knew that the childhood home she'd always loved had had to be sold and she'd been propelled, like a pea from a shooter, into the unknown harum scarum of London. He'd known that she hadn't liked the city. Not really. As soon as she was out of college, she'd used some of Ruby and Isaac's money to buy this flat, only two streets away from their old house on Belmont, and Dan, fresh out of medical school, had agreed to make a life with her away from the big red buses and black cabs he'd always been used to.

But there were lots of things Dan didn't know. Things Harriet had kept to herself for fifteen long years. An argument. An abortion. A boy called William Cartwright. And then, of course, the biggest thing of all.

The fact that, as far as she knew, Hermione was very much alive.

Harriet had said some terrible things after the funeral. She'd blamed Hermione for the crash. Told her it was all her fault their parents were dead. The truth was that Hermione hadn't been in the car at all. Isaac and Ruby had been on their way to pick her up from a party. Harriet, who had been in a black mood all evening, had almost gone with them. She'd wanted to confront her sister about Will. In the end, she'd decided it could wait. So she'd stayed at home to watch a *Top of the Pops* special and escaped death by a whisker.

She'd always meant to get in touch. After the accident, after she'd moved to London, it had always been on her mind to say sorry for the terrible things she'd said. But she'd never quite been able to pluck up the courage. And then Dan had come along and it had been all too easy to just go with the flow. But she'd never imagined they would end up like this. Not having spoken for fifteen years.

Fifteen years! Was it really that long?

She wouldn't even know where to find Hermione now.

She went to the tall chest of drawers over by the window and slid open the bottom drawer, rummaging between the colour coordinated piles of dozens of T-shirts until she found what she was looking for. And suddenly, there it was. As familiar as *Blue Peter* badges and Mr Benn's shopkeeper.

Hermione's diary.

Isaac had given it to her for her thirteenth birthday, a big handsome book bound in butter-soft leather. You could lock it with a tiny silver padlock to keep out prying eyes. Harriet had spent a good proportion of her teenage years trying to find the key to this book, in which her sister, who had aspirations of becoming a writer one day, recorded every single little thing that happened to her. She'd never succeeded. And then, one day, as she was going through the boxes of stuff Pip, their father's sister, had got together for them when the house on Belmont was cleared out, she'd come across it. It must have been put in the wrong box in the panic to get everything packed up before the house was sold.

The key was missing. Thus far, Harriet had resisted the temptation to break the lock. But now she didn't care any more. She might find something in those pages full of loopy peacock scrawl that would help her make sense of it all.

If only she knew what it was she wanted to make sense of.

She picked up a paperweight from the dressing table and took a deep breath before bringing it down hard on the tiny silver lock. It sprang open immediately. Opening the book, Harriet was amazed to catch a heady whiff of *Paris*, trapped within the pages for all this time. It made her want to cry.

As she picked up the book, two squares of paper fell from the pages, spinning like sycamore helicopters to the ground. Photographs. A black and white snap of Hermione sprawled on the back steps of the house in Bath, wearing beaten-up Converse boots and faded jeans, ripped at the knees. There was a New York Yankees baseball cap perched on her head. Harriet couldn't remember who had taken the photograph. But she remembered the Converse boots well. They had been bright bubblegum pink. Hermione had worn them everywhere that summer.

She turned the picture over. On the back, Hermione had written in her loopy hand, 'Sweet sixteen at last'.

The other photograph was the colour of old tea and depicted two tiny babies, wearing doilies and lying side by side. On the back of this one, in shaky, old-fashioned hand-writing, somebody had penned, 'Ruby and Emerald, 1952'.

She stared at it. Her mother as a tiny baby. Presumably with a baby born in the same hospital. Funny, them both being named after jewels.

She sat up straight.

What if . . .

Twins ran in families, didn't they?

What if Ruby had had a twin? A twin sister who had died.

Was that why she'd always made such a song and dance about Hermione and Harriet always being there for each other? Why she hated it so much when they pinched and bit and pulled each other's hair?

If so, what was Hermione doing with this photograph? Did she know? And why had she never shown it to Harriet?

There was only one way to find out. Dan forgotten for now, she brushed her teeth, climbed into bed and started to read her lost sister's diary.

My dear Gigi,
Harriet's acting weird. *Well* weird. Ever since I got back from Greece, it's like I

haven't existed. And I've got so much to tell her. I want to tell her how much she'd love it there. The sea is really the most incredible colour. I don't know really what you'd call it. Green? Blue? Greeny-blue? Or bluey-green? None of them sound right. A colour as beautiful as that should really have its own name. Something lovely and amazing. Something that isn't real. Like sky blue-pink . . .

Harriet shimmied further under the duvet, rearranging the big French pillows behind her head and dipping into the little capiz shell bowl beside her for another black olive. Hermione's diary was bringing memories flooding back. She could still picture her sister, kissing Will at their eighteenth birthday party. She could still feel the terrible sense of betrayal and the hot flush that crept up her cheeks as she stood at the bottom of the garden steps.

She'd discovered, days later, that she was pregnant. She'd told Will immediately. He had shown a callous lack of interest in his unborn child and gone to the cash point on Milsom Street to give her the money to get rid of it.

'Why?' Harriet, her pride forgotten, had asked him. 'Why did you stop calling me?'

'I dunno.' Will shrugged. 'Things had just gone a bit flat, that's all. We had fun, didn't we? While it lasted.'

Harriet had thought about confiding in Ruby. Ruby had once been in a similar situation. She would know what to do. She'd been working up to telling her on the night of the accident, when the phone call had come from Hermione to ask one of them to come and collect her. She'd also been planning to confront Hermione, who plainly knew nothing about any of it and thought Will was the bee's knees, zooming up to the front of the house to pick her up on his new motorbike, when he knew Harriet was inside. After the accident, Harriet had felt she might confide in her even then. Will hadn't been at the funeral. He hadn't been at the house much either, as she and Hermione tried to make sense of the frightening place their world was now. Harriet had thought optimistically that he was long gone. She'd thought perhaps she and Hermione could find a flat together in Bath when the house was sold. Perhaps she could have the baby after all. Hermione would help her look after it.

She pictured the way her sister must have looked as she wrote the diary. Sprawled on her front on the floor probably. A tangle of limbs and hair encircled by the chaos of her bedroom.

Harriet had always loved Hermione's room. Scrupulously tidy herself, incapable of using a jar of Marmite without replacing the lid and putting it back where she'd found it, she'd often wished she could be a bit more laid back. In contrast, Hermione's room had seemed to have a life of its own. Harriet remembered banana skins stuffed into empty yoghurt pots; coffee mugs furred with perfect discs of mould; a wicker hamper overflowing with a glorious jumble of cosmetics; little pools of pants positioned exactly where Hermione had stepped out of them before going to bed. There had even been a guinea pig once, until Snowflake the cat had got her. A sweet little thing named Lottie, who squeaked to communicate and left a trail of smooth Tic-Tac droppings everywhere.

There had been scarves, bags and belts looped over the end of the bed. Hermione had inherited Ruby's talent for accessorizing. She was never without the right belt or brooch with which to jazz up an outfit. She'd always had an instinct as to what suited her. Harriet had been pretty clueless. It was odd. Give her a fabric sample and she would instantly produce a selection of paint swatches to complement it. Clothes, however, were a whole different ball of wax. She hated having to decide what to wear in a hurry and big occasions caused days of worry. Which was rather inconvenient. She was due at her godson's christening next week and she had absolutely no clue what she was going to wear.

She decided on a silk wrap dress in the end. Apple-green with splashes of white; it gave her curves where she was as flat as a skateboard and made her look a bit jauntier than she actually felt. She fastened her pale brown hair in a ponytail at the side, in accordance with the jaunty theme, and fixed her face with the minimum of make-up. She was even clueless at that. Of the two of them, Hermione had definitely been the lipstick queen.

Edie, the old lady who lived on the ground floor, was on the landing when she went downstairs. Harriet always felt a bit sorry for Edie. Sandwiched between herself and Jesse and Joe in the basement, she seemed to live a kind of half-life at the mercy of her husband. Harriet saw Edie often, shuffling up the hill, her big string bag bulging with tins of ham and fruit cocktail. But the husband seemed to remain in the flat, shuttered from view. Occasionally, he was audible – when he shouted for his tea, for instance. But he was otherwise as elusive as Sowron. Harriet couldn't remember a time when she'd actually clapped eyes on him.

There was something different about Edie today. She looked brighter. Her hair, usually thin as candyfloss, looked freshly washed and perky. There was colour in her papery cheeks. As Harriet came down the stairs, she stopped what she was doing and cocked her head to one side, like a robin.

'Wotcher.'

'Hi, Edie.' Harriet nodded at her neighbour. 'How are you today?'

'I'm tickety-boo thanks, duck.' Edie said. 'I've just buried me 'usband.'

'Oh!' Harriet's hand flew to her mouth. 'I'm sorry. I didn't know.'

'Not to worry,' Edie said breezily, nodding at the huge cardboard box she was struggling with. 'I'm hooking me up to the World Wide Web.'

'Oh. Right.'

'Did you know?' Edie straightened, so she was about level with Harriet's chin. 'You can actually talk to someone in Orstralia on one of these.'

'I know . . .'

'And they got these chat room wotsnames,' Edie informed her. 'You go on and talk to people you've never even seen before. I could find meself a nice seventeen-year-old.' She cackled. 'I can tell him I look like that Jordan and 'e'll be none the wiser.'

'Can I give you a hand with it?' Harriet nodded at the box. 'It looks heavy.'

With much puffing, Harriet shunted the box with Edie's new PC in it through the doorway of Edie's flat.

'Where do you want it?'

'Just in 'ere.' Edie opened the door of the spare room. 'Stick it there. On the wotsname.'

Harriet put the box on a Formica-topped table next to an old black and white photograph. The two girls in it, all doe eyes and waved hair, looked like Hollywood film stars.

'Is that you, Edie?'

'This one.' Edie pointed at the smaller girl on the left. 'This is me.'

'Wow.'

'Little corker, wasn't I? That's what my Stan always used to call me. His little corker.'

'Your husband?'

'Eee, no.' Edie laughed. 'Not Cyril. Miserable bugger 'e was. Even on our 'unnymoon. We 'ad three days in Marlborough,' she said. 'Borrowed 'is brother's house, we did. Course it was all we could afford in them days.' She pointed to a photograph on the opposite wall: a handsome man in army uniform, his dark hair slicked back off his face with pomade. 'That's Stan, there. Little Bobby Dazzler, 'e was. We was engaged.'

'What happened?'

'He was killed in the war, duck.' Edie's eyes misted over. 'Like all the good 'uns. Course 'e were with Doris when I met 'im.'

'Doris?'

'Me sister.' Edie pointed at the second girl in the photograph. 'That's 'er there. Course she never forgave me. She went to Orstralia after the war. Never heard from her again.'

'And you married Cyril.'

'I 'ad to.' Edie's eyes glinted with mischief. 'I were pregnant with my Ann. Course 'e never knew she weren't 'is. If 'e did, 'e never said so.'

'Is that why you've got the computer?' Harriet asked. 'To find your sister in Australia?'

'No, duck,' Edie said. 'I tried to find 'er before. I wanted to tell 'er how sorry I were. Daft, ain't it? Letting a man come between you. Even a Bobby Dazzler like my Stan.'

'What happened?'

'She'd just gone. I found 'er son. Graham. He told me she'd had cancer. Riddled with it, she was. She'd passed over a month or so before I found 'im. I were too late.'

'That's so sad.' Harriet thought of herself and Hermione. How stupid she'd been to say all those things. And to let them fester for so long. 'Too late.' A terrible expression. The worst. She didn't want what had happened to Edie and Doris to happen to her. She knew she would have to find Hermione sooner or later.

But for now, she had a christening to get to. Or, at least, a christening of sorts. Lizzy and Conrad had decided, after christening their second child in church, that they would just have a big party to celebrate the coming of Oscar. They hadn't much liked the way their parish church in Bath had embraced modernity, with hymns they'd never heard of projected onto a big screen at the front instead of proper hymns, remembered from school assemblies, sung from hymn books.

'Are you going to be OK with that?' she asked Edie. 'How are you going to get it set up?'

'Eee.' Edie crackled like a bonfire. 'I got me guardian angel for that.'

'You have?' Harriet wondered if Edie might be going a bit dotty. She had just lost her husband, after all.

''Im downstairs.' Edie pointed at the floor. 'Jesse?'

'That's 'im.' Edie nodded. 'The one what don't wear the T-shirt with FUCK on it.'

'You mean FCUK,' Harriet said kindly.

'No,' Edie said decidedly. 'I'm sure it said FUCK. Anyway, 'e's coming to 'elp me tomorrow.'

Harriet left Edie to her computer and went outside to where Vin Rouge, her elderly maroon decorating van, was parked precariously on a slope. Dan always teased her that the bloody thing had so many holes in it you could use it as a colander to drain pasta. But Harriet was loath to part with it. The trusty Vin Rouge had got her through her early days as a painter and decorator, when she and Dan had first moved to Bath. It was an old friend.

Lizzy's house sat on the edge of the Kennet and Avon canal, out towards Avoncliff. Despite being a Londoner at heart, Lizzy had followed Harriet down here some time after finishing university. Bath was a bit like that. It captivated you with its beauty. It drew you in and spat you out again when you realised there weren't really any jobs that paid you enough to be able to live in one of the tall vanilla-fudge houses that lined its streets. It was one reason Harriet had set up on her own. Not that Lizzy needed to worry. Not now she'd married Conrad, a heart surgeon at a hospital in Bristol. When Jemima was born, she'd let her land-scaping business go and she was now a full-time wife and mother. Harriet often wondered why she never seemed to get bored. She had been a bit up and down lately. Sometimes, she was really quite vague. When Harriet had told her about Dan going to Scott's, she'd barely reacted, which came as quite a surprise. After more than ten years of marriage, you'd expect your best friend to do more than say, 'Oh, right,' while flapping about her kitchen like a giant manta ray, in search of Frubes and mini Babybels for Jemima's packed lunch.

Harriet thought about Dan as she drove through the windy lanes, steeped in the scent of wild garlic, to Lizzy's. She missed him. You couldn't share your life with the same person for that long and not find it strange when they weren't there any more. And it was difficult not to mind when she kept finding little reminders all over the place. Bits and bobs that Dan liked to eat, tucked at the back of the kitchen cupboards. Cheerios. Chocolate milk. Weird-tasting Japanese crackers. Lime marmalade with bits in. The other day, she'd come across a shirt, scrumpled up down the side of the bed. Instinctively, she'd picked it up and sniffed it. It had smelt so intrinsically Dan-like that she'd burst into tears.

She missed his cooking, too, although not having to worry about clearing up afterwards was a bonus. When she got back from Blue Ginger, completely knackered and covered in paint, Dan was usually pottering around in the kitchen, zesting lemons, chopping parsley and slicing squid into rings for a quick seafood pasta.

But there was another part of her that found she didn't mind quite as much as she'd thought she might. She found she could look at the photographs, still dotted about the flat in their various frames, without regret. The two of them, drinking beer on holiday in Thailand. Dan, in sunglasses and a checked shirt, leaning against the beribboned prow of a longboat. Herself, in baggy khaki shorts and a pale pink T-shirt, looking nervy on the back of an elephant. Both of them, wreathed in smiles on their wedding day. Dan's crimson cravat had clashed unfortunately with the posy of pink and mango gerberas she'd chosen to complement Gabby's pink silk creation. She'd just bowed down to what everybody else wanted. Gabby. Lizzy. Dan's mother, who'd insisted on what she called 'volley-vons', filled with a vomit-inducing chicken and mushroom slush, instead of the oriental buffet Harriet had had in mind. Without Ruby, or any of her own family in her corner, she'd found it easier just let them get on with it.

Perhaps it was a sign, she thought, as Vin Rouge crunched over the gravel in Lizzy's grown-up driveway. Perhaps the fact that she and Dan hadn't even thought to ensure their colours at least complemented each other was indicative of something else. Something far more sinister. Perhaps she and Dan just weren't meant to be. A bit like Edie and Cyril.

Lizzy's garden was festooned for the occasion.

The ancient stone feeding trough by the fence was a mass of floating peony heads and there were jam jars crammed with sweet peas on the white linen-bedecked tables lined up under the pear trees. Some people had arrived already and were standing about nursing tall glasses of Pimms laced with fresh fruit. Children bounced about like popcorn in a pan as Harriet removed Oscar's nearly christening present, a bucket of Lego, from the back of Vin Rouge and looked around for a familiar face.

'Harry.' Conrad spotted her as she wandered towards the house. 'Great to see you.'

'You too.' Harriet kissed him on both cheeks. She was fond of Conrad. Despite his Fisher Price hair and his funny bumbling ways, he was a sweetie.

'No Dan?' Conrad looked over her shoulder.

'Well, no . . .' Harriet said awkwardly. 'We . . .'

'Of course!' Conrad looked horrified. 'Lizzy told me. God, I'm an idiot. I'm sorry. How are you?'

'I'm OK.' Harriet said.

'Really?'

'Yes, weirdly. I mean, I miss him . . .'

'Of course you do.'

'But it's not as though anything's decided. And I've been so busy with everything at Blue Ginger.'

'Aha!' Conrad said. 'This bar I've heard so much about. When do we get to drink in it?'

'Soon,' Harriet told him.

'Fabulous.' Conrad rubbed his hands together.

'Right. Well. Best get on.' He nodded towards the barbecue. 'Hungry hordes to feed and all that. Do you fancy something? I've just plonked some ribs on.'

'No thanks.' Harriet held up her contributions to the party. 'I might just find Lizzy. See if she's got anywhere for me to put these.'

'Ah.' Conrad nodded. 'Of course. Well. See you later.'

Lizzy was in her big, messy kitchen, tending to a circle of sponge.

'Harry. Thank God. Look at the sodding cake.'

'It doesn't look too bad.' Harriet picked up a pile of clean laundry and dumped it on Lizzy's kitchen table, where it sat, defiant, amid a tide of family flotsam. Marmite soldiers. A potato print, splodged lime-green and yellow. Dog-eared picture books. A marble. A packet of mustard and cress seeds. A sock, grubby and bereft of its partner. Sequins. Plasticine. A peacock feather. A single pink jelly shoe, the soles packed with glitter.

'Harry,' Lizzy said firmly. 'It has a ruddy great well in the middle. You could chuck a cat down it and never see it again.'

'I'm sure no one will mind,' Harriet reassured her.

'*I'll* mind,' Lizzy said.

She didn't seem to be coping very well since Oscar had been born. She'd been fine with Jemima and Lucy, her two eldest, but now, one minute she would be high as a kite, the next her good

73

mood would collapse like a sandcastle. It was sometimes hard to reconcile the post-Oscar Lizzy with the glamorous bar fly of old. What had happened to the slick chick who had always refused point blank to look both ways when she crossed the road because she was going to an important party and she didn't want her hair getting stuck to her lip gloss? The kitten-heeled lovely whose mascara counted as excess baggage when she flew cattle class? Sometimes, it was hard to recognise her any more.

Harriet had been a tiny bit disappointed when Lizzy and Conrad got married. Lizzy and Dan had always got along brilliantly. The three of them had done things together. Dinners. Picnics in Victoria park. They'd even cycled from London to Brighton together for charity. And then Conrad had come along and everything had changed.

They'd had a lovely wedding. Lizzy had worn a strapless two-piece in pure white fabric rinsed in a blue bag to make it shine like silver. Conrad had been otter-sleek in a tailored indigo suit and rose silk tie. Even his hair had been a bit less Lego than usual. There had been pure white orchids. Tiny bridesmaids in gasps of pale plum chiffon. Oysters served from swans of sculpted ice. Dom Perignon, in flutes of delicate vintage crystal, had flowed all day and Harriet, in a wisp of sea-green sprinkled with sparkles, had guzzled her fifth glass and allowed herself the secret hope that nothing need change. Perhaps the newly double-barrelled

Lizzy Armstrong-Jones would turn out to be no different from plain old Lizzy Bone after all.

The early signs hadn't exactly been great. In the run-up to the big day, Miss Bone had been a pain in the proverbial. She'd worked herself into a frenzy over the most insignificant things. Should they have ribbons or roses? Crystals or pearls? Angels on horseback or pigs in blankets? Asian fusion or meaty French? On more than one occasion, Harriet had sat back and waited for her to go postal with the party poppers.

The only area of calm had been the making of her wedding outfit, and that had been down to Gabby. Gabby's wedding dresses really were fantastic. Harriet's own was packed in layers of tissue in an acid-free box on top of her wardrobe. Gabby was a real paragon. She always managed to look amazing, even on two hours' sleep when Luke had first come along. And she had willpower of steel. She recorded everything she ate on a spreadsheet, ensuring she stayed pin thin.

The day after Dan had packed his bag and left, Gabby had rung to see if Harriet needed anything.

'I am *so* sorry,' she'd gushed down the phone. 'Scott's just told me. Do you want me to give that idiot brother of mine a call? See if we can't get to the bottom of this?'

She'd almost sounded disappointed to hear that Harriet didn't require her help. To make up for it, she'd started sending things. A muffin basket, filled to the brim with sticky blueberry creations.

Harriet had spent a pleasant afternoon scoffing those in the garden. Yesterday, a bunch of lilies, which had already started to stink the house out, had come with a note, offering help of any kind. It had almost made Harriet feel guilty for not being more miserable about Dan having gone.

'Perhaps you could fill the hole with sweets,' Harriet said now, looking at the cake.

'Great idea.' Lizzy yanked open a cupboard and was hit by a deluge of packets and boxes. Crisps. Sunmaid raisins. Fruit bars.

'Shite. Ah. Here we go. Trusty Smarties. Lucy gets one every time she deigns to use the potty. I knew I had some more somewhere. Right.'

She emptied a tube into the hollow in the middle of the christening cake, just as the kitchen door opened and Luke waddled in with Gabby hot on his heels.

'Here you both are.' She wafted over in a cloud of Coco to swamp them in kisses. 'Conrad said you were here, Harry. How *are* you?'

'I'm fine.' Harriet felt guilty again. She'd been thinking more about Hermione than Dan. What Edie had said about her sister had really struck a chord.

'Really?' Gabby wrinkled up her pretty nose. 'Oh Harry, you *are* brave.'

'I'm not,' Harriet said. 'We've just got some things to sort through, that's all. We'll probably be back together again in a month.'

'Right.' Gabby didn't look convinced. 'Here,' she

said to Lizzy, putting a glossy eau-de-nil green box on the table. 'Present for you.'

'What is it?'

'Open it and see.'

Lizzy opened the flap on the lid to reveal a chocolate cake as large as an Ascot hat and glazed with chocolate ganache icing. Hot pink gerberas studded the edge for decoration. It smelt delicious.

'I didn't think you'd have time to make one.' Gabby looked at the sorry creation on the counter and didn't comment.

'It's gorgeous,' Lizzy said. 'You didn't *make* this?'

'Oh, it only took me an hour,' Gabby said breezily. 'It's no problem.'

'God,' Lizzy said, when Gabby had gone back outside to help Luke find a playmate. 'Why doesn't she just come right out with it. I'm a Bad Mother. Everyone thinks so. I can't even cook. Shit!' She made a dash for the oven and pulled out a tray of what looked like coal.

'Fucking butterfly cakes.' She banged the tray into the sink, sending charred black lumps skittering all over the place. 'Ruined.'

'So what?' Harriet said loyally. 'I don't think you're a bad mother at all. You've got three children. Gabby only has one. And you've got all those pets to contend with.'

'One less now.' Lizzy swiped clumps of her own cake into the bin. 'Nice Mary topped herself. Launched herself off the kitchen table. I'm not surprised, the way Jemima kept mauling her about. I think she was depressed.'

Nice Mary, Jemima's guinea pig, wasn't the only one who was depressed. Over the course of the afternoon, Harriet sank further into gloom as she was faced with a dozen babies, each one fatter and more smiley than the last. Soo, who had been at St Martin's with them, arrived in a taxi from the station, with Annabel, her bouncing baby girl, tucked under her arm like a loaf.

'Harry.' She plonked down all manner of paraphernalia, including what looked very much like a portable juicer, and kissed Harriet on both cheeks. 'I'm so sorry,' she said to Lizzy. 'Stu's working. He couldn't make it.'

Lizzy squeezed Soo. 'Don't worry. Bloody Conrad's on call. Today. Of all days. Silly sod. This *can't* be Annabel. She's so *big*.'

'Isn't she scrummy?' Soo grinned. 'I can't believe nobody's stolen her yet.'

'She's gorgeous.' Harriet took Annabel and balanced her on her hip, inhaling the heart-breaking scent of baby powder and innocence. It was hard to believe she might never have one of these of her own.

'Broody?' Soo beamed at Harriet. 'About time you got started, isn't it?'

Harriet felt Lizzy's hand squeeze her arm in reassurance.

'Oh God.' Soo's hand flew to her mouth in horror. 'Have I put my foot in it? Oh Crackerjack.

78

I have, haven't I? I'm so sorry, Harry. Are you and Dan having problems?'

Jemima came to Harriet's rescue. Clad in a baggy pea-green vest teamed with lurid magenta tights, acid-yellow flip-flops adorned with plastic lilies and a violet knitted beret, she pouted, hands on hips, from the dizzy heights of the garden wall.

'I'm the queen of the car-stle.'

'You're a little witch,' Lizzy muttered under her breath. 'GET DOWN BEFORE I COUNT THREE.'

'Or what?'

'Or I'll have you adopted. Yes. That does mean you'll be sent away to live with someone else. No. Not with Charlie out of Busted. He won't want you. No. I shouldn't have thought Ant and Dec would have you either. I expect you'll have to go and live with someone horrible. Yes. Like Claudia's mum.' She bit the end off a sun-dried tomato sausage. 'You see, Harry? They're not sugar and spice all of the time. Even Lucy's found her dark side. She's discovered she's got an opinion and she's apparently unafraid to use it. I could happily throttle the pair of them sometimes.'

Harriet wandered off on the pretext of finding something to eat. In truth, food was the last thing on her mind. Her stomach felt like a tight ball of elastic bands. She found the old wooden bench, tucked out of sight at the bottom of Lizzy's garden. She wouldn't be disturbed here. The silent, penny-brown waters of the canal were too close for comfort. No mother in her right mind would allow her offspring to venture this far. Here, she would have space to think.

She dug deep into her bag and retrieved the photograph of Hermione. She'd been carrying it around with her ever since she'd found it tucked into the pages of her sister's diary.

'I wonder what you would think of all this,' she whispered to the carefree spirit, clad in tattered jeans and baseball boots. 'Do you still think all this baby stuff is a waste of time?'

Hermione had been adamant, from the age of about ten, that she was never going to succumb to marriage and children. Harriet could remember her announcing it one day. Ruby had taken them to the beach hut for a girlie picnic of crab sandwiches and Victoria sponge. There had been a bride and groom on the beach, having their photograph taken. The bride had been wearing a huge cream puff of a dress. Ruby and Harriet, caught up in the romance of the occasion, had jumped up to get a better look. But Hermione had stayed where she was, perched on the white Lloyd Loom chair, licking buttercream from her fingers in the manner of a cat washing her paws.

'Aren't you coming, sweetheart?' Ruby had asked.

'Nah.' Hermione cut another slice of cake, sending cream oozing down the sides. 'Think I'll just have this. I don't really see the point of all that stuff.'

'Don't you want to get married some day?' Ruby had asked in surprise.

'Nah.' Hermione threw a clump of cake at a cruel-looking seagull. 'Think I'd rather be a spinster.'

'What about babies?' Harriet had asked, shocked.

Hermione considered it. 'I'd rather have a chinchilla. Helen's got a chinchilla. They're cool.'

Harriet stared at the photograph for so long she went into a sort of trance. When she looked up again at the people milling about, she saw a familiar figure crossing the garden towards the barbecue.

She blinked hard. Surely not.

Will?

She blinked again and looked at the spot where she thought she'd seen him, fully expecting him to have vanished like a mirage. But he was still there, striding purposefully towards Lizzy, an enormous bunch of sunshine-bright tulips in his hand. Behind him trotted a little girl in a scarlet flannel dress, her dark hair snaking behind her like seaweed as she tried to keep up.

Harriet's heart flipped like a Tiddlywink. It *couldn't* be him. It must be someone who looked a lot like him.

But there was no mistaking the slight swagger in his gait or the way that Lizzy instantly became a fawning fool when he handed over the flowers. He'd always had that effect on women.

It was him all right.

What the hell was Will Cartwright doing back in Bath? After all this time . . .

Harriet's composure started to unravel like old knitting.

The last time she'd seen Will, he'd been about to embark on the trip of a lifetime with Hermione. And here he was, back in Bath, with a small child trailing in his wake.

'Smile,' said a voice behind her. 'It might never happen.'

Harriet started. Jesse was standing by the clematis arch clutching a glass of something fizzy.

'Sorry,' she said. 'Am I not being entertaining enough for you? I could flap about in big comedy shoes and honk a horn if you like.'

'Excellent,' Jesse said. 'And perhaps you could wear a big red nose and a squirty flower in your lapel. That should just about cover it.'

'Loon.' Harriet grinned. Despite the shock she'd just had, she couldn't help feeling ridiculously pleased to see Jesse. Somehow, he never failed to cheer her up when she was feeling down. Recently, he'd gone from being the bloke who lived in the basement to a pretty good mate. He confided in her a lot. She knew all about his mad family. His brother, Joe, who drove him to distraction. Joe was staying with Jesse until he went travelling. There had been some sort of rumpus at home, apparently. So he'd come to treat Jesse's flat like a free hotel.

Jesse had told her all about his girlfriend, Clare, who lived and worked in Italy. It was a really sweet story. He'd known her since schooldays. Her father had been a house master at his boarding school and Clare had been around as long as he could remember. The only girl in a building where the testosterone was practically bouncing off the walls. She'd been much coveted, Jesse said. But he had won her heart. They'd been together on and off ever since. Harriet knew the distance got him down sometimes. But absence, as they said, did make the heart grow fonder. When they saw each other, Jesse said, it was worth it.

'What are you doing here?' she asked him. 'I didn't know you were coming.'

'I thought you might want some company.' Jesse shrugged down beside her. 'After what you said the other day about you and Dan, I thought you might find this a bit hard.'

'Thank you.' Harriet, genuinely touched, gave him a hug. As she did so, the photograph of Hermione fluttered to the ground. Jesse picked it up.

'Wow!' He whistled. 'She's gorgeous. Who is she?'

'My sister,' Harriet said. 'Sickening, isn't it? She was amazing. A real head-turner. We were so different. Penny Plain and Twopence Coloured.'

'Was?' Jesse's eyes clouded. 'So she's . . .'

Tears pricked Harriet's eyelids.

'Hey.' Jesse looked at her with concern. 'What's the matter?'

It was like opening floodgates. Harriet told him everything. The dreadful accident that had killed her parents. Hermione and Will's betrayal of her. The abortion. And then, that fateful day, a few weeks after their parents' death, when she'd come downstairs to breakfast and heard voices coming from Ruby's sitting room, the one she kept for best – Saturday night bridge parties. Cocktails in twinkly glasses. Little silver bowls of salted peanuts and pimento-stuffed olives. That morning had been a sunny one. The French windows had been open and the scent of nicotiana from Ruby's tobacco plants in their pots on the patio had been wafting in from outside.

Harriet remembered watching a fat bumblebee buzz around the red-hot pokers in the strip of soil by the fence as Hermione, beautiful in a black spaghetti-strap vest, dozens of Indian gold bangles and faded jeans slung just below her jutting hipbones, which emphasised the scoop of her stomach, talked excitedly to Will. As Harriet pushed open the door and came in, Hermione had turned and given her the news that had been the last straw. Her glossed toenails shimmered like ten miniature jellies in the early morning sunbeams as she told Harriet that she and Will were going.

'Going?' Harriet, trying hard not to look at Will, had stammered. 'Going where?'

'Anywhere we want.' Hermione beamed. 'Will's got us round-the-world tickets. We'll be gone for a year. Isn't it great?'

To Harriet, the news had been anything but great. Finally, something inside her had snapped. She'd turned on her sister. Called her all the names under the sun. Told her . . .

'I told her I never wanted to see her again,' she said to Jesse. 'Isn't that horrible?'

'God,' Jesse said. 'No. I mean, I'd say it was pretty normal under the circumstances.'

'But she went,' Harriet said. 'That day. She packed up the rest of her stuff and just got on the back of Will's bike. That was the last I saw of her. And I didn't mean it.' She was crying now. 'I didn't mean it.'

'Hey,' Jesse said. 'Of course you didn't mean it. You were in shock. It's OK.'

Harriet wiped her eyes. 'I think I blamed her, more than anything, for changing everything. I mean, if she hadn't called, my mum and dad would never have had the accident. And, maybe, if they hadn't died, she wouldn't have gone away with Will. I could have told her about the baby. She could have been there when I got rid of it.'

'I'm sorry.' Jesse squeezed her arm. 'I'm so sorry.'

'Dan thinks I can't be close to him in the way he wants because I haven't dealt with losing my parents yet. I think he thinks I married him because I wanted someone I could call my family. And maybe I did.'

'Perhaps it might help if you spoke to your sister. Did Dan not suggest that?'

Harriet shook her head. 'He thinks she's dead.'

'Dead?' Jesse said. 'But why?'

'Everyone just assumed it,' Harriet said. 'At university, they assumed I'd lost my whole family. And it was easier to let them think it. That way, nobody asked any questions.'

'Dan, though,' Jesse said. 'Your husband.'

'I know,' Harriet said. 'Mad, isn't it? What does that say about us? I couldn't even tell him the truth.'

'You poor thing. I had no idea.'

'I thought I was OK.' Harriet sobbed. 'But I'm not. I miss my sister.'

'Have you no idea where she is?' Jesse asked.

Harriet shook her head. 'She could be in Timbuctoo for all I know.'

'Right,' Jesse said firmly. 'Then we have to find her.'

HERMIONE

Toronto, 2003

In a house on Amelia Street, Hermione placed Josh's last Malteser on the milky flesh of her stomach and watched it gravitate towards her belly button like water swirling down the plughole. It was difficult to believe that, were she do to exactly the same thing a month or two from now, the little ball of crunchy chocolate would simply roll down the side of her tummy and bounce off the sofa cushions onto the floor for Lady Penelope, Josh's spoiled Siamese, to pounce on and gobble up whole.

It was all a hell of a lot to take in.

She was only bloody well pregnant!

Had been, apparently, for almost three months. For eighty-three days, a brand new life had been unfurling, like a sea anemone inside her. And she hadn't felt a flipping thing!

It was true that she'd been feeling a bit tired lately. And she'd been eating more over the past few weeks. But she'd put that down to the time of year. Canadian winters were glacial. It was just her hibernation instincts kicking in.

Sylvie, her friend back in London, had swelled from a svelte size eight to an eighteen when she'd been pregnant with her daughter, Daisy. She'd experienced some pretty weird and wonderful cravings to boot. She'd once got them thrown out of Robert Dyas in Kensington for sniffing doorknobs. She'd crunched ice cubes incessantly while her husband Ted was trying to watch the Superbowl on TV. And she'd eaten the most revolting combinations. Crisps dipped in Lucozade. Gherkins sunk in chocolate cake. Arctic Roll with ketchup. Jam doughnuts with salad cream. Quite disgusting.

She probably should have seen this coming. For some reason, she was the sort of person things just seemed to happen to. Her childhood years, for instance, had been characterised by a singular lack of organisation. Forgotten swimming things. Lost textbooks. At the age of nine, as everybody else in her class had been changing into costume for the Christmas play, an unintentionally hilarious rendition of *The Twelve Days of Christmas*, Hermione had reached for the tutu she was to wear in 'Seven Swans a-Swimming' and had suddenly had an image of the filmy, gauzy layers of tulle hanging on the newel post of the stairs at home. Another time, as she and Harriet swung from the school bus, minding the cracks in the pavement as they made their way to Assembly, she'd suddenly had a distinct feeling that she was missing something. As the green double-decker bumped and squeaked round the corner and out of sight, a mental picture of her cello on the luggage rack at the front popped into her head.

'I wish you would THINK,' Ruby had said in exasperation, after a flurry of panicked calls to the lost property office in Penzance had turned up nothing but a glove with one of Hermione's red name tapes sewn into it and a tennis racquet with 'Hermione Harker' burnt into the handle with a compass.

The trouble was, she told herself now, examining her flat tummy and trying to imagine what she would look like when she was an Easter egg with legs, she preferred to live in the moment and deal with the consequences later.

It was living in the moment, she supposed, that had made her run off with Will so soon after her parents had died. Such a dumb thing to do. No wonder Harriet had never got in contact. How must she have felt, being left in Bath alone, while her sister went gallivanting halfway around the world? How stupidly insensitive was that?

Mind you, she always got itchy feet if she stayed in a place too long. Unlike Harriet, who'd always been more than happy to stay at home, flipping through Ruby's copies of *Good Housekeeping* magazine and dreaming of the house she would live in when she grew up. By the time she was six, Harriet had already had the names of the four perfect children she was going to have neatly logged in her mind. She was probably happily married with a family by now.

Hermione smiled, picturing her sister walking purposefully towards a pair of school gates, her children trailing behind her like ducklings as she distributed the day's essentials: lunch boxes, PE bags, reading books. She would make a great mum. She'd always been such a gentle soul. Far happier baking a chocolate cake with Ruby than flirting with boys in pubs. Her children would be a lucky brood indeed.

She and Harriet had been so close once. Often, each seemed to know what the other was going to say before she'd even opened her mouth. They finished each other's sentences. They'd shared a bedroom until they were thirteen. They liked going to sleep knowing that the other was there.

They'd bickered, as only siblings can. But it had always been over silly little things. Who'd read *Smash Hits* in the bath and got it soaking wet so the pages had melded together. Who'd used the crimpers last and left burnt hair stuck to it like cinder toffee. Once, when Ruby had gone to the hair-dresser, Hermione had made Harriet so angry she'd taken a running jump at her when she was lying on her back on the floor, landing with both feet in the middle of her stomach. She could still remember the look of horror on Harriet's face when she'd sat up and started to retch. She'd thought she'd done some permanent damage.

Hermione wondered when, exactly, they'd started to drift apart. When had the first cracks appeared? Fourth year at school, perhaps? Fifth form? Certainly, she'd hit puberty at the speed of an Inter City train, while Harriet had almost shied away from it altogether. Suddenly, they seemed to have nothing in common any more. Harriet had no interest in the parties, fuelled with Blue Nun and Bensons, that Hermione went to on Saturday nights, preferring to stay at home and help their mother bake brownies. Hermione would have given her eye teeth to be able to confide in her as she once had. But, suddenly, it had become difficult to know what to say.

It had occurred to her to try, the day she lost her virginity. It would have been nice to be able to take Harriet into her confidence. But she couldn't. Her sister wouldn't approve. What if it drove her away?

On the one hand, she felt that what Mr Sinclair had done that lunchtime rendered him weak and despicable. On the other, however, she didn't really give a flip. For one thing, it was a relief to know that, to someone at least, she was irresistible. For another, she'd used him just as he'd used her. She'd been desperate to be rid of her virginity ever since Lisa had let Tim Vickery screw her in the bathroom at a party.

She remembered getting home that day after double French and racing up to her room, taking the stairs two at a time in her eagerness to study herself in the mirror to see if she looked any different. Her room was exactly the same as it had been that morning. The pastel duvet on her bed still bore the indentation from where she'd crawled out of it that morning. The omnipresent collection of coffee cups, filled with an inch of fuzzy green mould, lurked by her bed. The chair beside her dressing table was heaped with discarded items of clothing. Her favourite studded leather belt was draped over the back.

Last time I wore that belt, she told herself. I was a virgin.

Disappointingly, there had been no outward signs of her progression to womanhood. Her face, in the mirror, had been exactly as usual. Her dark brown eyes, set quite far apart, had stared back at her, just as they always had. Even Harriet, who as usual had already changed out of her uniform into Levi's and a red and blue striped shirt, hadn't noticed a thing. As Hermione had come windmilling into the kitchen, she'd merely looked up from the elaborate sandwich she was making, comprising layers of crispy bacon and squidgy avocado, and asked, 'All right?' before consuming her feast in the neat, orderly fashion that only Harriet could.

Suddenly, Hermione hadn't felt so sure of herself after all. The little domestic scene had jarred uncomfortably with the sordid lunchtime incident and she'd suddenly felt horribly uneasy. It was tempting to blurt everything out, so that Harriet could tell her it would all be OK. But, deep down, she was worried her sister wouldn't understand.

In Toronto, Hermione's gaze came to rest on the

photograph on the mantelpiece. It was one of the few family photographs she possessed. When Pip had packed everything from the house in Belmont into boxes and given them half each, the intention had been for them both to go through them at a later date and decide who got what, so it was fair. But they had gone their separate ways soon afterwards. She'd gone to Southeast Asia with Will and Harriet had moved to London. Somehow, somewhere along the line, they'd managed to lose each other. It was mad.

The photo sat on the mantelshelf between an ostrich egg and a picture of herself and Josh at some industry awards bash. It must have been taken on a Saturday morning because in the background the interior of the café Isaac had always taken them to as a treat after swimming was visible. Orange blobs, pendant globes of light, hung so low over the tables it was hard to see who you were eating with, made up most of the background. In the foreground, Harriet, her straight brown fringe hanging in her eyes, was giggling at the camera because her mouth was encrusted with sugar from the doughnut she'd been eating. Just looking at it now brought back the giddy excitement of feeling once-a-week Coca-Cola bubbles fizzling in her nostrils. It was such a happy memory.

It occurred to her that it would be good to be able to phone her sister the way her friend Sylvie in London called hers. How nice it would be to be able to take her out for a cup of coffee and ask her advice. Hear her say that everything was going to be all right, just as she'd done in those first few agonising days after Ruby and Isaac's accident.

It still shocked her to think about how she'd gone to pieces like that in the hospital. She was supposed to be the strong one. Harriet had been the fragile baby bird. The one who nearly hadn't survived. The one who got glandular fever and whooping cough. And yet, somehow, when the pressure was on, she'd come into her own.

Hermione could still see her now, her chin thrust forward with grim determination as, clad in a bizarre costume of winceyette pyjamas, an old and holey fleece and a pair of yellow Wellingtons, she'd gone in to identify their parents' dead bodies. The image was branded on her brain. If only she could go back to that brief snatch in time and somehow furnish herself with the guts to stand up and take her sister's hand so she wouldn't have to be strong all on her own; maybe then they might still be sharing secrets, just as they always had. She'd meant to stay in touch. But every time she thought about it, she lost her nerve. The longer she left it, the harder it became. And then, one day, she woke up and realised that three years had passed. Harriet would have moved on. She wouldn't be able to contact her now even if she wanted to.

She peeled the sliver of cellophane from a box of Camel Lights and slid a forbidden cigarette from the package into her mouth. Why was she thinking about Harriet now? After all this time. Perhaps it was her hormones.

A lump came into her throat as she remembered how she'd let her sister down when she'd needed support more than she'd ever needed it. She'd let her do that difficult, brave thing all on her own and then she'd run away. She wasn't strong after all. She was as frilly as a leaf of lollo rosso.

How on earth was she going to look after a baby?

She flicked the Zippo Josh had given her for Christmas and watched as the paper caught and a curl of blue smoke floated towards the ceiling. She was supposed to be giving up. For the baby's sake, if not her own. Her doctor had outlined all possible detrimental effects. But there had been a loophole. He had said that, if the stress of giving up out-weighed the health benefits, then it might be all right to have the odd one. And so it was that, with that loophole fixed firmly in her mind, Hermione had smoked the odd cigarette no less than five times this morning. She was quite sure that, without the familiar crutch her Camels provided, she would be climbing the walls by now.

Thus far, her life had been a hedonistic whirl of launch parties, awards bashes and clubs. Sometimes, if the fancy took them, she and Josh drank champagne for breakfast. For whole week-ends at a time, they got their required calorie intake purely from alcohol. How on earth was she going to keep a baby alive? She would have to stop her from running out into the road and sticking her fingers into electrical sockets. She was going to have to remember to tell her to eat her greens. Stop her from wandering off. She was going to have to remind her to thank people for having her at parties and make sure she wore knickers to school.

It wasn't even as though she had anybody to help her. She couldn't reasonably expect Josh to stick around. Which was a shame. In the aftermath of Greg, she'd come to the conclusion that now, more than ever, Josh was her perfect man. Being a gay man, he couldn't provide her with a sex life, which was admittedly a bit of a fly in the ointment. But then again, before Greg, she'd never been much of a one for monogamy. And Josh was there for everything else. Theirs was a fully functional relationship everywhere but in the bedroom. And even that was far from a no-go area. They snuggled up in bed on Saturday mornings to watch cartoons just like any other couple. After a hard day at work, they would often crash on Josh's huge white bed to chip and dip together like any husband and wife. The only thing that made them any different from a normal married couple was the lack of sex.

She'd never really believed in fate. The idea that there was someone out there for everyone had always seemed a bit too Mills and Boon for her liking. But the longer Josh was in her life, the more she started to doubt her convictions. Perhaps Josh *was* the one for her. Maybe fate thought it was OK to deal a Joker occasionally.

She and Josh had been inseparable since the day they met, as juniors in a Soho advertising agency. Hermione had just returned to London from Lyons, where she'd been living in an apartment in a gorgeous old block by the Saône. When life without Marmite had started to really get to her, she'd put some of the money she'd inherited from her parents into a sweet Victorian house in Fulham and started applying for jobs. She hadn't really needed the money. Isaac's business had been booming when he died. There was nothing in life as sure as death, after all, and people always needed headstones. On top of that, he'd bought a life insurance policy from a door-to-door salesman a week or so before the accident. She could still remember him telling them about it over Ruby's first attempt at Hungarian goulash that night. He'd been annoyed with himself for going along with it because, once he'd eventually shut the door, he'd had to admit to himself that he'd only been sucked in because the man had seemed down on his luck and he'd been too soft to say no.

As it turned out, Isaac had had the last laugh.

Back then, Hermione hadn't known a soul in London. The majority of her friends were in France and she thought the best way to meet people was through work. Three months later, however, she had nothing to show for the dozens of applications she fired off every week but a wall covered in rejection letters. It seemed that her failed A-levels, not to mention her lack of degree, mattered quite substantially in a climate where there were three million unemployed. One night, full of desperation, she decided to take matters into her own hands.

She lied.

The new Hermione Harker had passed four A-levels before going on to study modern languages in Oxford. Hermione had never actually been to Oxford. But she was blessed with a very vivid imagination. Six days later, her efforts paid off. She got an interview with Pritchard Smythe, a successful advertising agency in Beak Street. To be on the safe side, she'd worn a short skirt to the interview. She was offered a position as a junior copywriter on the spot. Initially, she'd been apprehensive. She had no idea what being a copywriter actually involved. But, as it happened, she'd turned out to be rather good at it. One promotion led to another. In time, she'd got so used to the money and the excellent perks of the job that she almost forgot to watch her back in case someone decided to run a few checks and realised she wasn't quite the brainbox she'd made herself out to be.

Two years ago, when Frank Pritchard had asked her into his office for a 'chat', she'd thought her goose was cooked. Perhaps someone had finally decided to pull their finger out and check her references.

Instead, Frank had told her that everybody at Pritchard Smythe UK was impressed with her work. They were expanding into Canada soon and they would be delighted to offer her the position of Creative Director at Pritchard Smythe Canada – or PSC as it was going to be known. Would she care to accept?

Hermione had jumped at the chance. By then she was sick of London. The black bogies and painted-on personalities had started to get to her. She had no family to speak of. No ties. She would miss Sylvie. But she was always so busy with Daisy. And, when it turned out that Josh was being offered a position on the new team too, it had seemed as though it was meant to be.

She'd grown to love Toronto. There was so much more space here than on the crowded pavements of Oxford Street. And she loved the way the city could seem glitzy yet down-at-heel at the same time. Loved the colourful neighbourhoods, jostling side by side in apparent harmony. Chinatown, with its plentiful dim sum restaurants and its fruit and vegetables spilling all over the sidewalk. Little India, bursting with perfumed spices and jewel-bright saris. Little Italy, packed with smoky espresso cafés and crowded pool halls. The Beaches, dotted with quirky antique shops and pretty clap-board cottages. And the Islands, which studded Lake Ontario like jewels.

Last September, she and Josh had bought a tiny cabin, way up in Northern Ontario. It had been an impulse purchase. She'd always been a city girl at heart. But she and Josh had gone up for a weekend last summer. It had been so peaceful, just sitting at the lake surrounded by pine trees and total silence. So, when it transpired that one of the cottages, a sweet little Hansel and Gretel place with a pitched roof, was up for sale for a song, they'd gone ahead and put the money down. They were going to do it up this summer so they could have friends up for weekends.

If she had this baby, she doubted very much that she'd still be able to do that. Her staying in Canada depended on her job. And, in this industry, people were generally about as deep as your average crisp packet. Image was everything. Nobody wanted a walking Humpty telling them how best to market their products. They wanted something fairly easy on the eye.

Usually, when somebody went on maternity leave, they tended not to come back. They might *think* they were coming back. They might have made arrangements with Human Resources to agree on a return date as soon as the stitches were out and they'd got the hang of the breast pump. But advertising didn't quite work like that. You were only as good as your last campaign. And, while you were at home, learning the names of the Tweenies off by heart and discovering that, actually, rusks were pretty damned edible when there was nothing in the fridge but follow-on milk, there would always be someone better than you willing to offer that extra pound of flesh. Which, on the face of it, was laughable. Most of the women there were pretzel-thin. Even the men were adrenalin junkies, feeling the burn every lunchtime in the company gym as they pounded the tread-mills like stressed hamsters. There really wasn't that much extra flesh to go round.

As long as you took it for what it was – a world as fake as Willy Wonka's chocolate factory – PSC was a nice place to be. Everything was big and bright and clean, from the sleek glass doors to the funky exposed brickwork. The floors were all crafted from smooth limestone and the reception desk, which was the first thing you clapped eyes on when you walked in, was a block of black marble, which was always adorned with a vase filled with punchy flowers. Even Silke and Marley, who answered the phones, somehow fitted in with the décor. It didn't take a genius to work out that if Silke had been like the side of a house and Marley had had a face like a cobbler's thumb, they wouldn't have got jobs here, no matter how advanced their switchboard skills.

In this business, once you joined the pudding club, you were history. No sooner were you out the door, trailing squirly ribbon and clutching your wad of Mamas and Papas vouchers, than at least three people were swarming around your pen pot, swooping on Tippex and biros that hadn't gone blobby. And that was just the begin-ning. A week later, somebody else would bagsy your nice spot by the window. Six months in, if anybody asked why you hadn't come back to work, somebody higher up would say that you'd left to pursue 'other goals'. Meaning that, as far as they were concerned, you were on the scrap heap. After that, if you ever came up in conversation at all, nobody would remember your name. You would be the one who brought doughnuts in on Fridays. The one who once found a piece of windpipe in his steak and kidney pie. Or the one who picked his nose and ate it.

She wondered what they would say about her.

She would probably be the one who spent lunchtimes catnapping under her desk, she decided. She'd been feeling terribly tired lately. At least now she knew why.

Or she might be the one with all the shoes. She'd had a thing for shoes, ever since Ruby had bought her her first pair of silver party sandals in Freeman, Hardy and Willis when she was six. Yesterday lunchtime, she'd bought herself a frivolous pair of mules in pale pistachio silk to wear to the office spring party last night. They were still wrapped in the fluffy white tissue they'd come in. The news from the doctor had floored her rather. She'd only gone in for some iron tablets because she'd been feeling a bit lethargic lately. She'd certainly never expected to discover that, in just six months, she was going to have a tiny creature dependent on her for every single little thing. So she'd given the party a miss.

Having a baby on her own hadn't really been on the agenda. She'd never really thought about having children at all.

She still wasn't sure what she was going to do. If only she could speak to somebody about it, she might feel a bit better. But Josh was in Belfast for his brother's wedding and she was forbidden to call him. His mother would be dragging him to Mass every five minutes to make up for his dreadful Bacchanalian lifestyle and he wasn't going to have the energy to think about anything else.

As she flipped through her address book, her finger hovered over Harriet's name and she allowed herself a brief fantasy in which she called her up out of the blue and was rewarded with a joyful whoop, followed by a promise to be on the next flight over.

She snapped the book shut. Stupid! She had no idea where her sister was, let alone how to get hold of her. The last number she had for her was a flat in Battersea. She was hardly likely still to be there fifteen years later, was she? She could be in Timbuctoo for all Hermione knew.

She could always call the child's father. Tell him he'd left something behind when he last visited.

She smirked. Greg would be across town like a shot, in case it was something important. His favourite cashmere scarf. An Ozwald Boateng three-piece he'd thought was still at the dry cleaner's. How funny it would be to get him over here, only to tell him that what he'd actually landed her with was a foetus.

Actually, she told herself, Greg wasn't that bad. He did have a bit of a reputation in the industry as an arrogant son of a wotsit. But that was all front. During their affair, Hermione always felt she'd managed to tap through the slick exterior to find the gooey centre within. And it had come as rather a surprise, two or three months in, to find that it was the soft marshmallowey bit she was falling for, not the sleek, impeccably dressed Adonis she'd initially made a beeline for. Usually, she didn't like it when men opened up to her. It tended towards weakness, which always made her feel sorry for them. And once she'd felt any sort of pity for someone, she found it pretty hard to want them sexually.

She smiled wryly. A therapist would have a field day with her.

She'd met Greg on a freezing evening in January. The company he worked for – a huge soft drinks multinational – was making inroads into the sports drinks market and Pritchard Smythe were pitching. Spurt! was worth a few million and everyone in the office was buzzing. Hermione had come up with the brilliant idea of getting Brad Martini of the Toronto Maple Leafs to promote the drink in Canada. He was known from Alberta to Nova Scotia. And his star was just rising. By the time the advertisement came out, he would be huge.

Jeff, a cocky account manager at Pritchard Smythe, had decided that he and Hermione should do a bit of schmoozing on the client front. And so it was that Hermione found herself standing at the side of an ice rink, freezing her butt off and watching a game she didn't have a hope of understanding.

It had gone down a storm. The marketing guys from the Canon Corporation had had a ball. They'd loved every minute of it. The pizzas. The hot dog shooters. The plastic pitchers full of beer. At half time, Brad had stood there, his fat ass poured into a pair of über tight pants, and signed pucks for everyone. Jeff had high-fived her at the bar afterwards. It looked as though they were game on.

After a couple of beers, Greg Finch, the head honcho at Canon Corps, had suggested they all go get something to eat. Hermione, flushed with success, had proposed Chinatown. She loved the place, with its cabbages spilling out all over the streets and its weird, wonderful and often down-right freaky-looking delicacies in all the shop windows. But, one by one, Greg's minions had dropped out, pleading other commitments. Even Jeff had bailed, pleading an early start in the morning. Hermione had blushed puce with embarrassment. She'd been far too eager. And now she just looked uncool.

But Greg had simply grinned at her and said, 'Looks like it's just you and me then. Lead the way.'

Hermione took him to her favourite place. It was nothing fancy. The décor was worn and faded. Even the fish, swimming lethargically around the tank behind their table, looked bloated and depressed. But the dim sum was out of this world. She and Josh went there on a regular basis to stuff themselves silly with steamed pork dumplings and fried onion blossom.

Greg ordered the wine without consulting her. This pleased Hermione. She liked men who were confident enough with themselves to take charge. She couldn't stand the sort who shilly-shallied over where to sit in case they made a mistake that would blow the date out of the water.

She'd had to remind herself that this wasn't a date. OK, so Greg was good-looking. The appreciative glances he'd drawn from Emilie and Marcelle in the typing pool hadn't escaped her notice. And she'd definitely detected a certain chemistry during the hockey game. The proximity of his forearm as they'd stood, packed on the benches, had made the whole of her left side crackle with tickly electricity. But this was business. Certain rules applied. Fraternising with the clients wasn't encouraged at Pritchard Smythe. People had lost their jobs over it. Hermione didn't particularly want to be one of them.

'Bit lame.' Greg poured her wine.

'Sorry?'

'Your colleague. Dipping out like that. He's supposed to be trying to impress me.'

'He's a wanker,' Hermione told him. 'I can't stand him, to be honest with you.'

Greg's lips twitched.

'Shit!' Her hand flew to her mouth. 'I probably shouldn't have said that. It wasn't very professional.'

'Don't worry.' Greg grinned. 'Wan-kerrrr!' He enunciated it carefully. 'So funny.'

Hermione took a sip of her wine and hoped she hadn't blown it.

She needn't have worried.

'Tell you the truth,' Greg grinned, 'I can't stand him either. Arrogant little peckerwood, isn't he?'

Hermione burst out laughing. He had a really lovely grin. All twinkly. She'd always been a sucker for a twinkle. A half-decent twinkle had been Hermione's downfall on many an occasion.

'I probably shouldn't really be saying this either,' Greg confided, 'but I think I'm going to really enjoy working with you.'

'Steady on,' Hermione said. 'We haven't got the contract yet.'

Greg smiled. Raised his glass. 'I vote we have a toast. To a happy working relationship. *Santé.*'

'Cheers.' Hermione gulped her wine. 'Oh God. That's disgusting.'

'Disgusting,' Greg agreed. 'Shall we get some more?'

'Absolutely.'

The dim sum was excellent. The more they ate, the more Greg talked. Hermione wasn't quite sure if it was the effect of the alcohol or the fact that Greg was so handsome, but she was finding herself more and more attracted to him as the evening wore on. He was intelligent, in that, unlike a lot of the men she'd been with, he actually read books. He was attractive, obviously. And he had a sense of fun that was really refreshing. He didn't take himself too seriously.

When they'd finished eating, he suggested a game of spoof.

'We need more than two people,' Hermione protested, as a tingle of possibility shot up her spine.

'We'll improvise.' Greg counted out a fistful of loonies and gave her six. 'Whoever guesses nearest. OK? Your go.'

Hermione lost three times in a row and found herself getting more and more drunk.

'Another game?'

'We don't have any wine left,' Hermione pointed out.

'OK.' Greg scanned the table for more forfeits. 'Tell you what. Whoever loses this time drinks the dipping sauce.' He pointed at a polystyrene cup, filled to the brim with gelatinous red gunk.

'You're kidding.'

'I'm deadly serious. So come on. How many?'

Hermione stared at his hand. Which wasn't as easy as it sounded. She'd drunk so much wine she was seeing double.

'Four.'

'It's two.' He uncurled his palm. 'My turn.'

Hermione stretched out a clenched fist.

'How many?'

'Two.'

'Six,' Hermione said gleefully, grabbing the cup of gloop. 'I win.'

Greg put his hand on hers and her stomach spun like a Frisbee.

'Best of three?'

To her delight, he lost again and Hermione held out the dipping sauce. It looked truly disgusting. The colour was virtually radioactive.

'Yours, I believe.'

'Oh well.' Greg stood up and downed the whole pot in one go, putting the cup back on the table with a flourish. 'Never say I'm not a man of my word.'

'Gaah.' Hermione giggled. 'That's gross.'

'My thoughts entirely.'

With nothing left to drink, the game dwindled to a close. The waiter brought a pot of jasmine tea and Hermione sipped it gratefully as Greg asked her about herself. It was odd. Usually, she clammed up when people wanted to probe. With the exception of her closest friends, she didn't tend to tell people about the crash. In her experience, once you told people your parents had been killed in a car accident, you would always be the girl whose parents died. They could never get past feeling sorry for you long enough to get to know you.

But there had been something about Greg that put her at ease. He had a noble face. Long, aquiline nose. Frank brown eyes. And he wasn't afraid of talking about himself. As they sipped their tea, he told her that he'd lost somebody too. His brother had been killed in an accident when he was fifteen. The skiddoo he'd been riding on his parents' lake up north one Christmas had gone straight through the ice and the weight of it had sucked him down and dragged him away from the hole so he hadn't been able to come back up again. Horrified, Hermione had known immediately why she felt such a connection with Greg. He knew how it felt to lose someone close to you in tragic circumstances.

When he'd asked if there was a significant other in her life, her coccyx quivered with possibility.

It must have been about five minutes after she'd told him there wasn't that he'd gone to the bathroom and not come back. Disappointed, because she'd been so sure he was different, Hermione had sat, twiddling her thumbs and smoking one cigarette after another until she'd managed to convince herself he'd climbed out of the window to escape. She must have bored him to death.

She picked up her mobile phone and toyed with the idea of calling Josh. She didn't feel like going home just yet. Perhaps they could meet up in Sneaky Dee's. They could order huge pitchers of beer and she could cheer up and forget this whole sorry episode.

She was just dialling when her phone bleeped.

A text message.

It was a number she didn't recognise. Curious, she blipped the message open. It was short but sweet.

'You sure know how to keep a man waiting.'

Her stomach whirled with panic. What did it mean? Had she somehow missed him? Had he walked past the table as she'd been absorbed in lighting her cigarette? Was he waiting outside?

She swivelled her head around and glanced at the door. But there was nobody there, apart from the waiter counting checks. And the place was so narrow, it really was highly unlikely he could've squeezed past without her seeing.

She smiled at the waiter and made her way towards the back of the restaurant. The men's bathrooms were tucked away at the back. Her heart clopping like a pair of castanets, she opened the door a crack.

'Anyone here?'

'I thought you'd never get here.' Greg grinned at her.

Hermione was confused. 'How did you get my mobile number?'

'I called your office.' He grinned. 'Told the security guy I was supposed to meet you to discuss business but that I was running late. The crazy shmuck blabbed straight away.' He put his hands on her shoulders.

'Wait.' Hermione wriggled away. 'I haven't paid the bill.'

'Fuck the bill.' Greg pulled her into a cubicle and pushed her against the wall, cupping her buttocks with both hands. 'Tell me you don't want to do this and I'll stop.'

Hermione felt a tug on the invisible puppet string that led from her belly button down to her most intimate part. There was no doubt that she was incredibly attracted to him. The chemistry was mind-boggling. But she really liked Greg. And a part of her – admittedly a boring, sensible part – told her that if she wanted to see him again, she should hold out.

And then, of course, there was the small fact that below the waist contact with clients was strictly forbidden at Pritchard Smythe. After all, you could hardly call yourself something as patently proper as Pritchard Smythe and then allow your employees to behave like fishnet tarts, could you?

Greg lowered his lips onto hers and kissed her. It was a smoky, cidery kiss that tasted of teenage parties, when just the act of touching someone else's tongue and feeling the shock of their saliva on yours was electrifying.

His breath was coming in soft rasps now as he slipped his hands down under her waistband and hooked his fingers under the sides of her Strumpet and Pink thong, lifting it slightly so that it exerted a slight pressure on her clitoris, almost sending her into orbit.

'You like that?'

Hermione nodded. She was toast. And she knew it. She could hardly speak as Greg slowly rocked his thumbs back and forth until the thong was slippery wet and she had to beg him to take her.

When he did, he did so slowly, pushing himself inside her an inch at a time and then, just as she thought she really couldn't take any more, slamming himself home so that bolts of electricity shot up her spine and she couldn't stop herself from crying out. By the time it was over, she felt as though she'd lost all sense of who she was.

As she straightened her skirt, she wondered how many people were left in the restaurant. She knew she hadn't been able to stop herself from whimpering with delight. It wasn't like her. She always remained in control. But sex with Greg had taken her to another level completely. She'd totally lost it.

She was still shaking like a jelly as, cheeks burning, she picked her way through the restaurant to pay the bill. The waiter was too polite to say anything but she thought she could detect a faint twitch at the corners of his mouth.

Pritchard Smythe won the contract. Hermione, realising that she would never really know if it was her brilliant idea or her brilliant bedroom skills that had swung things in their favour, accepted a hearty pat on the back and a hefty pay rise with aplomb. It didn't matter. Because Greg had already rung to ask if he could take her out to dinner. Life, she'd told herself, as she popped out later that morning for her extra hot caramel macchiato, was pretty flipping perfect.

Over the next few months, they'd gone out to

dinner a lot. They both enjoyed eating good food in fabulous restaurants. Greg said there was something about watching a woman enjoy her food that drove him crazy with lust. One night, he'd leaned over his Caesar salad and, running his foot up her leg to massage the tiny corner of flesh at the top of her inner thigh, whispered, 'In a minute, I'm going to take you to the most expensive hotel in town and fuck you. And then I'm going to fuck you again. By the time you leave that hotel room, Little Miss Harker, you are going to be walking like John Wayne.'

He was dynamite in bed. There was no doubt about it. Three months in, everything still felt shiny and new. Hermione suspected that it was partly to do with the fact that, because they worked together, they had to keep their relationship quiet. Even Josh didn't know. Conducting a sexual relationship right under everyone else's noses certainly gave things a boost. Sitting in a room full of people and having to pretend nothing was going on was a sure-fire way to galvanise things in the bedroom. Not that the sex was always the dirty, blue movie sort they'd had that night in the Chinese restaurant. Sometimes it was. Sometimes, he wanted her so much he was like a crazed animal, his eyes glazed with lust. But some of the best sex they had was the slow, gentle kind, when Greg's brown eyes seemed to lock onto hers and she'd felt as though she could stay like that forever.

In the event, it came as quite a shock when,

after one particularly drawn-out meeting, at which Hermione's mind had been more on the exquisite curve of Greg's forearm than the Canon Corporation's projections for the next six months, Rob Smythe, over from London for a series of client conferences, had shaken Greg's hand and asked to be remembered to his wife.

Hermione hadn't trusted herself to speak. She'd watched the rest of the proceedings through a gauze of humiliation. Afterwards, she'd grabbed her new suede coat from the lobby and, without stopping to pull it on, even though it was minus ten degrees outside, had marched towards the subway, her eyes swimming with tears. How stupid could one person be? How come she hadn't figured it out?

She didn't go back to work that day. All she wanted was to be at home in Cabbagetown with Josh. She wanted to scooch over and put her head in his lap so he could fiddle with her hair, the way he always did when she was feeling down.

It all made sense now. Though she'd been fairly adept at dismissing the thought that had occasionally burrowed through her mind, like a maggot through an apple, she had occasionally wondered. Wondered why it was they never seemed to do normal stuff together. With Greg, it had always been flash restaurants and nights in elegant hotels. She'd often thought it might be nice to just go back to his. Curl up on the sofa with a bottle of wine, maybe. Listen to music. Cook pasta. Not all the time. There was plenty of time to turn into a couch potato when your veins were like ropes and her house smelled of dry skin. But, just occasionally, it would have made a nice change.

She'd reached the next block when she heard footsteps pounding the pavement behind her.

'Hermione. Wait.'

'Don't.' She spun round, eyes glittering with a mixture of upset and anger. 'Just. Don't. OK? I don't want to hear it.'

'Please.' Greg looked so forlorn even his jaunty sunshine-yellow tie seemed to droop. 'Let me explain.'

'I would have thought it was pretty cut and dried.' Hermione's voice shook. 'You're married. How much explaining does that need?'

'Don't do this.' Greg moved round the side of her and popped up in front. 'Look. Can we go for coffee?'

'I'm meeting Josh,' Hermione told him. 'It's about time I spent some time with him after lying to him for the last three months.'

'Please . . .' Greg begged. He looked so dejected that Hermione was tempted to give him the benefit of the doubt. Perhaps it had all been a mistake. Rob had got it wrong. Maybe – it was a long shot but it was possible – maybe Greg was pretending to be married because he thought he needed a wife for assorted social functions. Maybe . . .

She was clutching at straws. And she knew it.

She was so angry, her knees were knocking. It wasn't so much Greg she was angry with as herself. She was livid that she'd been sucked in. She'd actually allowed herself to fall for him. And now she was going to have to let him go.

'It's just coffee,' Greg pleaded. 'Please?'

She looked at his brown puppy dog eyes and her resolve collapsed like a soufflé.

'One coffee.' She held up her index finger. 'That's all.'

'So,' she said when she'd temporarily stopped shaking and there was a large mocha, piled with whipped cream, on the melamine-topped table in front of her. 'You have a wife.'

'Well . . .' Greg looked sheepish.

'You never told me you were married.'

'To be fair,' he said, 'I never told you I *wasn't*.'

'That's a bit pathetic, isn't it?' Hermione took a sip of her coffee and hoped the froth hadn't given her a moustache. 'Surely you can come up with something a bit better than that.'

He put down his cup and grabbed hold of her hands. 'It's difficult. Lena and I—'

'Don't.' She held her hands to her face as though to protect herself from the name. 'Don't say her name.'

'We're not in love any more. We've talked about a separation.'

Hermione stared at him. She wanted to believe him, if only because she felt so bloody foolish.

'So why didn't you tell me then?' Her hand shook as she picked up her cup. 'If that's true – about you getting a separation, I mean – why not just tell me? I might have understood.'

'Because we haven't separated yet,' Greg said quietly. 'We thought it would break the kids' hearts.'

'Kids?' Hermione echoed. 'Oh, this just gets better and better.'

'What can I say?' Greg shrugged. 'They're great kids. I'm proud of them. I'm not going to pretend they don't exist.'

'You've managed it for three months.' Hermione felt her fragile heart, the heart that had been dancing like a ping-pong ball balanced on a jet of water for three months, come pitter-pattering to an uncertain halt.

'Look,' Greg said. 'It's not as bad as you think.'

'How do you work that one out?'

'We can still see each other . . .'

Hermione pushed her coffee aside. It tasted acrid all of a sudden. She was in shock. Greg was the first man – apart from Josh, of course – that she'd really *felt* something for.

Greg pulled a boo-hoo face. 'We can, can't we?'

Slowly, Hermione shook her head. It was tempting. She would have liked nothing more than to be able to ignore Greg's 'situation' and carry on where they had left off. But she couldn't. An image popped into her mind. She remembered finding Ruby one day in floods of tears as she'd hung out sheets to dry in the garden of the house

118

in Cornwall. She'd been upset because her friend Miranda's husband had run off with another woman. At seven, Hermione had had a mental picture of Mr Holland and this other woman holding hands as they absconded down the street together. And, although the subtleties of the situation had been lost on her then, she did know that it had caused an awful lot of upset. Miranda had seemed to be in their kitchen for weeks, crying and eating cake. Hermione couldn't do that to somebody else's children. She just couldn't. She might not have the strictest of morals. But she was no home wrecker.

'But we're great together.' Greg looked appalled.

'I know,' Hermione said. 'But the answer's still no.'

In the house on Amelia Street, she put one hand on her belly and opened the window a crack to get rid of the smoke from another illicit cigarette. It was still chilly. Spring took a long time to arrive in Canada. The snow had just started to melt, leaving a muddy slush everywhere. Soon, though, the first buds would appear, poking bravely through the earth as though to remind everyone that life did go on, no matter how downright bloody difficult everything might seem sometimes.

HARRIET

Dearest Gigi,

I can't believe it! I've been suspended. All for breaking an egg over Fiona Wallace's head. I wouldn't mind, but she deserved it. She laughed! At my name. Bloody cheek. Fiona's far worse. Such a moany, whiny sort of a name. Fee-own-ah! And now, because of her, I'm missing the play. The absolute best thing about this term. I will hate Fiona Wallace for ever . . .

Hermione's diary was compulsive reading. It was extraordinary to hear her voice again, crackling from the pages with her own distinctive brand of humour. Harriet was finding it almost impossible to put down. Her sister's account of being suspended from school had almost had her in stitches. She remembered the incident well. They would have been about twelve or thirteen, making pineapple upside-down cake in cookery. Hermione had been a terrible cook. She didn't have the patience. As Harriet remembered it, her sister hadn't actually been suspended for breaking the egg. It had been on account of her bare-faced cheek. When Mrs Ellis, the cookery mistress, had come in and asked, 'Who's been breaking eggs in here?' Hermione had whip-cracked, 'One egg.' And so her fate was sealed.

Downstairs, Edie cranked up the volume on her shiny new state-of-the-art CD player. She was a different person since Cyril had died. Parcels, containing items she'd won on eBay, arrived almost on a daily basis. She'd suddenly developed a predilection for power ballads. As Harriet lay in the bath, her toes shrivelling like dried apricots as she read on, a blast of Guns N' Roses came through the floorboards. If it had been anybody else, she'd have got out of the bath and marched downstairs to have it out with them. But it was nice to see Edie living the life she'd so clearly missed out on.

Harriet closed her ears and chuckled as she read Hermione's account of smoking her first cigarette. She remembered that one too. They'd spent the morning trawling the supermarket with Ruby, who was set on making stir fry for supper. Later Harriet had been in her room, working on a watercolour of Hermione running along the beach near the house in Cornwall, her hair snaking in tendrils behind her. In the photograph she was copying, the wind had stippled the sand by the water's edge so it lay in black-speckled ridges. Hard to reproduce on canvas. She'd been on the point of flinging down her brush in exasperation when her door had opened and Hermione had edged in, her eyes glinting with mischief.

'Look what I've got.'

'What?'

Hermione shook a flat jade and gold box from the sleeve of her sloppy grey cardigan.

'Cigarettes?'

'Someone left them on a table outside the pub. Coming?'

'OK,' Harriet said, hating herself for being such a sheep but knowing she was completely powerless to do anything about it.

They'd told Ruby, who was frowning over sherry and soy marinade, that they were off for a walk and wandered into Hedgemead Park. They found a bench and Hermione slid the little white stick out of the packet and fumbled for a match. Harriet's hands trembled.

'If Ruby finds out, we're dead.'

'So?' Hermione scoffed. 'She won't find out. Unless you snitch.'

'Of course I won't snitch.' Harriet's cheeks burned. 'Won't we stink of smoke though?'

'I've got Polos.'

'We'll get addicted.'

'No we won't,' Hermione said. 'Not after one puff. They just tell you that to scare you off. We're fourteen. It's about time we learned how to do this.'

'Why?'

'We might become film stars,' Hermione said.

'We might need to smoke for a part. We'd look pretty pathetic if we couldn't even inhale.'

'I'm not sure I want to be a film star,' Harriet had said meekly. 'I wouldn't like all that attention.'

'A writer then for me,' Hermione said. 'A tortured artist for you.' She sucked in her cheeks. 'Luke Richards said I could even be a model. What d'you reckon?'

'Guess so.' Harriet eyed the cigarette with trepidation. In a minute, it would be her turn. She didn't really want to do it. But she knew she had to. Hermione wouldn't respect her otherwise.

'Cool.' Her sister lit the end and exhaled a perfect plume of lilac. 'Anyway, I don't mind getting addicted. I think I'm definitely going to be a smoker.'

Harriet flipped over onto a new page and cricked her neck to glance at the clock on her bedside table.

Bloody hell! It was nine thirty. She'd been marinating in here for nearly an hour! She had work to do.

Tonight was the night – Blue Ginger's launch bash. The doors opened at seven thirty and there was a heck of a lot still to do.

She balanced the diary on the edge of the bath and climbed out, just as the door buzzer went. She wrapped a nutmeg-coloured towel round her and, dripping water everywhere, went to let Jesse in.

'Are we all set?' He came bouncing into the room like a hyperactive Tigger, then stopped dead as he took in her half-naked state.

'Whoah.' He covered his eyes exaggeratedly and backed out again. 'Shit! Sorry. Don't worry. I'm not looking.'

'I won't be a minute.'

Harriet rummaged in her dressing-table drawer for the moisturiser. For some reason, she'd become somewhat lackadaisical in her normally stringent organisation of the flat. Her products, usually arranged in neat rows and categorised according to brand and type, lay in a jumbled heap. Tubes and bottles of glorious, unctuous goo littered the top of her chest of drawers. It was pretty difficult to find anything. Nevertheless, she got ready as quickly as possible, running a comb through her plain brown hair and pulling on jeans and a sleeveless hooded sweatshirt.

She'd spent most of yesterday afternoon ringing round those people who obviously didn't quite understand the RSVP concept. Most of them were London-based. It had been frustrating beyond belief.

'I'm sorry.' An adenoidal secretary with a name that sounded suspiciously like a sexually transmitted disease answered one call. 'You're asking if Varsha Kincaid is available to attend a bar opening in Bath?'

Harriet said that, yes, she was.

'Where is Bath? Is that SW12?'

'No. Bath as in Bath. The city.'

'A city not in London?'

'Yes.'

It was the same every time. It was as though everybody who lived and worked in the capital had absolutely no concept of anything that went on outside it. It had reminded her a little of Hermione when they'd moved from Cornwall to Bath.

They'd moved because a girl had drowned. Just after their tenth birthday, a tourist, a girl their own age, had been swept out to sea by a freak wave. Harriet could still remember the horror of it all. The townsfolk had come out in their droves, hoping to find some sign of the poor child. The mother, a sinewy woman with arms shaped like runner beans and long black hair that reached her backside, had stood on Porthmeor beach, day and night, to no avail. After a month or so, the hard fact that her daughter wasn't coming back had sunk in and she went back to wherever it was she had come from. Gradually, people in St Ives forgot the incident and moved on.

For one reason or another, Isaac hadn't been able to forget. The tragedy had stirred up memories of losing his father, on a fishing boat off the coast of Mousehole, years before and he decided, quite suddenly, to move both family and business as far from the sea as possible.

Harriet had looked forward to the move with trepidation. She loved where they lived. Loved being able to walk on the beach every day. Adored looking for wild flowers and butterflies on the cliff tops. Cities were filthy, polluted places. She didn't think she was going to like Bath one bit.

Hermione had been over the moon. When Isaac told them about the move one evening, as the family sat down to devour one of Ruby's culinary experiments, she'd looked as though all her Christmases had come at once. She'd always loved the bright lights and glitter of big cities. In London, on a trip to the Natural History Museum, she'd been in her element. Harriet had enjoyed the museum. The huge brontosaurus, its ribs arched like the ceiling of an Elizabethan barn, had fascinated her. She'd adored all the knobs and buttons there were to press. Nevertheless, she'd been relieved when they'd eventually stepped off the train at Penzance.

She still found the frenetic pace of London a bit much. She much preferred Bath. In Bath, you got the best of both worlds. You got dinky shops and nice restaurants on a more manageable scale.

Hermione obviously hadn't agreed. As the Triumph Herald pulled up outside the house on Belmont for the first time, her disappointment had been palpable. It had seemed to ooze into the car's every crevice, sneaking into the ashtrays and taking up residence in the glovebox. She'd been expecting something bigger. Faster. Louder. She'd been expecting black taxis and big red buses, churning out billows of grey smoke. The slow, sedate pace of Bath had come as rather a shock.

'Are you decent?' Jesse appeared at the bedroom door, averting his eyes in exaggerated fashion.

'It's OK.' Harriet grinned. 'You can look. Although I wouldn't exactly say I was decent. These jeans are disgusting. It was all that extra painting yesterday.'

'The jeans look fine to me. Here.' He handed her a cup of coffee. 'I took the liberty of introducing myself to your coffee machine. And I'm glad to say she's a lot more cooperative than Bertha.'

Harriet laughed. Last week, Blue Ginger's high-tech coffee machine had been installed behind the bar. A hissing silver monster, with more valves and spouts than you could shake a stick at, it had refused to behave since the day it had arrived. On the second day, after being spat at for the millionth time, Jesse had finally christened the damned thing Bertha, after a cantankerous maths teacher he'd once had.

Harriet took the cup from him and had a sip. 'Cheers. I need this. I'm knackered. I didn't sleep at all last night.'

'Me too,' Jesse said. 'I've had the squiddles all night. It's just nerves.'

'Partly,' Harriet said. 'But I've been up half the night reading that bloody diary.'

'Your sister's?'

'Yep. I can't put the bloody thing down. She should have been a writer.'

'Perhaps she is.' Jesse drained his cup. 'Perhaps

she writes under a pseudonym. You could have read dozens of her books and not even known. Weird.'

'Very weird.'

'Do you not feel a bit guilty?' Jesse asked.

'Guilty?'

'Reading things that weren't meant for your eyes, I mean.'

'Not really,' Harriet told him. 'A bit, perhaps. Mainly, I just see it as a way of getting to know my sister again.'

'Shame you'll never get to find out how it ends,' Jesse said thoughtfully.

'I know. I'm almost scared to finish it because then she won't be with me any more.'

'You could always do what I said.' Jesse raised an eyebrow.

'Look for her?'

'Why not?'

'I don't know.' Harriet shrugged. 'What if I found her and she didn't want to know me?'

'Why would she not want to know you?'

'Because of the awful things I said before she went away.'

'So put it right,' Jesse said. 'Find her. Tell her you're sorry.'

Jesse had to pick up a few things from his flat before they left for the bar. Harriet stood in his hallway, between an abandoned traffic cone and a mountain bike, as he sloped into the living room to find the pile of cocktail menus they'd had printed the week before. Jesse had left Harriet to choose the design and, after much umming and ahhing, she'd settled on an Art Deco font in sparkling white reversed out of the aniseed green that was Blue Ginger's signature colour.

'Sorry.' He came out into the hall, waving a large buff-coloured envelope. 'Got them.'

'Great.' Harriet nodded at the traffic cone. 'Courtesy of Joe, I take it.'

'Who else?' Jesse shrugged. 'Lurched through the door at half past three this morning, completely larruped, clutching that and the hanging basket from number thirty. It's still sitting on the kitchen table. I told him to go and put it back before anybody noticed it was missing but he hasn't bothered. He's not even up yet, the lazy feck.'

'I *told* you.' Joe's voice came from the direction of the bathroom. 'I'll DO it.'

Jesse lowered his voice. 'He's got candles in there, you know. Scented ones. Kumquat and thingummybob. And he's using conditioner. Bloody gaylord. He'll be listening to Simply Red next. Or opera. And you know how I feel about that carry-on.'

'Have you ever been to the opera?'

'Clare took me once,' Jesse said. 'She's very au fait with it all, being in Italy. She's just sort of soaked it all up. I couldn't get my head round it, to be honest.' He screwed up his nose. 'I kept wanting to ask her if she was *really* enjoying it or if it was just a case of the Emperor's New Clothes. You know.' He adopted a high falsetto voice. '"Ooh, I'm loving the cut of your gib, Your Majesty. Great strides too, by the way. Were they Diesel? Oh, you got them in the sale! How fabulous." I reckon most people say they enjoy it just because they think they should. What do you think?'

'I think we'd better get a move on.' Harriet looked at her watch. 'We've got a ton of stuff to get through before tonight.'

Project Blue Ginger, in all its glory, hadn't been plain sailing. In the six months Harriet had been working on it, she'd overcome more hurdles than Colin Jackson on a very bouncy day. There had been asbestos, the discovery of which had put the kibosh on her plans for at least six weeks. Shortly after work had recommenced, her foot had gone through a rotten floorboard like a knife through dolcelatte and she'd been on crutches for another month. And then, just as she'd got better, Bob, her handyman, had decided to get married at short notice and buggered off to Ibiza on honeymoon. Which wouldn't have been quite so bad if it hadn't been for the fact that, as he and his new wife Annie got to the airport for the flight home, Annie, who, despite having reached the grand old age of fifty-one, had never been abroad before, had taken exception to the customs officer going through her handbag and attacked him from behind with an outsize Toblerone. As a result, they'd missed their plane and not got another flight for five days, which had set Harriet's plans back further.

Last night, though, she'd had to admit that all the blood, sweat and tears had been worth it. When she thought about the way it had looked six months ago, when Jesse had taken her down there to show her, it was difficult believe it was the same place. It had been a right dump then. Anaglypta paper had peeled, like strips of sunburned skin, from the walls. Part of the ceiling had caved in. It had lain, like pieces of a giant jigsaw, on the bare floorboards. Beams stuck out like cracked ribs and live wires spewed from the walls. The former owner, closed down when Public Health had found the hindquarters of a Jack Russell in his fridge, had ripped out the peach frosted glass lampshades in an attempt to make a few quid in a car boot sale. It had been a real mess.

Anybody who had eaten at the Intrepid Chapatti would be hard pushed to recognise this as the same place now. Harriet had had the ground floor knocked through to make one vast space. Yesterday, as she and Jesse were on the point of locking up and calling it a night, it had been diffi-cult to tear themselves away. They'd stood for ages, just surveying the huge room. At one end stood a curved bar, made entirely of cherry wood and mirrored glass. Along the far side, intimate seating booths, upholstered in soft chocolate leather, were lined against the wall, so customers could tuck themselves away for privacy. The walls were all painted in the beautiful aniseed green she'd come across in a quirky paint shop in Portobello, and the hundreds of tiny pinpoint lights set into the ceiling sparkled like a canopy of silver stars.

'I always love it when it's like this,' Jesse had said softly.

'What do you mean?'

'When it's quiet.' Jesse nodded at the room. 'When everybody's gone home and all the noise and chatter has died down. When it's just me and the bar. It takes on a whole different personality when it's empty, don't you think? It's warmer. Kinder. Sort of magical.'

Harriet had known exactly what he meant. She'd always loved Blue Ginger in the early mornings, when she arrived to find the sunlight streaming through the big windows in the front onto the polished wood of the floor and Jesse, a pencil tucked behind his ear, coaxing the temperamental Bertha into action. There was something about a bar with nobody else in it. As she and Jesse had stood and looked at the baby they'd made together, a slow warmth had crept through her. This must be how actors felt when a play they'd rehearsed for ages came together on the first night. She could feel something. Something good. And she could tell Jesse felt it too. He was glowing with pride.

A voice from Jesse's kitchen startled her.

'Why don't we go upstairs? Slip into something more comfortable.'

'What was that?'

Jesse was fiddling with the envelope which held the invitations, trying to take one out so he could show her.

'We don't have to do anything if you don't want to. We can just lie there.'

The tips of Jesse's ears turned a deep damson – purple. 'God. Sorry. That wasn't me.'

'I know it wasn't you!' Harriet flushed peony at the thought. 'What was it?'

'That,' Jesse smiled, 'was our new flatmate.'

'You have a new flatmate?'

'Sure we do.' Jesse laughed. 'Want to meet her?'

Harriet checked her watch. 'We haven't really got time.'

'It'll only take a minute. Follow me.'

Harriet wondered what on earth he was talking about. The flat only had two bedrooms. Was this new girl sleeping on the sofa? Or was she bunking in with Joe? The latter seemed unlikely. Joe was twenty-one. He thought women were like Starbucks paper cups. Intended for single use only. He was hardly likely to allow one of them to move in.

Perhaps Clare had finally called it a day over in Italy and come back to be with Jesse. He did seem very happy today. OK, so they'd been on and off since school. But there must be something there for it to have lasted so long.

Harriet had only met Clare once. She'd come into Blue Ginger, when she'd been over for the weekend; a public school type with hyper-clean blonde hair and very white teeth. Considering the fact that Jesse was supposed to be her boyfriend, she'd shown remarkably little interest in the project. She'd draped herself across what was going to be a banquette, upholstered in soft chocolate leather, and accepted a cranberry juice as she picked at her quicks. As Harriet excitedly prised open a can of paint with a coffee spoon to show Jesse the amazing green she'd found, Clare had twisted a perfect strand of ice-blonde hair around her finger and looked at Harriet's spoils without much enthusiasm.

'Did you not think about doing it Tiffany blue?'

'No.'

'Oh.' Clare let the strand of hair uncoil. 'Only that's very now. Still. I could imagine that green in, like, a dress. A really flippy one, with maybe a halter neck?'

'Right,' Harriet had said uncertainly, as Clare turned to Jesse and asked when he thought he might be finished, because she wanted to go shopping for boots. Harriet hadn't really warmed to the woman at all. But, just like Emily with Bagpuss, Jesse obviously loved her.

Jesse would have said something if she'd moved in. As far as Harriet knew, Clare was coming over this evening as planned, to come to the launch and spend some time with Jesse before she had to go to New York for a month.

So who was this mystery lodger?

Jesse led Harriet into the kitchen, where the remains of somebody's supper sat on the draining board awaiting clearance. Dolmio pasta sauce, by the looks of things. On the fridge, a handful of neon-bright letters proclaimed 'Jesse is gay', while the table was covered in Yop cartons and empty pizza boxes, which Jesse said were all courtesy of Joe. In the middle of all this stood a very large red macaw with beady black eyes and a cruel-looking beak.

'Harriet.' Jesse stuck out a finger to allow the bird to hop on. 'Meet Miss Scarlett.'

'Did she do it in the study with the lead piping?' Harriet quipped.

'I don't think so.' Jesse looked confused.

'She's good with chat-up lines,' Harriet said. 'Joe again, I take it.'

'Who else?' Jesse said. 'She follows him every-where. Copies everything he does. She adores him. I can't think why. I'm the one who makes sure she's fed and watered.'

'Where did she come from?'

'That's the funny thing.' Jesse frowned. 'We don't know.'

'You don't know?'

'She just arrived on the doorstep a week or so ago. Completely out of the blue.'

'Perhaps she escaped from someone's garden. They're very valuable, you know, parrots. My Aunt Pip had one when I was little.'

'She can't have escaped,' Jesse said. 'She was in

135

a crate addressed to me. I had to sign for her and everything. Apparently she's come all the way from Costa Rica. Or Colombia. One of those places. I can't quite remember. One thing's for certain. She can crap like there's no tomorrow.' He indicated the top of the door. Parrot poop was draped all over it like paper chains. Harriet felt her throat constrict.

'Is that legal?'

'I guess it's acceptable within the boundaries of one's own home.' Jesse shrugged. 'I did ask Joe to clean it up. But you know what boys his age are like. It's all I can do to coax him out of bed with a fried egg sandwich. He treats the place like a bloody hotel.'

'I meant sending a parrot by post. Aren't there laws about that sort of thing?'

'I've no idea. And she was pretty well hidden.'

'We thought she was a set of garden furniture from IKEA at first.' Joe came in, drying his spiky hair on a striped towel. 'Hiya, Harriet.'

'Hello,' Harriet said. 'Do you actually *know* anyone in Central America?'

'Why?' Joe frowned.

'That's where Costa Rica is,' Harriet explained.

'Jack's in Chile.' Joe brightened.

'Our other brother,' Jesse explained. 'Joe's going out to see him in a couple of weeks. His first stop on his round-the-world trip. We're easing him in gently.'

'Actually,' Joe popped the toaster and cut a brick

of butter an inch thick, 'I'm spending four days in Venezuela before I go to Jack's. I'm fine on my own.'

'Course you are,' Jesse said. 'Though it might help if you knew where Chile was.'

'I *do* know.'

'So you'll know it's not in Central America,' Jesse said.

'Fuckhead,' Joe said. 'You sound like Dad.'

'You're adopted,' Jesse retorted. 'Did Mum not mention it?'

To get to Blue Ginger, they had to walk past the house in Belmont, where Harriet had grown up. As they walked along the raised pavement in front, she stopped, as she always did. She couldn't help herself. Mostly, it looked exactly the same. Huge windows, running right through to the back at first-floor level. A solid-looking front door, two hundred years old. It was a different colour now from the pretty chartreuse green Ruby had painted it on a whim. The current owner had painted it a bright canary yellow. There were bay trees: two lollipop-shaped sentries on either side of the entrance. And the kitchen, down in the basement, was different now. She'd walked past one evening and seen a light glowing like a barley sugar lozenge in the window. A woman had been chopping vegetables at a vast island, topped with gleaming black marble, in the centre of the room. There was no sign of the scrubbed oak units Ruby had loved. Even the walls were a different colour: plain cream, as opposed to the gorgeous chalky-blue Ruby had chosen the year before everything changed.

Ruby had loved decorating, although, unlike Harriet, she hadn't gone about it at all methodically. Not for her the days of careful planning, gleaning scraps of material and snippets of paint charts and fastening them all to a board on an easel. Ruby had been a lot more slapdash. She could be sitting at the table reading recipe books one minute and leaping into her car the next to see if the DIY store had any flamingo-pink paint for the bathroom. Like Hermione, she'd had a thing for words. She often chose the colours for the way their evocative names made her feel. Silver Jade. Moroccan Velvet. Salsa Melt.

'Why have we stopped?' Jesse asked. 'Are we calling on someone?'

'Oh.' Harriet shook her head. 'No. I just used to live there. That's all.'

She looked up at the eaves, where her own and Hermione's bedroom windows sat side by side like watchful eyes, guarding the rest of the house. When Hermione had been grounded for a whole weekend in the fifth year for bunking off maths to drink Pink Lady in the multi-storey car park, Harriet had loyally rigged up a complicated pulley system between those very rooms, using an egg box as a sort of cable car to transport the things her sister might need. Jelly beans. More cigarettes, which Hermione smoked with her head stuck out of the window, oblivious to the acrid stink creeping down-stairs like a naughty toddler that didn't want to stay in its bed. In turn, Hermione would pass her notes, on which she'd scribbled her requests, like a waiter noting down orders. Welsh rarebit. Tea with two sugars. More cigarettes. A Bounty . . .

'Are you OK?' Jesse asked her.

Harriet nodded. 'Funny, isn't it?'

'What is?'

'That house is still there. Just bricks and mortar. People are still living in it, going about their everyday lives. I wonder if they ever stop to think about who lived in it before.' She pointed up at the top windows. 'That one used to be my room. The one on the right. I painted it all white. Floorboards. Walls. Ceiling. And then I hung a crystal just there in the window. When it was sunny, all these tiny rainbows bounced over the walls. I used to lie in bed and stare at them for hours.'

To her surprise, her eyes pricked with tears.

'Sorry,' she said, embarrassed. 'I don't know what's wrong with me. You don't want to listen to me prattling on.'

'It's fine,' Jesse said kindly. 'It's obviously been on your mind a lot lately. Perhaps it's Dan going. It's shaken you up a bit.'

Harriet nodded, as the door of her old house opened and a woman came out. She looked surprised to see Harriet and Jesse standing staring at her house. Harriet felt silly.

'Come on,' Jesse said. 'Let's get to the bar. See if we can bribe Bertha to produce a couple of lattes.'

As they moved off, Harriet's mobile phone, tucked into the back pocket of her raggedy jeans, started to moo like a prize Jersey cow. Jesse must have changed her ringtone again when they were finishing up last night. He did it every time she left her phone lying around. This time yesterday morning, it had been the theme from *Ballamory*. The day before, it had shrieked 'Ding Dong the Witch Is Dead' at her when she was trying to pay for her shopping in Waitrose. The woman at the till had looked at her as though she was as mad as a cake.

'Harry, is that you?'

'No. It's the Dalai Lama.'

'Who? Look, I'm glad I caught you. It's about tonight.'

'You are still coming?' Harriet felt a tiny crest of disappointment peak in her chest.

'Of course I'm still coming,' Lizzy said. 'I intend to get horribly drunk. I've even got Crack Nanny on standby in case Conrad is on call.'

'Crack Nanny? Are you sure that's wise?'

'Oh, it'll be OK. They won't be any trouble. I'll knock them out with Calpol so they sleep through. Anyway, there's nobody else. And Conrad says it's churlish not to give her a second chance. Innocent until proven guilty and all that.'

'You caught her jacking up in your bathroom,' Harriet pointed out.

'That was ages ago. And it's not as though she

140

was in charge of the kids at the time,' Lizzy told her. 'I was in the house. And she is off the drugs now.'

'How can you be sure?'

'She looks as though she's gone large once too often,' Lizzy said. 'That heroin chic look has gone completely. Her face is sort of set back in a roll of fat now. She's really gone to seed. I think I'd be tempted to go back on the smack if that's what happens when you come off it. Conrad says she's got an arse like a saddle of lamb these days. Such a shame for her. Anyway, what I wanted to ask you was – What do you mean it's gone on fire? Actual flames? Or just smoke? OK. I'm coming. Harry, I'm sorry. Emergency. I'm going to have to go. I just wanted to ask if you'd pick me up. The ruddy car's playing up again and I'm not expecting to be in any state to drive home later.'

Harriet looked at her watch. They were cutting it fine as it was. There were so many bits still to do. And Lizzy was Lizzy. She was always running late. Harriet couldn't be late tonight. She wanted to be there when people started arriving so she could gauge their reactions.

Even so. They were friends, weren't they? She couldn't not go and pick her up.

'Be ready by half past six.'

'You're a star.'

Harriet and Jesse spent the rest of the morning at the bar, seeing to all the last-minute little bits.

At some point in the near future, Jesse was planning on getting a chef, so they could add food to Blue Ginger's mix. To which end, he'd asked Harriet to source crockery which had an Asian feel to it. This had arrived the previous week and was boxed, ready and waiting, in the stockroom towards the back of the kitchen. They would be using it tonight because Jesse had hired a caterer for the occasion. It all had to be unpacked and rinsed. In addition, one of the men who had delivered the tables had gouged a bloody great chunk out of the wall, which needed to be filled and painted over.

By some miracle, they managed to do all this by three o'clock. At half past, Harriet and Vin Rouge were on their way into town to pick up the flowers.

She had a devil of a job trying to park. The weather had decided to get shitty. It was raining in sticks, so her windscreen was a wobbling mass of water. The giant fish scale of the weir was a churning frothy sea and the road outside the Podium was a raging torrent. There was dirty brown water everywhere. Every car park was rammed. In desperation, she tried the leisure centre.

She did a circuit of the cramped underground parking lot in vain. Coming out of the exit for another go, she discovered the entrance blocked by a woman driving what looked like a block of flats, chugging out puffs of black smoke. There was a queue building up behind her. Nobody could move.

Harriet huffed and puffed like the wolf in *The Three Little Pigs*. What did the silly cow think she was playing at? If she'd been one of those constipated Sunday drivers who puttered round the countryside solely for the pleasure of driving itself, she might have been able to understand it. But this woman couldn't be much more than thirty-five.

As the car directly in front of her gave up and drove off, Harriet revved her engine. Shortly afterwards, the car directly behind the four-by-four gave up and buggered off as well, so it was just Harriet and the offending vehicle left. Suddenly, Harriet realised her game. The woman was going to bloody well sit there until somebody came out. Which wasn't on. She'd been here first. Any space that materialised was rightfully hers.

Banging Vin Rouge into first gear, she screamed towards the exit and drove in that way, making another circuit of the car park and finally coming to a stop just as a woman in a silver Ford Focus reversed out of her spot. With Harriet sitting there, she had no option but to back up towards the woman blocking the entrance. And, with a whoop of triumph, Harriet zipped straight into the empty space.

Woohoo!

As she turned off the ignition and pulled up the handbrake, she became conscious of somebody thumping on the window of the driver's side.

'I hope you're proud of yourself.'

'Thank you.' Harriet smiled at her. 'I'm usually completely pants at parking. And that was a pretty tight turn back there. I did well to do it first time.'

The woman jerked her thumb furiously at the Jeep. 'I have three children in there.'

Harriet bit her lip. She probably had a Baby on Board sticker on the back windscreen as well. She'd never quite understood the point of those. Presumably the people who put them there thought it was OK for everybody else to drive like Mr Bean on smack the rest of the time.

'Did you hear me?'

Perfectly.

Not that she was letting on.

'I said I have THREE CHILDREN in the back of my car.'

Harriet smiled nicely and peered round her head rest. 'And I have . . . let's see . . . one pint of semi-skimmed and a small cob loaf in the back of mine. Did you want to swap or something? Because I think I'll stick with what I've got if it's all the same to you.'

At half past six, she drove out to Lizzy's, hoping fervently that her friend would be ready on time. Lizzy was so renowned for being late for everything that it had come as a massive surprise to everyone when Oscar had arrived a whole two weeks early. The general consensus was that he must take after his father.

Jemima answered the door. 'You look pretty.'

'Thank you.' Harriet smoothed down her dress. She and Jesse had agreed to coordinate for the evening so that, while they wouldn't be wearing a uniform as such, they stood out so people would know who to ask if they had any questions. Harriet had decided they should each wear something in Blue Ginger's colours. Not the green. She didn't want them blending into the background. After much deliberation, she'd told Jesse to make sure he wore a vermilion tie, to match the splashes of red she'd used as an accent colour. She herself was wearing cropped indigo jeans teamed with a vivid scarlet camisole and black spike heels she couldn't walk in to save her life. In keeping with the Asian theme, she had tied her hair up and skewered it with a scarlet gloriosa lily, the slender filaments of its petals splashed with citrus.

'Where's Mummy?' she asked Jemima.

Jemima pulled her thumb out of her mouth and jerked it in the direction of the staircase.

Lizzy was standing in front of the full-length mirror in her bedroom, looking distinctly pissed off.

'I look as though somebody's tried to squeeze me through a pair of tights and given up at my arse.'

'You look fine.' Harriet was twitchy. She wanted to get going. And Lizzy did look fine. Slightly more ample, after three children. But it suited her.

'Harry,' Lizzy said. 'I look like a human Dorito.'

Harriet checked her watch. Time was of the essence here. Quickly, she marched over to the wardrobe and started to flick through it. It was no easy task. At home, her closet was carefully arranged. Jeans at one end. Then smart trousers, daytime. Smart trousers, evening. Slops (casual clothes for lounging at home in). Skirts, divided further into sections comprising pencil, mini or flouncy. Dresses. Tops. And so on. Each section in turn was divided into several sub-sections according to colour. Purple through lavender and lilac to palest pink. Blue: from deepest navy to the pale, powdery blue of a summer sky. Then red, through orange, to yellow. Not that she had much in yellow. With her sallow skin, it made her look washed out. Last but not least there was green. It was all there, so she knew where everything was in a hurry. Even her shoes were all still in their boxes with a Polaroid photo of each pair stuck to the front of the relevant one.

'What about these?' She held up the oyster-pink silk trousers Lizzy had worn to Gabby and Ed's wedding.

'Too tight,' Lizzy said drily. 'They give me a camel's hoof.'

As they progressed further, it became evident that everything, in Lizzy's opinion, was too tight. As Harriet vainly yanked out hanger after hanger, Lizzy fretted that she was going to have to join Weight Watchers. Apparently, she was going to have to sit on an orange plastic chair in a church hall with a load of people called Carol. She was going to have to join a line and shuffle forward to be weighed like a piggy going to market. A woman with frosted peach lipstick would tell her to lay off the pies and charge her a fiver for the privilege.

'What about these?' Harriet asked hopefully, holding up a perfectly smart pair of black trousers. You couldn't go wrong with black trousers, surely.

'Too short.' Lizzy screwed up her nose. 'I could always try yoga, I suppose.'

'Yoga?'

'Fran swears by it. But I just don't see how a whole lot of lying down with trumping can make you skinny. Do you?'

In the end, they plumped for what Lizzy said had been a dressing gown. Which, Harriet pointed out, was hardly a problem, since Lizzy had been known to do the school run in flannelette pyjamas more than once. With much coaxing, Lizzy finally allowed herself to be enveloped in the wrap of slippery chocolate and aqua silk before casting a critical glance at herself in the long mirror by the fireplace.

'Well?' Harriet chewed the skin on the edge of her thumb.

'It's OK.' Lizzy looked surprised.

'Great.' Harriet breathed a sigh of relief. 'Now. Have you got any sandals? Yes. Here. Put these on.'

'I'm sorry.' Lizzy obediently slipped her feet into the mocha satin sandals. 'I'm being thoughtless.

This is your big moment and I'm making you late.'

'No problem.' Harriet smiled. 'Now *come on.*'

The moment she set foot through the door of Blue Ginger, the worries that had been knotting themselves like a cat's cradle in Harriet's stomach melted away like lemon drops. The place was already buzzing. An appreciative hum was discernible as the guests sampled Jesse's crazy martinis, flavoured with lemongrass, chilli and basil or mango puree. The Dixieland band they'd hired was playing smoky jazz classics over in the far corner to liven things up and the shoal of lemon peel angelfish Harriet had ordered for the huge glass tank, set into the wall by the staircase that led to the upper floor, had arrived and were in situ, flippering through streams of silvery bubbles. The vibe was classy and sophisticated, just as she'd hoped. Pure white moth orchids soared like birds from glass vases, delicate as soap bubbles, hand blown in pale lemon, sugar pink and turquoise. The square stone bowl that stood at one end of the bar glowed with floating candles and another huge mass of orchids. Even the square plates, crackle glazed in zingy turquoise and vivid green, looked exactly as she'd hoped. It was all perfect.

'Harry!' Jesse came bounding over like an enthusiastic puppy. Harriet stared at him in amazement. Everything was red. Red suit. Red shirt. Red tie.

'Wow!'

He did a twirl. 'You said red, so I thought . . .'

'I didn't mean everything.' Harriet smiled. 'But . . . you know . . . it actually really suits you. You look good.'

'Thank you.' Jesse dipped in a mock bow. 'You look pretty good yourself, if you don't mind my saying so. So what do you think of the old place? She scrubs up pretty well, wouldn't you say?'

'Everything looks fantastic,' Harriet breathed. 'I feel . . .' She put her hands together, overwhelmed. 'I don't know . . . a bit . . .'

'You don't have to say,' Jesse smiled. 'I know exactly how you feel. It's great, having so many people here. But I almost want them all to go again so I can just drink it all in. I feel quite protective. All these people blowing their smoke over my precious baby. It's not right.'

'I know what you mean,' Harriet said.

'I couldn't have got here without you.' Jesse bent to kiss her cheek. 'Thank you. For everything. I'd better circulate. We'll have a drink together to celebrate later, shall we?'

'OK.' Harriet smiled, as Lizzy came over bearing cocktails. 'That'd be nice.'

'Wow.' Lizzy handed her a martini and watched Jesse's retreating back. 'Is there something you're not telling me?'

'Sorry?'

'You and him!' She nodded at Jesse, who was politely chatting to a couple of brittle-looking women clad top to toe in black, which gave them the appearance of a couple of insects, waving their long, thin arms around like feelers. 'You look great together. Talk about chemistry.'

Harriet took a sip of her drink, wincing as it burned the back of her throat. 'Bloody hell!'

'Good stuff, eh?' Lizzy grinned. 'He *is* a bit of a dish, though.' Her eyes sought out Jesse again. 'I doubt many men could carry off that clobber.'

'He's a bit short.' Harriet watched him laugh politely at something one of the black-clad insects was saying. 'Don't you think?'

'Taller than you.' Lizzy slurped her drink. 'Yum. So: What's going on there then?'

'Nothing!' Harriet flushed furiously.

'Oh, come on,' Lizzy urged her. 'I won't tell Gabby.'

'What's Gabby got to do with it?'

'Well.' Lizzy shrugged. 'You know. With Dan being her brother and all that. I just thought . . . Well, she might get a bit snippy.'

'Dan left *me*,' Harriet said defensively. 'I think that pretty much gives me carte blanche to do what the hell I like.'

'Aha!' Lizzy said triumphantly. 'So there *is* something going on.'

'*No!*'

'But you wouldn't mind if there was?' Lizzy winked. 'Am I right?'

'Actually,' Harriet told her, 'you couldn't be more wrong.'

'I say go for it,' Lizzy told her. 'Nothing like a

new man to put a bit of distance between you and the old one.'

'I don't want to go for it,' Harriet said. 'Anyway, he's got a girlfriend.'

'So?'

'So he's completely loopy about her. They've been together since they were seventeen or something.'

'His loss.' Lizzy shrugged. 'You've never looked better.'

'Really?' Harriet was surprised. Every time she'd looked in the mirror lately, her eyes had been puffy from lack of sleep.

'Really,' Lizzy said. 'You've got a sort of glow about you.'

'Well, I don't know why.'

'If you don't like him,' Lizzy said, 'why do you keep looking over at him?'

'I don't.'

'You do.'

'I suppose . . .' Harriet hesitated. 'It's just . . . you know . . . A sense of achievement. There have been times when we thought we were never going to pull this off. And now that we have, it's . . . well, pretty cool.'

'Hon, it's seriously cool,' Lizzy said. 'The place looks amazing. I'm going to bring Conrad the first chance I get. Oh, look.' She waved her empty glass under Harriet's nose. 'I'm all out of martini. It's your turn to go, I believe.'

Harriet battled her way through the squash of

perfumed and groomed bodies to grab two frosted glasses. She was just about to turn back when Joe appeared at her left shoulder.

'Nice to see you've dressed up for the occasion.' She nodded at his grubby T-shirt and khaki combats. 'What's the toothbrush in aid of?' She pointed at a pocket, halfway down his leg, from which a head of bristles was poking.

'In case I get lucky.' Joe laughed. 'And if dressing up means looking like mon bruv, I think I'll stay scruffy, if it's all the same to you.' He nodded towards the far corner where Jesse was causing gales of tinselly laughter to erupt from a group of glossy brunettes in the corner. 'Look at him. Thinks he's bloody Benny Hill.'

'He's just being polite,' Harriet said.

'That what you call it, is it?' Joe grinned.

Harriet became conscious that the ice in the drinks was melting, causing sticky rivers to ooze down the sides of the glass and onto her hands.

'Is Clare not here?'

'Dunno.' Joe shrugged. 'Think she was supposed to be here ages ago. She probably won't turn up. It wouldn't be the first time.'

'Really?'

Joe pointed to where Jesse was engaged in animated conversation with a tall, haughty-looking woman who reminded Harriet of one of the flamingos they used as croquet mallets in *Alice In Wonderland*. 'That pathetic show of peacockery is undoubtedly him getting back at her.'

'But she's not even here.'

'It makes him feel better.' He grimaced. 'Told you he was pathetic. Too under the thumb by half, that one. He's got women falling at his feet and what does he do? He flounders about here waiting for Clare to finally get her arse in gear. Hell-o-o!' He spotted a pretty blonde standing on her own by the bar. 'I might go for some of that.' He lifted his glass. 'Cheers, Ears. Place looks great and all that. Nice one. Laters.'

Harriet put her head down and struggled through the scrum by the bar to find Lizzy. By the time she reached her, half their drinks had run out of the glasses and up her elbows and Lizzy was coquettishly batting her eyelids at a man in an immaculately cut aubergine-coloured suit.

'Here we go.' Harriet thrust one of the drinks at her friend. 'It's a bit awkward, I'm afraid. Best have a slurp now, before it—'

'Too late.' Lizzy triumphantly held up the glass in her hand. 'I've already got one.' She was drunk. That much was obvious. Her eyes were a bit too glittery.

'Oh . . .' Harriet looked for somewhere to put the extra glass down.

'Will found me one from over there. So clever of him. Have you met Will?' She hiccupped softly. 'Lovely, lovely Will.'

Harriet's tummy flipped.

Not again!

'Hello.' Will was apparently unabashed. 'Long time no see.'

'You two know each other?' Lizzy asked, surprised.

'Yes,' Harriet said tightly.

'I came with a friend,' Will told her. 'He runs the French bistro place just off Queen Square. We thought we'd have a nose. I hope you don't mind.'

Harriet did mind. Seeing Will had come as a shock. He'd exposed every nerve ending in her body. She felt as though she'd peeled off her skin and climbed into a bathful of vinegar.

'I was very sorry about your parents,' Will said. 'They were cool. You must miss them.'

'Yes.' Harriet's throat felt tight.

'Lizzy said this was your place. I'm impressed.'

'It belongs to a friend of mine, actually.' Harriet craned her neck to see if she could spot Jesse. 'I did the interior.'

'You're a designer?'

'Yes.'

'You always did have a knack with that sort of thing. You changed my bedroom around that time. It always looked better afterwards.'

Harriet was surprised he should remember. She hoped she looked calmer than she felt. Her heart was bopping so hard in her chest he was bound to hear it.

There were fine lines around his eyes now. But he was still gorgeous. Spangles for the eyeballs. If this had been the first time she'd met him, if she hadn't known any better, she might just . . .

But she *did* know better.

There were so many things she wanted to ask him. Even now, after everything that had happened, she wanted to know why he'd just dumped her like that. Had he ever wondered what their baby would have looked like? Had he ever looked at his own daughter and wondered if the half brother or sister she might have had would have looked anything like her? Had he wondered, like Harriet had herself, what colour hair he or she might have had? Sand-blond, like Will's, or light brown like her own?

Their child would have been fifteen years old now. It hardly seemed possible.

She staggered, almost spilling her drink.

'Hey.' Will looked worried. 'Are you OK?'

'I'm fine.' She steadied herself. 'Just a bit dizzy.'

'Come and sit down.' Will took her arm and steered her towards one of the seating booths that were nearby. 'There you go. Is that any better?'

'Thanks.' This was all too weird. Her heart was fluttering, like a bluebird trapped in a cage. 'I'm OK.'

'Are you sure?' He eyed her with apparent concern, his lips perilously near her own. Suddenly, she was horribly confused. Half of her still hated Will with a passion. But the other half was curious to know what it would feel like to kiss him again. To feel those big hands skim her hips, working their way down until – at last – the thick, sturdy thumbs found their way under the silk of her knickers to her most intimate place, peeling

155

her apart like two segments of an orange as his head bobbed and his tongue found her . . .

'Harry!'

Dan, looking bewildered, was standing two feet away, cradling a drink. Harriet jumped as though she'd been stung and Will, sensing he wasn't wanted, moved hurriedly away.

'Dan.' Harriet struggled to her feet. 'It's good to see you. I missed you.'

'So I see.'

'No,' she said helplessly. 'It's not what you—'

'It's OK, Harry,' Dan said. 'I understand.'

'No!' she insisted. 'You don't.'

Dan held up his glass. 'Thought I ought to, you know, come and show my support. It looks great.'

'Thank you,' she said. 'And I'm glad that you did.'

'Well,' Dan said. 'I'd better . . .'

'Fine.'

She watched him walk away. Talk about bad timing. Part of her wanted to run after him. Tell him he'd misconstrued the situation. That she was waiting for him to come home. But another, more impish part of her wanted to knock his block off. He'd walked out on their marriage, for heaven's sakes. Did he expect her to wait around like a sap until he decided to come back?

Still, it was probably just as well that he'd interrupted her and Will. For a moment back there, she'd almost taken leave of her senses. What had she been thinking?

'It's gone a bit quiet in here.' Lizzy wobbled over and flumped down beside her. 'Should I start a Mexican wave, d'you think?'

'How many of those things have you had?' Harriet nodded at the glass in her friend's hand.

'Dunno.' Lizzy squinted at it. 'Four? Five? They just keep on coming.' She hiccupped. 'And I just keep on drinking. What are you looking at now?'

Harriet was watching Will pick up a fat butterfly prawn from the green-glazed dish on the end of the bar. It all felt rather surreal. She could still remember the last time she'd seen him, in her mother's sitting room in Bath. The image had become grainy with time. The edges were fuzzy and the colours had an acid trip quality, like those in seventies photography. But most of the detail was still discernible.

As she watched him, she imagined him skewered on a hog roast, an apple stuffed in his mouth as his eyes went slitty and his skin bubbled up, then blistered and split. Because of that bastard, she'd lost her own sister.

But, even as the thought floated into her mind, she knew it wasn't strictly true. She'd managed that on her own. Nobody had made her say those terrible things that day. She could have done the grown-up thing. She could have watched Hermione and Will waltz off into the sunset and wished them well. She could even have sat Hermione down and explained. Perhaps she might have changed her mind. Seen Will for the snake he really was.

157

Even so, it was still really rather surreal to see him back in her home town. It struck her now that, whether she liked it or not, Will was party to the next section in Hermione's diary.

He might even know where she was now!

'That man . . .' she said to Lizzy. 'He was at Jem's party, wasn't he? I saw him.'

'Will?' Lizzy followed her gaze. 'So what if he was?'

'How do you know him?'

'Alice is at nursery with Lucy,' Lizzy said, almost defensively. 'That's all. There's nothing more to it.'

'I wasn't suggesting there was,' Harriet said. 'Do you know anything about him?'

'No.' Lizzy shook her head firmly. 'He moved here from London about six months ago.'

'Is there a wife?' She was getting ahead of herself now. It wouldn't be Hermione. It would be too much of a coincidence. But coincidences did happen, didn't they?'

'Look, I don't know the ins and outs of the personal lives of every single child in the nursery,' Lizzy said, quite snappily, Harriet thought. It was a perfectly reasonable question, after all.

'Probably shouldn't try anything anyway,' Lizzy said. 'Dan's here.'

'I wasn't going to try anything,' Harriet said. 'And, even if I was, why should I care what Dan thinks?'

'Whatever.' Lizzy frowned suddenly.

'Lizzy? Are you OK?'

'No.' Lizzy shook her head firmly. 'I'm horribly drunk. I think I'm going to be sick.'

Harriet manhandled her outside and got her to take big gulps of crystal night air. She was feeling rather sick herself. It was the shock of seeing Will again. It had made her think about Hermione even more. The thought that Will probably knew more about her sister's life than she did herself didn't sit comfortably with her. It struck her that she knew nothing about Hermione now. The Hermione she thought she knew was the exotic bird of paradise she'd been at eighteen. What was she like now? Did she have a good job? Did she like where she lived? Was she happy?

Her thoughts curled around her like ribbons around a Maypole as she stood on the pavement, watching girls with silver halter-necked tops and miniskirted legs, tinged blue with the night chill, come spilling out of the bar opposite. As they clattered off down the street, Blue Ginger's door was flung open, sending out a warm blast of beery, nicotine-scented air. Just too late, she realised that the person coming out was Will. Before she could stop him, he flagged down a taxi and got in and Harriet, one hand on Lizzy's shoulder as she vomited over her shoes, had to watch as he sped away.

'Lizzy?'

Lizzy straightened. She looked confused. Frightened, almost. She pointed at the puddle in the gutter.

'Someone's been sick.'

'Loon.' Harriet sighed. 'It was you.'

'Don be stupid.' Lizzy looked bewildered. 'I wouldn't do that. I'm a wife and mother.'

'Come on.' Harriet took her friend's hand. 'Let's get you home.'

HERMIONE

All the things that were supposed to have happened to Hermione in the first three months of pregnancy seemed to kick in all at once, as though her body had some insane skewiff timescale of its own. Her breasts suddenly took on the appearance of ripe grapefruits and started to throb like submarine engines. She developed a mad craving for doughnuts, which had her stopping off at Tim Horton's for a box of Timbits or a couple of apple fritters at least once a day. A week after finding out she was pregnant, her waistband was definitely on the snug side and she stepped on the scales to find she'd gained a whole kilo in the space of five days. It was insane.

On Friday lunchtime, despite the fact that her head was still churning with the shock of it all, she dipped into the World's Biggest Bookstore and bought a big book on pregnancy. She still wasn't really sure what she wanted to do about this baby. She'd always considered herself to be about as maternal as a box of matches on a low shelf. But if she was going to go through with it, it would be as well to know what she was dealing with.

Back in the office, she told Kevin to hold all her calls and absorbed herself in her new book. It was hard to believe but it seemed that the baby she was carrying already had discernible features. Nose. Ears. Eyes. Mouth.

For the first time, her tummy filled with butter-flies of excitement. Perhaps she *could* do this. After all, she'd already done the hard part. She'd created a whole new life. It had been inside her, quietly going about the business of acquiring its own unique genetic characteristics, while she'd been going about her own business. Which, when you thought about it, was really rather clever.

She did no work that afternoon. That evening, she slid the baby book into her desk drawer for further reference and made her way home to Amelia Street, where she put a call through to Sylvie in London.

'Hermione?' Sylvie sounded delighted. 'Blimey. We are honoured. How *are* things with you?'

'Complicated,' Hermione told her.

'Oh?'

'It's a long story.' She took a deep breath. 'Tell me about you instead. How's Daisy?'

'Enormous.' Sylvie laughed. 'She's a shocking pig. Just like her father. You just missed her actually. Ted's taken her to his sister's. She's spending the night. Imagine. It'll be our first night away from her since she was born. I'm torn between not being able to wait to spend time alone with my lovely husband and feeling guilty for dumping my scrummy baby girl on JoJo.'

'I'm sure she'll be fine.'

'That's what I'm afraid of,' Sylvie said. 'Stupid, isn't it? She'll be so taken with JoJo's big garden and their new black lab puppy, she probably won't even notice we're gone.'

'Is she walking yet?'

'No,' Sylvie said. 'She likes to sit and be brought things, like a fat queen summoning her subjects. Can you believe she's one already?'

'No!'

'Last month,' Sylvie told her. 'We had champagne and pink cup cakes with sparkly candles. JoJo bought her a fairy castle and she sat on the box crowing with delight. We couldn't get to it to unwrap it for an hour and a half. I don't think she's quite grasped the concept of presents yet.'

'She will,' Hermione said.

'That's what everyone says. Wait until next year and there'll be no stopping her.'

'Do you not miss work?' Hermione asked her. 'The old crowd? That buzz?'

'Not for a minute,' Sylvie said. 'I know it's not very cool, being a stay-at-home mum. But I'm in total awe of Daisy. I still can't quite believe she's here. It's an amazing feeling. I love watching her change. At the moment, she's the spitting image of Ted's dad. Although last week, when I tried to give her prunes and custard, she got this stubborn look that was very definitely Ted.'

Hermione wondered who the tiny creature growing inside her would take after. Would she be sort of tall and kooky-looking like herself? Or perhaps she would be small and dainty like Harriet. It would be lovely to see a flash of either one of her parents every so often. It was mad, when you thought about it. That the smile of someone who'd been dead for years could suddenly produce itself on the face of a brand new person. It was really . . . well . . . just really sort of wow!

'Were you not worried?' Hermione asked Sylvie. 'Did you never worry you might not be able to cope?'

'Of course I did,' Sylvie told her. 'For the first few months, just going to Sainsbury's was like planning an Arctic expedition. I worried constantly. Was she too hot? Too cold? Should I take a spare fleece, in case she spewed down the one she had on? How many nappies was she likely to get through? Was she getting enough milk? Was she going to give up breathing in protest if her mashed carrots weren't organic? If I woke up and the house was quiet, I assumed she'd died in the night. And our sex life was virtually nonexistent. But, you know, Hermione, none of that really matters.'

'It doesn't?'

'Not a jot. Once you've held your own baby in your arms, it's like a switch has been flipped. You stop caring about yourself, because there's this brand new person that depends on you for everything. It doesn't matter that you can't just pop out for last orders any more. You know, I can't even remember the last time Ted and I ate out.'

'Not even the Blue Elephant?'

'*Definitely* not the Blue Elephant. We can't afford it.'

'It sounds awful.'

'Yes,' Sylvie said. 'But it isn't.'

'It isn't?'

'Daisy's brought far more to our world than Thai cuisine.' Sylvie laughed. 'She's like this giant splash of colour that lights up our lives. The moment I held her in my arms, I realised that nothing else mattered. Why are you so interested, all of a sudden?'

'I'm pregnant,' Hermione blurted before she had time to change her mind.

'Oh my God,' Sylvie squealed. 'But that's fantastic! God. Wait till I tell Ted. He'll be delighted. So how far gone are you?'

'Three months,' Hermione said.

'And you kept it quiet all that time?'

'I only found out yesterday.'

'A surprise then,' Sylvie said. 'Oh, Herm, that's brilliant. You . . . you are pleased about it?'

'I'm still trying to get my head round it.'

'What about the father?'

'Complicated.'

'It always is, with you.' Sylvie laughed. 'OK. I won't ask questions. But you will phone me if you need anything. Anything at all. Promise?'

'I promise,' Hermione said warmly. 'And thanks.'

It wasn't just Hermione's body that was changing. The Saturday morning of Josh's return found her

165

dressed in grey tracky bottoms and an old sloppy Joe T-shirt, her hair pulled into a Mrs Pepperpot topknot as she scrubbed down the floor of the spare room. She supposed that this must be the nesting instinct. According to her new baby book, it was likely that she'd feel more lively as she entered the second trimester. This must be what she was experiencing now. She'd never had an urge to spring clean in her life before.

She'd already been out once this morning, to buy groceries with which to welcome Josh home. His favourite purple Gatorade. Cookie Dough ice cream. Peanut butter cups. And now she was humping packing crates out of the box room and onto the landing. Not that she'd actually made any decisions yet. But she'd just wanted to see what the box room might look like as a little bedroom.

Some of the crates hadn't been opened for so long, she didn't have a clue what was in them. A lot of it could be got rid of. The plastic lobster she'd got in the Secret Santa at work, for instance. Why had she kept that? And there was the bolt of hot pink silk she'd bought all those years ago in Thailand. She'd been meaning to make it into something useful for fifteen years now. If she hadn't done it by now, she was never going to.

Although . . .

She grabbed it back from her 'Discard' pile and put it onto the pile she'd mentally labelled as 'Pending'. If the baby was a girl, she could make all sorts of cute little garments with it. A bandanna, perhaps, to keep the sun off her delicate skin. A frock with smocking, like the ones Ruby used to make for her and Harriet when they were little . . .

She was just opening a large leather hatbox the colour of Parma violets when there was a loud crash downstairs and, with a loud 'Buggeration', Josh's presence filled every nook and cranny of the house on Amelia Street once more.

'*Josh.*' Hermione's face split into a grin.

'Where are you?'

'Up here.'

'I bring tidemarks of great joy.' Josh peered around the landing, brandishing a bottle of bubbly. 'Perrier Jouet was fifteen per cent off in the duty free. Blimey.' He nodded at the piles of stuff that had mushroomed all over the landing. 'Are we being evicted?'

'No,' Hermione told him. 'I'm sorting through some stuff.'

'Jeepers.' He touched her forehead. 'Do you know how? I thought you just lumped it all in there and let it sort itself.'

Hermione laughed. 'I don't seem to be getting rid of any of it. How was Dublin?'

'Chocka bloody block with branded sportswear. Somewhere in America, a trailer park is looking decidedly sorry for itself right now. All its residents are hanging around McDonald's on Grafton Street. And they've got a ruddy great big wolfhound at number seventeen, you know. Barking its head off. I swear people only buy dogs like that because they're too afraid to bite people themselves.'

He threw his Louis Vuitton steamer bag into a corner and plonked a huge kiss on her forehead.

'I have MISSED you, Hermy One.'

He called her that because, until she'd told him how to say her name, he'd only ever seen it written down and thought that was how it was pronounced.

'How've you been?'

'OK.' Hermione stretched and smiled at him. 'I missed you too.'

'I'm jolly glad to hear it. Do we have plans for tonight?'

'Not that I know of.'

'Great. Because I'm jiggery buggered. And I can think of nothing I'd like more than a night in with my favourite girl. Can I play with your hair?'

'Of course you can.'

'Great. We'll do plaits. You wouldn't be an angel and fetch us some glasses, will you?' He nodded at the champagne. 'I'm parched.'

Hermione went to get a crystal flute from the kitchen and came back to find Josh peering under the lid of the lilac hatbox.

'What's this?'

'No idea,' Hermione told him. 'I've been lugging it around for that long, I've forgotten what's in it. Here.' She handed him a glass filled with golden bubbles.

'You not having any?' He looked wary.

She shook her head.

'Why not?'

'I don't feel like it.'

'Blimey.' Josh shook his head. 'You must be sickening for something. You look a bit peaky actually. You're not coming down with SARS, are you?'

'I'm fine.' Hermione wasn't quite ready to tell Josh her news yet. She wanted one last moment of normality with him, before the subject of the baby was raised and their friendship changed forever.

'How was Freddie's wedding?'

'Weddingy!' Josh sipped his drink. 'Lots of men in kilts. A girl in a white trouser suit, clearly trying to upstage the bride. Guests trying to outdo each other over who'd had to spend the most to attend. Oh, and my Aunty Cissie over from Strabane was caught on the official video, filling her big handbag with puff pastry sundries.'

'Bridesmaids?'

'Only one.' Josh rummaged in his bag. 'A whippet.'

'Even thinner than Coco in client services?'

'Not a thin girl, Hermy One.' Josh took another slug of champagne. 'An actual whippet. A horrid shivery grey one with a big silk ruff round its neck and a little tea towel holder bottom.'

'No way!'

'Way!'

Hermione snorted.

169

'Of course, the best bit was my speech. Everybody thought so. I did a poem. "First I was afraid, I was petrified. To be Best Man at the wedding of a ginger bride . . ."'

'I bet that went down well.'

'Like a cup of cold sick.' Josh grinned.

'So you had fun then?'

'Not as much fun as I would've had if you'd been there.'

'Flatterer.'

'It's true. I spent half the night before the wedding surfing the net, I was that bored. Did you know there's this site you can go on where you can just talk about weddings all night if you want to? I found it on Georgina's laptop. I gave myself a login and everything. Vicky from Bromley,' he said proudly. 'I'm marrying Darren in a civil ceremony in June and my bridesmaids will be wearing duchesse satin in Pastry. The flower girl is bellyaching because the shoes I've chosen squash her toes, but I've put my foot down. It's MY day.' He pouted. 'I should have what I want. I'm only going to be doing it the once, after all.'

'OK,' Hermione said. 'You're scaring me.'

'Sorry. You know how I get carried away. God, I really thought I was Vicky for a minute then. I'm clearly wasted in advertising. I should go into films.' He drained his glass. 'Right. Are you ready for a drink now?'

'I might have one a bit later.' Hermione watched

as he poured himself another glass of champagne and then dived into the purple hatbox.

'What's this?'

'What's what?'

She peered over his shoulder at a book made of sheets of scrap paper, all bound together with staples and covered in garish seventies wallpaper.

'It looks familiar,' she said. 'I don't know why. I can't remember having seen it before. But I must have.'

'Shall I open it?'

'Go on.'

The page at which the book fell open was divided in half horizontally with a thick black line. Above the line, somebody had drawn a series of matchstick people. Tiny ping-pong heads on big triangle bodies. The arms were twiglet-thin and spread wide, adorned at either end with a huge hand. Underneath, in careful pencil, somebody had written, 'My Family'.

'Listen to this.' Josh laughed. '"My daddy is called Isaac and we wave to him when he goes to work and he gives us fizzy tablets and when he eats his dinner he looks strange."'

'Let me see.' Hermione took the book from him. The wallpaper it was covered in had a familiar foamy texture that set her teeth slightly on edge.

'It's Harriet's news book,' she said wonderingly. 'I never knew I had that.'

'What is it?' Josh hoovered more champagne. 'I don't get it.'

'From primary school. We had to write our news in them on Monday mornings to let everyone know what we'd done at the weekend. I wonder how that got in there. I guess Pip must have packed it.'

'The one who helped you sort out the house.' Josh took a few strands of her hair between his fingers and started to separate it out. 'The nice one, as opposed to the nasty one.'

'Yes.' She looked at the wallpaper book again and her eyes filled with tears. 'She's drawn all four of us. Look. That's my dad. With the hammer and chisel. And that must be Ruby.'

'Which one is you?'

'This one.' Hermione pointed to what could only be described as a Weeble. 'At least, I think so. I'm the only one with curly hair. You wouldn't have thought she'd turn out to be a talented artist, would you?'

'Hey.' Josh stroked her cheek. 'Don't get upset.'

'Sorry.' She wiped her eyes. 'Don't know what's wrong with me. I've been really teary lately.'

'Oh, God.' Josh clapped a hand over his nose and mouth. 'I was right. You're sick.'

'No . . .' Hermione said lamely. 'It's not . . .'

'Is it catching? Because, you know, I am awfully susceptible to bugs. It's not that awful retro virus, is it? You know, I thought I felt a bit of a sniffle coming on earlier.'

'No,' Hermione told him. 'No. It's not catching.'

'Then it's cancer.' Josh threw his hands in the

air. 'And I'm terrible around ill people. I don't like the smell.'

'Josh,' she said desperately. 'Will you listen? I'm not sick.'

'Thank God.'

'I'm pregnant.'

Josh gulped. 'Holy Hannah. Is it yours?'

'Of course it's mine. Who else's would it be?'

'Sorry. Silly question. Does it hurt?'

'No.'

'So who's the father?'

'That's the thing.' Hermione said. 'It's a bit sensitive.'

'Oh God.' Josh threw his hands in the air. 'You didn't.'

'Didn't what?'

'You sly fox. You *did*, didn't you? I always knew it was a risk, leaving it in the bathroom bin like that. Did you get it off that programme? The one where the girl just picked a random bloke and then turned it inside out.'

'Now hold on . . .' Hermione said.

'Oh God. We'll be just like Richard Gere and Madonna in that film. I'm going to have to come to the birthing classes and watch fat women nesting all night. *And* I'm squeamish. Oh God. Oh shit. Holy guacamole. I have GOT to calm down. I'll make myself ill.'

Hermione stared at him.

'I want no misunderstanding, by the way.' He held up his hand like a lollipop lady stopping traffic. 'If it's a boy, I WILL play football with it, if it's that way inclined. I may not know the outside rule . . .'

'Offside.'

'But I *can* kick a bloody ball. David Beckham can do it. How hard can it be? Who do you think it'll look like? I mean it would be OK either way, wouldn't it?' Josh added hopefully. 'I know I'm a bit of a gingery blond, which isn't to everyone's taste. And I've got sloping shoulders and a slightly weak chin. And I had acne on my back until I was twenty-one, which crippled my sex life, I can tell you. But my mum says I've got a lovely smile. And I'm ever so light on my feet. And you . . .' He waved a hand at Hermione. 'Well, you're just lovely all over, aren't you? You're top-shelf material. You're wasted in advertising. So, what do you reckon?'

'Josh,' Hermione began. 'This baby. It's not—'

'Oh God.' Josh clapped a hand over his mouth. 'You're absolutely right. It might not have been mine. We both . . . you know . . . had a . . .'

'Josh . . .'

'What colour was it? The condom, I mean. Because I think mine was strawberry flavoured. Did you—'

'JOSH,' Hermione shouted, exasperated. 'I did not sneak into the bathroom the night you had sex with thingummybob with the express intention of going through the bin in search of your sperm. If I'd wanted a baby with you, I would have asked. OK?'

'What's wrong with me?' Josh looked huffy.

'Nothing,' Hermione told him. 'Nothing at all. And if I was going to *choose* to have a baby, I can't think of anybody I'd rather have it with than you.'

'Really?' Josh seemed appeased.

'Really,' Hermione said. 'You're my best friend. I love you.'

'I love you too.' Josh squeezed her. 'Sorry. Did that hurt?'

'I'm pregnant, Josh,' Hermione told him. 'I'm not made of sugar. I won't melt.'

'So whose is it then?' Josh asked her. 'Anyone we know?'

Hermione cleared her throat.

'Oh dear Lord,' Josh said. 'It's not your assistant, is it? The one that sits outside your office and squonks like a seal?'

'It's a nervous tic,' Hermione told him. 'And no. Of course it's not him.'

'Who then?'

'Greg Finch.'

Josh snarfed champagne everywhere. 'Old Bumface, from Canon Corps? Tell me you're kidding.'

'No.' Hermione shook her head. 'Why Old Bumface?'

'He's got one of those chins with a crack in it,' Josh explained. 'So was it a one-night stand, or . . . ?'

'It was a few months,' Hermione told him.

'Ruddy hell.' Josh whistled. 'So that was what you were doing when you were working late. I did wonder. You do know he's a total wanker, don't you?'

'So it would seem,' Hermione said.

'So you're not seeing him any more.'

'No. I dumped him when I found out he was married.'

'Good.' Josh appeared satisfied. 'Rumour had it he was shagging half the secretaries over at Canon Corps anyhow.'

The back of Hermione's neck prickled with goosebumps. Had Greg really been that bad? Had their liaison been just one of a string of sordid affairs? God. What a complete airhead Greg must have thought her.

Bastard.

Josh patted Hermione's tummy affectionately. 'Poor little mite. Destined always to think with its prick and have a bugger of a job shaving.'

'Not if I can help it,' Hermione told him. 'Anyway, I've decided it's a girl.'

'What makes you think that?'

'I'm getting lots of fluffy pink vibes. And we were all girls in my family. Ruby. Harriet. Me. Even Isaac had sisters.'

'Pip and Vinegar,' Josh remembered.

'That's them.' Hermione flipped once more through Harriet's news book, glimpsing several gold stars along the way. That was Harriet all over. If the book had been her own, it would have been covered with red biro scrawl: 'You have rushed this. Take more care.'

'Do you not think she might like to know?' Josh asked. 'Your sister, I mean. Won't she want to know she's going to be an aunty?'

He looked at the bunch of stick figures that were supposed to represent Hermione's family and, with the tip of his finger, drew an imaginary bump on the stick picture that was her.

'Just seeing if it suits you,' he explained, in answer to her questioning look.

'And does it?'

'You know,' he squeezed her hand, 'I rather think it does.'

HARRIET

The night after the launch party, Harriet couldn't sleep a wink. Her heart was drumming a paradiddle behind her eyeballs and her mind refused point blank to close down. Every time she tried to shut her eyes, her thoughts raced around her brain, like ball bearings in a pinball machine. She could feel her heart thumping behind her eyeballs, like the indignant ticking of a very loud grandfather clock. It was infuriating.

Her role in Blue Ginger was over. She had no excuse now for spending time there, unless, of course, she went as a customer like everybody else. The next time she went in, somebody else would be sitting at her favourite table by the window, dunking almond biscotti into their latte. She was going to have to find something else to do.

There was no point even trying to sleep now. Edie would be up soon, cranking up the Utah Saints on her new CD player as she pottered about making tea. Or Joe would come crashing through the front door and thump up the stairs to the flat below.

It occurred to her that finishing work on project Blue Ginger was going to leave a gaping hole in her life. She'd got so used to the routine of it all. She loved arriving in the mornings and wondering what sort of mood Bertha was going to be in when Jesse flipped the big silver switch on her side. Would she be accommodating and provide a steady stream of dark, fragrant espresso? Or would she decide to have a cob on and refuse to oblige?

She shook herself. She was being ridiculous. Blue Ginger was only a bar, for heaven's sakes. It was bricks and mortar. It was people that mattered. And she would see Jesse again. She could hardly avoid him, seeing as he lived downstairs. Things just had an odd, slightly hallucinogenic feel to them because it was the middle of the night. That was all. Things always seemed worse at this time. It must be low blood sugar or something. She wasn't quite firing on all cylinders. This time next week, she would have found another job. Everything would be fine.

She closed her eyes again. But Will loomed large in her mind. He confused her. She couldn't forget his hand on her arm as he'd steered her towards the safety of the seating area. There had still been something there. She'd felt it. A distinct crackle of attraction. He'd even smelt exactly as she remembered. That same lemony scent. One whiff of it, and she'd been eighteen again, squashed into her narrow single bed at the top of the house, her duvet discarded like a great white slug on the

179

floorboards as, with her feet twisted around Will's, she read the postcard from Hermione that had plopped onto the doormat that morning. That day, they'd had the house to themselves. Ruby and Isaac had gone to visit Pip, who was in London for a whirlwind grand tour of the relatives. They'd left at the crack of dawn and wouldn't be back for ages, which meant she and Will could have sex all day. They'd taken full advantage, of course. By the time Will left, her bed smelt of oysters mingled with rubber. She'd looked at it and felt a bit guilty.

The image of Will retreated and bumped into one of Dan, his face creased in puzzlement as he watched her and Will last night. Thus far, she had managed to banish him to the back of her mind by dangling the carrot of his probable return. Now, though, she wasn't so sure. If he thought she'd moved on already, he wouldn't want to come back. Would he?

She wasn't even sure now that she wanted him to. Three weeks ago, that state of mind would have been an impossibility. She'd felt so raw without him, she'd been worried what on earth she was going to do if he declared he wanted a divorce. More recently, though, with all the chaos of getting Blue Ginger ready, she'd thought about him less and less. This morning, as she and Jesse had collided in their haste to get all the bottles behind the bar sparkling in time for tonight, a big shiny bubble of possibility had surfaced. She wasn't sure why banging into Jesse had caused this. She hadn't even thought about it rationally. It had been something to do with his engaging smile as he'd apologised and rubbed her arm where the bruise would come. It had seemed to signify that life did move on. You could meet other people. You could fall in love again. And wasn't there always something gloriously exciting about the start of something new? Not with Jesse, of course. It seemed that he and Clare were inextricably linked. Ties that had bound them since schooldays weren't easily broken. Besides, she didn't want to break them. Jesse was a friend. Nothing more.

But Dan was her husband. She'd married him. For better, for worse. He'd come to the launch to support her. He hadn't been there for Jesse, had he? Despite the fact that Jesse had lived downstairs for the past six months, they hadn't had an awful lot to do with one another. If they met on the stairs, or in the communal garden at the back of the house, they would grunt briefly to one another, perhaps mentioning football scores or the outcome of the Bath rugby game at the weekend. But Dan didn't know the ins and outs of Jesse's private life. She only did herself because they'd spent so much time working together over the past few months.

So Dan had been there, nursing that ridiculous sparkly cocktail that she knew full well would have made him feel self-conscious, for her benefit.

Why?

It was just possible that he'd made up his mind about the direction in which their future lay. And he'd come to tell her.

She sat up in bed, her thoughts whirling around her brain like ribbons around a maypole. All these changes were doing her head in. It wasn't just Dan. It wasn't even Will. For the past fifteen years, she'd gone through life assuming that, one day, Hermione would just turn up. Harriet would mumble her apologies for saying all those terrible things. She would explain about Will, at which point Hermione would throw up her hands in horror and say she would never have gone off with him like that if she'd known. It had all been there, locked tightly in one of the honeycomb cells of her brain. A whole future incident, just waiting to be played out.

But what if it wasn't?

What if she and Hermione were destined never to meet again?

She picked up her sister's diary, feeling the now familiar butter-soft leather beneath her fingertips and inhaling the faint traces of Paris that still lingered within its pages. This morning, something stopped her from opening it. Something Jesse had said about not knowing how it all ended.

She didn't want to reach the point where her sister had put down her pen and stopped writing. Coming to the end of the diary would be like reaching the end of a road they'd travelled together and having to say goodbye.

And she didn't want to say goodbye. Not again.

She got out of bed and padded over the white plush of her bedroom carpet to Isaac's old writing desk, tucked in a nook by the fireplace. She snapped on the light and rummaged in the alabaster bowl on top of the desk, looking for the key to open it. There was a faint click as the lock, unused for years, sprang open.

Pulling down the polished walnut lid was like stepping back in time. The familiar scent of pipe tobacco hit her like a smack, sending cobwebby spokes of nostalgia through every fibre in her body. Swallowing hard, she slid her hand under a pile of papers until it came to rest on what she was looking for. A brown oblong box with a hinged lid. Shivering, she pulled it out of its hiding place and carried it carefully back to bed. She slid into the warm nest of her duvet, trying to ignore the way her heart was dancing a polka as she opened the box and stared at the treasures smuggled from her past.

There was the ballet shoe. A threadbare slipper of apricot silk, curled like a cotyledon from the hours Ruby had spent pointing her toes. She'd always been going to be a ballerina. And then she'd gone away and had babies instead. By the time Ruby was Harriet's age, she had two fifteen-year-old daughters. If Ruby and Isaac hadn't died in the car that night, Harriet might, depending on what Ruby's advice had been, have had a daughter or son of the same age by now. It seemed almost impossible.

Had her mother really never regretted getting pregnant at eighteen and missing out on a glittering career?

It was the sort of question you tended to reserve for later. When you were in your thirties, perhaps, and had children of your own. A life phase fate had denied her.

How different would things have been now if Hermione hadn't had a headache that night? If Ruby and Isaac had gone to bed early and slept through the phone call that summoned them out into the night? Would she, Harriet, still have got married so young? Would she even have looked at Dan twice?

Ruby's parents, devastated at their daughter's death, had seen to the clearing out of the house on Belmont. Harriet remembered watching them, pink-eyed with grief, as, aided by Pip and Vinegar, they packed family treasures into boxes. They'd never expected to have to bury their only daughter.

Harriet had wanted control over what was and was not kept. But everybody promised that nothing of any sentimental value would be disposed of. Ruby and Isaac's personal effects, with the exception of most of their clothes, had all gone into boxes. Some had gone home with the grandparents to be passed on in turn when Len had died of a heart attack at the ripe old age of eighty. Others were neatly labelled for Harriet and Hermione to take away with them. Things Len and Grace thought they might like. Ruby's silver hairbrush and comb. Isaac's pipe. Letters. Photographs. And when Harriet had walked past the house a week later and seen the velvet cushions that had adorned the chaise longue in Ruby's sitting room being flung out of the window by the removal people, she'd been glad she hadn't had anything to do with it after all. They might only be cushions but they had been part of a home once. The removal men's indifference to what had been their life as a family had only added to the horrible vulnerability she felt already.

Photographs. That was what she was looking for now. Photographs of herself and Hermione as children. Here they were. Squares of crackle-glazed celluloid, white-edged and slightly faded with age.

Here was Hermione, aged about two, sitting in a hole Isaac must have dug on the beach, with chocolate smeared all around her mouth.

Harriet in the back garden in Cornwall, proud as punch of her shiny red bike with the stabilisers.

Hermione on the beach again, proudly holding a brightly coloured beachball.

Here were Harriet and Hermione winning first prize in the Silver Jubilee fancy dress, thanks to the Beefeater costumes Ruby had slaved over. Neither of them had known what a Beefeater was but they'd been pleased with the prize. A £5 W.H. Smith token, which they'd spent on plasticky pencil cases, stickers and fruit-scented felt-tipped pens.

Hermione aged fourteen, singing with her newly formed band. She'd sprayed the ends of her long chestnut hair electric blue specially for the occasion.

And here they both were on their fourth birthday, blowing out barley-sugar twist candles on the merry-go-round cake Ruby had baked specially.

There were photographs of the whole family at

the zoo. They were all smiling, Harriet saw, as her heart slammed into her chest wall. Filled with hope for the future. None of them could have known then that Ruby and Isaac would die such violent deaths.

A salty tear rolled down her cheek and stung her lip. Had it already been going to happen? Way back in the seventies, when Bay City Roller mania had hit Britain in all its tartan glory, were Ruby and Isaac's cards already marked?

Pank!

At first, Harriet thought the noise was her own heart, lurching with nostalgia in her chest. But then it came again. A snickerty sort of noise. It was coming from the window.

She stiffened as blood rushed to her ears. Had she imagined it? Was she just freaking herself out for no reason?

It was the wind, she told herself. That was all. Just because she'd been sitting here wallowing in her past, it didn't mean it was actually coming back to haunt her. It wasn't a ghostly Ruby knocking at the window. It was an entirely natural phenomenon.

Here, tucked at the bottom of the box, was their school yearbook. Flipping through it, she noticed, not without irony, that on the questionnaire she'd filled out just before everybody left the safety of the common room, spreading like Spillikins into the great unknown, she had answered the question, 'What are you most afraid of?' with a frank, 'Losing the people I love.'

Hermione had put, 'Not having my lipstick.'

She settled back against the pillow to relieve the crick in her neck. She wasn't abreast of Hermione's current lipstick situation, though she suspected that, unless she'd changed beyond recognition, all was very much under control there, with a spare on hand for all eventualities.

She smiled, despite herself. For one glimmer-bright instant, her sister had been there before her, vain as a peacock, strutting in front of the mirror in her bedroom in a curtain-pelmet skirt and tiny vest.

Pank!

It was that noise again. Unmistakable this time. She listened, her heart pounding.

Pank.

She crept towards the window, her heart oscillating like a butterfly's wings.

Someone was out there!

Shivering, she pulled back the curtain an inch.

There it was. A black hump in the darkness. As she watched, a figure stepped into the light of the street lamp.

Bloody hell!

She yanked up the sash window and leaned out. 'What the hell do you think you're doing?'

'Sorry.' Jesse, still in the scarlet suit, looked sheepish. 'I'm locked out. I've been throwing rocks up at your window for the past half hour. Did I wake you?'

'No.'

'You're not . . . *busy?*'

'Some chance,' Harriet said as her heart slowed to a waltz. She shook her head. For a stupid second she'd really thought it had been Hermione. But it couldn't have been. Her sister had no idea where she was.

'How come you're locked out?'

'Forgot my keys.' Jesse shrugged. 'And Joe's nowhere to be found. I think those kumquat and wotsit candles might have done the trick tonight. I think he must have pulled. Either that,' he grinned, 'or he's passed out in his clothes again. You know what he's like.'

'What about Clare?'

'She must've missed her flight. She was supposed to get a cab at the airport and come straight to the bar but she didn't show up.'

'Did you call her mobile?'

'Switched off.'

Poor Jesse. She knew how much he'd been looking forward to seeing Clare. Nevertheless, there was a small, slightly twisted part of her that couldn't help feeling a tiny bit pleased that she didn't have to be on her own. She and Jesse could hold a proper post mortem of the evening's events and then it wouldn't all feel such an anti-climax.

'Are you worried?'

'I don't know.' Jesse frowned. 'I phoned the airport and there were no problems with the flights. But she can be a bit . . . well . . . dappy sometimes. She gets sidetracked.'

188

'She probably just missed it and went home,' Harriet reassured him. 'She probably knew you'd be really busy tonight. I expect she'll call you in the morning.'

'Maybe,' Jesse said. 'Look. Can I come in? I'm freezing my nuts off out here.'

'God.' Harriet came to her senses. 'Sorry. Of course you can. Hold on.'

She buzzed him in. A couple of seconds later, she heard footsteps on the stairs and opened her own front door to admit him.

'So what are you up to?' he asked. 'What's keeping you up at this hour?'

Harriet pulled her fluffy white bathrobe tighter around herself and nodded at the box on the bed. 'I was just looking at some stuff.'

'What stuff?'

'Nothing,' Harriet said hurriedly, piling her private bits and pieces into the box. But it was too late. Jesse saw some of the photos and swooped.

'I *love* old photographs.'

'You do?' Harriet was surprised. She wouldn't have thought for a minute that Jesse would have any interest in a pile of family history. Especially when it wasn't even his own family.

'Of course I do.' Jesse picked up a picture. 'Doesn't everyone? Oh, look at this one. This has to be you. Don't you look sweet?'

Harriet looked at the photograph he was holding. A picture of herself, taken in her maternal grandmother's garden in Kent. She recognised the rose trellis, spilling over with blowsy, old-fashioned blooms. Antique rust. Lemon yellow. Pale lilac. It must have been a special occasion, because she was wearing a purple and orange dress with pansies and puffed sleeves and her legs were encased in white lacy tights that made even her skinny ninepins look like two chipolatas in a string bag. Her straight brown hair had clearly been cut, pudding-basin fashion, by Ruby at some point because her fringe shot up at a forty-five degree angle, giving her a slightly surprised look.

'You look all worried,' Jesse said.

'Do I?' Harriet looked. 'I guess I do a bit. I didn't like having my photo taken.'

'You were so cute. Old-fashioned looking. There's no sign of the big, scary Harriet that yells at me when I leave my bike in the hall.'

'I'm not scary.'

'You can tell it's you a mile away. Look at those shy brown eyes. And that sad little face. It makes me want to go back in time so I can pick you up and tell you everything's going to be OK.'

'Is it?' Harriet sighed.

'Of course it is,' Jesse told her. 'Why shouldn't it be? Look at you. Beautiful. Successful.'

'Hardly. I'm completely skint. If I don't pull my finger out and find some more work, I'll starve.'

'You're not the only one,' Jesse told her. 'If Blue Ginger isn't a success, I'm up shit creek with your proverbial. Everything I own is sunk into that place.'

'What about your flat?'

'Mortgaged to the hilt. Joe's supposed to pay half. But he's off to see the world in a couple of days. And he's twenty-one. He's still sponging off the olds. He might think he knows a thing or two about real life but he doesn't have a flipping clue.'

'It'll be a success,' Harriet told him. 'You wait.'

'You sound very sure.'

'I am.' She felt lighter, suddenly. 'I bloody decorated it, didn't I? People will be falling over themselves to admire it. I'll have you know my egg-shelling is second to none.'

'They did all say it looked good, didn't they?' Jesse said happily. 'And that's all down to you, you know. Nobody could have done it better. I think you're fantastic.'

'Thanks.'

She watched as Jesse took off his jacket and tie and propped himself against a mound of pillows. It was funny. A few months ago, she hadn't really known him. Now, it felt completely natural to see him slumped at the other end of her bed. She supposed there was nothing like a common goal to draw people together. It was nice just having him here as a friend.

'Sorry I didn't stay around to help clean up tonight,' she said. 'I had to sort Lizzy out.'

'No problem. You'd done your bit.' He grinned. 'She was *blotto*, wasn't she?'

'She sure was.' Harriet laughed. 'Poor Lizzy. She

hasn't drunk much since the baby. I think it went to her head.'

'You're telling me.'

There was a sudden awkward silence, as though neither of them knew what to say next. Which, on the face of it, was daft. They'd spent every day together for the past couple of months.

She opened her mouth to ask if he wanted anything, just as he shivered and said, 'It's bloody chilly in here.'

'I'll shut the window.'

'Listen,' Jesse said when she came back to bed, propping herself up at the opposite end. 'You don't mind if I get my head down, do you? I'm pretty whacked. And I'll be gone first thing. I have to get to the cash and carry and then I have to put an advert in the *Chronic* for a chef.'

'It's fine,' Harriet said. 'You can kip here, no problem.'

'Dan won't mind?'

'Of course not.' The nape of Harriet's neck prickled. 'Why would he mind?'

'I saw him last night,' Jesse said. 'I thought perhaps you two had worked things out.'

'If we have, I'm blissfully unaware of it,' Harriet told him. 'Did you want a T-shirt to sleep in? He left dozens.'

She found him one and watched as he slung the funky red suit over the back of the sugarplum velvet chair she'd taken from Ruby's bedroom in Belmont. He had a nice body. Perfectly in

192

proportion with his height. Looking at him, it occurred to her that Lizzy was right. He wasn't actually *that* short. He was several inches taller than her, at least. They wouldn't look out of place walking along the street hand in hand.

She shook herself. Where had that come from?

Jesse climbed back onto the bed. It was light outside now. The dawn chorus was creating a right old racket outside. Even so, Harriet felt herself drifting into a rejuvenating, dreamless sleep.

Moments later, Jesse's voice jerked her awake again.

'Is this her?'

He was sifting through the photos again.

'Sorry,' he said sheepishly. 'You don't mind, do you? My mind was racing suddenly. And I got curious.'

She peered at the photograph Jesse was holding up. Herself and Hermione poking about in a rock pool on the beach near their old house. They were about seven, wearing knobbly knitted swimsuits. Harriet was bending to examine a razor clam shell that Hermione was holding up.

Tears pricked her eyelids.

'Hey.' Jesse looked at her with concern. 'I'm sorry. I didn't mean . . .'

'It's OK,' she told him, meaning it. 'It's just . . . I mean . . . I haven't looked at this stuff for so long.'

'And now you have, it's unleashed a whole lot of emotion.'

'Exactly.'

'Perhaps that's a good thing.' He picked up another photograph. 'Who's this?'

'That's Ruby,' Harriet told him. 'My mother.'

Ruby was dressed up. Her dark, glossy hair was piled loosely on top of her head and constellations of rubies sparkled in her ears and at her throat. She wore a low-cut dress of deep red silk. Seeing the picture again, Harriet could almost smell her perfume and powder as she bent down to kiss her goodnight and tell her to be good for the babysitter.

Jesse whistled through his teeth. 'She was a real stunner.'

He carried on sifting through the photos, sending memories flooding back. Harriet, glowering on a fat black seaside donkey. Simon, the malevolent marmalade-eyed cat who'd got run over when they were small. Photo upon photo of Hermione. Eating a blue meringue, stuffed with cream, on the promenade at Margate. In the bath, wearing a comedy beard made entirely from Matey bubbles. Triumphantly learning to surf on Porthcurno beach. Dressed as Madonna, her mouth painted silver-pink and an assembly of crosses dangling from her ears.

At some point, she wasn't sure when, his bare feet somehow found her own, steepling against them for just a second before his toes curled over the tops of hers. The gesture was subconscious. It was probably something he did with Clare. It

194

wasn't meant for her at all. But she found it reassuring nonetheless. It made her feel cocooned.
Safe.

'Will you tell Dan?' Jesse wanted to know. 'About
your sister, I mean.'

'Nothing to tell.' Harriet shrugged. 'It's not as
though she's made contact, is it?'

'She might.'

'I doubt it. I said some terrible things.'

'You were upset.'

'It was unforgivable.'

'You'd just lost your parents,' Jesse said. 'You
were looking for someone to blame. It happens.'

'Even so. If she hasn't contacted me in fifteen
years, she's hardly likely to start trying to find me
now.'

'So find her. Like I said.'

'How?'

'You'll find a way. If you want to. Harry, can I
ask you something?'

'Sure.'

'Why me?'

'Sorry?'

'That day, in Lizzy's garden. Why did you tell
all this to me?'

'I don't know,' Harriet admitted. 'Because you
were there, I suppose, and it was on my mind.'

'Right.'

He fell silent. It wasn't surprising. He must be
exhausted, after all. It had been a long day.

At some point, Harriet drifted into a crumby,

starchy morning sleep herself. She woke up at lunchtime, unable to figure out where she was. Then she realised. She was in her own bed. She was just the wrong way round.

The box of photographs was still on the floor. Jesse had put everything back tidily and closed the lid. There was a folded piece of paper on top with her name scribbled on it.

> Thanks for sharing your memories with me. And thanks for the refuge. I'm not sure where this box goes so I've left it for you to put away. Don't be a stranger now we're not working together any more. I've left a little present on your phone to show my gratitude. Oh, and I'll return the T-shirt when I've washed it.
> P.S. You snore!

She found her mobile under a pile of clothes on the squashy raspberry-pink sofa Dan had so hated and pressed the button to let the ring tone sing out. The Beatles, 'Here Comes The Sun'. She grinned. It was one of her favourites. She always loved the way it made her feel as though everything was going to be all right. And it made a nice change from the usual farmyard noises. Pigs oinking. Cattle lowing . . .

The thought that Jesse had been here in her bed seemed surreal in the cold light of day.

Even weirder was the thought that she had

nothing to do. Blue Ginger was up and running. She felt bereft. This must be what it was like for an actor the last night of a run, when the curtain had come down for the last time and the pan stick was just a dirty blur on a ball of cotton wool. You would do your job again. But you would never do it in the same place, with the same cast.

She looked at Jesse's note again and stretched out like a starfish under the duvet. What on earth was she going to do with herself today?

The phone on her bedside table shrilled. Once her bones had stopped rattling, she managed to pick it up.

'*Never* let me drink vodka again.'

'Lizzy.' She grinned. 'How are you feeling?'

'Completely banjaxed,' Lizzy told her. 'And very firmly in the dog house, I think it's safe to say. Lucy was sick in the night. Crack Nanny let her eat four Penguins on the trot. And guess who got the blame when Conrad had to go to her because I was out for the count? The air was blue at breakfast, I can tell you. And you don't want to know what it's like changing a nappy with a hangover. WHAT? RIGHT OFF? OH GOD. Harry, I'm going to have to go. I'll call you later.'

She left Harriet staring, dumbfounded, at a buzzing handset. Poor Lizzy. She really didn't seem to know whether she was coming or going at the moment.

The phone jumped in her hand.

'Harry?'

'That was quick.'

'You busy?'

Harriet looked down at the duvet. 'Hardly . . .'

There was a strangled sort of gulp on the other end of the line.

'Lizzy?' she asked. 'Lizzy? Is everything OK?'

'I don't know,' Lizzy sobbed. 'Oscar rolled off the table when I was on the phone to you.'

'OK.' Harriet jumped out of bed. 'Is he hurt?'

'Yes. No. I don't know. He banged his head.'

'Is he conscious?'

'Yes.'

'Crying?'

'No. But Jemima said he went down with a right clonk. He looks a bit dazed. Oh God.' She was almost hyperventilating now. 'Conrad said I was an unfit parent last night. I told him he could bloody well talk. He's never bloody here. But he was right. Wasn't he?'

'Of course he wasn't.' Harriet felt a surge of loyalty rise in her chest. It was a bit rich of Conrad to suggest that Lizzy wasn't capable of looking after her own kids. She worked just as hard as he did. Harder, probably. She might not be mending broken hearts all day but she'd done a pretty good job of mending Harriet's over the years. She was a good friend. She couldn't bear to hear her sounding so upset.

'What do you think I should do?' Lizzy was sobbing too much to catch her breath now. 'Sh-sh-should he go to hospital, d'you think?'

'Shouldn't you perhaps ring Conrad?' Harriet suggested. It was awful, hearing her friend in this state. 'I know he's cross with you. But he does work at the hospital. Wouldn't he know what to do?'

'I don't want him finding out,' Lizzy said. 'Not if it's nothing.'

'I think you should take him,' Harriet said. 'Just to be on the safe side. Are you OK to drive?'

'The car's g-gone in for a s-service.' Lizzy blew her nose. 'I'd ring Mum, but I know she's gone to look at a show home this morning. You know how she is. And she always turns her mobile off when she goes out, to save battery.'

'I'm not doing anything,' Harriet told her. 'I'll come.'

'Thanks, Harry.' Lizzy's voice was full of gratitude. 'Are you sure?'

'Of course I'm sure,' Harriet said. Poor Lizzy sounded beside herself. She knew just how she felt. Hospitals were terrible places. Particularly this one. The hospital to which they would have to take Oscar was the same one in which she'd stood, numb with shock, in that cold, hostile room and stared at the dead bodies of both her parents. She wasn't sure she could handle it.

HERMIONE

Bath, September 1988

In her bedroom, high up in the skinny house on Russell Street, Hermione awoke with a start. Something was wrong. Her heart was clanging, like a school bell, in her chest. Her head was thumping.

She sat up slowly, trying to piece together the events of the previous night.

She'd had a headache! That was it. At that party with Will. Black spots had floated in front of her eyes and her stomach had started to roll like a ship with nausea. Everybody had laughed and said she'd had too much Thunderbird. But she knew it hadn't been that. She'd only had a couple of sips, because five minutes after arriving her head had felt as though a jack rabbit was thumping his back feet on the inside of her skull. As the evening wore on, it had only got worse. In the end, she'd had to call Isaac. Will was having too great a time to leave and she'd felt too wobbly to get a cab home on her own. She knew her father would always pick her or Harry up if they called. It didn't matter what time of night it was. He was only a phone call away, he told them. That way, he said, he could always sleep at night. If the phone rang at one in the morning, he would at least know that it was one of the girls wanting a lift home from a party and not a policeman phoning with the news that, thanks to some bloody drunken idiot, one of his daughters was on a life support machine or worse.

Last night, Hermione had waited for him for an hour outside the party before hailing a taxi. It was cold and dark and she felt dreadful. She wanted to be at home. But it wasn't like her father to keep her waiting. What if she got in a taxi and he turned up? He would worry if she wasn't where she'd said she would be.

'Yes, love?' The taxi driver had wound down his window. 'Where to?'

Hermione hesitated.

'Come on, love.' He looked slightly irritated. 'I haven't got all night.'

'Bath,' Hermione told him. 'Only . . . My dad was supposed to pick me up an hour ago,' she confessed, feeling suddenly small.

'Coming from Bath, woz he?' The driver's face softened.

'Yes.'

'Well, he won't get through. Bin a terrible accident on the road out. Queues a mile long. If he's got any sense he'll have turned back. Come on. Jump in. He's probably waiting at home.'

When she'd finally arrived home, everybody had already gone to bed. There had been a note from Harriet to that effect. She'd felt miffed, somehow, that they hadn't waited to see she was in safely. But she knew that Ruby never slept until she heard the front door click shut. Only then, secure in the knowledge that both her girls were home safe, would she allow herself to drift off.

Now, Hermione checked her watch. It was only six thirty. Her headache still thudded dully behind her temples. What had woken her up so early?

She heard the front doorbell jangle. That must have been what had woken her. Isaac would answer it in a minute. He was always up before everybody else. Sparkly Autumn mornings like this one, when there was a tang of toothpaste coupled with a distinct bonfire underbelly in the air, were his favourite time to be alive. He liked to get up early and crunch through the leaves to sit and drink his tea on the gin and tonic wall at the bottom of the garden . . .

The bell jangled again. It was far too early for someone to be shattering the peace like this. Perhaps Isaac had gone to his workshop already. Even so, she was surprised the noise hadn't woken Harry. Bloody hell.

She yanked down her shortie pyjamas from where they'd ridden up in the night and went downstairs. There was still a dull pain behind her temples. She would ask Ruby later if there was anything she could take for it. She would just find out who this was and then she'd make herself a nice cup of herbal tea and go back to bed.

Her bare feet sank into the new hall carpet as she made her way to the front door. The carpet had been a present to Ruby from Isaac. She'd been complaining for so long about the threadbare offering she'd had to put up with since they moved here from the house in Cornwall that'd he'd gone out and chosen one and had it laid one day as a surprise. He was always doing silly little things like that for her. Last year, on her birthday, he'd blown up two hundred red balloons and released them in the garden so that the first thing. Ruby saw when she opened the curtains was a mass of them floating past her window. And every year on Hermione and Harriet's birthday he gave her two dozen old-fashioned roses. They were the most amazing colour. About as close to sky blue-pink as you could get. An impossible fantasy colour that shouldn't really exist. This year's bunch was still on the hall table, singed and curled at the edges now, like a sheaf of old sepia photographs, but still with splashes of pink here and there. Hermione knew that Ruby wouldn't throw them out until they were brown and crisp as old tea bags.

A chilly, back-to school-sort of smell came swirling into the hall as Hermione yanked open the heavy front door and, before she'd had time to consider the implications of the presence of two blue policemen on the front doorstep, it occurred to her that the schools must be going back about now. How strange not to be going back with them. She would have to do something at some point. Halfway through August, her worst fears had been confirmed when the A-level results had been posted on the noticeboard next to the school gymnasium. She had failed everything except English, which she'd scraped with a D. But that wasn't going to be enough . . .

'Miss Harker?'

Hang on. Policemen on the front doorstep at this ungodly hour meant something bad. The younger constable looked nervous, which made Hermione know for certain that something terrible had happened. Her first instinct was to slam the door in his face and run away so he wouldn't be able to tell her whatever it was he'd come to tell her. Instead, she covered her face, like a child who thinks that, by doing so, she is obscuring herself from view.

'What . . .' Her mouth was as dry as chalk. 'What is it? What's happened?'

'Is there somebody here with you, Miss Harker?'

'My . . .' Hermione was finding it difficult to make sense. She wanted to say 'My parents' but found she couldn't get the words out. Her stomach seemed to be spinning like a top somewhere in the region of her throat. 'My sister,' she managed. 'Harry. She's asleep.'

'Perhaps you wouldn't mind waking her.'

The elder of the two gently steered Hermione

back into the house. 'And then perhaps we could all go and have a sit down somewhere.'

Feeling as though she might be going to throw up any second, Hermione ushered the policemen into Ruby's sitting room, where the signs of one of her parents' drinks evenings lingered. A dainty capiz-shell bowl, half filled with pistachio shells, sat on the low coffee table. The scent of the French cigarettes Isaac's friend Guillaume always smoked hovered in the apricot velvet of the cushions on the chaise longue. Her heart leaden with dread, Hermione offered the policemen a seat on the squashy eau-de-nil sofa and went upstairs to wake Harriet.

HARRIET

Afterwards, Hermione would say it had all been a blur. That, even as she'd swung open Ruby and Isaac's bedroom door, hoping against all reason to find them snug in the big white expanse of their antique bed, her mind was already shutting down. Shrouding itself in a protective glaze.

For Harriet, snatched from a cosy dream in which Will loved her – and only her – after all, things were very different. As she and Hermione sat, holding hands, in the back of the police car, she noticed the oddest things in acute, magnified detail. The guy from number thirty, walking his dog. Hermione's feet, clad in fuzzy spearmint-green socks with bobbles on the backs. She'd been in such a hurry to clamber into the police car and get to the hospital that she'd forgotten her shoes. Somebody's BLT, half eaten, had been hastily tucked into the slot on the front of the dashboard. Presumably, bacon breath wasn't considered de rigueur when you were informing victims' relatives of a car smash.

It was unthinkable to imagine that last night she'd been working up the courage to tell her mother she was pregnant. From her perch at the kitchen table, she'd watched as Ruby stirred scrambled eggs for Isaac's late-night snack. Twice, she'd tried to say something. But her mouth felt as though it was gummed together with Plasticine. And then, when Hermione had phoned to say she felt unwell and needed a lift home, everything had fallen into place. She would wait until they got back and tell them all together. Hermione would dump Will in disgust. Ruby would know what to do about the baby. Everything would be all right again.

Except she hadn't told them, had she? In the end, she'd chickened out. They were gone a long time. She told herself that Hermione had probably changed her mind and was refusing to leave the party. It wouldn't be the first time. So she'd scribbled a vague note and hit the hay.

As the car sped towards the hospital, she played the old cracks in the pavement game with herself. If I remember not to stand on the slab with the spider's web crack on the way home, there'll be chips for tea. If I get to the shop before it shuts, Will will call tonight and everything'll be OK. I've been worrying about nothing.

If the lights don't change before I can count to ten, Ruby and Isaac will be sitting up in bed when we get to the hospital.

Onetwothreefourfivesixseveneightnine . . .

The traffic lights flashed amber.

Too late!

★ ★ ★

According to the police, Isaac's Triumph Herald had been wiped off the road by a couple of drunken yobs driving a Ford Escort. It seemed ironic to Harriet, as the policemen ushered them through the hive of bright lights and activity that was the hospital foyer, that it was the thought of such people that had made Isaac put on his funny Afghan coat at ten o'clock at night and climb into his car to rattle through the Wiltshire countryside to collect his daughter. He hadn't wanted any of his family to get hurt. And yet somehow these inconsiderate loons had still managed to hurt them. By paying no attention to Isaac's little yellow car, coming carefully up the hill, they had hurt Harriet and Hermione more than they could know.

Beside her, Hermione was twitching like a leaf. Her brown eyes were as wide as dinner plates and staring somewhere into the unknown. It was almost as though she wasn't actually here at all. For once, it was left to Harriet to be the strong one. As the policemen ushered them into a waiting room, where a portable TV was babbling inanely in the corner, she braced herself for the worst. A moment later, when a doctor in a white coat entered the room, accompanied by a lady who looked safe and sensible, she gripped Hermione's hand as though her life depended on it and waited obediently to be given the news she dreaded most.

'Your father . . .' The doctor's throat seemed to close up. Even he seemed to be holding back tears.

'Your father's car was badly damaged. It . . .' He gave a sort of gulp. 'When it was forced off the road, it flipped over and skidded through a fence into a swimming pool. I am . . . I'm telling you this because we will need you both to be very brave and identify the bodies . . .'

A terrible sound split the fusty air in the waiting room. For a second, Harriet thought the noise was coming from her and then she realised that Hermione had closed her eyes and was wailing as she rocked back and forth on the nasty plastic chair.

'They're . . .' Harriet knew she had to be strong, even though her world had imploded. 'You mean . . . they're . . . dead?'

'I'm sorry.' The doctor looked horrified. 'I thought . . . You mean you weren't told? You didn't *know*?'

One of the policemen who had brought them cleared his throat. 'We were waiting for the counsellor. We thought it might be better coming from her.'

'What did you mean?' Harriet said sharply. 'What did you mean when you said you had to tell us about the swimming pool?'

The lady who, so far, had not spoken, came over and put a hand on her knee.

'Did they drown?' For some reason, in spite of the fact that it was killing her, Harriet felt compelled to know every single little detail. Hermione was still rocking on the chair next to her. She wasn't going to be much help. 'In their own car? Do you mean they couldn't get out?'

'It was a very old car.'

'It wasn't *old*,' Harriet said. 'It was classic. It was a classic car.'

'Even so. It would have filled up with water very quickly. There wouldn't have been much time.'

Harriet thought of her parents' faces. Had they known what was going to happen? Had they come to after the initial impact, and been filled with relief to discover themselves both alive? It would have been a wonderful feeling. And then, with mounting terror, they would have felt the car lurch. They would have heard the rush of water, pouring in through the vulnerable roof. Had they tried the door handles in vain, banging and rattling them in panic? And then, when it became obvious that they weren't going to get out, had they hugged, seeking comfort in each other? Or had it not happened like that at all? Had one of them been unconscious? Had the other been forced to watch, all alone, as his or her lungs filled with water?

How long had she been asleep last night, hovering, like a fly in amber, between knowing and not knowing? How long had Ruby and Isaac been lying dead while she slept on, blissfully oblivious to the horror that was waiting for her when she woke up? What if Hermione hadn't heard those two policemen ringing the front doorbell? She would probably be calmly going about the business of making her breakfast right now. She would have assumed Isaac had got up early to go to the workshop and that Ruby had gone to the supermarket because they'd run out of eggs. Ruby and Isaac would still be dead. Would not knowing make it any better?

But she'd always have to find out eventually.

As soon as she saw Ruby, lying on a mortuary slab, she knew why some people believed in souls. Ruby wasn't there any more. Everything that had made Ruby Ruby was gone. With the exception of a gash on her forehead, her face was completely devoid of colour. She looked as though she was made of wax.

Isaac had been in the water for longer. His poor face was swollen, so that it almost didn't look like him at all. It was so difficult to relate the body lying on the block of marble with the loving ball of energy that had been her father that it was almost bearable. But then, with a pang, she noticed something in his hair. Something they'd missed when they'd cleaned him up for identification. Lurking in Isaac's thick, black thatch was a translucent white bean sprout from the Chinese takeaway he'd promised her in an attempt to cheer her up. It hadn't escaped his notice that she'd been in a grouch all day. She'd hardly touched the moussaka Ruby had made for lunch. Usually, it was one of her favourites. Yesterday, though, she'd looked down at the discs of potato, swimming in their sauce speckled with opals of fat, and felt sick

211

to her stomach. She was working up to telling Ruby the news that she was pregnant.

And now she would never be able to.

They must have picked up the takeaway from Kwok Sing's before they'd gone to collect Hermione. The thought of them both waiting patiently in the queue as the little bald man brought out the brown paper bag filled with treats made her want to cry. They would have been looking forward to eating it. Looking forward to sharing it with their girls, unaware that, in less than an hour, they would both die in the most horrendous manner.

Gently, she reached across and plucked the bean sprout from her father's hair. It didn't seem right, somehow, to let him lie there dead with bits of food in his hair. She held the offending item between her finger and thumb and examined it carefully, just to be sure it was what she thought it was. And in that moment, the awful reality of what had happened crystallised in her mind. Her parents were both dead. They were dead and they weren't coming back. She, Harriet, was never going to see them again. Never. Not ever. It seemed impossible. Unfathomable.

HERMIONE

Toronto, 2003

Life, Hermione reflected, could be pretty amazing when it wanted to be.

As she reached the four-month mark, she started to put on weight at the rate of a kilo every few days. It was almost as though her baby knew she was now expected and had decided to make her presence well and truly felt. And the bigger Hermione got, the more it dawned on her that there was a tiny little person growing inside her. It was funny to think that, only a month or so ago, that very thought had freaked her out. Now that she'd had her scan and seen her baby's heartbeat, she was really looking forward to it.

She only hoped she could manage to keep the whole thing under wraps for a little while longer. She wanted to stay at Pritchard Smythe for as long as possible before she went on maternity leave. She wasn't going to starve if she lost her job. She still owned her little house in Fulham. And there was money from Isaac's life insurance in her savings account. She and the little one would be OK for a while. But she didn't want to leave Canada. She'd fallen in love with this great big country. They had proper seasons here. Thick snow in winter. Stunning colours in the fall, when the trees that fringed the highway on the drive to the cabin were a crackling blaze of vermilion, crimson and orange. Proper hot summers. She hoped that she would be allowed to stay.

She didn't particularly want Greg to find out either. If word got round that she was expecting a baby, he might put two and two together. It would make things awkward.

Once or twice, since their break-up, she'd seen Greg around the building as he dropped by for various meetings. Her heart always gave a sort of skippety thump whenever she caught a glimpse of him laughing with Emilie in the typing pool or talking to one of the fat tie brigade over by the water cooler. But he never put his head around the door to say hi. She supposed she couldn't really blame him. She'd made it pretty clear she wanted nothing more to do with him. She was still pissed about the whole affair. Greg had seemed different, somehow. OK, so he was a red-blooded male. He liked to buy her raw silk underwear the colour of crushed raspberries and then ravish her while she was wearing it. But he had been slow and tender sometimes. She still remembered the look she'd glimpsed in his eyes when he'd told her about losing his brother. She'd been so sure they understood each other. She'd even allowed herself, for one crazy moment, to believe that they'd been meant to meet. That it was destiny, somehow.

She couldn't get him out of her head. It was as though, at some point during their brief affair, he'd found a way to unzip her skin and crawl inside, as though she were a human sleeping bag. It was a feeling that didn't sit comfortably. Usually, after a hiatus like this one, she just dusted herself down and moved on to the next man. Since arriving in Toronto, she'd had a few brief flings. Usually, her liaisons were paper thin. Men she saw a few times, then drifted away from. A cocktail waiter over from Vancouver. A bell hop. A year or so back, she'd had a brief understanding with Art, who was her friend and attorney. But it hadn't lasted. They'd both decided they were better off as friends.

This time around, however, it hadn't been as easy to move on. She had tried. Shortly after finding out Greg was married, she and Josh had gone to a bar in Queen Street because Josh had heard they made a wicked dirty martini. Hermione had wound up with the most beautiful man in her bed. Olivier, his name was. Ebony black, with skin so glossy it looked almost wet. A body to die for. But Hermione had watched those blue-black shoulders pumping above her and felt nothing. Olivier was gorgeous. But he wasn't Greg. And that was that.

At least she still had Josh, she told herself one afternoon, taking a chocolate glaze from the box of doughnuts on her desk and feeling a grateful rush of saliva fill her mouth as she took a satisfying bite.

She hadn't been able to do up the buttons on her suit jacket this morning. Her body was happily letting itself go, sliding down the slippery slope to rack and ruin. And, surprisingly, she was enjoying it. It was actually rather refreshing not to have to think about watching her weight for a change.

Josh had been brilliant about the baby. When she thought about how she'd been expecting him to react, she felt guilty for underestimating him. She'd honestly thought he would see it as an unwelcome intrusion. A cog in the wheel of their hedonistic lifestyle. Instead, once it had sunk in that the affair with Greg was over and done with, he'd begun to talk excitedly about what it would be like to have a baby in the house. He'd even started to ask what she might call it.

'I like Tallulah for a girl,' he said. 'Jack for a boy. What about you?'

Hermione thought. 'If it's a girl, Lola.'

'And for a boy?'

But Hermione hadn't been able to think of any boys' names she liked. They were all so penny plain. Steve. Mark. Paul. Alan. That was a good one. Who on earth looked at a tiny baby and thought to themselves, 'I know. Alan's a good name. We'll call him Alan.'

Because they couldn't agree, they'd decided to call her the Bean for now. Josh's excitement had been infectious. Hermione tried not to get ahead of herself. She told herself that, while Josh might be willing – and she truly believed he was – to play Daddy now, when he met someone, it might be a different matter. More to the point, what if *she* met someone? It wasn't likely, given her present size and shape. But it was possible. And what would happen then?

Even so, she couldn't help but get excited. Over the past week or two, she'd started window-shopping for baby clothes. The top drawer of the chest in her bedroom in Amelia Street had been cleared to make way for the little one. She knew it was supposed to be bad luck to buy things for the baby before he or she arrived. But, this lunchtime, she hadn't been able to resist a tiny pair of cashmere dungarees in zingy lime green and a little white bobble hat.

She couldn't focus on work this afternoon. The air conditioning was down and it was starting to get very warm outside. She felt fat and queasy.

She pressed the button on the phone to tell Kevin to hold all her calls because she was catching up on paperwork and started instead to catch up on what her baby was doing.

'Gotcha!'

'Bloody hell.' Hermione whipped round to see Josh grinning at her. He plonked a chocolate brownie on her desk. 'Where did you spring from?'

'I came through the door.' Josh laughed. 'You were engrossed.'

'I *told* Kevin not to let anybody in.'

'Yes.' Josh wagged his finger at her and made

himself comfortable on what he always called her 'Director's sofa'. 'But I'm not just anybody, am I? I'm the father of your baby. Sort of. So.' He got up again and came to peer over her shoulder. 'What's our little one up to? Can she suck her thumb yet?'

'Josh Mulligan, you are *way* behind.' Hermione pretended to scold him. 'The Bean was sucking her thumb weeks ago.'

'She was?'

'Yes,' Hermione said proudly. 'She's very advanced. She takes after her mother.'

'Naturally.' Josh took a walnut crunch from the box on her desk and broke it in half.

'Did you want anything in particular?' Hermione asked him. 'Or are you just skiving?'

'Bit of both.' Josh opened the file he was carrying and spread it out on her desk. 'Skiving, obviously. Goes without saying. But I just wanted to run through this with you.'

'What is it?'

'I've been doing some research,' he said earnestly. 'And I've made a list of all the things you can eat and all the things you can't.'

'Right.' Hermione's lips twitched. He was adorable.

Of course, she'd already done her own research. She knew exactly what she should and shouldn't be eating. But she decided to humour him. He was trying so hard. Deep down, he knew she missed Greg. And he was trying to make up for it.

'You can still have eggs,' Josh told her. 'But only

if they're cooked properly. You can't eat cookie dough any more.'

'Why not?'

'Because it has raw egg in it. You can't eat Camembert. And you'll have to stay away from seafood for now.'

'Right.' Hermione assumed a serious expression. 'I'll bear all of that in mind. Thanks, Josh.'

'Oh.' Josh fumbled in his jacket pocket and pulled out a little purple box. 'I got you these.'

'Pills.' Hermione took the box and examined it carefully. 'Anything good?'

'Don't be silly,' Josh said. 'You can't do any of that now. Not now you've got the Bean to think about. Nope. This is folic acid. You should have been taking it months ago.'

'What's it for?'

'It helps prevent developmental defects,' Josh said. 'Spina bifida. That sort of thing.'

'Thanks, Josh.' Hermione eyed the doughnut box and wondered if she should make a start on the last maple dip now or save it for later.

'And you should swim,' Josh told her. 'The birth will be easier if you're fit. And then there's the smoking.' He nodded at the carton of Camel Lights on her desk.

'What about it?'

'You're still doing it.'

'So?'

'So you really mustn't. It's pure poison, you know. Travelling through the placenta straight into the Bean's bloodstream. We're going to have to knock that on the head, I'm afraid.'

'It's only the odd one. The doctor said—'

'Even so,' Josh interrupted. 'This is the Bean's health we're talking about.'

'OK.' She held up her hands in defeat. 'I'll try.'

'Good.' Josh looked relieved. 'And I've decided I would quite like to be at the birth. I mean, obviously, I won't be looking at your Spam fritter. But it's important to be there from the moment the baby's born. It cements the bond, apparently. If I'm the first person the Bean sees, she'll accept me as her parent immediately.' He paused for effect. 'I looked it up on the internet. And I think it's a good thing if she does see me as a father figure,' he added anxiously. 'Don't you? It'll be a whole lot easier when we come to discipline further along the line.'

'Bloody hell.' Hermione was amused. 'I haven't got that far yet. To be honest, I still can't quite believe this is a baby I'm carrying. I keep thinking I'm just going to keep on getting bigger and bigger until I explode. Like Mr Creosote.' She looked at him, touched by his consideration. 'You've really thought about this, haven't you?'

'I made you a promise,' Josh said. 'I told you I'd be there for you and the baby and I will. It'll mean I have to come to the birthing classes,' he added. 'So I know how to help you do your breathing and everything.'

'I thought you said that was just a load of fat women nesting.'

'Well.' Josh looked sheepish. 'They won't *all* be like that, will they? Surely some of them will be like you?'

'I hope so.' She smiled. 'Thanks, though. I'd like it if you came to the birthing classes with me.'

'That's settled then.' He tweaked at his tie. 'Does this look a bit Fun Tie Friday to you?'

'No. Why?'

'I've got a sort of date.'

'Oh, you have, have you?' Hermione teased him. 'I hope you're not going to misbehave. I'm not quite sure what the Bean would have to say about that.'

'Should I cancel?' Josh looked panicked.

'I'm joking,' Hermione told him. 'To be honest, Josh, I'm just grateful you still want to live in the same house as us. I certainly don't expect you to stay celibate. So come on.' She rubbed her hands together. 'Who is he?'

'Bloke called Bernie. He's a bit . . .' Josh crinkled his nose up.

'What?'

'A bit young. But he looks gullible enough to succumb to my ginger urges, so I thought.'

'Where are you taking him?'

'He's taking me. That new Icelandic place. Ptarmigan, is it? Something like that.'

'I know the one,' Hermione said. 'Kelly's husband took her there for their wedding anniversary. You have to eat puffin and rotting shark meat.'

'I don't mind about that.' Josh said. 'I just didn't

want to look like the sort of tosser who has one of those signs above his desk. You know. You don't have to be mad to work here . . .'

'But it helps,' Hermione finished for him.

'Exactly. So do I?'

'No.' Her internal line buzzed. 'Yes?'

It was Kevin, squonking like a seal with nerves between sentences.

'Are you still, *squonk*, h-h-holding your calls?'

'Did I say I wasn't?'

'No. I just, *squonk*, thought you might have forgotten to say.'

'Kevin. When I want you to un-hold my calls, I'll tell you. OK?'

'I'll tell him to go then, shall I?'

Hermione rolled her eyes. Sometimes, she wondered what planet Kevin was on.

'Tell *who* to go?'

'Greg Finch. Only it's not in the diary.'

'Greg's *here*?'

'He says it's important.'

'Send him up.'

'So am I, um, un-holding your calls now?'

'No,' Hermione said firmly. 'This is a one-off.' She put the phone down. 'Shit!'

'What?'

'It's Greg.'

'Greg Finch?' Josh looked horrified. 'Here? Now?'

'Afraid so.' Hermione hastily pulled on her jacket. 'How do I look?'

'Why does it matter?' Josh pouted. 'I thought it was all over between you and him.'

'It is,' Hermione told him. 'I didn't mean do I look beautiful. I meant, can you *tell*?'

'Oh, right.' Josh looked relieved. 'No.'

'Good.'

'Although . . .'

'What?'

'Perhaps you should try and stay sitting down.'

'Right.'

'You want me to stay?' he asked her. 'In case he tries it on?'

'I'll be fine.'

'Because I can, you know. I don't mind.'

'Don't be daft,' Hermione said. 'Why should he try it on? This is probably business. Nothing more.'

'As long as you're sure.' Josh placed his hand on the door handle. 'Oh . . .'

'Yes?'

'Ditch the jacket. It's a bit Gucci does Bar Mitzvah.'

'Josh?'

'Yep?'

'Have a lovely time with Barney.'

'Bernie.'

'Bernie. Now scoot.'

The second Josh left, Hermione raced around like a demented bee, locating mascara, lipstick and a little silver atomiser filled with her favourite perfume. She knew it was over between her and Greg. But that didn't stop her from fancying him.

And she didn't particularly want him looking at her and thinking she'd gone downhill. She might be pregnant but she had her pride.

Greg sat down, loosening his lavender silk tie so that his crisp Thomas Pink shirt rucked up at the waist to reveal a square inch of flat mahogany stomach. Hermione felt the puppet string in her belly jerk with lust.

'Greg.' She tried to look professional. 'What can I do for you?'

'We have a problem.' His face was giving nothing away.

'We do?'

'We sure do.'

Tendrils of fear wove themselves through Hermione's entrails. For a stupid moment, she thought the cat was out of the bag. Greg knew. He knew she was pregnant and he'd come to tell her he wanted nothing to do with it. Which was fine, of course. She didn't want him to have anything to do with the baby in any case. She just didn't want to actually hear him say it.

'Is it the campaign? Someone didn't like our ad?'

'God, Hermione,' Greg scoffed. 'Of course it's not the ad. I couldn't give a fuck about the ad.'

'You couldn't?'

'Of course I couldn't.' Greg took off his tie and rolled it into a neat Swiss roll. 'This is about me and you.'

'I told you,' Hermione tried to remain firm, even though the carbohydrate-laden contents of her stomach were jerking about like a lobotomised Mr Punch, 'there is no me and you.'

'That's my problem,' Greg said.

'What do you mean?'

'I can't stop thinking about you. About us.' He leaned forward, his eyes locked on hers. 'I was on the subway the other day and someone was wearing your perfume. The first thing I had to do when I got to the office was jerk off in the bathroom.'

Hermione crossed her legs. It was hardly the most romantic thing anyone had ever said to her. She was almost disgusted by it.

Disgusted and incredibly turned on.

Pregnancy was playing havoc with her hormones. She was unbelievably horny at the moment. And it was only going to get worse as she got bigger. It just went to show that Mother Nature had to be a guy in disguise. What sort of woman would decree that her sisters should be deranged with lust when, due to the fact that they were at their most physically repulsive, no bugger would come near them? It was completely topsy-turvy. A man had to have had a finger in the pie somewhere there.

Last weekend, things had got so bad she'd had to take a walk down Yonge Street, where she'd gone into a sex shop and bought herself a slim silver vibrator. She'd used it that night under the duvet, praying that Josh wouldn't hear the embarrassing giveaway buzz. Now she was using the damn thing at least twice a day.

'So you *do* miss me,' Greg said.

'Of course I miss you,' Hermione told him. 'But I told you, I don't make a habit of sleeping with married men.'

'But—'

'It hurt,' she told him bravely. 'I thought . . . we were good together.'

'We were. We were more than good. We really had something.'

'But you're married.' Hermione reeled herself in from temptation. 'End of story.'

'What if I told you I wasn't,' Greg said.

'What?' Hermione allowed herself a small, marmalade shred of hope. 'You're *not* married now?'

'Sorry,' Greg said. 'Bad choice of words. Of course I'm married. But—'

'You already told me,' Hermione said. 'You have to stay together for the sake of the kids.'

'That's what I'm trying to tell you. I changed my mind.'

'What do you mean, you changed your mind?'

'We talked about it. Lena and I. I told her . . .' He looked sheepish. 'I told her I was in love with somebody else.'

A starburst of hope exploded in Hermione's chest. 'You . . . You mean . . .'

'I'm in love with you, Hermione. I want to be with you.'

'But why now?' Hermione asked him. 'You seemed perfectly OK last week.'

'Last week?' Greg looked perplexed.

'You were here. For a meeting with Jeff.'

'Ah!' Greg's face cleared. 'The wanker!'

Hermione had to hide a smile. 'If you knew you were in love with me, why did you never once even come in here to see how I was doing?'

'You dumped me,' Greg said simply. 'Did you think it was easy for me? Seeing you again was only going to make things worse. I missed you.'

It still didn't sit well with her conscience, knowing that Greg had hurt his family because of her. But she was relieved and glad to know that her feelings were reciprocated. At least now she didn't feel so damned foolish.

'What made you decide?' she asked. 'Why did you change your mind?'

'Does it matter?' Greg came around to her side of the desk. He took her head in his hands and pulled her towards him so her forehead rested on his taut stomach. He smelled deliciously of freshly cut grass and lunchtime vino. There was something about the smell of alcohol on a man's breath that made her weak at the knees. It reminded her of discovering boys for the first time. Fumbling behind the sofa at teenage parties. Rough hands, trying to unhook the clip on her bra. Fingers sliding under the shiny satin of her best French knickers until they found the soft, wet spot they were looking for and stabbed gratefully, desperately in its general direction.

Greg knelt down and leaned his forehead against hers.

'It's you I want to be with,' he told her. 'Your face I want to see first thing in the morning and last thing at night. I want to be with you all the time.'

'What are you saying?'

'I'm saying let's live together. Let's make a life together.'

Hermione didn't quite know what to say. 'What about your kids?'

'They'll understand,' Greg said. 'They won't be the only kids in school with divorced parents. And they're not stupid. They know we've been having problems for a while.'

'And work?' Hermione said. 'What are we going to tell them?'

Greg's hand moved slowly down the knobs of her spine, giving her goose bumps. 'I'll just tell my lot I've moved out of the family home. They won't ask questions. They don't have to know I'm with you.'

'Josh will have to know,' Hermione said.

'That's fine.' Greg said. 'It's only fair that we give him a bit of notice.'

'Notice?'

'Well, obviously he'll want to find somewhere else. He won't want to play the gay gooseberry for the rest of his life, will he?'

'I don't think . . .' Hermione began, then stopped. It hadn't occurred to her that Josh might want to move out.

She was happy, of course, that Greg wanted to move in. And there was something about the way he'd said 'for the rest of his life' that had made her tummy dance its own little boogie of happiness. But . . . wasn't this all a bit quick?

And Josh had been so sweet, offering to help with the baby and come to her birthing classes. She'd been really touched to discover just how good a friend he was. And the truth was that she wanted him to be involved with the baby . . .

Oh God! The baby.

Greg didn't even know about that yet. It was all going to come as a huge shock.

She opened her mouth to tell him, but Greg stopped her, bringing his mouth down on hers and kissing her in his own inimitable style, making her gasp. She'd forgotten the way he always caught hold of her bottom lip, oh so lightly, as he broke away, prolonging the contact until the last possible moment.

'What do you say?' he asked, when he finally pulled away. 'Shall we go for it?'

Hermione told herself that this was her one chance of happiness.

OK, so the situation was far from ideal. They hadn't really spent enough time together to really *know*. Living together was a far cry from dinner in lavish restaurants and fucking on designer sheets in swanky hotels. Plus, she still wasn't hugely comfortable with the thought of Greg's wife and kids. They made her feel guilty.

But Greg was the first man she'd ever really felt something for. Apart from Josh, of course. And she could never have Josh, could she? One day, he was going to meet somebody special. And then where would she be? On her own with a baby.

The thought terrified her.

Perhaps Josh would even be relieved at being offered a get-out clause. Who knew? Something might even develop with this Bernie guy. Who was she to stand in his way if it looked as though things were going along that route? If he lost out on the chance of something good he would only end up resenting her in the end.

'Please?' Greg's soft brown eyes searched her own. 'Can we make a go of it, do you think? Come on. I could move in tonight. We can finally be together. Properly.'

Hermione's face broke into a smile. She couldn't help it. She knew this was mad. But perhaps it could really work.

'OK,' she said. 'But on one condition.'

'Anything.' Greg grabbed her and lifted her up. 'Bloody hell. Have you put on weight?'

'Thanks a lot.' Hermione pretended to look offended.

'So what's the condition?' Greg grinned at her.

'It's Josh,' Hermione said. 'This is going to come as a bit of a shock for him. Would you mind . . .' She hesitated. 'Would you mind *not* moving in tonight. I could cook him a nice meal, perhaps. Break it to him gently. Having a new roommate is going to take some getting used to.'

'He won't want to *stay*, surely?' Greg said. 'Won't he feel a bit . . . surplus to requirements?'

'Amelia Street is his home,' Hermione said loyally. 'We found it together, when we first came here. I don't want him to feel he has to move out of his own home.'

'You might find he wants to leave anyway,' Greg said.

'Fine,' Hermione said. 'If he wants to, that's fine. But if he doesn't, then he stays.'

'OK.' Greg held up his hands in defeat. 'OK. Josh stays. I don't have a problem with that.'

Unfortunately, Josh didn't quite see things the same way.

'I'm sorry,' he huffed as Hermione dolloped his favourite garlic mash on his plate. 'I just don't think complex carbohydrate is going to make this any easier to deal with.'

'It might be fine,' Hermione pleaded with him. 'You might find out you get on really well once you get to know each other better.'

'Oh look.' Josh peered out of the dining room window. 'Flying pigs.'

'Please don't be like that,' Hermione begged. 'Here. Have some wine.'

'I couldn't.' Josh shuddered.

'It's Pouilly Fumé.'

'OK. Perhaps just a small glass.'

In the end, Josh begrudgingly agreed to give it a go. But the next night, as Greg unpacked his things, he stood in the doorway, pouting like Shirley Temple as the endless parade of crisply

231

ironed shirts and pure silk ties made their way from Greg's brown leather holdall to Hermione's closet. Later, when Greg was taking a shower, he shambled into the kitchen looking so doleful that Hermione couldn't help but feel sorry for him, even though he was clearly not prepared to make an effort.

'Why are you doing this?'

'I like him.' Hermione shrugged.

'He's married.'

'He left his wife.'

'And you feel responsible.' Josh opened a bottle of sparkling water.

'No.' Hermione shook her head. 'Not at all. I mean, obviously I feel a *bit* responsible. If it wasn't for me he'd be at home with his wife and kids right now. But I like him, Josh. I mean *really* like him. He makes me feel alive. And the sexual chemistry between us is mind-boggling. I really think this could work.'

Josh looked sceptical. 'What does he say about the baby?'

'I haven't actually mentioned it yet.' Hermione told him.

'Are you *mad*? Why the hell not?'

'It just seems too crazy.'

'You mean you don't know how he's going to react.'

'It's not that.' Hermione shook her head. 'I will tell him. I guess it's just a case of letting him settle in a bit. I'll have to pick the right moment.'

'Do you want me to go?' Josh said.

'No.' Hermione patted his arm. 'Of course not. This is your home as much as it is mine. And when the baby comes, I'll need you more than ever.'

'Really?'

'Really. This doesn't change anything, Josh. You'll still be a part of my baby's life.'

'That's just it, though, isn't it?' Josh looked sad. 'She's your baby now. Yours and Greg's. She isn't ours any more.'

For the next week or so, Josh circled Greg like a bird of prey, picking him up on every little thing.

'Spurt! is causing a bit of a buzz,' Greg would say.

'Bluebottles buzz,' Josh would retort. 'Around shit.'

To be fair to Josh, Greg did have an unfortunate habit of winding him up sometimes. If Josh made her a morning cup of tea, Greg would pick up angel food cake from the deli on the way home. If Josh ran her a bath, Greg would give her a foot massage. The pair of them were so territorial around her, she half expected them to cock their legs and start spraying her. Josh's jibes got more and more acidic the longer he was around Greg. One morning, Greg asked Hermione if she thought he ought to do something about his hair because he was going grey.

'Silver,' she said affectionately. 'I wouldn't

bother. I quite like grey hair. I think it's distinguished.'

'Even so.' He peered into the hall mirror. 'I must be able to get some sort of product to cover it up.'

'How about brake fluid?' Josh sneered.

'Stop it, Josh,' Hermione told him. 'Or I'll have to put you in a home.'

'It's not fair,' Josh said later when Greg had gone to the liquor store to buy a bottle of wine to go with their evening meal. 'You don't have time for me any more.'

'Of *course* I do,' Hermione said.

'You're always doing things without me. That couples massage you had the other day . . .'

'That was sort of the point,' Hermione told him. 'We're a couple.'

'I know,' Josh said sadly. 'But that doesn't mean I have to like it.'

Two glorious weeks trickled past. Josh's bad moods apart, Hermione thought she'd never been happier. She still had her hormonal ups and downs. And there were times when she looked at the picture of her seven-year-old self eating doughnuts with her sister in that funny café with the orange lights and wondered if she wouldn't feel more complete if she plucked up the courage to make contact. Presumably, her sister hadn't vanished off the face of the earth. Someone was bound to know where she was. She might even still be in the Bath area.

The only problem was that if, as she suspected, Harriet had got married, she would have changed her name.

Most of the time, though, she pushed all thoughts of family to the back of her mind and concentrated on the present. She'd never lived with somebody before. She had been worried that part of Greg's earlier appeal had been the fact that he'd always seemed just that tiny bit out of reach. But living with him was more fun than she'd ever thought it could be. She loved waking up with him; opening her eyes to see him stretching like a delectable cat in the bed beside her, then nuzzling into him so they could make love before work.

It was the same at night. Greg reached out for her as she climbed into bed and slowly worked his hands and tongue over every inch of her body, dropping butterfly kisses on the crook of her knee or the nape of her neck before slipping inside her and moving with her to climax. As the days passed, the kisses, particularly when they were in the region of her tummy, made her feel more and more anxious. She was getting bigger. She still didn't quite look pregnant. It was more that she was starting to fill out around the middle. One night, as Greg's tongue leisurely made its way from her right nipple and down over her stomach towards the throbbing nub of her clitoris, he stopped in the region of her belly button and grinned up at her.

'Hermione Harker,' he said. 'I do believe you're getting fat.'

'Contentment.' Hermione smiled back, hoping the wobble of panic she felt didn't show.

She would tell him. Of course she would. She just wanted to find the perfect time. Meanwhile, the sex was amazing. The silver vibrator lurked, forgotten, in Hermione's bedside drawer until Greg, looking for a Kleenex one night, found it.

'And what, may I ask, is this?' He waved it like a flag under her nose.

'Oh God.' Hermione was embarrassed. 'That was just . . .'

'You,' he nibbled her ear, 'are one naughty little cat.'

'I don't . . .' Hermione was flustered. 'I mean . . . I . . . What are you doing?'

Greg had turned the handle at the base, watching as it purred into life.

'Here.' He handed it to her. 'Use it.'

'What?' Hermione said. 'Now? But we've only just . . .'

'Please,' Greg said. He was hard again, she noticed. His cock leapt like a salmon as he looked at her. 'I want you to.'

Hermione was tired. Tonight, for the first time ever with Greg, she'd faked her orgasm. She'd noticed herself getting tired a lot more easily over the past few days. And it would feel rather odd, writhing naked on the bed with a piece of metal stuck inside her.

'Come on, you dirty little bitch', Greg said thickly. 'Do what you used to do to yourself when I wasn't here to tell you off.'

Slightly embarrassed, Hermione lay back against the pillows and obliged. And it wasn't too long before the sensation of the vibrator itself, combined with the sight of Greg's eyes glazing over with lust as he grabbed hold of himself, sent waves of pleasure rippling over her.

'He's a wanker,' Josh told her, in no uncertain terms, over breakfast the following day. Hermione had decided to take a sickie. She couldn't even think about work any more. She felt sick. Which shouldn't still be happening. Not now. She was exhausted. And she felt fat and ugly.

Nevertheless, she couldn't help smiling at the irony of Josh's description.

'You do know what they say about him at Canon Corps?' Josh went on.

'How do you know what's going on at Canon Corps?'

'Belinda,' Josh said. 'That friend of Stanley's.'

'How *is* Stanley?'

'Hopelessly single,' Josh said. 'As always. Don't try and change the subject. Belinda said—'

'Josh.' Hermione was tired. 'I don't care what Belinda said. And you shouldn't go checking up on him. We're fine.'

'He'll shit on you,' Josh told her. 'You know that. Men like him never change. I should know.'

'I'm sorry?'

'I've been out with married men myself, you know. Not all married men are as straight as they might like to make out. And I've met men like Greg before. They never leave their wives. At least, not for good. I can't believe you're taking the risk.'

'I love him,' Hermione said. 'And I know he loves me. Anyway, isn't that what love is all about? Taking risks.'

'If you're so sure he loves you,' Josh spooned in Cap'n Crunch cereal, 'why have you still not told him about the baby. I can't believe he hasn't noticed. I mean has he actually *looked* at you?'

'Yes,' Hermione said, thinking of last night. He'd looked at her in acute detail. Though she *had* kept her steel-blue silk nightie pulled over her stomach. She'd been doing that for a while now. Greg kept complaining that he couldn't see her properly. He liked to watch her while they were making love.

'I am going to tell him about the baby,' she said defensively.

'When?'

'Tonight.'

'Good.' He kissed the top of her head. 'I've got to go to work. Make sure you get some rest. The Bean needs you to be strong.'

Hermione was still feeling sick when the phone rang at 11 a.m.

'Hermione?' It was Jon Lloyd. Her boss at Pritchard Smythe.

'Hi. Did Josh give you the message?'

'That you're sick.' He sounded awkward. 'Yes. I hope it's nothing serious.'

'Just a bug,' Hermione said. 'I should be better by tomorrow.'

'That's good to hear.' Jon cleared his throat.

'Is that it?' People were jumping out of their seats on some cable TV show. She didn't want to miss it.

'Not quite. Hermione, you know I'm more than happy with your work. You're a real asset to this company. Your insight is quite . . . astounding.'

'But . . .'

'But . . .' Jon took a breath. 'Word has reached me that you've been seeing rather a lot of Greg Finch.'

'Ah!'

'I'm told he's left his wife.'

'I see.'

'Is this true?'

'Yes,' Hermione said. There wasn't really any point in lying. The truth was bound to come out sooner or later.

'You do know that fraternising with clients is a dismissable offence.'

'Yep,' Hermione told him. 'I know.'

'I'm afraid I don't really have any choice but to ask you to clear your desk.'

'Right.'

'I'm sorry, Hermione.'

'Me too.'

The rug had been pulled out from under her. Her job at Pritchard Smythe was the reason she'd come to Canada. It was her link to everything. Josh. Greg. Without Pritchard Smythe, she wouldn't be carrying this child. She didn't even know anybody outside the company. Not really. She would miss it. She'd always known she would have to give up her job eventually. But she'd hoped for a little longer to sort herself out. At least she would be OK for money. The generous salary Pritchard Smythe had paid her meant she'd been able to save a bit.

How had Jon Lloyd found out, anyway? Nobody else knew. Apart from Josh. And Josh wouldn't . . .

Would he?

No. He might not like Greg. But he wouldn't deliberately lose her her job.

Even so, she asked him about it when he got home.

'You lost your job?' He was gobsmacked. 'Oh God. What a white trash thing to happen.'

'*Josh.*'

'I'm sorry. What did you want me to say?'

'I was wondering if you knew how Jon might have found out.'

'I've no idea.' He looked puzzled, then his face cleared. 'Hang on a minute. *You think it was me.*'

'No,' Hermione protested. 'I didn't say that.'

'You didn't have to.' Josh stood up. 'It's written all over your face.'

'But I didn't think . . . I mean . . . I know you wouldn't have done it deliberately.' Hermione panicked. She'd never seen Josh like this. 'Please don't be cross.'

'I'm not cross,' Josh said, looking cross. 'I'm hurt.'

'But—'

'How could you even have thought I'd do something like that to you? I'm your best friend.'

'I know.'

Josh thought for a minute. 'I think I'd be better off out of this situation.'

'What do you mean?'

'I think I should go. Move out.'

'No.' Hermione felt all the breath whoosh out of her in one go. 'You can't.'

'Why not?' Josh said. 'You've got Greg now. You don't need me.'

'I do,' Hermione protested feebly. 'I do need you.'

'You'll be fine.' Josh started shoving jeans and shirts into a bag. 'If Greg's as bloody wonderful as you seem to think he is, what can go wrong?'

'Where will you go?'

'Bernie's.'

'I thought you said he was too young for you.'

'He is,' Josh said. 'But he's also built like a brick shithouse and goes like a train. And, unfortunately, I can't be around you right now. I care about you too much.' His lip wobbled. 'I really wanted to be a proper father to that little one. It's crazy. But I was even a bit disappointed when I realised the Bean wasn't mine.'

'You would have made a great dad,' Hermione croaked.

'Well.' Josh picked up his bag. 'It wasn't to be.'

'You still can.'

'I can't,' Josh said. 'Not with Greg around. It's his baby. Not mine. He won't want me butting in every five minutes. And who can blame him?' He zipped up his bag. 'You know, I'll never understand what it is you see in him. I guess it'll just have to remain one of life's mysteries. Along with why people only ever take one case with them when they leave soap operas for good.'

'Josh . . . Please don't go. Let's sort this out.'

'I have to. This isn't going to work. I can't stay here. We'll end up hating each other.'

Hermione panicked. She couldn't imagine a life without Josh in it. She didn't want her baby to have a life without Josh in it either.

'Are we . . .' She sniffed. 'Are we still friends?'

'We'll always be friends,' Josh told her. 'Things are just different now. That's all.'

Hermione watched him go with a heaviness in her heart. He was right, of course. Things *were* different now. It had probably been too much to hope that Josh and Greg would obediently become one big happy family. When the baby came, things would change again. Her life – and Greg's too – would change irrevocably.

It really was high time she told Greg he was going to be a father again.

HARRIET

As it turned out, baby Oscar had fractured his skull when he fell from Lizzy's kitchen table. There was a considerable amount of blood around his brain, which was causing great concern. In the hospital, Harriet felt clumsy and useless. The sight of Oscar's tiny body, swaddled in bandages and hooked up to an array of bleeping monitors, was almost more than she could bear. She couldn't even begin to think how Lizzy must feel.

Lizzy blamed herself entirely. If she hadn't been out on the razzle dazzle the night before it happened, Oscar would now be perfectly safe at home in Ivy Cottage. Lucy would be at playgroup. Jemima would be at nursery. And she and Oscar would be making the most of the quiet time, tucked up on the sofa, eating iced fingers and watching *Teletubbies*.

'He always used to clap his little hands when the Noo-Noo came on,' Lizzy sobbed that first morning as Harriet handed her a cup of foul-tasting coffee from the machine. 'Oh God, Harry. What if he never wakes up?'

'You heard what the doctor said.' Harriet gave Lizzy's hand a squeeze. 'We have every reason to be positive.'

She wasn't sure if Lizzy could even hear her. Her right hand was picking methodically at the cuff of her navy fleece, sending little pills of fuzz all over the floor of the hospital waiting room.

'He was just learning to pull himself up,' she sobbed. 'When I went into his room this morning, he was standing up in his cot, waving Blue Teddy in the air. His little face looked so proud. And now . . .' She broke down again.

'He'll be OK.'

'How do you know?' Lizzy looked at her, her eyes streaked with tears. 'They haven't actually said so, have they?'

'They never do,' Harriet told her. 'They can't. They have to cover themselves, in case . . .'

'In case he dies . . .' Lizzy's lip trembled.

'No.' Harriet could have kicked herself. 'I mean—'

'It doesn't seem fair,' Lizzy said. 'He's so little. He hasn't even had chance to learn to talk yet.'

'He will.' Harriet smiled. 'He'll probably save it until you're having tea with the mother-in-law and then come out with some terrible swear word.'

Lizzy managed a watery smile. 'Lucy's first word was fucker.'

'I never knew that.'

Lizzy rubbed her eyes with balled fists. 'It's always the first thing I shout if some bugger cuts me up on the road. We were taking my mum to Tesco's when some bloody lunatic white van man tried to race me off the lights and she just came out with it. "Fucker!"'

'In context and everything,' Harriet said. 'I'm impressed.'

'My mother was delighted.' Lizzy gave her a wry smile. 'She said it showed exceptionally good judgement of character in one so young. You know my mother. She has a deep-seated dislike of the white van man.' She looked down at Oscar, small and pale against the starched hospital sheets, Blue Teddy tucked in beside him so it would be the first thing he saw when he woke up.

'Oh God,' Lizzy said. 'I love him so much. What if he doesn't make it? What if he's brain-damaged?'

'But we know he's not,' Harriet soothed her. 'They already told us that. And babies are resilient, you know. Remember when we took Lucy to the park to feed the ducks and that little boy came flying down the slide and almost knocked her into next week? She didn't even flinch. Oscar will get better. You'll see.'

'I wasn't looking after him properly,' Lizzy said dully. 'Conrad was right.'

'You made a mistake,' Harriet said. 'It happens.'

'Only to idiots.'

'You know,' Harriet confided. 'My sister tripped over the flex of the iron once, when Ruby had left. us with our dad. He'd stretched it across the kitchen doorway so he could listen to the *Archers* and Hermione came racing into the kitchen to get an ice-pop because she was thirsty and went flying. Somehow, the iron ended up clonking her around the back of the head.'

'Did she get burnt?'

'No, thankfully.' Harriet grinned. 'My dad wasn't what you'd call a domestic god. He hadn't thought to actually turn the iron on.'

'Sounds like Conrad.'

'She took quite a whack though. I distinctly remember having my nose put out of joint because everyone made such a fuss of her. It was usually me who got sick. And there she was, with just a silly little cut on her head, getting Neapolitan ice cream with Ice Magic in bed. I was livid. What?' Lizzy was looking at her, a Mona Lisa smile on her face.

'You never talk about your family.'

'I do. Don't I?'

'Not really. Not like that. I mean, I know you miss them. At college, you told us about the accident and how it made you feel. But you've never talked about what it was like before.'

'I haven't?' A twizzle of guilt spiralled through Harriet's chest. If what Lizzy said was true, it was a shame. She'd had a happy childhood. It deserved to be remembered.

Now that Lizzy mentioned it, she supposed she had shied away from thinking about the happier times. In her experience, when somebody died, it was often the happy things that got to you the most. For some bizarre reason, the thought of innocent pleasures was the worst. At the funeral, as she and Hermione threw red rose petals and golden angels onto the pair of coffins being lowered into the earth, she'd suddenly had a vision of Isaac, a week previously, sitting on a headstone made of speckled pink marble in his workshop, his face alight as he ate the ice-cream sandwich that was his afternoon treat. He'd been enjoying himself and now he was dead. The icecream sandwich had lulled him into a false sense of happiness. He certainly hadn't been expecting this. It was almost as though he'd been tricked.

'It's nice.' Lizzy's voice nudged at the edges of her memories, channelling them, like blobs of silvery mercury, away from Isaac and his ice cream and down a new path. 'Tell me some more.'

'About my family? But you don't want to—'

'I do.' Lizzy's hand, holding the hot coffee, trembled slightly. Harriet, who'd been about to suggest that Lizzy wouldn't want to listen to her unburdening herself, suddenly realised that was exactly what Lizzy did want. She needed something to take her mind off what was happening to poor Oscar. It didn't really matter what it was. She could sit here and read the shipping forecast and Lizzy would listen avidly. So Harriet told her. She told her about her idyllic childhood in Cornwall. She told her about Ruby's experimental cooking. She told her about the waves crashing onto the cliffs below their house. She told her about

Godiva and Daphne, the two white ducks, forgotten until now, who'd lived in their garden and attacked the postman on a regular basis. Big Red, the unfortunate cockerel, who had come to a sticky end. She told her about Hermione's winsome ways. And she told her about Ruby and Isaac, whose enduring zest for life saw them dressing up on a Saturday night for no particular reason. For Lizzy's benefit, she described everything at length. Ruby, dressed in a steel-blue dress, making gin and tonics with slices of lime. Isaac, in an old dinner suit, putting on a record. 'Pennies From Heaven', 'Over the Rainbow', 'Smoke Gets In Your Eyes'. She told her how she and Hermione used to creep in their rabbit slippers to peep through the banisters at their parents as they twirled around the sitting room like childhood sweethearts.

'That's the sweetest thing I ever heard,' Lizzy said.

'I know,' Harriet said fondly. 'It was real movie-star stuff. My parents were hopeless romantics. Both of them.'

'Did you and Dan ever have that, do you think?'

Harriet thought about it. 'I don't know,' she said honestly. 'I always thought so. But now he's gone, I sometimes wonder. I think I married him partly because he made me feel safe. Everybody said we were too young.'

'I remember,' Lizzy said. 'Soo said she gave it a year. Do you remember? In the Chequers, the night before your wedding. She was squiffy. And Gabby was fuming because Dan was her brother and she thought that was disrespectful to him. She threw a drink over her.'

'I'd forgotten that.' Harriet smiled. 'Gabby was so volatile back then, wasn't she?'

'Ed's calmed her down,' Lizzy said. 'And Luke, of course.' She smirked. 'Let's not forget the Little Prince.'

Harriet laughed. 'I knew we were young to be getting married,' she said. 'I just didn't care what anyone else thought.'

'Do you still think you were right for each other?'

'Yes,' Harriet said. 'No. Maybe. I think we just met each other too soon. I guess I kind of clung onto him.'

'You'd lost your whole family.' Lizzy nodded. 'It was only natural. You wanted to be sure he wasn't going to leave as well.'

'You think that's it?'

'It's possible,' Lizzy said. 'I mean, isn't that how life moves on? We all know we're going to lose our parents one day. At least, in the natural order of things. I don't mean like you did, of course,' she added hastily. 'I just mean it's partly why we go ahead and procreate. We're programmed to love others and to expect love in return. On the whole, we feel safer in groups. That's why we create families.'

'Do you and Conrad have it?' Harriet asked her.

'Have what?'

'That all-consuming passion. Like Isaac and Ruby.'

'Sometimes. Things have changed a bit, since Oscar was born. But then that's just life. And I'm not even sure if I'd be comfortable with that all the time anyway. I suppose everyone's different. Just because it's not all rainbows and butterflies all the time, it doesn't mean you're with the wrong person.'

'I guess not.'

'And having children changes things.' Lizzy's eyes darted momentarily towards her son, lying in the hospital bed. 'Your priorities do change. They have to. Oh, I'm sorry, Harry. I know you wanted . . .'

'It's OK,' Harriet said. 'You know, Hermione always used to say she never wanted to have children.'

'Do you think she really meant it?'

'Hermione never said anything she didn't mean.' Harriet smiled at the memory of her feisty sister.

'Do you think she would have changed her mind?' Lizzy asked her. 'Hermione, I mean. If she'd lived. Do you think she'd have settled down eventually, like the rest of us?'

'I'm not sure,' Harriet said guiltily.

'Sorry.' Lizzy detected the edge to her voice and shut up. 'You must miss her so much. I mean, Charlotte does my head in. We're so different. We're at each other's throats most of the time. But I don't know what I'd do if anything happened to her.'

Harriet bit her lip. 'Can I tell you something?' Suddenly, she didn't feel like lying any more. It seemed so stupid, not to acknowledge her sister. And it didn't feel right, letting Lizzy think Hermione was dead.

'Of course.'

'That accident,' Harriet said. 'It wasn't . . . I mean . . . Hermione wasn't . . . She didn't . . . She isn't dead,' she finished lamely.

'She isn't dead?' Lizzy echoed.

'No. At least, not as far as I know.'

'But . . .' Lizzy's mouth opened and closed again. 'Why did you tell me she was?'

'Because you assumed it,' Harriet said. 'That day in Freshers' Week, when we'd all just met. We were sitting in the refectory, talking about our families. You remember? Gabby was whingeing about Dan being at the same university, cramping her style.'

'Hells was telling us about her sister getting a part in *Grange Hill*!' Lizzy remembered. 'And you said . . .'

'I said I didn't have a sister any more. And then I told you about the accident. And you all sort of assumed Hermione had died in it too.'

'And she didn't?'

'No,' Harriet said carefully. Lizzy looked hurt. As well she might. She'd just found out she'd been lied to for the best part of fifteen years.

'So where is she?' Lizzy looked flummoxed. 'I don't understand.'

Harriet took a deep breath. 'You remember that bloke I was talking to. He was at Oscar's christening. I asked you about him at the party last night.'

'Will?' Lizzy looked confused. 'What about him?'

'I knew him. A long time ago. He was my boyfriend. At least, I thought he was. We were sleeping together, so I guess I kind of assumed.'

'Men!' Lizzy scoffed. 'So what happened?'

'It was the summer after we left school,' Harriet told her. 'Hermione went island-hopping in Greece with a friend. I was meant to go,' she said quickly. 'But I was working. I wanted to save up enough money for college. And I'd got the chance of my first exhibition. I'd kind of blagged it, so, when they said yes, I had to go away and come up with some masterpieces pretty quickly. But it was my future. Or so I thought then. I stayed at home.'

'And met Will?'

'Yes.' She nodded. 'I thought he was gorgeous.'

'He still is,' Lizzy pointed out.

'I know,' Harriet said. 'Annoying, isn't it?'

'Depends which way you look at it,' Lizzy said. 'You're a free agent now. Nothing to stop you rekindling the old flame, is there?'

'No way,' Harriet said. 'Will hurt me. Badly.'

'What happened?'

'It was all brilliant at first. You know what it's like, the first time you have sex. You think it's some big secret only you know about. You walk around feeling sorry for everyone else because you think they don't understand. It's almost as though you invented it all.'

'Steve Lilley in a tent on the Yorkshire Moors.' Lizzy nodded. 'Wouldn't recommend it. Uncomfortable and very chilly. But I know exactly what you mean. It's like turning on a tap. When you've done it once, that's it.'

'Exactly,' Harriet said. 'We couldn't get enough of each other. We did it whenever we got the chance. If Ruby went to the hairdresser's, we'd be straight into my room with a pack of condoms and a chair jammed under the handle in case she came back before we were done. We did it in his crappy Vauxhall Viva. We even managed it on a bus once. We spent every single minute together for three weeks. And then . . .'

'Go on.'

'He just stopped calling me,' Harriet said. 'It was as though I didn't exist any more. I couldn't believe it. One moment, I was the centre of his world; the next, I was nothing.'

'Horrid feeling,' Lizzy said.

'It was worse than that. A week later, I found out I was pregnant.'

'Shit!'

'At first, I was almost pleased,' Harriet admitted. 'I thought, if I called him and told him, at least he'd pay me some attention. But of course I could never get hold of him to tell him. It was always his mum who answered the phone. Or his sister.' She shrugged. 'I was naïve, I guess.'

'What's this got to do with Hermione?'

Harriet told her all of it. The party. How she'd seen Will and Hermione wrapped around each other in the garden. His reaction when she'd told him she was expecting a baby. And then she told Lizzy about coming downstairs after the accident to find him in her own house and realising with a shock that it was Will that Hermione was going travelling with.

'And that's why you've not seen her?' Lizzy shook her head in disbelief. 'Because of a bloke?'

Harriet shook her head miserably. 'I said some terrible things. I told her it was her fault Ruby and Isaac were dead. The next day, she went off travelling with Will. She hasn't contacted me since. Can you blame her?'

'But it all seems so stupid,' Lizzy said. 'To miss out on fifteen years of each other's lives. Can you not contact her? Tell her it was all a silly mistake? She'll understand, surely.'

'I have no idea where she is,' Harriet said sadly.

'Would Will know?'

'I don't want to ask him.' Harriet said.

'Why on earth not?'

'What if he *does* know where she is?'

'That'd be good,' Lizzy said. 'Wouldn't it?'

'Not if he tells me she never wants to see me again.'

'At least then you'll *know*,' Lizzy told her. 'You can get on with your life knowing you tried.'

'Isaac always said the things he regretted most

in life were the things he hadn't done,' Harriet said. 'The chances he didn't take, rather than the ones he did that didn't turn out as well as he hoped.'

'There you go then.'

'You think I should try to find her?'

'Nothing to lose.' Lizzy nodded at Oscar. 'We don't know what's around the corner. What if something unexpected happens and you realise you've left it too late?'

'That's what Jesse said.' Harriet shifted on the hard hospital chair.

'You told Jesse?' Lizzy's eyes were clouded with hurt.

'It sort of slipped out,' Harriet admitted.

'How does something like that just slip out?'

'It was after the party. I was going through some old photos in my room. I couldn't sleep.'

'I knew it,' Lizzy said triumphantly. 'What was Jesse doing in your room in the middle of the night?'

Harriet told her.

'Locked out, my eye!' Lizzy snarfed. 'He has a soft spot for you.'

'He *hasn't*.' Harriet's tummy flipped. 'He's got Clare.'

'Do you like him?' Lizzy wanted to know.

'Of course not.' Harriet felt her cheeks burn.

'Liar.'

'I *don't*.'

'So why have you gone red?'

255

'Because you're waiting for me to.'

'He was looking at you all night.'

'I'm surprised you were in any state to notice,' Harriet told her.

'You *do* like him,' Lizzy said. 'It's obvious.'

'Why is it?'

'Because of the way you said "Clare". You're jealous.'

'I'm not.'

'Why can't you just admit it? You like him and he likes you.'

'OK.' Harriet held up her hands in defeat. 'I do like him. A tiny bit. But it doesn't matter. Because nothing's going to happen. I'm married. And he's taken. This *thing*, whatever it is, will pass. OK?'

'If you say so.' Lizzy's eyes sparkled briefly with mischief. Then suddenly, as the air filled with the flippant plink-plonk of a children's television theme tune, her face crumpled.

'Lizzy?' Harriet squeezed her hand. 'What is it?'

'It's the *Tweenies*.' Lizzy started sobbing afresh. 'Oscar loves the *Tweenies*. He always likes to bob up and down when the music comes on. And now he's too sick.'

'He'll be OK.' Harriet laced her arm through her friend's. 'This time next week, he'll be bobbing up and down again. You'll see.'

For once, she was right. Oscar did get better over time. The next time Harriet visited, bearing a tiny plush octopus that jangled, crackled or burped, depending on which tentacle you squeezed, he was sitting up in bed, gurgling happily as Lizzy played 'This Little Piggy' with his fat pink toes. At some point, he had mastered the glottal stop. The tiny cubicle at the end of the paediatric ward reverberated with the sound of one happy chappy, delightedly shouting, 'GUH,' at the top of his lungs.

Harriet suspected that things between Lizzy and Conrad might take a little longer to heal. From her vantage point at the side of Oscar's hospital cot, she was able to sense that things between them were distinctly frosty. It was obvious that Conrad blamed Lizzy for the accident. Which wasn't fair. Accidents happened, after all. Oscar could have fallen off the table at any time.

One morning, as she watched Conrad cuddle his son, she was reminded of their first meeting, at a barbecue in Lizzy's higgledy-piggledy back garden. With an odd sensation in her stomach Harriet had watched her friend dress up in a floaty confection of rich jade silk. Jealousy, perhaps, because Lizzy's relationship was bright and shiny as a new penny and her *own* was just, well, her own.

Lizzy had flitted from kitchen to courtyard garden with bowls of potato salad and piles of couscous, jewelled with roasted Mediterranean vegetables. For some reason, she'd been terrified Conrad wasn't going to show.

'He isn't coming,' she'd said nervously, as Harriet tossed the salad. 'Is he?'

But Conrad had come. He'd walked nervously into the garden as everybody was digging into strawberries and chunks of dark chocolate. Clutching a crate of Stella and shielding his eyes from the bright sun, he'd looked almost comical in a pair of navy blue Bermuda shorts. Even Lizzy had been alarmed. Harriet remembered her pointing to his little sparrow's legs, complete with knees so knobbly they could have won first prize at Butlin's, and blurting out, 'Are they your legs?'

Now, sitting at Oscar's bedside, watching him punish Lizzy through his diffidence, she wanted to remind him of that sunny afternoon, when he'd had to walk through a garden full of strangers in order to make the woman he thought he might be able to love happy.

So Lizzy wasn't perfect. Who the hell was?

HERMIONE

Hermione spent so long worrying how to tell Greg she was pregnant, that it came as quite a shock in the end to find out she wasn't going to have to bother after all.

He already knew!

'Who told you?' Hermione put her cup of tea down on the breakfast bar. Her hands were shaking like skeleton leaves.

'Bumble.'

'Who the hell's Bumble?'

'My secretary.'

'How the hell did *she* know?'

'Everybody knows.' Greg loosened his tie and sat down. He looked tired.

'How?'

'Hermione,' Greg said, 'I've had a hell of a day! The figures for Spurt! have gone through the floor. There are necks on blocks all over the shop. My wife rang me this morning to inform me that my seven-year-old daughter is asking to get a belly button ring. And then I get a snide call from my bloody secretary to ask if I think we should be sending you flowers because she's heard from that bubblehead on reception at PSC that you're expecting. They all talk, those receptionists, you know. They go out for glasses of wine together on Friday nights. Like witches round a cauldron, the lot of them.'

'So your secretary knows about us?'

'Of course she does,' Greg said shortly. 'Everybody knows why you got fired.'

'But how did she know I was pregnant?' Hermione was bamboozled. 'Nobody knows.'

Greg pressed the heels of his hands onto his eyeballs as though he was trying to make it all go away. 'They cleared out your desk. They found this.' He held up Hermione's big baby book. 'I take it it's not a coincidence. I mean, it could just have been wishful thinking on your part. But you know how people gossip. And you have been putting on a bit of weight lately.'

'I'm sorry,' Hermione said. 'I did want to tell you. But you'd just left your wife.'

'It *is* mine, I take it.'

'Of course it's yours,' Hermione told him. 'What do you take me for?'

'Damn it, Hermione.' Greg slammed his fist down so hard on the table that Hermione flinched. 'Did you not think of mentioning it? How long have you known?'

'A few months,' Hermione said meekly. She'd never seen him lose his cool before.

'Months.' Greg threw his hands in the air. 'Oh, this is just great. So how long have I got to get used to the idea? More to the point, how long have my kids got? This isn't going to be easy for them, you know. Their mother and I split up and suddenly they've got this new brother or sister to think about.' He grabbed his jacket.

'Where are you going?'

'Out.'

'Where?'

'A walk. A drink. I don't know. God damnit, Hermione. You sure know how to make a man's day.'

Hermione burst into tears.

'Oh God,' Greg said. 'I'm sorry. It's just a shock.'

'I wanted you to be pleased.' Hermione wiped her eyes. 'I know it was a long shot. But this is our baby. I thought you might be able to love it.'

'Of course I'll love it,' Greg said. 'I've got three children already. One more won't make that much difference. Come here.'

Resting her head on his shoulder, Hermione tried to hide her disappointment. She'd wanted him to think that this one would be different. Because, unlike his other children, this would be theirs.

'I know one chap who's going to be over the moon about this,' Greg said.

'Really?'

'Spike,' Greg said. 'He's sick of being the youngest. You'll make his year.'

Hermione burst into a fresh round of tears.

'What is it now?'

'You don't want me to meet your kids.'

'That's not true.'

'You see them every week. And you never ask if I want to come along.'

'That doesn't mean I don't want you to,' Greg said.

'What then?'

'To be honest, I never had you down as a kiddie sort of person. You always seemed so . . . independent.'

'So I can meet them then?' Hermione sniffed again.

'Of course you can meet them.' Greg kissed the top of her head. 'They're going to love you.'

Greg was fiendishly busy at work over the next few weeks, which meant there wasn't time to arrange anything concrete. Hermione did offer to accompany him to McDonald's one Wednesday but, on the morning of the planned outing, Greg's eldest called to say she'd become a vegan and that all subsequent attempts to get her through the golden arches would be considered an assault on her civil rights. Greg said that, in that case, they could all go to the By The Way, where they did falafel. But the two little ones had kicked up such a fuss that he'd given his daughter fifty dollars to spend in her beloved Queen Street and taken the little ones for their weekly cheeseburger fix anyway.

On balance, Hermione had thought it was best

to meet them all in one go and had gone shopping instead. The list of things the baby would need was endless. Cot. Buggy. Sterilising equipment. Nappies. It was all very well buying cute little fleece dungarees and tiny bootees. But the big stuff was what her mother would have called Blue territory. She couldn't make a decision on her own. She needed Greg to help her. Unfortunately, the poor guy was flat out trying to keep his head above water at work. He came home too exhausted to do anything but flop. She even had to make it to her second scan on her own because Greg had had to fly to London at short notice. He was gutted to miss it, of course. But work was work. He couldn't afford to fuck up now. Not with two families to support.

'Can you tell if it's a boy or a girl?' Hermione asked as the nurse squidged icy lime-green jelly over her tummy.

'I can.' The nurse beamed. 'Would you like to know?'

'No, thank you.' Hermione shook her head. 'I think I already know what it is.'

She still craved nicotine. Smoking had always been a big part of her life. Since that day with Harriet in Hedgemead Park, she'd been a staunch smoker. At school, she could always be found puffing away behind the mobile classrooms at lunchtimes. These days, she was having trouble sticking to the one a day she'd promised herself. Greg teased her about it. But then he teased her about everything. He called her the squeaky-clean freak because of the sudden urges she got to feather her nest for the new arrival. She finished clearing out the spare room and painted it a gorgeous pistachio green, which seemed a pretty unisex sort of colour. She filled the room full of interesting things for her baby to look at. A mobile, made up of dozens of busy bees, swarming around a honey pot. A caterpillar of sky-blue concertinaed tissue paper hung from the ceiling. A brightly coloured alphabet frieze. A is for apple. B is for ball. C is for cat. And so on. She put the flatpack cot together herself. She even found an old wardrobe in Kensington Market and painted it white. It was already half full of bits. Vests the size of her outstretched hand. A tiny fleece hat. A sweet orange and red striped grow with a friendly snail appliquéd to the front. Harriet would have been proud.

It didn't stop there. Over the next few weeks, she turned out the whole house. With a pang of regret, she packed the rest of Josh's things into a big case and put it in the cellar for when he came back for it. She painted the spare room white and filled it with pretty things. She'd got it into her head, after going through all Harriet's school stuff, that perhaps, one of these days, she would find her sister and tell her she was going to be an aunty. She ought to have a room for her to come to, in case she wanted to come and stay.

One Saturday, she decided to spring-clean her

own room from top to bottom, ripping off sheets and pillowcases in a burst of energy and throwing them into a pile on the bare floorboards. That was another thing that would have to be seen to when the Bean arrived, she realised, looking at a raised nail that was sticking up by about a centimetre and wincing as she imagined it tearing through the soft pink pads of tiny feet.

Remembering how her own mother had always turned the mattress every week without fail, she decided to give it a go. It took all her energy to get it up on its side and even then it pinged off the wall and came crashing down on her back, almost winding her.

It was then that she saw them.

Magazines!

Three or four of them. Half repulsed, half curious, Hermione picked one up and started to leaf through the cheaply printed pages. *Blonde Bombshells*, it was called. True to its word, it was full of glittery blondes, all naked and staring directly into the camera lens with looks of yearning on their faces. Blondes pretending to be lesbians. Blondes pretending to be schoolgirls, their hair in pigtails and their faces painted with fake freckles. One page portrayed a blonde sitting on the toilet, her legs spread wide as she sucked on her fingers, which presumably had just been in the bright pink place between her legs.

Part of her wanted to laugh. It was so staged. So ridiculous. Did people really get off on this stuff?

And then she remembered Greg with the vibrator. He'd been so excited that night. He'd been almost like a wild animal as he watched her use it on herself. They said men were more turned on by visual imagery than women were. It was probably perfectly normal. The advice columns in magazines were always saying it was normal for men to want to look at porn. They could dissociate the women in the pictures from their real flesh-and-blood partner. And it would have been almost funny to think of Greg wanking himself silly over these ludicrous images, if only her own sex drive hadn't taken a nosedive these past few weeks.

She was starting to feel like a blimp. She dreaded to think how she'd feel when it got hotter. Summer in Toronto was generally humid in the extreme. It was going to be uncomfortable to say the least.

She wished Josh was here. This was the sort of thing they could giggle over. She could see him now, stuffing himself with taco chips and holding the magazine up to peer at it from all angles.

She missed him. Without Josh, there was nobody to gossip with. Nobody to analyse the significance of what Greg did or didn't say. He still rang her from time to time to see how she and the Bean were. But she couldn't talk to him. Not the way she used to. For some reason, he still disapproved of Greg. And that was that. These days, their conversation seemed to skate along the surface of politeness. One day, Josh would probably disappear from her life altogether.

She decided there was no point mentioning the magazines to Greg. Even if she asked him outright if he preferred these glossy celluloid fantasies to her own, too solid flesh, he would probably just tell her she was crazy.

Prising up the mattress, she replaced them exactly as she'd found them.

HARRIET

arriet's feet hadn't touched the ground for weeks. Word had got round that Blue Ginger's design was an unmitigated success and, suddenly, work was pouring her way. She was crazy busy. One day, she was painting a Chinese peony on the floor of a chi-chi boutique in town, the next she was deliberating between a delicious dusty grape and a fresh aquamarine for the walls of a beauty salon in Bartlett Street. It was great for her bank balance. But she couldn't help feeling a little unsettled. She missed the stability of working in one place. So much so that, occasionally, when she got a moment, she popped into Blue Ginger to see how things were going. It was never quite the same as it had been when it was just herself, Bob and Jesse, working together to get things done. It was always far too busy. But sometimes she would drop in early and Jesse would pull a leather-topped bar stool into the slice of sunlight that bisected the bar and make her a latte so she could talk to him while he bottled up.

This was one of those mornings. Harriet was

due at an apartment in the Royal Crescent later this afternoon. A woman wanted the fake poly-styrene pillars in her bathroom painted to look like marble. She seemed to think that the fact that she was loaded meant she could get by with the manners of a guttersnipe. Feeling in need of forti-fication, Harriet had dropped by the bar and was perched on her usual stool, while Jesse darted about like a spiky little mosquito.

'You're busy today,' she observed.

'Tell me about it.' Jesse slotted bottles of Schweppes tonic into the fridge. 'Joe was supposed to do the late shift last night. Course the little gobshite didn't turn up. It was only me and Catriona on last night and we were rammed. I didn't like to make Catriona stay to finish clearing up. She's only nineteen. It doesn't seem right.'

'Is Joe ill?' Harriet asked.

Jesse examined the seal on a carton of tomato juice. 'Is he hell. He was out gallivanting. Didn't come home at all. His mobile was off the whole time. I guess it's my fault. He's not interested in all this. And who can blame him? Blue Ginger isn't his responsibility. He's off to see the world.'

'He was supposed to go weeks ago.'

'He's actually got his ticket now.' Jesse pulled the omni-present pencil from behind his ear and scratched the top of his head with it. He looked stressed.

'Do you wish it was you?' Harriet asked him. 'Going off without a care in the world.'

'Not, really.' Jesse shrugged. 'I don't really get all this obsession with buggering off for weeks at a time. Makes me the black sheep of the family, I guess.'

'How do you mean?'

'Jack's in Santiago. And now Joe's off to seek his fortune out in the big wide world. It's never really appealed to me. I suppose I'm a bit of a home bird at heart. I like to feel settled.'

'I know what you mean,' Harriet said. 'I'm a bit the same myself. I sometimes wonder what would have happened if I'd gone on that trip to Greece with Hermione. Things might have turned out differently.'

'In what way?'

'I wouldn't have met Will.' She shrugged. 'Hermione probably never would have gone to that party. My dad wouldn't have gone to pick her up. Ruby and Isaac would still be alive. And I'd never have gone to London and met Dan. Or Lizzy.'

'You think that's how it all happens then?' Jesse asked.

'You think life is that random?'

'Don't you?'

'I don't know. I often wonder if it isn't already planned for us.'

'Like you and Clare, you mean?'

'What about me and Clare?'

'Meeting at school like that. Staying together, after all this time. It's obviously meant to be.'

'We've had our ups and downs,' Jesse told her. 'It isn't easy, trying to make a long-distance relationship work.'

'You seem to manage it though,' Harriet said. 'You must be doing something right.'

'Mmm.' Jesse looked thoughtful. 'I take it you haven't heard from Dan then.'

'Not since the launch.'

'He'll come round,' Jesse told her. 'I mean, I take it that's what you want?'

'You know,' Harriet admitted, 'I really don't know any more. I can't help wondering if it isn't time I did something completely different.'

'Like finding Hermione?'

'Something like that. Perhaps I'll go travelling. Do all the things I should have done when I was younger.'

'What about your business?' Jesse looked surprised. 'You said you've spent ages building that up.'

'I have. But it's only a business. I can always start another one.'

'You'd be missed,' Jesse said. 'If you went.'

'By whom?'

'Me, for a start. Lizzy. Oscar. You've been brilliant, helping out while he's been in hospital.'

'He's much better now.' Harriet grinned. 'He tried to say "hedgehog" today.'

'That's fantastic. I thought he looked quite bright and breezy on Sunday.'

'Sunday?'

'I was going past the hospital,' Jesse explained. 'Thought I'd nip in and say hello.'

'You went to see Oscar?'

'Sure,' Jesse said. 'Why not?'

'I don't know,' Harriet said. 'Just, I mean, you don't know Lizzy all that well. It was nice. Really nice of you.'

Jesse shrugged. 'To tell you the truth, I saw this elephant in Snooks and I couldn't resist it.'

'What were you doing in a toyshop?'

'Haven't you heard? I'm a big kid. Lizzy must be relieved, though,' he added thoughtfully.

'She is . . .' Harriet hesitated.

'But?'

'I'm not sure things are OK between her and Conrad. She seems . . . I don't know. Not herself. I called her last night and she was really distracted.'

'You worry too much.'

'You think?'

'Definitely.' Jesse looked at his watch. 'Bloody hell. Is that the time? I said I'd get Edie's shopping. What day is it?'

'Tuesday.'

'I always take her some M&Ms on Tuesdays,' Jesse said fondly. 'Fridays it's a Double Decker if I can get one. And I buy her a Flake Dipped when I go out for the paper on a Sunday.'

'I didn't know you did Edie's shopping,' Harriet said.

'It's no trouble. I'm usually going anyway. And it saves her legs.'

'I can do it,' Harriet told him. 'If you're busy, I mean.' She had to get groceries anyway. She had nothing in.

'You don't mind?'

'Course not.'

'That's brilliant.' Jesse handed her a list. 'You might need to go into HMV on the way down. She's after the Eminem CD. Saw him on *Popworld*, apparently. Says the man's got spunk.'

'Great.' Harriet groaned. '"The Real Slim Shady" at a million decibels. I can hardly wait.'

'She's eighty-three,' Jesse said fondly. 'I reckon she ought to get her kicks while she can, don't you?'

'Of course,' Harriet said quickly, in case he thought she was a killjoy. 'I didn't mean . . .'

Jesse's phone rang. 'Sorry. I'd better . . .'

Harriet turned to examine the bottles of flavoured vodka, sparkling under the lights set into the mirror behind the bar.

'Hello?' Jesse was saying. 'Hi, my love. Sorry. Today? Oh, I'm sorry, sweetheart, I can't. I'm at the bar all day.' He glanced at Harriet, who was pretending to be engrossed in one of the sample menus he'd run off for his meeting with the potential chef. She could hear an outraged female. Clare, presumably, giving him a stream of abuse.

'I'm sorry you feel like that,' Jesse said, 'but it's impossible. We'll do something next week. I promise.'

Harriet waved Edie's list at him to show she was

making a move and he mouthed, 'Thank you,' and waved back.

In Sainsbury's, Harriet went through Edie's list meticulously, putting the required items in the front section of her trolley. Four bananas. Toasted teacakes. Breaded ham. Tins of food for Leroy, Edie's beautiful glossy black cat. For herself, she got cold chicken, tomatoes and potato salad. Picnic food. Food that made her think of the sunny days spent at the beach hut when they were small. Ruby had bought the beach hut with money she'd won on her Premium Bonds. Because of this, she'd declared it Pink Territory, which meant that, as far as the décor went, it was herself, Harriet and Hermione who made all the decisions. For the purposes of the hut, Isaac had been declared a Blue, exempt from all decisions and required only to turn up for the celebratory picnic feast they'd held when the hut was ready.

Harriet picked up and rejected a carton of pineapple juice, remembering that Dan didn't like it. Then she remembered it didn't matter a toss what Dan liked or didn't like any more and threw two cartons into her trolley.

She dropped Edie's shopping in and went to unpack her own. She was unloading pineapple juice, marinated artichokes and double cream when her phone rang. She picked it up to see Jesse's name flashing on the digital display.

'Everything OK?'

'Yes,' she said happily. 'I've dropped off Edie's shopping.'

'Great. Are you still at the house?'

'Yep.'

'Can you do me a favour?'

'Of course.'

'Can you just go into the flat and check I turned off the hot water this morning. I don't know if Joe's home yet and the boiler's a bit temperamental. It gets like molten lava if it's left on too long. The key's under that awful pot thing on the floor.'

'No problem.'

She found the key and let herself in. Jesse's hot water tank was gurgling like a sea monster and she found the switch and turned it off. She was just about to get going when a letter, in a raspberry-coloured envelope addressed to Clare Pargiter in Milan, caught her eye.

Cautiously, she reached out a finger. She wasn't going to open it or anything. She just wanted to touch it. Make sure it was solid. Real, as opposed to a figment of her imagination.

'Harry! What are you doing here?'

Joe was standing at the top of the stairs, a banana-yellow towel slung around his nipped-in waist in a fashion that left little to the imagination. Quick as a flash, Harriet whipped her hand behind her back.

'Jesse asked me to turn off the hot water.'

'Cool.' Joe came downstairs in a waft of Herbal Essences shampoo. 'Want a coffee?'

Harriet checked her watch. She still had an hour. 'OK.'

She followed him into the kitchen and watched as he unscrewed the lid of a jar of Nescafe. It was nice and peaceful in here, without the blare of Edie's TV.

Too peaceful.

Something was missing.

'Where's Miss Scarlett?'

'Shit.' Joe looked around wildly. 'Oh bloody hell.' He indicated the open window. 'It was boiling in here this morning. I forgot. I totally bloody forgot. He's going to *kill* me. He'd got really fond of the stupid bird.'

'Don't panic.' Harriet looked out into the paved back garden, where the pink and white Nelly Moser clematis she'd planted when she'd taken charge of the communal area was in full, frothy bloom. 'I'm sure we'll find her.'

'How?' Joe asked. 'She could be halfway to Bristol by now.'

'Perhaps not.' Harriet indicated what looked like a crumpled red rag, hunched underneath the profusion of chocolate mint she'd planted last summer.

Joe followed her outside. 'What's wrong with her?'

'I think Leroy might have got her.' She squatted down. 'She looks bad. I think you should call Jesse.'

Jesse came home straight away and despatched

Joe to Blue Ginger. The place was apparently packed and there was only one member of staff on. Muttering 'It's only a bleeding parrot' under his breath, Joe obliged.

'I know it's only a parrot,' Jesse said to Harriet, when Joe had sloped off. 'It probably seems stupid, doesn't it? Rushing home for a bird.'

'Not at all,' Harriet assured him. 'We had loads of pets when I was little. Ducks. Cats. A cockerel. We got hysterical every time one of them died.' She nodded at Miss Scarlett. 'Do you think she's going to be OK?'

The poor creature was definitely looking a bit seedy. Her feathers had lost their sheen and her beak was decidedly droopy.

'What's the matter, old girl?' Jesse stroked the parrot's wing gently. 'Are you feeling poorly? Hey. That's it. That's the girl. Come and sit on my arm.'

The parrot made a feeble clucking sound and looked dolefully up at Jesse before nestling her head in the crook of his arm.

'Poor thing,' Harriet said. 'Do you think Leroy got her?'

'Doesn't look like it,' Jesse said. 'Let's try a sunflower seed.'

He took the parrot inside and proffered a humbug-striped treat.

'Come on, old girl,' Jesse crooned. 'No?' He frowned. 'She must be sickening for something. I think we ought to take her to the vet. Can you ask Edie if she has a number? She took Leroy a month or two ago when he got into a fight with that black and white lard tub from down the road.'

The vet's surgery was in Oldfield Park on the other side of town. As Harriet called the number Edie had given her, Jesse wrapped Miss Scarlett in an old towel and put her in a lettuce box.

'Can you hold her on your lap?' he asked. 'If I drive.'

Harriet should have been making her way to the Crescent for her meeting about now. She'd never not turned up for a meeting in her life. Her reputation depended on reliability.

But Jesse needed her too.

She picked up the box. 'Of course I can.'

The bubbly blonde receptionist took their names and asked them to sit down. There were only a few other people waiting. A couple, both extremely short and round, for some bizarre reason reminded Harriet of the man and woman on the weather vane in Isaac's workshop. When it was going to be fine, the man would come out of their little house, and when rain was expected, he popped back in to make way for his wife. The couple were tending to a sneezing Dalmatian, who was imaginatively named Spot. And there was a girl with a hamster. Soon enough, it was Miss Scarlett's turn. Clutching the box, Harriet, followed by Jesse, took her in.

'Oh God.'

'If I didn't know better,' Will looked up from

the sink where he was scrubbing his hands with carbolic soap, 'I'd say you were stalking me.'

'What's going on?' Jesse looked bewildered.

'Jesse, this is Will.'

'Ah.' Jesse's face cleared. 'Right. I have to do . . . something. I'll see you outside.'

'What about Miss Scarlett?'

'I trust you. I'll wait out there.'

'So,' Will said. 'Your boyfriend knows about us.'

'What little there is to know,' Harriet said. 'And he's not my boyfriend.'

'Whatever.' Will hesitated. 'I guess I owe you an apology.'

'For what?'

'For the way I treated you.'

'It was a long time ago,' Harriet said.

'I know. Even so. It was bad of me to take your sister away when you needed her. Your parents had just died. And then there was the, you know . . .'

'Termination?'

'Yes.' Will cleared his throat. 'I probably didn't handle it very well.'

'No.'

Harriet thought back to the day of the abortion. The image of the brown envelope, stuffed with crisp £20 notes, that Will had given her so she could terminate the life of their unborn baby, was still imprinted on her mind. She'd called him as soon as she'd discovered she was pregnant, leaving her sister's name with his mother in an attempt to get him to the phone. He'd come round immediately, sneaking in as Hermione played 'Sunday Bloody Sunday' at top whack in her room opposite.

'Here,' he'd said.

'What's this?'

'Money. To get rid of it. That's what you want, isn't it?'

Harriet hadn't known what she wanted. But she'd kept the money anyway. It was bound to come in useful for something. And then, when Ruby and Isaac had been killed just days later, it had seemed as though she had no option. Much as she wanted to, she knew she couldn't bring a baby up on her own. She didn't have the strength.

'I was young,' Will said now. 'I freaked out.'

'*You* freaked out!' Harriet said drily.

'I am sorry. What a bastard, eh?'

Harriet said, 'You avoided my calls for a week. Even before I told you about our baby.'

'Don't call it that.'

'Why?' Harriet challenged him. 'Does it make you feel bad?'

'It wasn't a baby,' Will said. 'Not really. It was just a tiny cluster of cells.'

'It makes *me* feel bad.' She met his eye. 'I wanted to keep it, you know.'

'Really?' Will raised an eyebrow. 'You wanted to tie yourself down with a baby so young?'

'I know it's not very cool. But to me, it was always a baby. Not a tiny cluster of cells, as you so conveniently describe it. I was going to tell

Ruby that night. The night you took my sister to a party and didn't bother bringing her home when she felt unwell. The night my parents got killed going to pick her up from the party you took her to.' Unconsciously, she balled her fists.

'Hey.' Will put his hands up like a shield. 'I'm sorry. OK? I'm really, really sorry. I didn't even know she was your sister. Not at first.'

'What I don't understand,' Harriet said, 'is why you even came to our birthday party. You obviously didn't want to know me. You avoided my calls for a week.'

'It was my sister,' Will said.

'Alison?'

'Yes. She called me a spineless bastard. Told me if I wanted to end it with you I could at least have the decency to tell you to your face. She said you'd been phoning nonstop.'

'Hardly nonstop.' Harriet bristled. 'I wasn't that desperate. Don't flatter yourself.'

'It doesn't really matter now,' Will said. 'Does it?'

'I think so,' Harriet told him. 'Because of you, I lost my sister.'

'You didn't make things up with her then?'

'No.' Harriet's hopes sank like cherry stones in custard. If he was asking that, then he probably hadn't seen Hermione in a while.

'She always wondered,' Will said. 'She never understood why you went off like that when you saw me in your mother's sitting room that day.

She thought it was her fault. She thought you were upset because she was leaving. She felt terrible. And I never had the guts to tell her the truth. I've always felt bad about that.'

'You do have a conscience then.'

'I've changed,' Will said.

'Easy to say.'

'It's true.' Will shrugged. 'I lost my sister too.'

'You did?'

'Alison.'

'Oh God,' Harriet said. 'What happened?'

'She took an ecstasy pill at a party.' Will said. 'We all did. Me included. It was my idea. Later that night, Alison collapsed. She died in hospital. I had to tell my parents. It pretty much shattered their world.'

'I'm sorry.'

'Not as sorry as the cunt who sold us the pills will be if ever I get my hands on him,' Will said. 'We had our own practice, you know. In London. Family business. I couldn't face carrying it on without her. So we moved down here.'

'We?'

'Me and Aidan.'

'Aidan?'

'Her husband,' Will said. 'Alice's father. He works all the hours God sends to make ends meet. I pick Alice up from school and bring her here so Melissa can play with her for an hour or two.'

'Your wife?'

'God, no,' Will said. 'Melissa's our receptionist.

I'm a confirmed bachelor. Anyway,' he said, clearly eager to change the subject. 'Shall we have a look at the parrot?'

'What do you think's wrong with her?'

'I can't say for sure.' Will lifted a droopy red wing. 'Not until I open her up. But I'd say it's some sort of amphetamine. Speed, maybe?'

'You mean, she's . . .'

'Drugged.'

'Will she die?'

'Almost certainly.'

'Oh dear.' Harriet's eyes filled with tears. 'Jesse will be upset.'

She watched Will examine Miss Scarlett. Had he really changed for the better? It was possible.

'I am sorry about your sister,' she said.

'Thank you.' Will's eyes met hers. There was a look in them she hadn't seen before. It was as though he really was sorry for all the pain he'd put her through. 'I'm sorry about yours.'

'It was a long time ago,' Harriet said.

'If it's any consolation, I got what I deserved,' Will said. 'She could be a bit of a minx, your sister. Buggered me about no end.'

Harriet told him what she'd read in Hermione's diary about Mr Sinclair.

'I'm not surprised.' Will laughed.

'What happened between you?'

'We ended up in France,' Will said. 'We stayed with my cousin for a bit. And then Hermione just left. She'd met someone else.'

'You don't know where she went?' Harriet asked him. 'I would love to track her down.'

Will shook his head. 'Actually . . .' he said slowly. 'I think she did share a flat with my cousin's girl-friend for a while. Audrey, her name was. It's a long shot. It must have been a good nine, ten years ago. I doubt either of them would still be there. But I should have an address somewhere.'

He leafed through an ancient-looking address book until he found what he was looking for, then ripped out the entire page.

'Here,' he said. 'I hope you find her.'

'Thanks.' Harriet rummaged in her bag for one of her business cards. 'Give me a call.'

'Sure,' Will said. 'We could have coffee some-time.'

'I meant about the parrot.'

'Ah,' Will said. 'Of course.'

It was a tiny victory. But it was victory nonethe-less. Harriet left that surgery feeling ten pounds lighter.

HERMIONE

Hermione stood under the lukewarm trickle of water that seemed to be the best the swimming pool showers had to offer and tried to rinse the soap out of her hair. That was the thing about having long, curly hair. It took ages. In an inadequate dribble like this, it was nigh on bloody impossible.

'Excuse me.'

She glanced up to see a pretty woman with a mist of amber Elizabeth I curls looking at her.

'I forgot my conditioner.' She tweaked at her hair. 'And I could really use some. If I don't tame this lot I'll end up looking like a poodle.'

'I know the feeling.' Hermione offered her the bottle of curl-taming, de-frizzing, oleaginous gloop she'd brought with her for that very same reason. 'Help yourself.'

'You're a star. Thank you.'

Hermione watched as the woman squeezed a polite, pearly dollop into her palm.

'Take as much as you want.,' she said.

'You don't have a whole lot left.'

'I'm just about done.' Hermione smiled. 'Saves

lugging the bottle home anyhow.' She nodded towards the swell of her stomach, where the Bean was happily performing what felt like a nightclub-style rendition of Riverdance. 'I'm weighed down enough as it is.'

'I noticed.' The redhead finished slathering conditioner through to the ends of her tresses and then started to rinse under the pathetic trickle. 'Hell in the summer, isn't it? And it gets so muggy in Toronto too.'

'Tell me about it.' Hermione rolled her eyes. Over the past couple of days, her ankles had started to puff up like vol-au-vents. And the weight of the baby was putting a strain on her back. When it started to get really hot, she was going to collapse like an over-egged Yorkshire pudding.

'When are you due?'

'Not for a while yet.' Hermione puffed. 'You wouldn't think it, would you? If I get much bigger I won't be able to get out of bed.'

'I was like that with my third.' The girl laughed like a drain. 'Four and a half kilos, he weighed when he was born. I used to look at all these women with their neat little bumps up front and wonder why I got to look like a galleon in full sail.' She picked up a striped beach towel and started to slot shampoo, shower gel and lotion into her sponge bag. 'Thanks so much for the conditioner. You've just about saved my dignity. My kids would never let me live it down if I turned up to collect them from school with a frizzball on my head.'

'You're welcome.'

'Best of luck with the baby.'

'Thanks.' Hermione smiled. It had only been a two-minute exchange but she didn't really want the woman to go. She didn't like to admit it but she'd been feeling a bit lonely these past few weeks. She missed the buzz of her job. It was so odd, having nothing to do when everyone else was at work. Greg was still working flat out. He often had to work until ten at night. The house on Amelia Street felt large and empty without Josh in it. She missed him. Missed vegging out on the sofa with him. Missed creeping into his room on a Saturday morning to bring him tea and French toast. She never thought she'd say it, but she even missed his dreadful singing in the shower. His misguided rendition of Oasis's 'Don't Look Back In Anger', which, surprisingly, involved him cater-wauling 'Whoah! Pelican Way' at the top of his lungs, had at least made her laugh. These days, although she was looking forward to meeting her baby, she felt as though she didn't have much to laugh about. Greg was lovely. She was really happy with him. But he was a man. It would just be nice to have someone to gossip with.

The redhead wrapped her hair in a turban and picked up her belongings. Hermione watched as she made her way towards the changing cubicles. She was being silly. She didn't know the woman from a baked potato. Why on earth would she want to share confidences with her?

She shook out her own towel and wrapped it round herself and the Bean. Perhaps it was the fact that the woman had mentioned her children. It was difficult, being pregnant, with no one to ask for advice. Most women had their mothers. Or their sisters. Hermione only had Sylvie. And Sylvie seemed very far away right now.

As the friendly redhead reached her locker, Hermione smiled ruefully to herself and got on with the business of drying her toes. Everything seemed to take twice as long these days.

She was just bending over to finish the job when there was a light tap on her shoulder.

'Hey. You dropped this back there.'

It was the redhead again, holding out the hair band Hermione had worn in the pool.

'Oh.' Hermione straightened. 'Thanks.'

The woman nodded at her tummy. 'Is it your first?'

'It's that obvious, huh?' Hermione said. 'I don't mind admitting that I'm terrified.'

'Of what?'

'All of it,' Hermione confessed. 'Being a rubbish mother.'

'Everybody worries about that.'

'The birth.'

'You'll be fine. Trust me.'

'I wish I shared your confidence.'

'You will.' Her new friend grinned. 'I'm Celine, by the way.'

'Hermione.' Hermione held out her hand.

'I've seen you in here a couple of times.'

'Josh said it would be good for me.' Hermione pulled a face. 'Although I have to admit I don't feel particularly good right now. I'm absolutely whacked.' She started to slap body lotion onto her thighs. 'Look at me. I've got pots of expensive cream at home and I'm still getting stretch marks.'

'You should see my stomach.' Celine laughed. 'He's right, though, your man. About the swimming being good exercise. Josh, was it?'

'Oh.' Hermione shrugged on her T-shirt. 'No. Josh isn't my man. He's a friend. He was kind of helping out.'

'Lucky you,' Celine said. 'Having such supportive friends.'

'I suppose so.' A shadowy pike flicked its tail beneath Hermione's solar plexus. Thinking about Josh made her feel uncomfortable. She knew it had been his choice to leave. But she couldn't help but feel that Josh's leaving had put a dampener on her happiness at being with Greg. And things did seem distinctly odd without him around.

'Will he be at the birth?'

'Josh?' Hermione looked up, surprised. 'I doubt it. Greg might. The father.'

'My ex was a Greg,' Celine said.

'Sorry,' Hermione said. 'Bad associations . . .'

'It's OK. I'm a big girl. I can handle it.'

'Was your Greg at the birth?' Hermione hoped she wasn't being too nosy. She couldn't help being curious.

'In body, he was.' Celine grinned. 'If not in spirit. He was always pathetically squeamish. He was there for the last two, anyway.' Celine said. 'I didn't know him when I had my first. Her father worked on the Chanel counter in Barneys.' She smiled. 'Gay, of course. My best friend. We painted New York red in our time, I can tell you. Then I decided I wanted a baby and darling Louis obliged. He saw it all as great fun. He made a pretty good dad, actually.'

'So what happened?' Hermione thought of Josh.

'The usual story,' Celine said. 'He met someone. Byron, I think his name was. Byron wanted Louis to go live with him in San Francisco. And who was I to stop him? They wanted to take my little girl with them,' she said. 'We had one hell of a fight. We haven't spoken since. I missed him. Still do miss him, as a matter of fact. But life goes on, doesn't it? And I'm sure you really don't want to hear me rambling on like this.' She grinned. She had a big gap between her two front teeth. It made a striking contrast against all that creamy skin and the dusting of coppery freckles on the bridge of her nose. It gave her a rather kooky air that made her seem all the more approachable.

'Does it hurt? The birth, I mean.'

'Yes,' Celine said. 'It hurts like hell.'

'Great!'

'But you forget about it afterwards. The moment you hold your baby, it all sort of fades into the background.'

Celine spritzed Eau Dynamisante behind her

ears and rummaged in her bag for a lipstick as Hermione made a valiant attempt at pulling her socks on. Her toenails were a disgrace, she noticed. All chipped and snarled. Pre-Bean, she'd always taken such care of herself. She'd had a pedicure, complete with paraffin wax, every two weeks. She wondered if Greg had noticed the difference.

If he had, he hadn't said anything.

She finished with her socks and slipped into a pair of emerald-green Converse All Stars. She couldn't be doing with heels any more. She couldn't seem to get past the fact that they made her look like a pig, trotting to market.

'I'm sorry.' She looked at Celine. What was she doing, blurting all her fears to a stranger? 'I'd better let you get on.'

'Don't be silly. Tell you what. Are you doing anything?'

'When?'

'Right now.'

'Oh.' Hermione floundered. 'Er. I was going to get groceries on my way home . . .'

She didn't want to admit she had nothing on in case Celine had a hidden agenda. She could be some crazed Myra Hindley, on the lookout for fresh blood.

Was that really likely, though?

'I've got an hour until the kids come out of school,' Celine said. 'I don't suppose you feel like grabbing a coffee.'

'OK.'

They went to the Second Cup at the intersection of Bloor and Spadina. Hermione ordered a skinny hot chocolate because the smell of full fat milk had suddenly started to make her feel nauseous. Celine asked for a fat cappuccino with extras, in the form of an energy-giving boost. Standing at the counter listening to Celine, Hermione was reminded of when McDonald's opened its first branch in Cornwall. It must have been just before they moved to Bath. A girl at school had convinced Harriet that, if you asked for a Big Mac with extras, they put drugs in it. Harriet had believed her. For years afterwards, she'd refused to set foot in the place. If they went there in a big group, she would wait outside and Hermione would bring her the gherkins out of her own cheeseburger to eat on the way home.

'Are you having a muffin?'

Celine was hovering, tongs in hand, over a pyramid of deliciously sticky-looking cakes.

'Look at me,' Hermione said. 'Do you honestly think I need to pack in any more carbohydrate?'

'You look just fine to me,' Celine told her.

'Maybe . . .'

It was stupid but she couldn't help but think of the perfectly honed and toned bodies in Greg's girlie magazines, lurking beneath her as she slept. She was starting to get a little bit paranoid.

'I'm the size of an apartment block,' she said. 'With adjacent residents-only gym and parking for a hundred vehicles . . .'

'Crap.' Celine rubbished her. 'You just went swimming. You deserve a sugar rush.'

Hermione bit her lip. She was starving . . .

'Tell you what.' Celine grinned wickedly. 'How about I get one banana and one walnut date and we share? It doesn't really count if somebody else orders.'

'OK.' Hermione grinned back. 'You're on.'

At their table, Celine cut one of the muffins in half and divided the pieces between two plates. 'You're British, right?'

'English.'

'Where from?'

'All over,' Hermione admitted. 'I was born in Cornwall.'

'Cornwall.' Celine looked delighted. 'We went to Cornwall when we were just married.'

'Oh?' Hermione was pleased. They had something in common! 'Where in Cornwall?'

Celine wrinkled her freckle-sprinkled nose. 'Oh, Jeez. Now you're asking. It was a long time ago. There was some castle.'

'Tintagel?'

'That's the one. It was so beautiful around there.'

'My sister cut her first tooth in Merlin's Cave,' Hermione remembered. 'Oh God.' She covered her eyes. 'Teething! Another thing to look forward to.'

'It's not so bad.' Celine smiled. 'Once you get used to it. You don't want to believe all you read, you know. Mind you, I did with my first, I did everything by the book. I had this sort of baby bible I stuck to rigidly. I thought if I deviated from it one iota something terrible would happen and I'd be branded a bad mother for all eternity.'

Hermione flushed as she thought of her own glossy baby book at home.

'All that mumbo-jumbo goes out the window when you're suddenly faced with this screaming crumpled rag.' Celine took a bite of muffin. 'You just have to pick out the bits you think suit you and then wing it from there. My mom was a big help, actually. I was lucky. She stayed with me for a month after I had my first. Single mother.' She cut the other muffin in two and gave half to Hermione. 'She was a godsend. I guess your family are all in England.'

'My parents are dead, actually,' Hermione told her.

'Oh God.' Celine looked horrified. 'I'm so sorry . . .'

'It's OK,' Hermione said. 'It was a long time ago.'

'Was it an accident?' Celine asked. 'Sorry. You don't have to talk about it if you don't want to.'

'They were driving to pick me up from some stupid party,' Hermione said. 'Some drunk hit their car. They didn't stand a chance, apparently.'

'Oh God. That's so awful.'

Hermione sipped her hot chocolate. 'It was pretty terrible.'

'You don't have any brothers or sisters?'

'A sister,' Hermione told her. 'Harriet.'

'Oh. Right.' Celine nodded. 'The tooth thing . . .'

'Yeah,' Hermione said. 'We were twins.'

'Were?'

'We don't really see each other any more.'

'That's too bad. Do you miss her?'

'It's been a long time but, yeah, I do. It's funny. It's been fifteen years. And I miss her more now than I ever did.'

'That'll be the baby,' Celine said sagely. 'They have a habit of bringing people together. I didn't speak to my mom for a year. Stupid differences. And then, suddenly, my little girl was there. Nothing seemed to matter any more.'

'I'm sorry,' Hermione said. 'We've only just met and here I am pouring out my life story.'

'Hardly your life story.' Celine smiled warmly. 'And I *did* ask you.'

'Well.' Hermione felt bashful. 'It's OK. I mean, if you're bored . . .'

'Not at all.' Celine licked her finger and pressed it down on the walnut and date crumbs left on her plate. 'I love hearing other people's stories. Is your sister in England?'

'As far as I know.'

'You don't know?'

Hermione shook her head sadly. 'We sort of drifted apart after our parents' accident. She blamed me.'

'Ah!'

'And then I just left her. I don't think she's ever forgiven me. I haven't heard from her since.'

'You think she still bears a grudge? After all this time?'

'I don't know.' Hermione shook her head. 'She's probably got her own life now.'

Celine said, 'You're very brave. I don't know what I'd do without my sister. Louise has been brilliant with the kids. Especially now.'

Hermione looked at her plate. It wasn't really a question of being brave. It was a question of not really having any choice.

'I've been through a pretty bad patch recently,' Celine admitted.

'I'm sorry to hear that.'

Celine scooped the froth from her second cappuccino. 'I'm going through a divorce.'

'What happened?' Hermione swallowed her coffee. 'If you don't mind my asking.'

'The usual. He had an affair.'

'I'm so sorry.'

'Don't be. Besides . . .' She broke off another piece of muffin. 'Some men just don't change. In a way, I probably had it coming.'

'How's that?'

'He had a girlfriend when I met him,' Celine said. 'They were engaged. It was two weeks off the wedding.' She grimaced. 'Imagine. Relatives gearing up for the big event. Friends buying fondue sets and silver candlesticks. The works. And then . . . there I was, in the middle of it all . . .'

'Did you know?' Hermione asked.

'I wish I could say no,' Celine said. 'But it would be a big fat lie, I'm afraid. I knew full well. And it made me feel terrible. But I just couldn't help it.'

'What happened?'

'She found out,' Celine said wryly. 'Called off the wedding. And there I was. Waiting to pick up the pieces.'

'It wasn't your fault,' Hermione said kindly. 'Perhaps it was just meant to be.'

'That's what I thought,' Celine said. 'What I didn't realise was that, once you've been the other woman, you're always on your guard. You're expecting another Other Woman. It might not be today. Or tomorrow. Or even the day after that. But one day, someone thinner or brighter or prettier than you will come along. And there won't be a damned thing you can do to stop it.'

'How did you find out about his affair?' Hermione pushed her muffin away. She didn't really feel like eating it any more.

'I caught him with the au pair just after my second was born.'

'No!'

'I told myself it was just pregnancy. I didn't exactly feel very sexy when I was expecting.' She laughed. 'You're supposed to have hair like silk and skin like a peach, aren't you?'

'Something like that.'

'You don't seem to have done too badly on that score.' Celine looked at her. 'You're glowing.'

'It doesn't feel like it,' Hermione said modestly. 'I feel rank, most of the time.'

'Oh, you can't out-rank me,' Celine said. 'I'll show you the photos some time. My hair was like straw. I gained thirty pounds. And I had this sort of clammy look. Like a dead fish nobody wants to buy. I told myself it wasn't any wonder he should be tempted to look elsewhere.'

'You took him back?'

'Yep.' Celine took more muffin. 'Sucker, huh?'

'You loved him. There's nothing wrong with that.'

'I guess not,' Celine said. 'And he suddenly became really attentive after that. It was like falling in love all over again.'

'Then what happened?'

'You want another drink?' Celine jerked her thumb at Hermione's empty cup.

'Sure.'

'There was this do,' Celine said, when the waiter had been dispatched. 'At his work.'

'Oh?'

'We'd been getting along so well,' Celine said. 'Our sex life was great. Better than great. And I'd been looking forward to this party. I'd had my hair done. New outfit. You know the score.'

Hermione nodded.

'I was sitting in a corner of the bar waiting for him to bring me a drink when I realised he was talking to a group of people I recognised.'

'Go on.'

'I thought I should say hello. I'd met them before. It seemed rude to just sit there and not say anything. So I went to join them. But before I got there, this girl I'd never seen before appeared from nowhere.' She hesitated. 'It would be gratifying to say that she looked like Gollum on a bad hair day. But I'm afraid that would be a big lie.'

Hermione laughed.

'She was very petite. Eastern-looking. Beautiful almond eyes and that lovely dusky skin. 'You know?'

Hermione nodded.

'There were lots of bottles of wine hanging around,' Celine said. 'And there was this one on the bar behind my husband.' She hesitated. 'It was funny, really. They didn't touch. Nothing like that. After all, *I* was there. They couldn't make it obvious, could they? But there was something in the way she just held her glass out to him and nodded at the wine on the bar that made me suspicious. It was too familiar. And then, when he turned round and refilled it without commenting, I *knew*. I mean, you have to be pretty intimate with someone to not even acknowledge them if they've just asked you for a drink, don't you?'

'I guess so.' Hermione nodded. 'What did you do?'

'I waited till we got home and confronted him,' Celine said. 'Of course he burst into tears. Just like he did when I caught him with Julica. He swore it would never happen again. Begged me to forgive him. But I'd heard it all before. It was like a stuck record. I felt as though suddenly something had snapped inside me. I'd had enough. And that was that.' She looked at her watch. 'Crap. Is that the time? I have to go pick up the kids.'

'It's been nice meeting you,' Hermione said, for want of something better to say.

'Nice . . .' Celine laughed. 'That's so British.'

'Well, it has,' Hermione said. 'I was feeling a bit down this morning. And you've really cheered me up.'

'Ditto.' Celine slapped an address card onto the table. 'Here. You can be the first to get one of these. I just had them printed out in my single name.'

'Celine Jacques,' Hermione read.

'That's me.'

'Thanks.'

'Think about what I said, won't you? About your sister. She'll want to know she's going to be an aunty.' She smiled. 'Weddings and funerals. That's normally when the clans gather, isn't it? Why not a brand new little person? What better excuse is there?'

Hermione smiled. She had a point.

'Anyway.' Celine tapped the card on the table with a French-polished fingernail. 'Call me. This has been so great. Let's do it again soon.'

'That'd be great.'

'I want to know what happens with the little one.' Celine picked up her bag. 'All the gory details, please. How much she weighs. What time she was born. You'll find you get a lot of that.' She grinned. 'Stupid, isn't it? People are always obsessed with a baby's weight. You'd think they'd be more worried about the important things, wouldn't you? Like, has it got a head?'

300

HARRIET

Jesse, sprawled against the dingy brick wall of the police station, looked like a doleful Jack-in-the-Box.

Harriet yanked up Vin Rouge's handbrake and parped the ancient horn, waving frantically as Jesse looked up. The poor guy looked exhausted. Anybody would, she supposed, if they'd just spent the night in a police cell.

She'd been downstairs in Jesse's flat last night when the drug squad had turned up to take him in. She'd promised to help him cook a Thai curry for Joe's leaving party the following evening and they'd spent a happy afternoon in the oriental supermarket in Weston village. They'd returned absolutely laden with goodies. Handfuls of aromatic Thai basil. Tiny green chillies, sitting in a polystyrene tray and covered in cling film. A green papaya as thick as a forearm. Little bricks of coconut cream. As they'd unpacked their spoils, laying them out on the kitchen table, Jesse had asked Harriet about the hunt for Hermione.

'This Will guy.' He sounded full of derision. 'Did he know anything?'

'He had an address,' Harriet told him. 'In Lyons.'

'France?'

'Yup.' Harriet found the piece of paper, tucked into the back of her jeans, and spread it out on the table.

'Place des Celestins,' Jesse read. 'Sounds nice.'

'It doesn't matter if it's nice or not, does it?' Harriet said. 'She's hardly likely to be there now, is she? Not after ten years.'

Jesse pounded a pale stalk of lemongrass as instructed. 'Is it not worth a try?'

'There isn't even a phone number,' Harriet said.

'We'll think of something.'

'I wish I had your confidence.'

The arrest had happened so quickly. Suddenly, the kitchen was full of policemen. Edie must have let them in downstairs and they'd kicked Jesse's door in. It must have come as something of a surprise to find him and Harriet serenely chopping herbs together in what was a relatively clean kitchen. They'd probably expected a bunch of crumblies sitting around talking shit.

'Can I help you?' Jesse sliced through a knob of fresh ginger.

'You can put that fucking knife down for a start.'

It had been horrible seeing Jesse cuffed and dragged off in a meat wagon. He'd looked bewildered and frightened. Harriet knew she wouldn't be able to sleep that night. Instead, seeing as Joe had gone walkabout again, she'd made sure the flat was secure and gone for a walk herself. She liked walking at night in Bath. The city never ceased to surprise her. Even now, there was still always something she hadn't noticed before in the higgledy-piggledy maze of limestone streets. A wrought-iron portico, perched on the edge of a tall skinny house. A sudden staircase, twisted like barley sugar. A gap in a wall, affording an unexpected vista of the rest of the city twinkling below.

Jesse climbed into Vin Rouge and drew a hand across his chin, which was peppered with stubble. She'd never seen him looking so rough.

'Is Joe OK?'

'He's fine,' Harriet told him. 'At least, he was when I called in this morning with croissants. He was packing.'

'Croissants!' Jesse said deliriously. 'What I wouldn't give for a croissant.'

'In that bag,' Harriet said. 'Croissants and pains au chocolat.'

'You star.' Jesse sank his teeth into a sticky almond croissant laced with icing sugar. He looked haunted, Harriet thought.

'Are you sure you're OK?'

'I'm fine.' Jesse munched on a stick of marzipan. 'I just wish I knew who'd done this. It wasn't me.'

'Of course it wasn't,' Harriet said. 'I know that.'

'Trust me to get landed with a pill-popping parrot.' Jesse groaned.

'Was that what it was?'

'Yeah.' Jesse slumped in his seat. 'When your Will opened her up, her stomach was full of little white pills. Apparently, whoever put them there had wrapped them in Sellotape packages and forced her to swallow them.'

'Poor thing. Why?'

'So they could wait at the other end when she crapped them out, I guess. Only thing is, they hadn't bargained on some of them splitting open. That was what killed her.'

'But who would do something like that?'

Jesse shrugged. 'The person who sent them, I guess.'

'Your brother in Chile?'

Jesse frowned. 'No way. Jack's straight as a die. And what would he get out of it? He could hardly get his hands on the drugs, could he? And the only other person who had contact with Miss Scarlett was . . .'

'Joe!' Harriet finished for him.

'Exactly.'

'He wouldn't, though,' Harriet said.

'I know,' Jesse said. 'But I'm fast running out of options.'

'Did they charge you?'

He shook his head. 'Not enough evidence. But they've impounded the body. Fortunately, I still had the box she came in, so they have that. They're hoping to trace the sender that way. Until then, we just have to wait and see.'

'Bet it was Edie,' Harriet said, more to make him laugh than anything.

It worked. Jesse threw back his head and roared.

'You're a diamond, Harry,' he told her. 'Did you know that?'

'Oh,' she said. 'I had a fair inkling.'

She parked Vin Rouge and they walked together along Camden Crescent, squinting against the sun.

'I suppose we can't blame Will,' Harriet concluded, as Jesse stuck his key in the front door.

'What for?'

'Telling the police.'

'No,' Jesse said. 'It was his duty. Anybody would have done the same. And he lost his sister to drugs, don't forget. AND he doesn't know me from a loaf of bread.'

'Still.' Harriet started up the stairs. 'You'd have thought the police would have had more sense. If you'd known the drugs were in there, you'd have hardly taken Miss Scarlett to a vet, would you? You'd have just chopped her up and helped yourself.'

They'd reached Jesse's front door.

'Thanks.' Jesse kissed the top of her head.

'What for?' Harriet's heart skipped a beat.

'For picking me up,' Jesse said. 'For being a good friend.'

'I should think so too,' Harriet chided him. 'I'm a busy girl. I'm scumble-glazing a table at three. Oh, the glamour.'

'And for making me laugh, of course,' Jesse said. 'You're good at that.'

'You're welcome.' She turned to go up to her own flat.

'Harriet . . .'

'Yep?'

'I wondered,' Jesse said, going uncharacteristically red. 'You are coming tonight, aren't you?'

'If you'd like me to.'

'Of course.'

'Right then.'

'Right.'

There was an awkward silence. For a moment, neither of them knew what to say. Jesse scuffed the toe of his tomato-red Converse boot against the skirting board and Harriet stared at her feet.

'I'll see you tonight then,' Jesse said eventually.

'Yep,' Harriet replied. 'See you tonight.'

HERMIONE

Hermione had no idea what a teenager, a six-year-old and a seven-year-old would enjoy eating, so she packed a bit of everything. Bagels, stacked with cream cheese and salmon. Lays chips in two flavours. Apples, Carrots. Cherry tomatoes. A package of strawberry twizzlers. Butter tarts. She was a bundle of nerves. What if Greg's children didn't like her?

What if she didn't like them?

They arrived, bang on time, at ten o'clock. According to Greg, the drive to Niagara Falls took an hour and a half. They should be there in plenty of time for lunch.

Her tummy swirled like a carousel with nerves as the doorbell jangled. Where the hell was Greg? Shouldn't he be here to make the introductions? He'd nipped out to the office at eight to do some paperwork. But he'd promised to be back in time for the kids.

She slapped down the hall in her flip-flops to answer the door. Flip-flops were about all she could bear to wear right now. As June dripped, like an overripe fruit, into July, the temperature

307

in the city had gone up a notch. The air was almost syrupy with heat, punctuated only by the odd down-pour that lasted for all of two minutes. As it got hotter, Hermione got bigger. Her ankles had started to look less like ankles and more like the great parsnip-shaped slabs of lamb you saw oozing oily gobbets in the windows of kebab shops all over Greektown. She was shattered.

She checked her reflection in the hall mirror. At least her cheekbones were still there. It was amazing how much weight you could pack on and still have them hold your face up for you. It was just a shame she couldn't say as much for the rest of her body. Whatever muscle tone she did have seemed to be obscured by a healthy layer of blubber. The swimming was helping. Josh had been right about that. But, seeing as her Saturday swimming mornings these days usually finished up in a coffee house eating white chocolate muffins with Celine, who was becoming quite a good friend, she wasn't sure she wasn't just undoing all the good work she was putting in in the pool.

Six bright currant-bun eyes observed her from the front doorstep.

'Hello,' she said uneasily. 'I'm just waiting for your dad.'

'Is there a problem?' The eldest, a tall, bony girl with pale green eyes, Peppermint Patty spectacles and a faceful of freckles, visibly prepared herself for disappointment. 'Is he not here?'

Hermione didn't know what to say. This was

hardly the fun meeting she'd hoped for as an introduction.

'I'm so sorry,' she told them, steeling herself for a wall of sulkiness. 'Your dad's at work.' She peered out into the street, curious to catch a glimpse of Greg's wife. 'Did your mom drop you off?'

'We got a cab,' the little boy informed her. 'Our dad has an account. Maud knows the password.'

'I go all over.' Maud looked proud. 'Specially Queen Street.'

'Maud loves Queen Street,' the boy piped up. 'She reckons the shops are cool. Are we going to Niagara now?'

'We'll go when your dad gets back,' Hermione told him.

'Right.' The boy seemed unperturbed. 'Do you have any candy?'

'You must be Spike.' Hermione smiled. 'I've heard a lot about you.'

Spike's big round face crumpled into a smile. He was a doughty-looking boy. 'That's me.'

'We thought you'd be short.' The younger girl, who, thus far, had remained silent, looked up at her. She had an angelic mop of white-blonde curls and a pair of remarkable pale silver eyes.

'You did?'

'Yes.' Spike nodded solemnly. 'What's your name again?'

'Silly,' Maud chided him. 'Her name's Bee, stupid. Like Mom said.' She nudged the smallest girl. 'Say hi to Bee, Maisie.'

'Hi, Bee.'

Hermione was confused. She had no idea why Greg's children should think she was named after an insect. Perhaps it was something their mother had said. She vaguely remembered Ruby referring to people she didn't like as 'Silly Bs'. Shorthand for bastard, she supposed. Or bugger. Perhaps that was it.

Either way, there was no point in saying anything. If they wanted to call her Bee, then Bee it was. And now that they were here, she might as well do something about getting to know them.

'Hello, Maisie.' She smiled at her. 'And I know you're Maud,' she said to the eldest girl.

Maud held out her hand politely. 'It's good to meet you, Bee.'

'Good to meet you too.' Hermione couldn't help feeling that this was all rather surreal. 'Would you all like to come in and get something to drink?'

'Cool.' Spike, needing no encouragement, hurtled down the hall like a bowling ball and spilled into the sitting room. 'Wow. Is this a real ostrich egg? Can I touch it? Will it break? Do you like *Slipknot*? 'Cos Maud does. She listens to it all the time. It drives our mom MAD. Do you have *Finding Nemo*? 'Cos ours got stuck in the DVD player and we can't use it. Have you seen *Toy Story 2*? Who's your favourite? I love Woody. Are you from another country? Have you been to DQ yet? Will you take us there one time? Do you have any Oreos?'

'I'm sorry about him.' Maud caught her eye. 'He talks a LOT.'

'It's fine,' Hermione told her. 'Oreos coming up.'

Spike followed her into the kitchen.

'What's that?'

Hermione stopped fanning Oreos onto a plate and looked up to see that Spike had fallen on the box of junk food Josh had left behind when he moved out. He always used to stock up on his favourites when he took a trip home. She tried to ignore the pang she got at seeing his carefully packed jars of Marmite and bottles of HP sauce poking out of the carton. Those are Monster Munch. Crisps.'

'Crisps?'

'You know, chips.'

Spike's forehead creased. 'We don't have these.'

'They're from England,' Hermione said. 'From Josh's goodie box.'

'Who's Josh?'

'My friend.'

God, she missed Josh. If he were here, this would be a whole lot easier.

'You're from England?' Spike's eyes almost popped out of his head. 'Is he from England too?'

'That's right.'

'And you have different stuff there to us? Like this?' He unscrewed the lid of an industrial-sized jar of Marmite and sniffed the contents cautiously. 'Eew.'

'Marmite.' Hermione laughed. 'For toast.'

'It smells gross.'

'It's an acquired taste.'

'Do you have Jubes back home in England?'

Hermione shook her head.

'You don't have Jubes?' Spike was incredulous.

'Not as far as I know.'

'Do you have Kraft Dinner? D'you have cheese popcorn? My dad buys us cheese popcorn when we go to the movies sometimes. D'you have O Henry bars?'

'Nope.'

'Oh wow.' Spike goggled. 'No O Henrys? I so don't think I'm gonna like it in England.'

'That's good.' Maud came into the room. 'Because you're not going, Dope. You've never even been out of Ontario.'

'So? Neither have you.'

Of all of them, Maud was the most reticent at first. She was nothing like her father. She wore big bovver boots under a pair of thick red pyjama bottoms and a T-shirt with PORN STAR scrawled across it. As Maisie and Spike twittered like a pair of budgerigars, Maud draped herself across the couch listening to her portable CD player. Hermione, though flattered that Greg's kids seemed more than happy to spend the morning with her, was worried that all three of them were bored. There wasn't much for them to do here. Clearly, they'd been told they were spending the day with their father and so it hadn't occurred to them to go home. It was quite sweet.

She nodded at Maud's layers and layers of clothing.

'Are you not a bit hot in all that?'

Maud unplugged herself. 'What?'

'I was wondering if you weren't boiling in those thick trousers.'

'What?' Maud looked blank.

'Sorry.' Hermione corrected herself. 'I meant your pants. Do you want to borrow some shorts? I've got a couple of pairs that might fit you. You can keep them if you like them. I'm not likely to get back into them again.' She patted her tummy.

'I'm fine.' Maud shook her head.

'You're sure?'

'Yup.'

'Maud won't get her legs out,' Spike explained.

'They're too fat,' Maisie added helpfully.

'She's got hair too.' Spike's eyes were as round and shiny as brass buttons. 'On her bottom.'

'We saw it,' Maisie said. 'Our mom always wipes hers off. But Maud hasn't yet. It's gross.'

'Shut *up*!' Maud's face was on fire. 'You two are retarded. You don't know anything about anything.'

Hermione didn't have a clue what she was supposed to say. It was all very well expecting a baby. But finding yourself with two under-tens and an adolescent under your wing was a very different kettle of fish.

Perhaps she should suggest that she and Maud spend the day together one weekend. They could have some pampering time. She could get her to have a wax. And a pedicure. Girls of thirteen liked that sort of thing, didn't they?'

Something told her that Maud probably wasn't your average thirteen-year-old girl. And if she took Maud to have her nails done, she would have to think of something special to do with the others. She was bound to bollocks that up quite spectacularly. She had no idea what sort of things a boy of six and a girl of seven liked to do in their spare time.

She was just wondering how best to approach the subject when her mobile started to ring. Leaving Spike and Maisie bugging their big sister, she ducked out of the sitting room and went to answer it.

It was Greg.

'Hi.' He sounded tetchy.

'Hi.' Hermione tried to sound breezy, even though her stomach was sinking faster than the *Titanic*.

'Are the kids there?'

'Yep. They're all here. They seem fine,' she said, suddenly anxious to please him. 'I've fed them. I'm hope that's OK.'

'What?'

'I fed them. Cookies and stuff.'

'Oh, right,' Greg said vaguely. 'Whatever. Look, sweetheart, it's like Armageddon in here. There's no way I'm going to be able to get away this morning. Can you tell the kids we'll have to do Niagara another time?'

'Right,' Hermione said tightly. 'And what am I supposed to do with them in the meantime?'

'Talk to them,' Greg said. 'Play. You'll be fine. It'll be good practice for you.'

She'd just put the phone down when it rang again and she snatched it up.

'What is it this time?'

'Charming!'

'Celine.' Hermione smiled. 'Great to hear from you. Sorry about that. I thought you were someone else.'

'No problem. How are you? I just wondered if you felt like getting a coffee or something. It's such a beautiful day.'

'I'm sorry,' Hermione said. 'I'm kind of tied up right now.'

It was too bad. Since that day at the swimming pool, she and Celine seemed to have settled into a casual friendship. Celine would call her occasionally when she found herself with a free moment and vice versa. Hermione found herself looking forward to seeing her. Their meetings went some way towards filling the hole Josh's departure had left. She couldn't tell Celine everything, like she had Josh. She didn't know her well enough yet. And Celine preferred to stick to certain topics of conversation, refusing to discuss her ex or the kids, almost as though, by mentioning them to Hermione, she would somehow tarnish the downtime they had together. They seemed to spend an awful lot of time discussing Hermione. Hermione's plans for the baby when it was born. Hermione's past. She loved hearing about Harriet. And the more Hermione talked about her sister, the more she realised just how much she missed her.

Still, nice as it would be to gossip over a caramel macchiato with Celine today, she couldn't do it. She had no idea how long Greg's children planned on sticking around and she didn't want to let them down. They seemed like nice kids. Things couldn't be easy for them right now.

'No problem,' Celine said. 'I'll take myself off to the health club. They do a rather delicious scrub up and bliss out treatment. And I could do with a bit of that at the moment.'

'Is everything OK?'

'Fine. Just the bloody ex, being difficult about the house. He wants to sell it, I want to keep it on. It's the kids' home. I don't see why they should have to live in a poky apartment some place awful just because he can't keep it in his pants.'

'I'm sorry.'

'Don't worry. It'll work itself out. I'll call you next week?'

'That would be lovely.'

In the sitting room, the rumpus over Maud's recently acquired public hair seemed to have died down and she was draped over the couch, twirling her hair around her fingers as she listened to something boppy on her headphones. Spike and Maisie were sitting on the floor reading a copy of *OK Magazine* that Josh had had sent over at some point. There was something rather nice about them being there. She couldn't quite put her finger on what it was. But it reminded her of home. She and Harriet had often spent time in each other's company like this. Each doing different things but choosing to do them in the same room. Apart but together.

'I'm sorry,' Hermione told them. 'Your dad's tied up at work.'

'When isn't he?' Maud didn't bother to look up.

'We could still do something nice though,' Harriet said. 'We could go to the park if you like.'

'We're OK.' Maisie examined a photograph of a celebrity. 'Is that the lady out of *A Bug's Life*?'

'No.' Spike peered over her shoulder. 'She was in that movie we saw with Mom. *E.T.*'

'Are you sure?'

'Of course.' Spike shifted from his kneeling position until his legs were stuck right out in front of him. 'You can tell it's her. Her head's too big for the rest of her.' He stared at his shoes. 'I've got that thing.'

'What thing?' Hermione asked him.

'Stars are walking all over my feet.'

'Pins and needles,' Maisie explained. 'His foot's asleep.'

'Here.' Hermione grabbed his foot playfully and wiggled it about. 'Better?'

'Much.' Spike smiled up at her. 'You're good.'

'Why thank you.' Hermione smiled back. 'Is Maud OK, d'you think?'

'Yeah. She always just lies down and listens to music. Even when we go to really fun places. Even,' his eyes were suddenly saucer-like again, 'when we go to Lake Bernard.'

'Lake Bernard is cool,' Maisie said. 'Mom's friend has a cabin there.' She adopted a concentrated expression. 'It's the biggest freshwater lake without an island.'

'But we found one.' Spike's eyes shone. 'When Mom and Maud went ski-ing and we sat in the boat.'

'It was only tiny,' Maisie said.

'So?' Spike said. '*We* found it. It's ours.'

'And it is big enough to have a wiener roast on. You should come with us next time,' Maisie said kindly. 'You can even bring your baby if you want. As long as it doesn't cry too much. Spike cried loads when he was a baby. All the time. Except for when he was milking Mom.'

'Don't be such a retard.' Maud unplugged a headphone and looked embarrassed. 'You *know* Bee can't come on vacation with us. Mom would just go insane.'

'Because she's slutty?' Spike asked innocently. 'Bee, d'you have any peanut butter cups?'

'*Spike!*' Maud looked mortified.

'It's OK,' Spike said. 'It doesn't have to be peanut butter cups. I'll settle for Reese's Pieces.'

'You shouldn't *ask*.' Maud's lip wobbled. This was excruciating for her, Hermione realised. She actually understood the complexities of all of this, while her brother and sister just made as much sense of it as they could at their age. It was OK for Maisie, still glued to the sparkly celebrities in *OK*. Most of this seemed to have gone over her head. And Spike. Dear Spike. Life was simple to him. He didn't seem to mind where he was, as long as there was a steady supply of cookies. But to Maud . . .

Not for the first time, she felt a whorl of guilt in her stomach.

She winked at Maud in what she hoped was a conspiratorial fashion to show that they were the ones who understood here. The adults.

Instantly, Maud's face relaxed.

'It's OK,' Maisie said. '*We* don't think you're slutty. And you don't need to worry about taking us to the park or anything. We can amuse ourselves. We're quite resourceful children really.'

HARRIET

Harriet rolled over onto her front and hugged her pillow, drumming her feet on the mattress in paroxysms of unparalleled delight.

Crazy!

Crazy, crazy, crazy!

Who in their right mind would have thought it? Her and Jesse!

Not once. Not twice. Three times in one night. And lots of times since.

It had all started on the night of the party for Joe. She and Jesse had worked like Trojans to get everything ready in time. Harriet had laced fairy lights, in old-fashioned colours, around the garden. They'd glowed prettily all night. Peppermint cream. Soft yellow. Bluebell. Pale rose. She'd been in her element, making the food. Waxy new potato salad, generously sprigged with mint and coated in glossy homemade mayonnaise. Red onion tart. A Spanish omelette, stacked with blue cheese and broccoli. A plain tomato salad.

It had been such a fun night.

She'd been a bit perturbed at first. Lizzy hadn't turned up, despite having promised to drop in for a drink. When Harriet had called Conrad, at nine thirty, to find out if everything was OK, he was just as surprised as she was because she'd left the house at seven.

'Right.' Harriet felt bad for worrying him. 'I'll sure she'll turn up.'

'Of course she will,' Conrad said. 'When she does, keep an eye on her, will you? She's been behaving a bit oddly lately.'

Lizzy never showed up, but apart from that the party had been brilliant. The food had been amazing. The atmosphere was relaxed. A garden filled with happy people drinking beer and having a laugh. Edie had made a grand entrance at half past eight, wearing an intriguing outfit consisting of a huge fifties-style skirt, napped with strawberry pink lace and teamed with a silver vest, little footless tights and skyscraper heels. She'd obviously been watching too much *Sex and the City*. By ten, she was clearly exhausted, but refused point blank to go home and miss out on all the fun. Jesse had had to steer her into his own flat, where he'd tucked her up on the sofa with a gory movie. Once, when Harriet went inside to go to the loo, she caught a glimpse of one of the characters holding aloft a severed head and distinctly heard Edie saying, with unadulterated scorn, 'That's not even a real head!'

When most people had gone home, and just a

few of Joe's madding crowd remained, Harriet had helped clear up.

'You really don't have to do that.' Jesse's head appeared at her shoulder. 'You've done enough for me lately.'

'It's fine,' Harriet said, as Leroy wiped himself around her ankles in the hope of acquiring a left-over chilli butterfly prawn. 'I was only going to go to bed otherwise.'

'Really.' Jesse took the plates from her and put them down on the picnic bench. 'It's about time I did something for you.'

'Like what?'

'A-ha!' He tapped the side of his nose. 'That's for me to know and you to find out.'

'That's not fair!'

'You really want to know what it is?'

'Yes.'

'It's inside.' He jerked his head towards the flat. 'Come in and have a coffee and I'll tell you.'

In Jesse's flat she waited for him to shut the door and pounced. 'So do I get it now?'

'Steady!' He pretended to push her away. 'You'll have me over.'

Wickedly, Harriet told herself that might not be such a bad thing. He was looking rather lovely tonight.

She shook herself.

'So where is it?'

'Here.' He reached into his jeans pocket and pulled out a folded piece of paper.

'*That*'s my present?'

'Why?' Jesse laughed. 'Were you hoping for a small box of crystallised fruit?'

'No.' Harriet turned the crumpled piece of paper over in her hand.

'Bath cubes, perhaps?' He laughed. 'I'm always told you can never go wrong with smellies.'

'What is it?'

'Oh dear,' Jesse said. 'You look disappointed. This is going to be like the time I bought my mum a frying pan for her birthday when she wanted something frivolous, isn't it?'

'It's a number.' Harriet stared at it.

'A *phone* number.' Jesse corrected her. He picked up a jar of mayonnaise and started to look for its lid.

'Whose phone number?'

'Well.' Jesse abandoned the mayonnaise and started to stack the dishwasher instead. 'I know you really want to find your sister . . .'

'Hermione?' Harriet gulped. 'But . . .'

'You left that address on the table,' Jesse said. 'I called international directory enquiries and they had a number.'

'But this is a London number.'

'I know,' Jesse said. 'I called the number in France.'

'Was it Audrey?'

'No, but it was someone who knew Audrey. She got hold of her and called me back. This is the number of a woman called Sylvie, who still keeps in contact with your sister.'

Harriet stared at the piece of paper. 'So I could just call this and get my sister's number?'

'That's the plan.'

'Thank you.' Harriet hugged him. 'Thank you so much.'

She tried to pull away. But Jesse didn't let go, so she buried her nose in the warmth of his sweatshirt instead. He smelt of barbecue smoke and black pepper. They stood there, hugging like teddy bears until Joe came sweeping through the kitchen in search of his rucksack.

'Get a room, you two. Put us all out of our misery.'

Jesse drew away from Harriet and his eyes searched her face.

'What do you think?'

'Should we?'

'What about . . .'

'For fuck's sake.' Joe picked up a blue sweatshirt and sniffed it. 'Of course you should.'

Sex with Jesse had been like nothing she'd ever experienced before. As they lay on their sides, her legs wrapped round his waist as he looked her straight in the eyes and moved slowly in and out of her, she realised that what she'd thought of as good sex in the past had actually been nothing of the sort. With Jesse, sex didn't even seem to be about sex. It was about being close. It was something of a revelation.

She'd thought she might feel guilty. As though she was somehow being unfaithful to Dan. But he hadn't been in contact for so long. He'd obviously made up his mind not to come back and hadn't had the guts to tell her. And being with Jesse had felt so right. That very first time, when he finally allowed himself to come, he'd fallen on her with a whimpering sound she'd never heard before. Afterwards, as she lay with her head in the crook of his arm, she'd felt as though she wanted to unzip his skin and climb inside.

It was hard to believe that had been two weeks ago. Since then, she had spent more time at Jesse's than she had in her own flat. Finally, she knew what people meant when they talked about the honeymoon period. She couldn't stop thinking about Jesse. She could be sanding a skirting board or painting a beam and an image of his face, contorted with ecstasy, would drift into her mind like a dandelion clock and simply refuse to budge. The thought that the delicious look on his face was all down to her sent shivers of delight down her spine. She was on cloud nine.

She'd never really had any of this with Dan. Then, it had been about securing herself a future. In Dan, she'd found somebody who was willing to make a life with her and for that she was grateful. If she was honest with herself, she had to admit that she'd always suspected they weren't the kindred spirits Isaac and Ruby had been. But she'd calmly accepted him as her fate anyhow.

And now this.

It couldn't last, this thing with Jesse. She knew that. There was Clare in Milan for a start. Jesse had unfinished business there, Harriet was sure, whatever Jesse said about finishing with Clare. But, somehow, Harriet found she didn't actually mind. At least she knew the score. And, in some ways, it just made things more exciting.

From her bed, she peeked through a chink in the curtains at an impeccable cerulean sky. It was going to be a beautiful day. And she was having lunch with Lizzy at Blue Ginger. She could catch up on gossip while copping an eyeful of Jesse. What could be better?

She stretched like a cat and got out of bed to run herself a bathful of filmstar bubbles in which she wallowed, accompanied by the dulcet tones of Edie singing along to her latest Fatboy Slim CD.

'Fatboy Slim is fucking in heaven.'

The idea of her neighbour, sitting in her Whimsy-infested flat, tapping her foot to the beat, made her laugh. She laughed all the way to Blue Ginger, where Jesse, dressed in T-shirt, jeans and a little white apron, dropped a kiss on her nose and showed her to the best table.

'Wow!' Lizzy said as she sat down, grinning like a Cheshire cat. 'You must be doing something right. You look amazing.'

'You don't look so bad yourself,' Harriet said. 'Should we get a bottle of wine? I feel like getting sozzled.'

'Fine by me.' Lizzy's face was serious suddenly. 'Listen, Harry, there's something you should know.'

'What sort of something?'

'I saw Gabby the other night. We had dinner.'

'I won't hold it against you.' Harriet watched Jesse pull a pint of Gem, his smooth capable hands expertly working the pump. The same hands that knew every inch of her body.

'She told me something. About Dan.'

'Like what?' Harriet still couldn't take her eyes off Jesse.

'Apparently,' Lizzy said, 'he's been seeing someone.'

Harriet snapped to attention. 'Really? Dan has? Are you sure?'

'I'm just telling you what Gabby said.'

'Fine.' Harriet held up her hand. 'Don't tell me any more. I actually don't want to know.'

'Ladies!' Jesse appeared, notepad in hand. 'What can I get you?'

'Oh.' Harriet blushed, all thoughts of Dan forgotten. 'What can you recommend?'

'Chef says the Vietnamese rice rolls are very good.'

'I'll have those then,' Harriet said happily. 'Lizzy?'

'The same.' Lizzy snapped shut the menu and watched as Jesse retreated to the kitchens.

'OK,' she said, when he was out of earshot. 'Dish.'

'What?' Harriet bluffed.

'I'm not stupid,' Lizzy said. 'I can tell when something's going on. It's obvious.'

'OK,' Harriet said. 'We've been having a thing.'

'A thing?' Lizzy squealed. 'I *knew* it!'

'Shh.' Harriet looked around her. 'I don't want everybody to know. As far as I know, I'm just a bit on the side.'

'No way,' Lizzy said. 'There's just no way. I've never seen him look so happy. So what happened to Clare?'

'He told me he broke it off.' Harriet sounded dubious.

'And you don't believe him?'

'I don't know,' Harriet said. 'She's so far away. And he wrote to her. Recently. I saw the letter lying on the hall table.'

'How do you know he wasn't writing to break it off?'

'You think I'm being an idiot don't you?'

'A bit.'

'Sorry,' Harriet said. 'I'm just not used to all this. Dan and I were together for so long, I'd forgotten what it's like for it all to feel brand new again.' She blushed.

'Ahhhhh.' Lizzy grinned, 'He's made you really happy, hasn't he? I'm so pleased.'

'I feel like a teenager,' Harriet admitted. 'Look,' she added quickly, as Catriona the barmaid swished past in a cloying cloud of Eternity. 'Can we not talk about this now? It's still all a bit . . .'

'New?' Lizzy sipped her wine. 'OK. Just tell me when it happened. Come on. I'm dying to know.'

'Joe's party,' Harriet said. 'The one you were supposed to come to. Remember?'

'Sorry,' Lizzy said. 'I meant to call. Crack Nanny was ill and I couldn't get anyone else at short notice.'

'That's funny,' Harriet said. 'Because I called Conrad. And he said you'd gone out.'

'I must have gone for a walk or something.' Lizzy said. 'I get cabin fever sometimes, being in the house with the kids all day and then having them all night as well.'

'How are they?' Harriet asked, as a waitress she hadn't seen before flounced over and plonked their rice rolls down in front of them. She couldn't have looked any less interested in the food if she'd tried. Which was a shame. It looked absolutely delicious.

'They're fine.' Lizzy dipped her first roll into the tamarind dipping sauce. 'Oscar said "bugger" the other day.'

'Delicious boy. You must be very proud.'

'Oh, I am.' Lizzy giggled. 'We both are.'

'How are the girls?' Harriet asked.

'Not bad. Lucy's had the snuffles a bit. And Jemima bit some poor kid at nursery the other day for screwing up her Plasticine man. I've had the mother on the phone, chewing me out. I don't quite see what she expects me to do about it. I'm delighted my daughter can stand up for herself.'

'She sounds like Hermione.' Harriet laughed.

'How are you getting on there?' Lizzy asked her. 'Did you check out that address?'

'Address?' Harriet was confused. She hadn't told

Lizzy about the address in France. She hadn't had a chance.

'The address in France,' Lizzy said. 'Will said he gave . . .'

'Go on?' Harriet said. 'Will said . . .'

'OK.' Lizzy held up her hands. 'You might as well know. Me and Will have been seeing a bit of each other.'

'What do you mean, "a bit"?' Harriet asked. 'How much, exactly?'

'Pretty much everything,' Lizzy said.

'An affair?' Harriet was shocked.

Lizzy nodded.

'But . . .'

'Please don't lecture me,' Lizzy begged. 'I know what it must look like. I mean, he was your—'

'Will, of all people,' Harriet said. 'He's a rattlesnake, Lizzy. He's poisonous. He gave me money for an abortion and fled the country with my sister when I needed her most. Doesn't that tell you something?'

'It was a long time ago,' Lizzy said. 'People change.'

'Not Will,' Harriet said.

'How do you know?'

'I just do,' Harriet said. 'Besides, you're *married*.'

'I know,' Lizzy said. 'I know it's wrong. But I can't stop it. There's just something about him . . .'

Though she was loath to admit it, Harriet did know what she meant. There was something about Will. He was the sort of person who made you feel good just by giving you his attention. When he looked at you, it was as though you were bathing in the warmth of a golden spotlight. You couldn't help but be drawn to him, like a moth to a flame. And then, when he turned his attention to somebody else, you were left shivering in darkness.

'How long has this been going on?' she asked gently. Lizzy was crying now.

'A w-while,' Lizzy stammered. 'He was at sports day with Alice. Jemima won the egg and spoon and I didn't n-notice, because I was so engrossed in what he was saying. He asked me out to dinner . . .'

'And?'

'And I went,' Lizzy said. 'I knew it was stupid. But Conrad was being so cold because of Oscar's accident. I was flattered by the attention. I just thought I'd treat myself.'

'But this is adultery,' Harriet said. 'Not a shopping trip to Cribbs Causeway.'

'I know,' Lizzy said. 'I kept telling myself the next time would be the last. But I can't seem to stop. And now Conrad's being all nice. And I wish he wouldn't because it makes me feel guilty. And . . .'

'Hey.' Harriet put her hand on Lizzy's. 'Calm down. Don't be too hard on yourself. I do understand.'

'You do?' Lizzy's large, watery eyes met her own.

'Of course I do,' Harriet said. 'I've been there, haven't I?'

'I s'pose.' Lizzy shuddered.

'If anything, it makes me realise why my sister went off with him like that,' Harriet told her. 'He has this magnetic quality. You know,' she confided, 'I was almost tempted myself. When I saw him at Blue Ginger's launch. I thought he was going to kiss me and for one minute I thought, what the hell? And then Dan interrupted us, thank God.'

'Poor Dan.' Lizzy said. 'No wonder he's seeing someone else.'

'What do you mean?'

'Do you not think he came to the launch to try and get back with you?' Lizzy said.

'Oh God. You think . . . ?'

'I'm not sure. But it seems likely. Gabby said he was like a lost pup without you.'

'And then he came and saw me with Will,' Harriet said. 'Bloody hell.'

'What would you have said? If he had asked to come back?'

'I don't know,' Harriet said honestly. 'I'm still confused, to be honest. A couple of months ago, I thought Dan was my lot in life, you know? And I was perfectly happy with that. Or at least I thought so. Now, though, it's like I've realised I have options. There's Jesse, for a start. And I do want to find my sister.'

'Of course you do.'

'I'm still terrified she won't want to see me. Not after what I said.'

'I'm sure that won't be the case,' Lizzy said. 'You never know. Perhaps she's trying to find you.'

'I doubt it. I'm not that hard to find. I've been in Bath nearly all my life. I didn't change my name when I married Dan. All she'd have to do is look me up in the phone book.'

'Even so. I reckon you should give it a go. You won't know unless you try, will you?'

'Guess not,' Harriet said. 'Lizzy? You will stop this thing with Will? Before it wrecks your marriage, I mean.'

'Of course,' Lizzy said, as Jesse, still in his sexy French waiter's apron, came over to see if they'd like anything else.

'Just the bill please,' Harriet said.

'On me.' Jesse grinned.

'Cool.' Harriet stood up. 'We must come here more often.'

'Hold it,' Jesse said. 'There's a condition.'

'What?'

'This!' He kissed her hard on the mouth. In front of Lizzy and everything.

'Blimey,' Lizzy said when he'd finished. 'We must definitely come here more often.'

'I'm glad to hear it.' Jesse, looking ridiculously happy, smiled at Lizzy.

'See you then.'

'See you.'

HERMIONE

Greg's children started to spend a lot more time in Amelia Street. They seemed to feel at home there and didn't appear to mind whether or not Greg was around. Hermione was glad. She must be doing something right.

If Greg was around, it was nice to see him with his kids. It sounded crazy. But she'd been worried she might find it hard to see him giving so much attention to others. On the contrary, watching him scoop Spike and Maisie up when he came in, twizzling them around until they got dizzy and staggered about like newborn foals, was a delight. Every other weekend, the five of them went to Dairy Queen, where Maud's vegan principles seemed to fly out the window every time she was faced with a hot fudge sundae. It was amazing what a heap of ice cream, sliced banana and a few chopped nuts could do to win a place in the affections of a thirteen-year old.

On the whole, life had been looking up recently. With the exception of Josh's absence, Hermione was happy. She wished Greg didn't have to work quite so hard. But then she'd been there. She did understand. Having Celine in her life helped. It was another adult to talk to at least. They met for coffee a couple of times a week now. Celine loved hearing about Greg and the kids. She'd wanted to know everything about them. She always asked what they'd been up to. Once, after Hermione had taken Spike and Maisie to the Eaton Centre for New York fries, she'd called sounding a bit panicked, Hermione thought. She'd wanted every little detail, down to the colour of Maisie's eyes. It had seemed a bit odd at the time. Especially seeing as she never seemed to mention her own children. But Hermione soon forgot about it. When they saw each other, they got on so well, there didn't seem any point bringing it up.

It was lovely having the kids around. They said the funniest things. One morning, after they'd all stayed over after a barbecue, Maisie had turned round and asked if she and Greg would be having any more children when this one came out. Hermione had said she didn't think so. One was probably quite enough.

'So.' Spike dipped his long spoon into his ice cream. 'You and Bee will only need to mate about once a month then.'

Hermione and Greg had both burst out laughing.

'Why d'you keep calling her Bee?' Greg asked, when he'd recovered himself.

'Because that's her name,' Spike said solidly.

They still all called her Bee, even though Greg

called her by her real name in front of them dozens of times a day. And, even though she didn't really understand why, she got to rather like having her own nickname. In particular, she formed a special bond with Maud, who often stopped by on her way back from high school for a chat, regardless of whether Greg was there or not. She used Hermione as a sounding board for her problems. She had fallen out with her friend Grace. There was a boy at school called Chandler. How did she know if she liked him or not? Were you supposed to shut your eyes when you kissed? Or was it OK to keep them open? One Friday, a week or two before Hermione's birthday, she'd been complaining how hard it was to do her maths homework with Maisie and Spike thundering up and down the stairs all the time when she'd suddenly asked Hermione if she had any brothers or sisters.

'I have a sister,' Hermione told her. 'A twin.'

'You do? Is she back in England?'

'I don't know.'

'You don't *know*? So how will you send her a birthday card?'

'I won't, I guess.'

The children had been excited about Hermione's birthday for ages. Greg had arranged to take time off and had cleared it with his ex to take the children on a boat to the Toronto Islands for the day. Hermione was fairly sure that other plans were underway, judging by all the excited whispers that seemed to stop when she came into the room.

She plaited the ends of Maud's hair and wondered how Harriet would be celebrating their birthday this year. In some mad, crazy way, she still saw her as the eighteen-year-old girl who got rather touchingly excited over banana and chocolate pancakes. What must she be like now?

She was probably preparing for her own children's birthdays these days. Hermione could imagine her, standing happily in a farmhouse kitchen somewhere, putting last-minute touches to a spectacular fairy castle, constructed entirely from vanilla sponge and fondant icing.

A lump rose in her throat.

'You won't send your own sister a birthday card?' Maud was horrified. 'Mom would *kill* me if I didn't get Maisie one. And you know what a pain in the butt *she* can be.'

It was touching to see Maud, teetering on the edge of adulthood, yet still placing a childlike emphasis on the whole business of birthdays. In so many ways, she reminded Hermione of Harriet at the same age.

'Won't she even get a cake?' Maud blinked.

'She might do.'

'I hope so.'

'You know what?' Hermione smiled. 'So do I.'

'What's Dad getting you for your birthday?' Maud wanted to know.

'I don't know.' Hermione shrugged.

'I do,' Maud said mysteriously.

'Will I like it?'

'Yup. At least,' Maud sucked her favourite grape soda noisily from the bottom of her glass, 'I *hope* you will. He thought of it all on his own.'

Hermione was touched. Greg had been so busy lately, she was surprised he'd had time to get her anything. One night last week, he hadn't come home from work at all. Hermione had paced up and down until four in the morning, with Celine's words clattering around her head like the wheels of a runaway train. She couldn't remember what it was she'd said, exactly. But it had been something about being the other woman. Always having to watch your back. Something like that.

In the morning, though, Greg had called. He'd been at a meeting that had gone on and on. By the time it was over, it had got too late to call and he'd got some kip on the couch in his office so he could make an early start. 'I hope you weren't too worried,' he'd said. 'I just didn't want to wake you.'

'No,' Hermione lied. 'I knew it would be something like that.'

'He works hard, your dad.' Hermione peeled the paper off an orange Popsicle and slid it into her mouth.

'He used to say he was working all the time when he still lived with us. But he wasn't.' She turned to look at Hermione. 'He was with you. Wasn't he?'

'Yes,' Hermione said. 'I'm so sorry. I would never have taken him away from you all on purpose.'

'I know.' Maud smiled.

'Really?'

'Really.' Maud's fingers, sticky with grape fizz, found hers and squeezed them. 'We like you. You're cool.'

'So are you.'

'They fought all the time anyways. It's nicer now we only see Dad weekends. And Mom is happier.' She paused to chase an ice cube around the bottom of her glass with the straw. Hermione hadn't known her long. But she knew her well enough to know when there was something on her mind.

'What's the matter?'

'*You're* not going to throw him out, are you?' Maud asked nervously.

'Of course not.' Hermione tugged her plait affectionately. 'Why on earth would I do that?'

'Because he's always working late.' Maud peeled a sliver of skin from the corner of her fingernail. 'You might think he's doing something bad again and sling him out. And then we wouldn't see you any more.'

'Of course you would,' Hermione said, as a shiver went down her spine. 'Anyway, it's not going to happen.'

'How do you know?' Maud asked her.

'Because I love your dad,' Hermione said simply. 'And your dad loves me.'

'What if one of you changes your mind?' Maud wanted to know.

'Why would we?'

'Chandler changes his mind every five minutes,' Maud said sadly. 'He likes Calypso now. She's heaps prettier than me. And heaps smarter.'

'Rubbish. I'm sure you're every bit as pretty as Calypso. And way smarter.'

'You reckon?'

'Of course.'

'You know,' Maud said, 'we really thought we might hate you. We were so relieved when you were nice.'

'Likewise.'

Maud left happy. But what she'd said about Greg using work as an excuse to have an affair had left Hermione with a squirmy feeling, like tadpoles wriggling their tails in her tummy.

It was true that he was busy at work. She knew that when you rolled out a new product across the whole of the USA, you were going to be up to your nuts in it. There were bound to be meetings. Conference calls. Quick dashes across whole continents.

But the small fact that she and Greg never seemed to have sex any more bothered her. She knew it wasn't the be all and end all of any relationship but she couldn't get his glittery blondes out of her head. The ones he thought she didn't know about. Lindy, with her nineteen-inch waist, on her hands and knees, rear end to the camera, licking chocolate mousse off the perky sit-up-and-beg breasts of pert little Suki.

She wondered if Greg had noticed the very small zit on Lindy's bum. It was almost tempting to encircle it with a black pen for further reference.

Puerile though it seemed, she was prepared to put up with Greg's celluloid infidelity. As long as this didn't extend to real women, she didn't really mind. It was fantasy, after all. Pure and simple. There was no point in getting all wound up about it.

But what if a real-life glittery blonde crossed his path? A nubile young thing with a pancake-flat stomach, instead of the watermelon that was protruding from Hermione's own. What would he do then?

From the upstairs window, she watched Maud make her way down Amelia Street. A redheaded Olive Oyl, with pigtails and big banana feet. She still walked as though she hadn't quite got used to her legs yet. She was such a sweetie. Perceptive too.

'You might think he's doing something bad again and sling him out. And then we wouldn't see you any more.'

The minute Maud rounded the corner out of sight, Hermione started to turn the house upside down.

She didn't know what she was looking for exactly. Restaurant receipts. Telephone bills. Anything that would prove that Greg wasn't where he'd said he was at any one time. She checked the pockets of suits. His briefcase. Every single drawer he'd ever used. She even checked under the mattress, remembering to say a quick hello to Lindy and Suki as she did so.

Nothing.

Relieved, she flumped on the couch in the sitting room to get her breath back. Thank God.

But wait. She'd missed something. Greg's jacket, hanging on the post at the bottom of her stairs.

Damn!

Her heart clackety-clacking like a pair of castanets, she heaved herself off the sofa and slipped her hand inside the lavender silk-lined pocket.

Bingo!

Seconds later, swamped with guilt at having had such squirmy, suspicious thoughts, she was back on the couch, beaming from ear to ear.

In a tiny dove-grey and pink box in her hand was a pair of the most beautiful earrings she'd ever seen. White-gold chandeliers, studded with diamonds.

Her birthday present!

HARRIET

Harriet found Jesse's key under the flower-pot and stuck it in the front door. The TV was blaring away to itself inside. Jesse must have left it on this morning. Downstairs, she could hear Edie's music. Edie was going through a boy band phase at the moment.

Harriet was still living on a high. Her life finally seemed to be coming together. Jesse was wonderful. She could tell him anything. She thought back to that time at Lizzy's, when Jesse had asked her why she'd chosen to confide in him about her sister. At the time, she'd put it down to the fact that he happened to be there when she was ready. Now, she wasn't so sure. He was so easy to talk to. He never seemed to judge. And he was paying her to do up his flat. It certainly needed doing. And her bank account could do with a boost. It was positively anorexic.

'What colours do you want?' she'd asked him when he'd suggested it.

'Surprise me.' He kissed the top of her head. 'Paint it any colour you want.'

'Really?'

'Really.'

'Sky blue-pink?'

'If you must.'

She'd been joking, of course. But, in the paint shop on Walcot Street, she had spotted a sample pot of lollipop-pink paint that would look great in the bathroom. That room needed urgent treatment. The wallpaper was coming off in lumps. Parts of it were black with mildew. She dreaded to think what lurked beneath the loo.

Today, she'd spent a happy morning choosing colour schemes for the other rooms as well. A dusty grape for the kitchen. Pale buttermilk for the hall. A soft dove-grey, teamed with classy taupe, for Joe's old room. The flat was a blank canvas, just waiting for someone to breathe life back into it. She couldn't wait to get started.

As she stepped into the hall, she was already envisaging it painted in the cool buttery shade she'd got in the paint shop.

There was something on the stairs. Something unfamiliar. A make-up bag, lilac and white striped and covered in drawings of women in Caribbean dress. Spilling from the bag was a glorious hotch-potch of girlie paraphernalia. Pots and tubes. A bright orange scarf. Dozens of Indian gold bangles. A pair of glittery green earrings.

She had a bad feeling about this.

Taking a deep breath, she went into the living room where the TV was still blaring. There, draped across the sofa, wearing a tiny black vest and powder-pink fifties-inspired shorts which left little or nothing to the imagination, was a girl. A girl with legs like a baby llama and a smooth, completely unlined face. A face that was still there in the morning. As Harriet came in, she barely bothered to look up from the TV.

Harriet tried not to gape. Inside, she was shaking like milk. She'd only been apart from Jesse for two nights since they'd got together. The night before her lunch with Lizzy, when she'd just felt like sleeping on her own, and last night, when Jesse had suggested she got her beauty sleep because he had to do a stock take and would only clatter in at three in the morning and wake her.

She shook herself. There had to be some perfectly innocent explanation. Jesse was one of the good guys. He wouldn't do her down. Would he?

The girl slid off the sofa and nonchalantly flipped off the TV. 'Did you want Jesse?'

'Not really,' Harriet said, determined not to let this girl, whoever she was, see how upset she was. 'I'm here to decorate the flat.'

'You Harriet?'

'Yes.'

'Thought so.' The girl smirked.

Harriet bristled. What did she mean by that?

'And you are?'

'Delilah.' Delilah stretched out a hand. 'I stay here sometimes.'

'Sometimes?'

345

'You know.' Delilah winked.

'So . . .' Harriet was unable to help herself. 'So, you and Jesse . . .'

'Me and Jesse what?'

'You're . . .'

Delilah indicated her state of half undress. 'What does it look like?'

'Right.' Harriet tried to ignore the bolt of pain that shot through her windpipe. 'Will you be here when he gets back?'

'It depends.'

'On what?'

'On how long I decide to stay.' The girl examined her nails, which were bare and bitten to the quick. She was very young, Harriet realised with a pang. She couldn't be more than nineteen. Her legs still had the suppleness of youth. There were no wobbly bits. No broken veins feathering out around the knees.

'Did you want me to give him a message?'

'Yes.' Harriet wanted Jesse to know she'd caught him out. 'Yes, I do. Tell him I've changed my mind, can you? Tell him I'm not sure about painting the flat any more. Tell him . . .' She rolled her eyes. 'I don't know. Tell him what you like.'

'Any particular reason?' the girl asked. 'About the flat, I mean.'

'Just tell him it's on account of him being an arsehole,' Harriet said. 'He'll understand.'

HERMIONE

'"The Toronto Islands were not always islands,"' Greg read from the book in his hand. '"They were actually a series of sandbars that originated at the Scarborough Bluffs. They were carried west by the currents." Did you know that, Spike? Maize?'

'I don't think they're listening.' Hermione laughed, as Spike and Maisie bounced like two eager spaniel pups towards the lakeshore. 'They're too excited.'

She loved feeling part of a family again. Granted, it was a disjointed family. She and Greg had to share the kids with his ex. And there were times when she felt guilty about that. But for now she simply allowed ripples of happiness to wash over her as Maud and Greg unloaded the picnic hamper from the back of the Dodge and followed the little ones to the beach.

It was funny to think that, a year ago, she hadn't subscribed to any of this. She'd always thought Josh was enough.

He'd phoned the other day, to tell her he'd heard a rumour about Greg bonking somebody at the Canon Corporation.

347

'I hate to be the bearer of bad news,' he'd said. 'But I've heard it from several sources. You know I wouldn't tell you unless I thought there was some truth in it.'

'It's nice of you to tell me.' Hermione thought of her diamond earrings, secreted in Greg's pocket. 'But you know what a cauldron of gossip that place is. Things between me and Greg have never been better. Honestly.'

She wished Josh didn't have to insist on being the harbinger of doom and gloom as far as Greg was concerned. If he could just see him now, racing Spike and Maisie along the finger of sand that pointed out into the lake, he might think differently. Josh only knew one side of Greg. The corporate side. The married man who'd abandoned his wife and family to go and live with his mistress.

There had been a card from Josh in the mail this morning. A photograph of them both in happier times. She remembered it well. It had been taken on a day trip to Brighton. They'd got the train down there from Victoria one summer, when the temperature had soared and the thought of spending the day in smoggy London had seemed too much to bear. In the photo, they were both laughing and eating candyfloss. She could still remember Josh asking a total stranger to take their picture. He'd told her they were just married and the woman had laughed and said she could tell because they looked so happy together.

Maud, still in the fleece pyjama bottoms and Doctor Marten boots that were a mainstay of her wardrobe, stopped dead on a patch of sand. 'This is a good place. Let's stop here.'

Hermione helped her spread out the picnic rug. She was glad to stop. She got tired so easily these days. Her ankles were swollen nearly all the time now. The skin on her stomach seemed stretched to the limit. Her navel, usually a penny-sized notch, like a gingerbread man's, looked like the flibbery bit on the end of a balloon. Her whole body was looped, like a road map, with thin, greenish-blue veins. Quite apart from anything else, it was becoming quite a struggle to move.

As they ate their picnic, the children gave her presents they'd made themselves. From Maud a bracelet made with glass beads that looked like sweets. She looked on anxiously as Hermione slipped it over her wrist.

'It's a friendship bracelet,' Maud told her. 'In case you're ever far away. It'll remind you of me. Do you think it's pretty?'

'Very pretty,' Hermione said. Maud was such a worrier.

'You know, you remind me of someone.'

'I do?' Maud's eyes sparkled. 'Someone good?'

'My sister,' Hermione told her.

'Harriet?'

'Yep.'

'Did you find her yet?' Spike wanted to know.

'Not yet,' Hermione said.

'You should.' Greg chewed on a piece of grass.

'Look at you.' Hermione teased him affectionately. 'Quite the countryside hick, aren't you?'

Maisie gave her a photo frame, painted black and surrounded with pasta shells, varnished in bright colours and covered in blobs of glitter.

'You can put a picture of us in it,' Maisie said. 'And then we'll always be with you, even when we're at Mom's.'

'I will.' Hermione was touched. 'Thanks, Maize.'

'And I got you this.' Spike opened his sweaty palm. 'It's a bird's egg.'

'Idiot.' Greg reached out to grab it. 'You shouldn't take eggs from nests. It's illegal. You stupid boy. Did you not know that?'

'Hey.' Hermione put a hand on Greg's forearm. 'Come on. He's only six.'

'I didn't take it from any nest.' Spike's lip wobbled. 'I bought it in a store. They put holes in it, see, to blow the yolk out. You've got to be really careful you don't squash it.'

'It's lovely.' Hermione shot Greg a furious look. 'I'll treasure it, Spike. Thank you.'

After lunch, she could see that Spike was still smarting from his father's outburst. She was pretty shocked herself. Where had that flash of temper come from? She didn't like it. She would have said something but she didn't want the day to be spoiled so she suggested that the two of them went off for a walk, while she and the girls looked after the picnic stuff.

'Go on.' She waved them off. 'Go and explore. We'll be all right here, won't we, girls?'

Greg didn't look sure.

'There are some calls I really should make.'

'Too bad,' Hermione said. 'It's my birthday. You have to do as I say.'

'Bloody hell, Hermione.' He almost stomped his foot in the sand. 'It's OK for you. You don't have to . . .'

'What?' Hermione dared him to bring up her unemployed status. 'What don't I have to do?'

'Nothing.' He looked sheepish. 'Forget it. I'm being unfair.'

'Darned right you are.'

'Come on then, squirt.' Greg tugged Spike's hand. 'Let's go see what we can find.'

'Great.' Spike, so easily forgiving, trotted after his dad. 'You think we'll find any water snakes? That'd be so cool . . .'

Hermione lay on her back on the hot sand while Maisie tried, not very successfully, to plait her hair the way Josh always had when she needed to feel calm.

'What do you think Harriet's doing today?' Maud, propped up on her elbows, her bare skin shining, moon-white, in the glare of the sun, asked.

'I don't know,' Hermione said. 'Do you have lotion on?'

'Factor thirty,' Maud said proudly. 'Did it myself.

Maisie's got it too, so you needn't worry. We did it all before we came out, didn't we, Maize?'

Maisie nodded. 'Do you think there will be children to buy your sister presents?' she asked, her pale silver eyes wide with intrigue.

'I expect so.' Hermione smiled, imagining four robust kiddiewinks, pink-cheeked and clad in knobbly knitted jerseys, playing in a garden filled with chimneypots and marigolds. There would be a washing line, perhaps, filled with rows of tiny vests. Inside, Harriet's house would be a tidier version of their mother's. Ruby had loved nice things but she'd never been very house proud. She'd always ridiculed people who were. Once, when they'd gone for tea at Aunt Vinegar's, Hermione had dropped two grains of rice salad on the carpet and Vinegar had gone straight for the Hoover. Ruby had laughed about it all the way home. Harriet had always been a very tidy sort of person.

'So they would be sort of our cousins then,' Maud said.

'Who would?'

'The children,' Maud said simply. 'The children who are giving your sister presents. They'd be our step cousins, wouldn't they?'

'Yes,' Hermione said. 'In a way, I suppose they would.'

'Will we be able to play with them one day?' Maisie stopped plaiting her hair.

'Well . . .' Hermione said. 'I guess that depends.'

'On what?'

'On whether I can find my sister.'

'You have to.' Maisie blinked. 'I mean, Maud isn't even my whole sister. But I'll always know her. I'm gonna speak to her every day of my whole life. Even if I'm a top explorer and I have to go to the jungle on a secret mission. I'll just get a cell phone.'

'Thanks, Maize.' Maud smiled.

Hermione struggled to sit up, which wasn't easy, considering her tummy was like an Edam cheese.

'What do you mean?' she asked. 'Maud isn't your whole sister?'

'We're half-sisters.' Maud said. 'Dad isn't really my dad.'

'Not bio-lo-gickly speaking.' Maisie pronounced the word carefully. 'But we'll always be friends. Won't we, Maud?'

'Course.'

Hermione shook her head as if to try and shake water out of her ears. She had a vague feeling that Maud not being Greg's biological daughter should mean something to her. But she couldn't think what it was.

'It doesn't make any difference,' Maisie said, 'us only being halves. Do you think our new cousins will mind being steps?'

'I don't know,' Hermione said.

'Can you not just ask them?' Maisie's breath was hot on her neck, her pink tongue poking out of the side of her mouth with concentration as she had another go at the plait she'd been working on for ages now.

'Well . . .' Hermione began. 'It isn't as simple as . . .'

'I could show them how to play horseshoes,' Maisie chirruped happily. 'Would they like that, d'you think?'

'Is there no way you can contact Harriet?' Maud picked at the frayed end of her bootlace. 'Think how cool it would be if you just called, out of the blue, on her birthday.'

'She's probably thinking about you anyway,' Maisie said staunchly. 'I know I'd be thinking about Maud if it was her birthday and she was away. I'd still make her a cake.'

'That's nice, sweetheart.'

'I might bake her those cookies we made with you one time,' Maisie said. 'The ones with Reese's Pieces in. Do you think your sister bakes cookies with her children?'

'Oh yes.' Hermione imagined Harriet presiding over a row of chocolate-covered faces. 'I'm quite sure she does.'

'There must be someone,' Maud urged her. 'There can't be nobody left on the planet who knows where your sister is.'

'You're right,' Hermione said. 'Maud, you're a genius. I know exactly how to find out where my sister is.'

She rummaged through her capacious handbag until she found what she was looking for. A battered silver address book. Ruby's. She'd taken it when she left the house on Belmont, just in case.

She still couldn't believe she'd left Harriet all alone like that. It wasn't surprising she'd never bothered to get in touch. She must have felt so alone. So abandoned.

Pip's number was scribbled in lavender ink in the top corner of the back cover. Ruby had always written in brightly coloured ink. Pink. Carmine. Jade. It was what had given Hermione the idea to write in peacock blue. It was her signature colour, if you like. It was a habit she had yet to break.

Holding the page open with one hand, she looked again in her bag.

'Bugger.'

'What's up?' Maud asked.

'I've left my phone at home.'

'No problem,' Maud said. 'Have mine.'

'I don't know,' Hermione said. 'It'll cost a lot. I'm calling Ibiza.'

'Mom put a load of credit on it,' Maud explained, her eyes shining. 'She likes us to be safe. Go on.'

'Are you sure?'

'Sure.' Maud laughed, wrinkling her nose up so all the freckles joined together in a rusty mass.

'It's a long shot,' Hermione confided. 'This person might not even be there any more.'

'What person?' Maisie wanted to know.

'My Aunt Pip,' Hermione told her. 'I'm supposed to contact her every year to let her know I'm OK. So is Harriet. She made us promise.'

'SO CALL HER,' Maud and Maisie yelled in unison.

'OK.'

Hermione dialled Pip's number in Ibiza. If – and it was a big if – she was still there, she would be amused to hear from her after all this time. Pip had always said Hermione was the most like her of anybody in the family. They both got the same itchy feet. That same urge to travel. Hermione could remember her coming back from India once. She couldn't have been more than seven or eight. But she could still picture Pip as she'd been when she'd come to stay that time. She'd dressed in bright saris. Lots of orange, purple and jade, splashed with gold. Her thin brown arms had jingled with bangles and there had been a tiny diamond stud in her nose.

She wondered what Pip looked like now.

'Hello?'

The voice startled her.

'Pip?'

'Yes.' Pip's unmistakable voice crackled like a bonfire over a thousand miles of ether. 'Who's this?'

'It's Hermione,' Hermione said. 'Your niece.'

'About time too,' Pip whip-cracked. 'You're a naughty girl. Every year, I said. Your poor mother would be spinning in her grave. Leave it in the refrigerator.'

'What?'

'Sorry,' Pip said. 'That's Antonio. He's been out milking the goat. He'll make an honest woman of me yet.' She crackled with laughter.

'You've got a man?' Hermione was surprised.

'I have,' Pip said. 'But enough about me. What about you? Where are you? How are you?'

'I'm fine,' Hermione said. 'Pregnant.'

'You're never.'

'Yes,' Hermione told her. 'Almost eight months now.'

'Well, you look after yourself,' Pip said. 'And make sure you keep me up to date in the future. I want photos, mind.'

'OK.'

'Promise?'

'Promise.

'Good girl.' Pip inhaled sharply, probably smoking a cigarette. That was another thing she and Hermione had always had in common. 'Now. What can I do for you?'

'I wondered . . .' Hermione hesitated. 'Do you still hear from Harriet?'

'Of course I do,' Pip said. 'She was always such a good girl. Sends me a card every year, she does. Prints her number on the back. You know Harriet. Hold on. Here.' She read out a number preceded by a Bath code.

'Does she ask about me?'

'You two still haven't made things up then,' Pip said. 'You know your father would be unhappy. It would make them both unhappy to know you'd been fighting all this time. They loved you both so much.'

'I'm going to call her,' Hermione said.

'Good girl,' Pip said. 'Life's too short. You never know what's around the corner. You of all people should know that.'

'I will,' Hermione said. 'Speak to you soon, Pip.'

'As soon as ever you like,' Pip said warmly. 'And don't forget to send me those photos. It's the old address. If you call to let me know to expect them, I'll make sure the goats don't eat them.'

Hermione clicked off Maud's phone and turned to the girls, who were both looking at her with bated breath.

'Did you get it?' Maud's eyes sparkled.

'Yes,' Hermione said.

'Are you going to call?'

'Yes.' She looked at Maud. 'It's a bit . . . I wonder if you could . . .'

'Sure.' Maud leapt to her feet. 'C'mon, Maisie. Let's go look for eager beavers.'

'But we never saw a beaver in Lake Ontario,' Maisie protested.

'Ice creams then.' Maud winked at Hermione. 'I'll buy you one.'

'Turtles?'

'Done.'

It was now or never.

Hermione stared at Maud's phone, which was covered in glittery stickers and dangling ornaments and, with trembling hands, dialled the number Pip had given her.

It was ringing.

It rang three times.

Four.

She imagined her sister stopping whatever it was she was doing and going to answer it. Wiping flour from her hands onto her apron perhaps. Lifting a child out of the bath, just to be on the safe side.

The phone rang and rang.

There was always the possibility that Harriet was at work.

Eventually, the line clicked into automated voicemail and a haughty female voice welcomed her to BT Answer One Five One.

Hermione hesitated. Did she leave a message and risk it being heard by the wrong person? If she did that and the call was never returned, she would never know why.

Then again, if she didn't leave a message . . .

Somewhere, deep inside her, her baby kicked, as if to urge her to just do it.

'Er. Hi.' She blurted it out before she got cold feet. 'I'm trying to reach Harriet Harker. This is Hermione Harker.'

She hesitated. She sounded idiotic.

Maud's face, stern and freckled, loomed large in her mind and she pressed on.

'I'm calling to wish you a happy birthday. And to tell you that you're going to be an aunty shortly. At least . . . I sincerely hope it's going to be shortly. I'm absolutely enormous. If I get any bigger I won't be able to get out of bed . . .'

She sounded mad as a box of frogs, she realised. When Harriet heard this, she would probably conclude that her sister had finally lost her marbles and stay well away. And who could blame her?

'Anyway,' she said. 'I don't expect to hear from you but if you would like to get in touch, then . . . well . . . that might be nice.'

She sounded like Bridget Jones now. Still, she'd started, so she might as well finish.

'I'm living in Canada at the moment. Toronto. I know you were never one for big cities. But I think you might like it here. And it would be nice . . .' She hesitated. 'If you came for a visit. It would be nice to see you. We'd all like to see you.'

She'd just hung up when Greg returned with all three children. He looked so fit and handsome, bounding up the beach. She wished she had his energy. It would be a relief when the baby came and she could get back to normal.

'There are more presents.' Spike's eyes shone, bright as apple pips.

'Yes,' Greg said. 'But there is one present I want to give Hermione on her own, if you three would be so kind as to go play on the tyres for a bit. Is that OK?'

'OK.' Maud nodded. 'I'll keep an eye on them.'

'Good girl.' Greg patted the top of her head.

As they watched the children barrelling towards the tyre swings at the edge of the lake, Greg slid his arm round her waist and kissed her on the cheek. He smelt of ginger cake from being outside in the sun with Spike. Hermione thought of the earrings and realised she hadn't been this happy in ages.

She'd finally plucked up the courage to do something she should have done years ago. On top of that, she was expecting a baby with a man who loved her. She had three wonderful step kids. Even Josh, the only grey cloud scudding across her perfect blue sky, had remembered her birthday.

'So.' Greg patted Hermione's tummy gently. 'You want your present now?'

'Yes please.' Hermione clapped her hands together.

'OK,' Greg said. 'Close your eyes and hold out your hands.'

Hermione obeyed, remembering, for some bizarre reason, a time when she'd instructed Harriet to do the same. Poor Harriet, thinking she was in for some sort of treat, had eagerly spread out her palms, only for Hermione to drop a wriggling daddy longlegs into her hands. Harriet had been terrified.

God. What a bitch!

She wondered whether she'd got her message yet. If she had, what was she thinking?

'There.'

'Can I open them now?'

'Sure.'

The box was much larger than she remembered. Cunning. He'd obviously played that box within a box trick. Isaac had done that once, when he'd bought her a watch for Christmas, enjoying the fleeting disappointment on her face when she clocked the huge gift, and the obvious delight when she'd unwrapped layer after layer to discover the slim silver timepiece within.

'Do I get to open it now?'

'Of course.'

She scrabbled at the gold paper with her hands, surprised as just the one layer came away to reveal a long, flat box.

'Open it.'

She levered off the lid and delved into the layers of scarlet tissue within, her face clouding with confusion as she pulled out a pair of red and black crotchless knickers, complete with matching bra and suspender belt. The knickers especially were like something one of his secret glittery blondes would wear. Thin black nylon, with a slutty red frill around the split crotch.

'Underwear!' She could hardly mask her disappointment.

He must have changed his mind. He must have taken the earrings back to the shop.

'Do you like it?' Greg looked pleased with himself.

'It's . . . lovely.'

'I knew it was you,' Greg said. 'The moment I saw it.'

'It's too small.'

'That's the point.' Greg skimmed his forefinger over her thigh. 'It's for when the baby's here. I thought it would spice things up a bit.'

'Oh.'

'You like them, don't you?'

'Of course,' Hermione said. 'I love them. They're very sexy.'

'Sexy!' Greg said. 'That's what I thought.' Slowly, he ran his fingers further up her thigh until they brushed the silk of her knickers.

'*Greg*!' Hermione couldn't help feeling pleased.

'What?' Greg's breath was coming in rough gasps as he unzipped his fly.

'The kids,' she said. 'Someone might see.'

'They're miles away,' he grunted. 'And nobody else is looking.'

'But . . .'

'I want you,' Greg growled. 'Please, Hermione.'

His fingers eased the knickers she was wearing to one side and – oh so gently – brushed the tight bud of her clitoris, making her twitch with desire. She wanted him too. So much. It was such a relief to know he still found her attractive. Suddenly, the slutty underwear didn't matter. She didn't even care that he'd bought it several sizes too small on purpose. She just wanted to feel him inside her.

'Sit on top of me,' Greg ordered. 'Pull your skirt down so it . . . Oh. Oh God. That's it.'

It was over in seconds. But it was long enough. Hermione had come so hard she was left shaking like a leaf. They'd only just had time to rearrange themselves when Spike came thundering back up the beach.

'Hey, Dad.' He wheeled like a seagull. 'Can we give her our present now?'

'Your present?' Hermione asked. 'You already gave me a present. My egg.'

'We got you a special present,' Spike panted. 'From all of us. Can we, Dad? Can we?'

Hermione's spirits lifted. Even during the sex, those ear-rings had been playing on her mind. She hadn't been able to shift the thought that they might have been for somebody else. Somebody secret.

After all, she'd been his secret once.

'Of course.' Greg beamed. 'Did you think that was all you were getting?'

Hermione grinned with relief. He'd been teasing her. The underwear was a joke. She might have known. Even Greg wouldn't buy her something so . . . well . . . *obvious.*

'I wouldn't just buy you sexy underwear!' Greg grinned.

'You wouldn't?' *Thank God.*

'Of course not. Not when you're expecting my child.'

Hermione's heart soared like a kestrel.

'Spike,' Greg said, as Maud and Maisie appeared from nowhere. 'Do the honours.'

'Close your eyes,' Spike said.

Hermione did as she was told. She was sure she must still be flushed from the knee-trembling orgasm she'd just had. It didn't seem quite right, somehow, to have done it while the children were so close by. Especially Maud. But . . .

'There.'

She closed her fingers round a small box, about the same size as the one she'd found in his jacket pocket.

'Open them,' Maisie squeaked.

There in her hands lay the dove-grey and dusky pink box. Hermione hesitated for a moment. She wanted to make sure she looked appropriately surprised. It would spoil it for them all if they knew she'd been peeking. Greg would want to know why she'd gone through his pockets in the first place. And it wouldn't do to admit that, even for the maddest of funny five minuteses, she hadn't trusted him.

'Open it.'

Hermione did so, pulling out a layer of tissue to reveal the silver rattle within.

'Oh.'

'Look.' Spike picked it up and shook it. 'It jingles. Isn't it great?'

'Fantastic.'

'We knew you'd love it,' Maud said.

'Do you think Spiderman will love it too?' Spike asked.

'That's what he wants to call our new baby when he arrives,' Maisie added helpfully.

'Oh,' Hermione said, as her heart went kerplunk with disappointment over the lost earrings. 'Yes. I'm sure Spiderman will love it.'

TWINS

Harriet spent her birthday alone, the piece of paper with Sylvie's number on it forgotten in the pocket of her jeans as she lay, like a sausage roll in her duvet, with just the top of her head poking out. The fact that Jesse had turned out to be another Will, utterly incapable of encountering a beautiful girl without doing something about it, made her blood boil. She wanted nothing more to do with him.

Which pretty much left her with nobody.

Even Lizzy had forgotten her birthday. In fact, she hadn't heard much from Lizzy at all. Not since that day at Blue Ginger, when she had told her she'd been seeing Will.

It just went to show. You couldn't rely on anyone but yourself.

For days now she'd been in the sort of fragile state that had her bumping into things and then crying because she'd bumped into them. She hadn't been out of the flat except to feed Leroy. Edie, with her new-found lease of life, had gone on a coach tour of Russia and left her in charge. She hadn't fed him at all today. She'd tried. But she'd heard Jesse and the girl on the stairs as she'd been about to go out. She couldn't face them.

She should have seen it coming, of course. Jesse was far too good-looking to be reliable. She'd thought she was safe. Just as she had with Dan. Perhaps, with Dan, she had been. Perhaps Lizzy was right. Perhaps he had come to Blue Ginger that night to say he wanted to come back. They might have been together now if it hadn't been for bloody Will.

And bloody Jesse.

She hated being alone on her birthday. At home, as kids, they'd always made such a big thing about birthdays. There had been special breakfasts and treasure hunts. Parties, when they were tiny, with magicians and wobbly jellies. This had to be the worst birthday since her eighteenth, when she'd caught Will snogging Hermione's face off at the bottom of the garden. This year, there had been no treats. Lizzy, it seemed, had forgotten her birthday altogether. Dan was clearly too busy with his new love. The only person who had even tried to contact her was Jesse. And he'd been trying to call her every hour for the past seven days, so he didn't count.

She'd given up even listening to his messages. She was sick of listening to him try to 'explain'. What was to explain? She'd invested all her trust and belief in Jesse and he'd gone and thrown it away. She hated him for being so weak.

She waited until she heard the front door bang

and peeped behind the curtain to watch him walk in the direction of Blue Ginger. Then she sneaked downstairs to feed Leroy, enjoying, for a fleeting moment, the physical contact of his tail whipping against her knees as he demonstrated his obvious pleasure at seeing his bowl filled with meaty chunks, glistening with jelly. As he bent to eat, still purring like a motorbike, she patted the sleek Egyptian head and went back up to the flat to wallow in self-pity once more.

The red light was blinking on the answer phone.

Her finger hovered over the erase button. She didn't want to hear any more of Jesse's wheedling excuses.

But what if it wasn't Jesse? What if it was someone calling to wish her a happy birthday? Dan, for instance. Lizzy might not have had it right when she'd said he'd got himself somebody new. Even if he had, he might still want to wish her a happy birthday. He was nice like that.

She wished he was here now. He might not have been her soul mate but at least he'd always been there for her.

She pressed the play button.

'Hi.'

The voice was uncertain at first. But there was no mistaking it. Harriet's heart bobbed like a Halloween apple as she listened to a voice that was still as familiar to her as breathing. She could hear it, soaring high above the others in the playground in a jumble of long-forgotten rhymes.

'*Crocodile, crocodile, may we cross the water? Om pom poodle. Whirly whirly whisky. One banana. Two banana. You're OUT.*'

And now. Hermione at thirty-three.

'I'm calling to wish you a happy birthday. And to tell you that you're going to be an aunty shortly. At least . . . I sincerely hope it's going to be shortly. I'm absolutely enormous. If I get any bigger I won't be able to get out of bed . . .'

She listened to the end of the message, then rewound the tape and listened to it again, tears pouring her face. Somehow, despite everything, her sister had managed to phone her when she most needed it. She'd been at her lowest ebb this morning. She'd never felt more alone.

She cried for ten minutes and then had a good old blow of her nose. It was obvious what she had to do. She had to call her sister back. She had to tell her she'd been thinking about her too. She supposed she ought to confess to reading the diary as well. It was only fair.

But at least – and her spirits soared like a kite at this – at least she knew now. She could stop worrying. Hermione still wanted to see her. After everything she'd said.

She was just about to pick up the phone to call the number her sister had left, when it rang. Instinctively, she picked it up, then wished she hadn't.

'OK,' Jesse said. 'I haven't been entirely truthful—'

'I don't want to hear it, Jesse.'

'But it's not what you think,' Jesse said. 'Honestly. If you'd just let me—'

'You're starting to sound like a broken record now,' Harriet said.

'But—'

'Goats butt, Jesse. Please get off the line, will you? I have better things to do than listen to you.'

A thousand miles away in Toronto, Hermione was dreaming she'd given birth to a pig. A Gloucester Old Spot, by the looks of him, splotched pink and chocolate and with a squirly-whirly tail. In the dream, it hadn't seemed like a big deal. The doctor, masked and gowned in a colour she would have described as Prussian Blue, seemed to think it was all very run of the mill as he wrapped the piglet up and handed it over. Then, just as Hermione thought things couldn't get any worse, Maisie, in her drum majorette's outfit, and Spike, in scarlet soldier's uniform complete with fuzzy black busby, marched in, clashing cymbals and shrilling on whistles.

'Stop!' Hermione shrieked. 'Stop it. Can't you see? My pig's trying to sleep.'

She shot up, covered in a thin film of sweat, only to find herself alone, safe in Amelia Street and still pregnant, hopefully with a human baby. And the noise she could hear wasn't a whistle after all. It was the phone.

Groaning, she got up to answer it. It was probably

Greg, calling to say he was on his way home from dropping the kids off. She hoped everything was OK. She was worried Spike might have got a bit sunburnt. She'd tried to keep him covered up. But he'd kept squiggling away.

It wasn't Greg. It was Celine. She sounded a bit odd.

'Hiya,' Hermione said, aware that her voice was gluggy with sleep. She'd conked out as soon as she got back. The day had worn her out. And the business of the earrings was still whirring through her mind. The seeds of fear, planted in her mind by Celine and then Maud, had grown shoots. Perhaps he was being unfaithful. Perhaps . . .

'Sorry,' Celine said. 'Did I wake you?'

'It's OK,' Hermione said. 'I'm awake now. How are you?'

'Not too bad. I got an interview for a job.'

'That's great. I didn't know you wanted to get back to work.'

'Spur of the moment decision,' Celine said. 'I've been drawing a lot lately. Thought I might as well put it to good use. It's for book jackets downtown.'

'Congratulations. I'm really pleased for you.'

'Thanks. Anyway, that wasn't why I called.'

'Oh?'

'Doh. I wanted to wish you a happy birthday.'

'Thanks.' Hermione couldn't remember having told Celine it was her birthday. After all, she wasn't at the age where you expected cake and balloons from your friends. Still, she supposed she must have. Perhaps last week, when Harriet had been on her mind a lot. She must have mentioned it then. 'That's so sweet. Thank you.'

'No problem. Coffee's on me next time, OK?'

'Great,' Hermione said. 'Good luck with the interview.'

'Thanks.'

She'd just put the phone down when it rang in her hand, making her jump.

She almost ignored it. The question of the diamond earrings was still bugging her. She didn't feel like talking. But something compelled her to snatch up the phone nonetheless.

'Yup'

'Hello?' The voice was timid. 'Hermione?'

'Oh my God,' Hermione said. 'Harry? Is that you?'

'Yes.' Harriet's voice caught in her throat. 'It's me.'

Hermione suddenly found she couldn't speak. A huge achy rush had filled her throat. Tears stung her eyes. The words wouldn't come.

'H-h-miney?' Harriet sounded as though she might be sobbing too. 'It's really you?'

'Yes.' Hermione took a deep, shaky breath. 'It's really me.'

'Thank goodness.' Harriet burst into tears. 'I really . . .'

'Go on,' Hermione said. 'It's OK.'

'I just needed to hear your voice,' Harriet said.

'Ditto,' Hermione told her.

'Did you mean it? About me coming over?'

'Yes.' Hermione's heart offered itself up in a silent Hallelujah. 'Yes, I did.'

'And I'm really going to be an aunty soon?'

'I sure hope so,' Hermione said. 'At the moment, I can't imagine this ever ending. I'm like the side of a house.'

'Wow, though.'

'I know. It's mad. I still can't quite believe it myself.'

'So when can I come?'

'Whenever you like. Come tomorrow. Or the next day. Come whenever you can. Just come.'

HARRIET

The silver nose cone of the Boeing 747 pointed skywards and the plane soared into the clouds, leaving Harriet's tummy balled in a tight knot on the tarmac below.

It was too late to back out now.

She was on her way!

After speaking to Hermione – a surreal, emotionally charged experience – she'd phoned Soo, whose husband ran a small travel agency in Guildford, and asked her to book her on the first available flight to Toronto.

She'd spent a fortune in the duty free shop. Shopping in the light, bright environment had helped take her mind off the flight. She'd always hated flying, ever since the first time, on a family trip to Scotland. Pip had been living in a flat in Edinburgh at the time and Isaac had thought it might be fun to visit her there during the festival. As the plane took off, she'd chirruped nonstop to cover her nerves. Hermione, who had been desperately excited at the idea of flying, had put a hand on her arm and said, 'Can you please be quiet, Harry. This is my first flight.'

The plane banked west, sending the carrier bags at her feet skittering in all directions. One eschewed its contents completely, sending them sliding under the seats all around her. Cellophane-wrapped boxes of perfume and body lotion. Glossy magazines for the journey. A box of chocolate Brazil nuts went rolling towards the cabin and the tiny cardigan she'd bought in Monsoon for the new baby got hooked on the expensive-looking suit of the man next to her.

'Here.' He handed her the cardigan and bent to retrieve a glossy crimson and white box from the aisle, as people around her popped up like Jack-in-the-boxes, holding aloft an assortment of Body Shop comestibles.

'Clarins bust-firming gel,' he read. 'Interesting.'

'It's for my sister.' Embarrassed, Harriet snatched it back.

Hermione had provided her with such a long list of things to bring over from England that Harriet had found herself wondering what her sister was looking forward to most. Marmite or her?

As the seat belt light above their heads went out, Harriet found herself worrying again. It was becoming her specialty. Nevertheless, she'd whacked a flight costing just shy of seven hundred pounds on her credit card even though she had absolutely no money in the bank to pay it back, especially now that Jesse wouldn't be paying her to paint the flat.

She had absolutely no idea what awaited her at the other end of this flight either. Would there be a Waltons-style reunion? Or would they be more like the Simpsons? Things were bound to be a bit stilted. She had a lot of explaining to do.

And then there had been that phone call. One more thing to worry about. It had come just twenty minutes before her flight was due to be called, as she paid for a bottle of Evian and a Chapstick in Boots. Cursing, she'd handed the till woman a tenner, ignoring the filthy look she got in return for answering her mobile mid-transaction.

'Hello?'

The call was from Lizzy's mobile phone but it wasn't Lizzy's voice that asked if she was Harriet Harker.

'This is Chloe,' the voice on the other end informed her.

'Chloe?' She didn't know any Chloe.

An image of the girl on Jesse's sofa popped into her head. Was this her? Was she Chloe? If so, what the hell did she think she was doing?

'Has something happened to Jesse?' Harriet asked without thinking. Get a grip, she told herself. Why would that girl be using Lizzy's mobile? And why should she worry about Jesse? He was out of her life now.

'Jesse?' The voice was confused. 'Who's Jesse?'

'Never mind. I thought—' She was being dim. Jessie's bit of fluff was Delilah. She'd said so herself.

'You might know me as Crack Nanny.' The voice on the other end of the phone sounded worried. 'Although I swear I am off the crack now.'

'I'm sorry,' Harriet said. 'I didn't know your name was Chloe. Is everything all right?'

'I'm not sure. Is Mrs Armstrong Jones with you?'

'No. Why?'

'She hasn't come home.'

'Since when?' Harriet thought she could hear her flight being called over the tannoy.

'Since she went out at lunchtime and said she'd be back at four.'

Harriet looked at her watch. 'But it's six o'clock. Where's Conrad?'

'He's in Leeds,' Chloe said. 'On a course or something.'

'What about Conrad's mother? You could try her.'

'I don't think Mrs Armstrong Jones would like that,' Chloe said.

This was true, Harriet realised. The last thing Lizzy would want was being outed as a Bad Mother in front of the in-laws.

'She'll probably be home soon,' Harriet said kindly. 'Try not to worry.'

'I wouldn't usually,' Chloe said. 'She's been doing this sort of thing quite a bit. One night, she didn't get home until five in the morning. But there's something wrong with Lucy.'

'What do you mean?' Harriet's heart bopped.

'She's burning up. And she's just been sick. Like, really sick. And she's gone all floppy.'

'Right.' Harriet tried to think quickly.

'Can you come?' Chloe asked desperately.

'Not really,' Harriet said. 'I'm at the airport. I'm supposed to be boarding a flight to Canada in ten minutes.'

'Oh God.' Chloe started to panic. 'What am I going to do?'

'Where are the other kids?'

'Upstairs,' Chloe said. 'They're upset. They want their mum.'

'Can you drive?' Harriet asked her. 'Is Lizzy's car there?'

'Yes, and yes. But I've had three Archers. You won't tell, will you?' she asked anxiously. 'I'm not supposed to drink while I'm in charge of the kids.'

'I think that's the least of your worries,' Harriet told her. The poor girl was only eighteen. She couldn't believe Lizzy had just gone off and left her with her beloved kids.

Bloody Will. This had his stamp all over it. Clearly, Lizzy had disregarded her advice completely. She was still sneaking off to see him when Conrad was at work.

'What shall I do?' Chloe sounded on the verge of tears.

Harriet thought laterally. There was only one thing she could do. And there was only one stick of battery left on her phone. She was going to have to act quickly.

'Hold on.' She hurried to the public phone on the concourse and dialled Dan's surgery. She wasn't quite sure how pleased he would be to hear from her. But he was Dan. The one person she knew she could rely on. She'd been crazy to let him slip through her fingers so easily. She knew that now.

'St Catherine's Surgery. Can I help you?'

'Dan Collyer please.'

'He's with a patient at the moment. Can I help?'

'I really need to speak to him.'

'I'm afraid that's not possible.'

'Just try,' Harriet pleaded. 'Please. Tell him it's his wife. And it's an emergency.'

'Are you still there, Chloe?' She spoke into her mobile phone.

'I'm here.'

A second later, she was connected.

'Harry!' Dan sounded worried. 'Are you all right?'

'I'm fine,' Harriet told him.

'Thank God,' Dan said. 'I was worried. I thought . . . well, never mind what I thought. I'm sorry about not having called,' he began. 'Things have been a bit—'

'It's OK.' Harriet explained the situation as quickly as she could, grateful when Dan's voice switched over to his efficient doctor mode. There wasn't time for regrets. Not when Lucy's life very possibly hung in the balance. Lizzy would never forgive herself if anything happened to her daughter. And Conrad would never forgive Lizzy. They might not survive this. And they had to. They just had to. If only to spite Will bloody Cartwright.

379

'Does she have a rash?'

'Chloe? Does she have a rash?'

'I don't know.'

'She doesn't know.'

'Tell her to look on the chest.'

'Look on Lucy's chest, Chloe.'

'Hold on.' There was a rustling sound as Chloe put the receiver down then the sound of her voice again as she came back on.

'Yes. There's a rash.'

'There's a rash.'

'Tell her to roll a glass over it.'

'Can you roll a glass over it, Chloe?'

'I've only got a shot glass.' Chloe said. 'Will that do?'

'I'm sure any glass will be fine.'

'I've done it.'

'She's done it.'

'Did it disappear?'

'Did it disappear?'

'No.'

'No.'

'Right,' Dan said briskly. 'Tell her not to wait for an ambulance. Tell her to get her straight to a hospital.'

'She can't drive.'

'Then tell her . . . Oh, SOD it,' he said. 'Tell her I'll call an ambulance. And, just in case, I'll go over there.'

'Are you sure? Will you get there in time?'

'It's not too far,' Dan said. 'It won't take me any

longer than an ambulance. I might even get there faster.'

'Thanks, Dan.' Harriet was filled with relief. 'I owe you one.' The final call for her flight came over the tannoy.

'You're welcome,' he said. 'And Harry?'

'Yes?'

'Take care of yourself.'

As the plane levelled out at thirty thousand feet, Harriet tried to put the thought that she was hurtling through the air in a pressurised canister to the back of her mind. Which was easier than it sounded. Especially when terrible images of Lucy lying dead in a hospital bed kept racing around her brain. What if something happened to her while she, Harriet, was blithely flying across the Atlantic in search of . . . what, exactly? Lizzy wouldn't be able to get hold of her. She'd be frantic.

She closed her eyes and breathed a silent prayer for Lucy.

Harriet was actually afraid of flying. It wasn't so much being high up in the air as the thought that she wasn't in control of the plane.

Perhaps it would help if she tried to imagine she was.

She'd already scanned the cabin for likely terror-ists. She felt bad doing it. But there was a shifty-looking man by the emergency exit she wasn't quite sure about. Although that was a copy of Jilly

Cooper's *Rivals* he held in his hand. Hardly the Koran.

She focused on steering the plane straight ahead in her mind. If she could just imagine she was flying it all the way across the sea, everything would be OK. All she had to do was keep her mind firmly on the . . .

Before she knew it, the drone of the plane's engines had lulled her into a deep sleep. The sun was coming up when she eventually woke. Through the tiny porthole window she could see the navy blue sky, shot with dazzling streaks of colour. Gold. Crimson. Bright marmalade. Deep tangerine. She was safe. The plane hadn't dropped like a clay pigeon from the sky after all. She was going to survive this.

They must be nearly there.

Her mind wobbled as she thought of Lucy. Hopefully, they would have managed to get hold of Lizzy by now. They would all be at the hospital being told it was a false alarm.

She remembered Lizzy, when Jemima was born, saying that holding her for the first time had been like nothing else in the world. 'Can't you feel it?' she asked, as Harriet held the child woodenly. 'Watch her head.'

At the time, all Harriet had felt was a dead arm from trying desperately not to let Jemima's head loll. Now, though, now that she knew a family baby was expected, she couldn't help wondering if the feeling Lizzy had talked about applied to extended family members. Would Hermione's baby feel like family? Or was that just for mothers? Something she herself would never be.

The pilot's voice crackled over the loudspeaker system to tell them that the plane had begun its descent into Toronto Pearson airport. As they got lower and lower, Harriet's ears popped and her stomach lurched with nerves. She was so apprehensive, she realised, that her joints were in spasm. Her wrists were twitching.

What if Hermione was completely unrecognisable to her? What if she, Harriet, no longer knew what made her tick. She knew nothing about her sister any more. She didn't know what sort of house she lived in. What did the air smell like in her street? Was it choked with traffic fumes, like the narrow bottlenecks of Bath? Could you smell the tang of toothpaste and bonfires on the air when the nights drew in and autumn crept up? Or was Toronto totally different?

She didn't even know if her sister was married. Presumably there was a partner, because of the baby. But she hadn't even thought to ask his name.

The plane bumped and dipped through pillows of cloud. As they came into still, clear air again, the sun made an appearance, rinsing the whole sky in a pure lemony light.

They banked to the west. Suddenly, Harriet saw it. A vast expanse of water, stretching as far as the eye could see.

Lake Ontario, glittering in the morning sunshine.

There was the CN Tower. Next to it, the SkyDome, crouched like an armadillo on the shoreline. And somewhere down in that vast city by the lake was her sister.

Harriet stretched in her seat, arching her back like a cat. A frisson of anticipation of the sort that comes with early starts and new places rippled through her. So what if it didn't work out? So what if she and Hermione had nothing in common any more? They might be tearing each other's hair out by the end of the day. Hermione could well lean over and pinch her, as she'd done in the bath when they were small, leaving a perfect crescent-shaped scar on Harriet's cheek. But did it really matter? At least they would have tried.

She tried to remember the times they'd been closest. Summer holidays, probably, when they were very young. After they moved to Bath, the whole family had packed into the peppermint-blue Cortina they'd had then and taken off somewhere for two weeks every August. Back to Cornwall, where they'd grown up. Devon. The Norfolk Broads. Once, they had got a ferry to France. Harriet remembered a swimming pool: a vast oblong of pure azure. Stubby bottles of beer. Huge peaches oozing golden juice. French children, spinning on the roundabouts in the play area, wearing dusty clogs on their feet.

The plane rolled on its final approach to the airport and Harriet rested her head on her upright seat back and let go.

384

At the carousel, she hoyed her bag, which bulged at the sides like a banana, onto a trolley. Her mobile rang. She checked the screen to see who it was and saw Jesse's name flash up.

She dropped the call and pushed her trolley through the sliding glass doors into the arrivals hall, blinking like a mole in the bright lights as she looked for the sister she hadn't seen in fifteen years.

HERMIONE

It was only once you'd started cleaning, Hermione decided as she scrubbed the skirting boards with an old toothbrush, that you realised exactly how disgustingly dirty a place could get. She might have been nesting for the past few months, but there were bits she'd missed. In the morning sunlight, the big bay window in the sitting room looked awfully smeary. The light switches were filthy. Dust motes danced in the coloured slices of light that filtered through the panels of stained glass in the front door. She was going to have to Hoover again.

As she scrubbed, Greg came downstairs, streaming an assortment of ties behind him.

'Do you think this one?' He held up a pale lemon kipper concocted from raw silk. 'Or the Paul Smith? I can't decide.'

'Does it matter?'

'Of course it matters,' he said irritably. 'It's the first day of the sales conference. I'm the marketing director. Do you want me to look as though I've crawled out of a garbage bin?'

She wasn't sure if she was just noticing it more

386

since he'd snapped at poor Spike over the bird's egg but Greg definitely seemed more irritable these past couple of days. Hermione wasn't quite sure how he did it but he managed to make her feel as though she was imposing on his privacy every time she asked him a question. It didn't even matter what the question was. It could be anything. What did he feel like doing for supper? What time would he be back? How long would he be in San Francisco for the sales conference, because Harriet was coming over from England and she really wanted him to meet her?

Greg pulled on his jacket. The same jacket in which, just a week or so ago, Hermione had found the diamond earrings she'd assumed were for her. She longed to march over to him to see whether or not the dusky pink and grey box, tied with pink velvet ribbon, was still there. If it wasn't meant for somebody else, why take it all the way to San Francisco?

Greg was ready. As Hermione handed him his bag, he skim-kissed her cheek and patted the giant watermelon of her tummy.

'Look after yourselves.'

'We will.'

Hermione longed for him to pull her towards him in a desperate, passionate clinch as he'd done just two days ago at the lakeside. But he didn't. He picked up his bag and walked out into the sunshine, his shiny shoes tapping the sidewalk as he made his way to his waiting cab.

When his car had pulled away, she stood at the front door in the Chinese silk kimono that always made her think of Josh because he'd coveted it so. Perhaps Josh was right. Perhaps Greg wasn't the man for her after all.

She didn't really want to ponder the significance of the earrings too much. Perhaps, when the baby came, things would change for the better again. They said all newborns looked like their fathers for the first year of their lives. She'd read that in her book. It was nature's way of ensuring the male parent stuck around or something. Which, whether you liked it or not, did hint at the male's predilection for variety.

Perhaps it was inevitable then. Perhaps it was only a matter of time before Greg strayed. Perhaps they all did it.

The air was filled with the promise of a beautiful day. Even though it was still early and dew glistened like raindrops in the lilac tree in the front, she could feel that ripe, syrupy potential, just waiting to burst out the moment the sun emerged. She closed her eyes to enjoy it and opened them again to see a familiar figure plodding up the street. A skinny balink with big banana feet, an enormous bag slung over its back.

'You just missed your dad. He's gone to San Francisco.'

'I didn't come to see Dad.' Maud kissed her on the cheek and slung her bag down in the hall. 'I came to see you. To wish you good luck. With Harriet.'

'Thank you.' Hermione was touched. 'That's so sweet.'

The children had all been excited at Harriet's imminent arrival. Spike, in particular, had been anxious to ensure that their guest got enough to eat.

'What about some chips?' he'd asked hopefully, as Hermione made a list the previous evening. 'Should we get extra?'

'I think we'll be fine.' Hermione smiled.

'A banner then.' Spike's eyes were bright as a gerbil's. 'A welcome home banner.'

'This isn't really her home,' Hermione told him. 'She doesn't live here.'

'She might want to,' Spike said. 'When she gets here, I mean. I can't think of anywhere better than Canada to live, can you? I'm glad I'm Canadian.'

'Only because you've never been out of Ontario,' Maisie rebuffed him. 'I'd rather be an African.'

'Are you sure?' Spike had looked doubtful. 'I don't reckon Santa can see as far as Africa. They don't get many presents there.'

'I wouldn't care,' Maisie said happily. 'I'd have zebras, wouldn't I?'

'Did you have your breakfast yet?' Hermione asked Maud now.

'A bagel.' Maud followed her into the kitchen. 'Holy Moley. It's clean in here.'

'That's good,' Hermione said, thinking of

Harriet's childhood bedroom with its immaculate rows of paints, all lined up according to colour. 'You want a soda?'

'For breakfast?' Maud looked doubtful. 'Mom doesn't usually . . .'

'Grape?'

'Is there any other kind?'

Hermione stacked the dishwasher as Maud slurped happily from the can, a grape moustache gradually spreading across her top lip. She was such a precious girl. Sometimes, she could be charmingly innocent. At others, she was astonishingly perceptive.

'Are you worried?' she asked now.

'Worried?' Hermione wiped her hands on a tea cloth. 'About Harriet?'

'About Dad.' Maud tipped the soda can up to catch the last purple droplets. 'Being in San Francisco without you.'

'He'll be OK.' Hermione ruffled her hair affectionately. 'He's a grown-up.'

'I don't mean that.' Maud stuck her tongue through the triangular-shaped hole in the top of her can. 'I just meant . . . well . . . Mom always used to get really snippy whenever he went away. She used to worry. She was always calling the hotel and stuff. Sometimes, he wasn't where he said he'd be.'

Hermione felt the colour drain from her face. Her stomach revolved like a chicken on a spit. Bubbles of nausea floated up her oesophagus.

'Are you OK?' Maud's freckled face crumpled into a frown.

'I'll be OK,' Hermione said. 'Just a bit of wind or something. That's all.'

'I've made you worried,' Maud said. 'I'm sorry.'

'No. I'm just very pregnant. I get indigestion sometimes.'

'Are you sure? Because I'm positive Dad wouldn't do that to you.'

'I'm sure.' Hermione looked at her watch. 'Jeepers. Look at the time. You'd better get yourself to school.'

'OK.' Maud slid off her stool and came to kiss Hermione. 'Have fun with your sister. You will text me later, won't you? Let me know how it goes.'

'Of course.'

'Cool.' Maud patted Hermione's tummy. 'Bye little bro.'

'You're still sure it's a he?'

'Damn skippy I am.' Maud grinned. 'Aren't you?'

'I'm fifty fifty.' Hermione laughed. 'Now go on. You'll be late.'

When Maud had gone, she rang Greg's office. She didn't want to speak to him, particularly. She just wanted to be sure he was where he said he was. So, things between them weren't always perfect. So he could be snappy sometimes. He'd proved that. But he was her baby's father. And besides. It wasn't just him any more, was it? It was Maud and Maisie and Spike. Little Spike, who had a heart so innocent it sometimes made her want to burst.

'Canon Corporation.' The voice sounded bored and tinny.

'Could you put me through to Greg Finch please.'

'Sure. Hold the line.'

Hermione's heart thundered like hooves as she waited. Eventually, the line clicked through to Greg's voicemail. Clicking her tongue with irritation, she dialled again.

'I was hoping to speak to Greg Finch.'

'I'm sorry, caller,' the bored voice intoned. 'Greg Finch is on his way to San Francisco right now. We have a sales conference there. Can anyone else help you?'

'No, thank you.' Hermione's heart sang in relief. 'I'll call back another time.'

TWINS

With hindsight, Hermione decided the placard with Harriet's name on it might be overkill. She might not have seen her sister for fifteen years, but they were twins. They'd shared a womb for nine months. Surely she would recognise her anywhere.

What on earth was she going to say to her?

As the sliding glass doors disgorged another load of red-eyed passengers into the arrivals hall, it occurred to her that she still knew relatively little about her sister's life now. That first telephone call had been so emotionally charged, the details of their lives hadn't seemed relevant. Apart from the baby, of course. Harriet had sounded pleased about that.

Subsequent communication had been a brief exchange of flight numbers and arrival times, with very little light shed on their situations. In one way, it was probably good. It would give them plenty to talk about.

The arrivals hall was full of people. People drinking big cups of coffee. Mothers. Grandmothers. Brothers. Sisters. Really, she thought, watching a family of Hassidic Jews making their way

393

sedately through the throng, airports were the same all over the world. You could be surrounded by live chickens and mangoes in India or shows of patriotic opulence in Dubai but essentially they were the same. People hoping. Waiting. Meeting and greeting.

Her heart pinged with expectation every time the doors slid open to admit more passengers onto Canadian soil. Time and time again, she was disappointed. It was an elderly lady, shuffling back into the bosom of her family. A sleek blonde. A drunk. Two people, perhaps husband and wife, speaking to each other in sign language. She had to wait for so long, she started to worry that this might all be a big joke. Harriet wasn't coming at all.

By the time Harriet eventually did come out, Hermione almost missed her. But, when she eventually saw her, teetering shyly on the edges of the crowd, she realised she'd been looking for the Harriet she'd known at eighteen. A pair of bleached Levi 501s and a casual white vest. Bony shoulders. Long eyelashes, like a shy llama.

This Harriet was different. She still would have recognised her anywhere. But she exuded a confidence that hadn't been there before. And her hair was darker.

But it was her. It couldn't have been anyone else.

Before she could stop it, a huge sob erupted from nowhere. And, as Harriet pushed her trolley towards her, the tears started pouring down her face.

★   ★   ★

The sun was streaming in through the windows behind Hermione as Harriet emerged into the arrivals hall, so that her sister was backlit. It gave her the impression of being surrounded by a halo of light, which, for one reason or another, seemed in keeping with the enormous tummy that contained her sister's precious cargo.

This was so surreal. Her tummy was on a spin cycle of nerves. She felt silly now for bringing presents. Baby clothes for a baby that hadn't even arrived yet. A bottle of Paris perfume in a glossy boudoir-pink box for a sister she hadn't seen for fifteen years. Hermione wouldn't be wearing the same perfume any more. It was ludicrous to expect that she might. But it had jumped out at her as she'd passed through the duty free shop, crowded with people filling baskets with things they didn't need. Amid the orgy of consumerism, the glamorous pink box had somehow seemed to encapsulate Hermione. The scent that wafted from the tester bottle she'd sprayed on her wrist had whipped up nothing but happy memories.

Hermione was weeping openly by the time Harriet reached her. As Harriet steered her trolley into a vacant space, Hermione wiped her eyes and stared at her.

'I'm sorry,' she said. 'I can't believe it's you. After all this time. My sister.'

'I know.' Harriet was crying too now. 'And look at you. I can't believe you're having a baby.'

'Neither can I.' Hermione looked down at her

tummy. 'I've been enormous for so long, I've almost forgotten this isn't my usual state. The baby seems almost incidental.'

'You look fantastic,' Harriet said. She did too. All the way here, she'd tried – and failed – to imagine what Hermione would look like pregnant. She'd never seemed the type. She'd always been far too glamorous. But now, looking at her, she could see a softness that hadn't been there before. It suited her.

'I don't look as good as you,' Hermione said. 'You look amazing.'

'Now that does surprise me,' Harriet said. 'I've spent the last week bawling my head off. Bloody men!'

'Really?' Hermione was shocked. She'd imagined Harriet as a happily married mother of four for so long now that, in her mind, that was what she'd become. Sure enough, there on her wedding finger was a slim band of gold. So she was married at least.

'Ah.' Harriet followed her eyes, twiddling the ring nervously. 'Not quite as simple as it looks, I'm afraid.'

'Nothing ever is,' Hermione said. She was dying to ask more. But she could see that Harriet was tired.

'You've had a long journey,' she said softly. 'Come on. Let's get some coffee. We can talk in the car.'

HARRIET

'It's funny,' Hermione said as she eased the car into the streams of traffic on the highway. 'In one way, you and I probably know more about each other than any of our friends know about us.'

Harriet clutched her seat belt as Hermione swapped lanes. She was still getting used to seeing her sister driving an enormous Dodge ram on the wrong side of the road. Nope. Scrap that. She was still getting used to seeing her sister drive full stop. She'd failed her test three times when she was seventeen for driving without due care and attention.

'I mean, I know you had that blanket thing when you were little. What was it called?'

'The Wolleydodd,' Harriet said. 'From that Ponder and William story.'

'Of course.' Hermione looked tearful again. 'Ponder and William. I wonder if it's still in print. I must get a copy for the Bean.'

'The Bean?'

Hermione tapped her tummy. 'It was Josh's name for her.'

'The father?'

Hermione shook her head. 'Josh is my best friend. Or at least,' she frowned, 'he was. We've drifted apart a bit recently. He doesn't approve of Greg.'

'Is Greg the father?'

'Yup.'

Harriet rested her eyelids. She was exhausted. But she couldn't just go to sleep. Not now. There was too much to find out. She needed to get to know her sister all over again.

'Greg was married when I met him,' Hermione said shortly.

'Oh dear.'

'I mean, I didn't know,' Hermione said quickly. 'Not until it was too late. But Josh seems to think it means he's a waste of space.'

'Are you kindred spirits?' Harriet asked her.

'I thought we were,' Hermione said. 'I mean, I connect with him. Or at least, I did. But I miss Josh.'

She smiled. 'I used to think Josh was my soul mate. We always did everything together. Parties. Clubs. Watching the TV. But Josh is gay. So we could never . . . you know.'

'It sounds complicated.' Harriet put her hand on her sister's arm. It was strange. She actually felt quite calm. She'd expected to be a nervous wreck. But somehow, being with Hermione felt quite normal. They still fitted.

'I'm sorry,' Hermione said. 'Listen to me going

on. My life isn't quite the mess I've made it out to be. I have three wonderful nearly stepchildren. And a baby on the way.'

'I still can't believe that,' Harriet said. 'You were always so adamant that you never wanted children.'

'I know. And you were going to have dozens. You even had all their names planned out.'

'They kept changing.' Harriet smiled ruefully. 'I never could stick with one. It's probably just as well I never actually had any children.'

'You didn't?' Hermione looked shocked.

'No.' Harriet shook her head. 'It didn't work out.'

'Oh my God.' Hermione swerved to miss a Chevy. 'That's so sad. You're married though, right?'

'Not any more. At least, I don't think I am. We separated,' she explained. 'A few months back.'

'Was he your soul mate?'

'I thought so,' Harriet told her. 'We met in college. He was this calm, efficient medical student and I was this chaotic wreck. He made me feel safe. Sort of put me together again, if you know what I mean.'

Hermione nodded.

'I wanted babies straight away. But he made me wait. Said we were too young. That I was trying to replace the family I'd lost. And he was right, in a way.'

'Did he make you happy?'

'He made me feel safe,' Harriet said. 'Does that count?'

'I don't know. Life doesn't quite work out the way you expect it to, does it?'

'No.' Harriet shook her head. She was thinking about Lucy again. The image of the poor little mite all alone in a hospital bed, as Oscar had been, had been nagging at her since she left the UK. She needed to phone Lizzy. Put her mind at rest.

'Listen,' she said to Hermione. 'Would you mind if I made a call? It's kind of urgent.'

'No problem,' Hermione said. 'I'm going to pull into Tim Horton's anyhow. Get us some breakfast. Here.' She steered the car onto a forecourt. 'I'll hop out and get the coffee. Give you some privacy.'

Harriet got through to Lizzy on the first ring. She sounded terrible.

'Harry?' Her voice was all shaky. 'Thank God. Can you come over?'

'Oh God.' Harriet's stomach pitted. 'I'm in Canada. Lizzy, please don't cry. What is it? I've been worried sick. I tried to call from the plane but the air hostess said I couldn't use my mobile. It interferes with their equipment or something. Is she OK?'

'Who?' Lizzy sounded vacant.

'Lucy.' Harriet frowned. 'Chloe was worried. I had to get Dan to take her to hospital.'

'Oh.' Lizzy sniffed. 'Yes. Of course. Thank you.'

'Is she OK?'

'She's fine.'

'Thank God. What was it?'

'A viral infection.' Lizzy sniffed again. 'A twenty-four hour thing. It was touch and go at the start though. You did the right thing.'

'So what is it?' Harriet asked her. 'What's wrong?'

'Conrad's left me.'

'*What?*'

Surely not. If steadfast Conrad had left Lizzy, then her faith in men hadn't just gone down the toilet. It had rounded the U-bend, never to return.

'Conrad's left me.' Lizzy hiccuped.

'Oh God. He found out.'

'Yes.'

'Oh, *Lizzy.*'

'I know.' Lizzy sobbed. 'You warned me. You said this would happen. And what did I do? I thought I knew better. I tried to stop it. But I couldn't. I thought I'd never get found out. I thought I was invincible. That's how Will made me feel.'

Harriet wished she could just give Lizzy a big hug. OK, so she'd been in the wrong. But she could understand how it had happened. Will was one of those dangerous men who made perfectly rational women take leave of their senses. And Lizzy hadn't exactly been perfectly rational. She'd been wobbly ever since Oscar was born. He hadn't been supposed to come along so soon after Lucy. Perhaps Lizzy had had a bit of post-natal depression.

'How did Conrad find out?'

'He was at the hospital when I got there.' Lizzy's voice shook. 'I lost track of time. Crack Nanny couldn't get hold of me. By the time she did, they were all frantic. She had to tell him I'd been out all night. He was furious with me for leaving the kids all night on their own.'

'Perhaps you should explain.' Harriet watched Hermione come out of the store, clutching two brown paper bags with the tops rolled down. 'He might understand.'

'I doubt it.' Lizzy sobbed. 'Oh, Harry. He's packed a bag and gone. What am I going to do?'

Hermione wedged herself back into the Dodge.

'I'm so sorry I'm not there,' Harriet said.

'What are you d-doing in Canada?'

'I found my sister!' Harriet smiled at Hermione.

'You d-did?' Lizzy sounded as though she was shivering. 'That's f-fantastic. Is it going well?'

'I think so. I'll ring you tomorrow. Is Crack Nanny still there?'

'She had an appointment at the c-clinic.'

'Right. I think you should call your mum.'

'She'll kill me.'

'Charlotte?'

'She's in Italy. Gone off with this new bloke of hers. They've discovered a shared love of the place apparently. It's enough to make you sick.'

'Gabby then,' Harriet said. 'Call Gabby. I don't think you should be on your own tonight.'

'OK.'

'Promise?'

'I promise.'

'OK.' Harriet's mouth watered as the delicious scent of coffee reached her nostrils. 'I'll call you tomorrow to find out how you are. All right?'

'All right. Bye.'

'Doughnuts and coffee.' Hermione passed her a bag. 'The Canadian staple diet. I got you what I always have. Caramel macchiato . . .'

'Extra hot,' Harriet finished for her.

'How do you know?'

'Because that's what I always have.'

'No! Really?'

Harriet nodded.

'Weird.'

'But not that weird,' Harriet said. 'We always had similar tastes.'

'I guess.'

They fell silent as Hermione negotiated the streets of Toronto, a not unimpressive feat given the streetcars that seemed to hurtle by with seemingly little regard for anything smaller than themselves. Harriet hadn't realised how hungry she was until she bit into that first apple fritter, a delicious combination of sweet stodge and sour fruit filling that had her salivary glands tingling in appreciation. She couldn't speak for at least ten minutes because she was too busy filling her face.

But there was something else. She thought they were probably both afraid of saying too much. Now that the pleasantries were out of the way, the subject of the fifteen-year breach hung like a

403

gaudy Christmas tree bauble between them. They were both happy as long as the conversation was skimming along, leaving just the odd dent in the tranquil surface of politeness. But at some point they both knew they had to delve deeper. It was inevitable.

'Here we are.' Hermione pulled up outside a pretty Victorian terrace in a row of gracious bay-fronted houses. 'Home sweet home.'

'It's nice.'

'You like it?'

'Definitely. It's not what I imagined.'

'What did you imagine?' Hermione stuck her key in the front door.

'I always imagined you living in a trendy loft somewhere,' Harriet said. 'All white walls. That sort of thing. This is really quite British.'

Hermione explained that this part of the city had once been an enclave for Irish immigrants. She and Josh had chosen the neighourhood because it had so many nice parks and gardens.

'For the baby?' Harriet said.

'God, no.' Hermione guffawed. 'That was ages ago.' She winked. 'We just wanted somewhere to loiter and make a nuisance of ourselves.' She threw her keys onto the table in the hall. 'I've gone for shabby chic, as you can see. More shabby than chic, actually. I was never as good as you at that sort of thing. But it sort of works, don't you think?'

Harriet nodded. 'I love it.'

'You will make yourself at home while you're here?' Hermione said. 'Greg's away at a sales conference for at least a week.'

'That's a shame.' Harriet was quietly relieved. Meeting Hermione's significant other straight away would probably be a bit much.

'He'll be back,' Hermione said. 'In the meantime, we've got lots of fun things planned. My friend Celine wants to meet you. I called her last night. And Greg's kids can't wait to come and get a look at you. I'm sorry,' she said. 'That makes you sound as though you're in a zoo.'

'It's OK.' Harriet smiled. 'How old are they?'

'Six, seven and thirteen,' Hermione said. 'You're already a legend in their eyes. They've spent the last two days worrying whether we've got enough special food in. Anyone would think you were J-Lo. And they've got your whole trip planned out for you. Maud wants to take you to Peach Berserk. Her favourite shop,' she supplied as Harriet looked blank. 'And Maisie's got her heart set on taking you to DQ.'

'DQ?'

'Dairy Queen. It's an ice-cream place. Maisie's obsessed. That little girl would eat ice-cream and chopped nuts until they came out of her ears. And then Spike. Well, Spike will probably just settle for you buying him some fries. I'm sorry,' she said hastily. 'I'm wibbling.'

'It's OK.' Harriet looked around her. 'Is there somewhere I can have a wash?'

'Of course. I got Josh's old room ready for you. In here.'

She led Harriet into a white-painted room filled with pretty Cath Kidston fabrics.

'I hope it's OK,' she said shyly.

'It's lovely,' Harriet said.

'The bathroom's just across the hall.' Hermione pointed. 'I'll leave you to it. Have a nap if you like. I made lunch.'

'You did?'

'Don't get too excited,' Hermione warned her. 'You remember my legendary bean bakes?'

Harriet nodded. 'And your cakes,' she said. 'You made that lemon drizzle cake for Pip one time.'

'Was that the one that was more of a biscuit?'

'No.' Harriet shook her head. 'It was the one you put all the baking powder in. Loads of people came to the house in Bath to see Pip party and you came out with this great big cake. Everyone was saying how delicious it was and then someone said . . .'

'No one drink water while eating this cake.' Hermione guffawed. 'Who was it said that?'

'Vinegar, I think.' Harriet laughed.

'Well, let's just say that things haven't progressed much from there. Luckily we have the most amazing food markets in Toronto. Most things come ready prepared. Just come down whenever you're hungry.'

'OK.'

'Harry?'

'Mmm?'

'It really is great to see you.'

Harriet smiled. 'It's good to see you too.'

It was dusk when Harriet woke up. For a minute, she couldn't quite figure out where she was. Then, as her eyes grew accustomed to the dim light in the room, she remembered. Of course. She was at Hermione's.

She must have been asleep for ages. She showered quickly and pulled on some clean clothes before going to find her sister. It didn't seem quite right, somehow, to have found Hermione after all this time, only to have conked out for hours on end.

She padded through the house, surprised at how homely it all was. The kitchen was gorgeous, with black and white tiles all over the floor, a family-sized table and lots of mismatched chairs. Part of the ceiling was made from glass. It would be lovely and light in here in the daytime.

'Hermione?' she called tentatively.

'Out here.'

Harriet poked her head out of the back door into a tiny courtyard garden. Hermione was sitting in a deckchair, smoking a cigarette.

'Hello, Sleeping Beauty. You missed lunch.'

'Sorry.' Harriet stretched guiltily. 'I didn't mean to sleep for so long. I think it was being in the car. I always feel sleepy in a car.'

'Ruby and Isaac used to put you in the car and

drive you around the block when you were small,' Hermione said. 'They used to say it was the only way to get you to sleep. Do you remember?'

Harriet shook her head. 'Do you still miss them?' She pulled up a chair.

'Every day.' Hermione exhaled a column of blue-tinged smoke.

'Me too,' Harriet said. 'I can be jogging along quite happily with my own life and then . . . WHAM.' She shivered in the thin cotton jumper she'd pulled on over her jeans.

'Cold?' Hermione struggled out of her chair and went into the kitchen, returning with a big fleece. 'Put this on. I should warn you, it can get really cold here at night. The temperature can just plummet. Even if it's boiling during the day, you'll always need a sweater at night.'

'Thanks.' Harriet snuggled into the fleece. It smelled familiar. She smiled.

'What?'

'It's funny,' Harriet said. 'After all this time, your clothes smell just the same.'

HARRIET

For days, Harriet and Hermione picked around each other, like cats on a hot tin roof. Harriet wasn't sure exactly what she'd been expecting. A big bust-up, perhaps? Anything but this. She felt like a polite house guest.

No mention was made of the accident or of the time they'd last seen each other. They both avoided the subject like the plague. Hermione hadn't pressed her for information. Hadn't demanded an apology for that terrible outburst that day in Ruby's sitting room. And although it was a bit disappointing, Harriet also felt slightly relieved. She wasn't sure she was quite ready to explain about Will. For the moment, she had to be content for Hermione and herself to just be. They'd both changed, after all. They needed time to adjust. To come to terms with their parents' death as a unit as they hadn't had the chance to before. Not with Pip and Vinegar butting in every five minutes.

Vinegar, in particular, had been a pain in the neck in the days leading up to the funeral. As Harriet and Hermione wandered like ghosts around the house on Belmont, too shocked to speak even to each other, let alone either of their aunts, Vinegar had made extensive preparations for the funeral. There had been a great deal of whispered conversation about the tea. Harriet could remember wandering past closed doors and hearing Vinegar ask Pip, 'And what about afterwards? Will they come back here?'

Harriet hadn't been able understand it. So much palaver over a few fish paste sandwiches. What did it matter? Ruby and Isaac were dead. Rotting in coffins. She knew what happened when you died. Bacteria that was already present started to eat its way out of you. Soon, Isaac's kindly face and Ruby's beautiful one would be little more than grinning skulls. At the funeral, as she and Hermione had thrown rose petals onto the pair of coffins, she had wanted to hurl herself into the grave and beg them not to cover them up with earth. To do so would mean never seeing their faces again. But she'd known they had to.

And sooner or later she and Hermione would have to face each other over the cause of their fifteen-year rift.

In the meantime, she loved being in Hermione's house. It was only rented, as Hermione put it. But it was light and airy. And Hermione had accumulated some amazing stuff over the years. Harriet particularly liked her collection of coloured glass. She had a lot of emerald-green St Louis wine goblets that must have been worth hundreds of pounds. Her old job must have been pretty lucrative, to say the least.

Every so often, she came across something that brought a jolt of recognition. A childhood photograph. A pottery hedge-hog. An exquisite carved angel, standing in the fireplace in Hermione's room.

'Oh my God,' she breathed, stroking the smooth alabaster feathers of the creature's wing. 'I didn't know you'd kept this.'

'Pearl's angel?' Hermione said. 'I took her from the workshop when the place was sold. I don't know why really. I suppose it was just a part of Isaac. I couldn't bear to leave her behind.'

'Pearl,' Harriet said softly. 'That's it.'

Isaac had made the angel for a man called Bert Lack, who had just lost his wife, Pearl, to cancer. He'd wanted a whole host of angels guarding her grave. Isaac had finished the first one and then Bert had changed his mind. He wouldn't be needing them after all. They'd never found out why. The angel had stood guarding the entrance to Isaac's workshop in Bath for years. Harriet had completely forgotten about her.

What Harriet found really strange was the big collage of photographs Hermione had stuck in a clip frame on the kitchen wall. It was full of pictures of a Hermione she didn't know. A Hermione whose life she hadn't been a part of. Hermione, raising a glass in a giggly toast at somebody's birthday party. Hermione and a smiley, sandy-haired boy on a boat, both wearing forest-green baseball caps that, for some reason, had Fogle's Irish Peat stamped across the front. Hermione wearing a paper hat at a Christmas party. Had she, as Harriet often had, wondered what her sister was doing during times of celebration? Or had she simply blocked the past out of her mind?

They weren't in the house all the time. Harriet liked what she saw of Toronto. It was a great city. Friendly and not too overcrowded. Like Hermione, she enjoyed the rich cultural mishmash of the place. And she liked Greg's children. Maud would drop by for a chinwag before school every morning, and Spike often popped in for his second breakfast. Harriet found herself looking forward to their visits. Maud was a sweetie. The sort of daughter she'd have liked to have had herself if things had worked out differently. And Spike made her laugh, with his glassy green eyes that threatened to pop out of his head every time he got excited about something.

On Saturday, Hermione took Harriet and the three children to the Second Cup on Bloor Street to eat muffins and drink more coffee. As far as Harriet could see, the whole of Canada must run on the stuff. There were coffee houses everywhere.

They did other things too. Maud took her to Peach Berserk, which was tucked away on a street filled with quirky shops selling vintage clothes, records and an eclectic jumble of other stuff.

'This is my absolute favourite shop,' she said happily. 'It has the cutest stuff.'

Spike and Maisie were still treating her like an exotic exhibit. They loved hearing about England. To them, it was a land as mysterious as any at the top of Enid Blyton's Faraway Tree. One day, over strawberry sundaes in Maisie's beloved Dairy Queen, they quizzed her on the subject of British zoos.

'Are there zebras?' Maisie licked the end of her spoon.

'Maisie is obsessed with zebras,' Spike, his face smothered in strawberry syrup, supplied helpfully.

'I am not,' Maisie slurped. 'I just think they're beautiful. That's all. Are there any, Harry, in your zoo?'

'Actually, we don't have a zoo.'

'You don't have a zoo?' Spike goggled. 'You don't have zoos in England? No zoos? No O Henry's? No Jubes?'

'Of course we have zoos in England.' Hermione laughed. 'Harry just means there isn't one in Bath.'

'There's one in Bristol,' Harriet said.

'Is it a good one?'

'Do they have zebras?'

'I don't know,' Harriet said truthfully. 'I've never been.'

'You've never been?' Maisie echoed. 'Holy cow! If I was a grown-up I'd go with my own money every day.'

'Actually,' Hermione said, 'you have been.'

'Have I?'

'We went when we were little,' Hermione said.

413

'Don't you remember? We fed the penguins with those little fish and chip crisps. We must have been about nine. Vinegar took us.'

Vaguely Harriet did remember. It came as a surprise to her that Hermione could remember certain events that had taken place in their childhood better than she could herself. She'd always assumed Hermione hadn't cared as much.

The weekend wore on. Maud, Maisie and Spike left, doling out sticky strawberry hugs and kisses on their way out. That night, they were expected for dinner at Celine's. And the following day, Hermione thought they might all go to the cabin. Celine might have to bring her kids. But that would be OK. They sounded as though they were pretty well-behaved.

'Cabin?' Harriet was intrigued.

'It belongs to Josh and me.' Hermione pulled on a crimson cardigan to keep out the evening chill. 'We bought it last summer.'

'Where is it?'

'Northern Ontario, three hours from here,' Hermione said. 'You can only get to it by boat, so we'll have to pick up the canoe from Uncle Ott's place on the way. But it's glorious. You'll love it. What?' she asked, as she caught Harriet looking at her.

'You've changed,' Harriet said. 'You always used to be such a town mouse.'

'I know.' Hermione laughed. 'I still am. I go stir crazy if we stay up there for too long. I have to come back so I can be near a shop. Josh thinks it's hilarious.'

'Will Josh be there?'

'No,' Hermione said sadly. 'Things are still a bit difficult there.'

Celine's house was in a long, tree-lined avenue, slightly west of Hermione's neighbourhood. To get there, Harriet and Hermione took a subway train and then walked along a street lined with nice shops. Aveda. Roots. Banana Republic. Harriet, who had been asleep all afternoon, felt rejuvenated and slightly apprehensive as they reached the house. Hermione, on the other hand, just looked utterly exhausted from the walk.

Celine was lovely. Hermione had been right about that. She welcomed the two of them into her large red-brick villa and fed them shrimp bake and zucchini brownies. Her kitchen was amazingly glamorous. Lots of floor-to-ceiling units with turquoise glass worktops, all cunningly lit from below so that Celine's elegant crystal glasses sparkled as she poured them all wine.

'This is gorgeous.' Harriet gulped the wine gratefully to cover her nerves and nodded around the kitchen.

'Isn't it?' Hermione agreed. 'Your ex isn't still trying to get you out, is he?'

'He can try all he likes.' Celine cackled with laughter. 'I'm not budging.'

'I love all the clean lines.' Harriet was still looking at the kitchen units. 'Very ergonomic.'

'Harriet's a designer too,' Hermione said proudly.

'Oh?' Celine looked pleased. 'Then I imagine we two will get along very well. What sort of design?'

'Interiors, mostly,' Harriet said shyly. 'I just decked out a new bar in Bath. I guess I'm still feeling my way a bit. What sort of thing do you do?'

'Book jackets,' Celine said.

'You got the job?' Hermione looked thrilled.

'Yep. I start Monday.'

'But that's brilliant.'

'I know.' Celine raised her glass and grinned. 'Cheers.'

When she grinned, Harriet noticed, it showed the jagged gap between her teeth that gave her face its character. It was the difference between plain beautiful and beautifully plain.

'Come through.' Celine led them both into a sitting room, painted in a neutral palette of creams and greys. The whole house was decorated in the style Harriet might have chosen for her flat. Except in her flat, there would be no friendly additions as there were here. No books. No piles of computer games. No squidgy dinosaur light pull in the bathroom. On Celine's fridge, a poster-paint girl with an orange triangle dress, huge cauliflower hands and club feet resided between a strip of lime-green grass and bright blue sky.

'Do you have any photographs?' she asked suddenly.

'Sorry?' Celine said.

'Photos,' Harriet said. 'Of your children.' It had just struck her as odd. This was the sort of house that would normally be filled with family snaps. Yet she couldn't recall seeing one in any of the rooms she'd been in.

'Dozens,' Celine said airily. 'All neatly catalogued in an album somewhere. We'll dig them out later. So . . .' She patted Hermione's tummy. 'How's the little princess? Still sure she's a girl?'

'I think so, although Maud is sure it's a boy.'

'How is Maud?' Celine asked her.

'Lovely as ever,' Hermione said. 'Isn't she, Harry?'

'She's delightful,' Harriet said.

Harriet drank far too much wine. She couldn't help it. She was still worried about Lizzy, for one thing. Since arriving here, she'd spoken to her every single day. She sounded as if she was cracking up. Gabby was so worried about her she'd sent Dan over.

Bless Dan. She did miss him. He might not have been exactly right for her. She might even have married him for the wrong reasons. But did it really matter, in the grand scheme of things?

Hermione and Celine were still talking about children.

'It must be nice,' Harriet said, 'having a family of your own.' She was drunk now. She wasn't

417

even sure what she was leading up to. She had no particular desire to hurt Hermione. But she did want to get everything out in the open.

'It is,' Celine said. 'It's hard work, though. Especially when they get colic and refuse to sleep through the night.'

'Three of them,' Harriet said. 'Must be quite a job.'

'Yes. I only have to look at a man and I fall pregnant.'

'What about you, Hermione?' Harriet asked. 'You got pregnant by mistake, didn't you? That's what you said, isn't it?'

'Well, yes.' Hermione looked bewildered. 'But I'm pleased now, obviously.'

Harriet rested her chin on her hand, wincing slightly as her elbow slipped off the table. 'I only ask,' she slurred, 'because having children is something I won't experience in my lifetime.'

'I'm sorry.' Celine looked upset. 'That's too bad.'

'It's my own fault,' Harriet said.

'Don't be silly,' Celine said. 'How can it be?'

'I had an abortion and caught an infection. When I was eighteen.'

'You what?' Hermione looked horrified. 'When?'

'Just after you left to go travelling,' Harriet told her. 'You didn't really leave me any choice, did you? I was all alone.'

'Oh God.' Hermione's hands flew to her mouth. 'What about the father? Did he not give you any support?'

'Hermione,' Harriet said, 'did you never wonder why I said all that awful stuff to you? The day I came downstairs and you told me you were going away?'

'Of course I did,' Hermione said. 'But I guess I always kind of knew.'

'You did?'

'Of course. It was terrible of me to go away like that. I've always been worried to call you. I thought you'd never forgive me.'

'You thought I yelled at you for going away?' Harriet was shocked. 'You thought I would blame you just because of that?'

'Well, yes.' Hermione looked upset. 'That and shock.'

Harriet shook her head. 'You really don't understand at all.'

'What then?' Hermione asked her. 'What happened?'

Harriet cleared her throat. 'I was with Will,' she said simply.

'Will?' Hermione said. 'Will Cartwright?'

Harriet nodded. 'It was before you came back from Greece. He dumped me. At least,' she said bitterly, 'that's what he thought. He didn't actually have the decency to tell me about it. I was waiting for him to turn up. That night at our party. And then I saw him with you.'

'Oh God,' Hermione said. 'I didn't know. Please believe me, Harry. I didn't know.'

'I know you didn't,' Harriet said. 'It was just a

shock, that day in Ruby's sitting room. I'd managed to convince myself he'd gone away. He came over, you know. When you were seeing him. I asked him to. He gave me money for an abortion.'

'Bastard,' Hermione said.

'I knew I was pregnant that day we went to the hospital,' Harriet said. 'I was going to tell Ruby the night before. I knew she would have been good about it.'

'Yes.' Hermione had tears rolling down her face. 'She would have.'

'But then they had to go and pick you up. And they never came home.' Harriet's face crumpled.

'Oh God.' Hermione rocked. 'It was my fault. If I hadn't gone to that party . . .'

'No . . .' Harriet gasped. 'It was just one of those things.'

'There was sticking plaster,' Hermione wept, 'on Isaac's glasses, when they gave them to us at the hospital. D'you remember?'

'Yes.' Harriet envisaged the sorry-looking plastic bag, filled with what the police had been able to salvage from the wreck of Isaac's Triumph Herald. 'I think about it all the time.'

Hermione's face was distorted. 'I miss them so much.'

'So do I,' Harriet sobbed.

HERMIONE

ermione eased the car across the lumps and bumps in the gravel and parked up by Uncle Ott's, where she and Celine had agreed to meet to untie the aluminium boat the old man let her and Josh borrow last summer.

Last night had been a revelation. Poor Harriet. To have to go through all that on her own. It didn't bear thinking about.

At least now they'd cleared the air. Last night at Celine's, they'd hugged and cried for almost an hour before noticing that Celine had slipped away at some point. Afterwards, they'd both admitted they felt a lot better. This morning, they'd both come down to breakfast in sunglasses to hide their puffy eyes and got the giggles. At last, the awful veneer of politeness that had glossed over everything for the past few days was gone. They could be normal siblings again.

'Here we are.' Hermione grinned. 'Are you OK?'

'Fine.' Harriet looked out at the lake, which was almost emerald in colour and fringed with palm trees. 'This is beautiful.'

'Isn't it?'

Hermione got out of the car and started to heft bits and bobs out of the trunk towards the patch of ground by Uncle Ott's boat. Harriet helped her, lugging a polystyrene cool box across the gravel and throwing down a couple of sleeping bags. They'd brought everything, down to thermal socks. It could get very cold in the middle of nowhere at night. Not one to miss out on her home comforts, Hermione had brought five pairs for three days. Just in case.

Harriet pulled her overnight bag out of the car and went to put it by the boat. Hermione saw her pull her mobile phone out of her pocket and check her text messages, furiously deleting whatever she found there.

'Everything OK?'

'Fine.' Harriet smiled up at her. She was already getting a bit of colour on her face. She looked really pretty.

'Look,' she said. 'The others have arrived.'

Celine's Jeep, bulging with children and belongings, bumped and squeaked over the rough road. There was a canoe tied to the top with string and, before Celine had had a chance to stop the vehicle properly, the doors burst open and two small figures hurled themselves out and started to bounce about like ping-pong balls. With a twist of shock, Hermione looked at the curly blonde head and the mousy brown one and realised they seemed very familiar.

Very familiar indeed.

Her stomach lurched like a fairground cakewalk as the significance of what she was seeing sunk in.

'Bee?' Spike's clear green eyes almost popped out of his head. 'What are you doing here? We thought we were meeting Mom's friend.'

'This *is* Mom's friend.' Celine, wearing a floppy straw hat and big sunglasses, got out of the Jeep, closely followed by Maud, who was sporting a khaki fishing hat with a luminous orange sticker stuck to the front, with the words 'Thank You' printed on it. 'And her name isn't Bee. It's Hermione.'

'We know that.' Spike stuck out his arms and ran around the Jeep in a circle. 'Neeeeeeeeeeeooooor.'

Hermione found she couldn't speak. Not even to explain to Harriet, who was clearly completely stumped. Celine, on the other hand, seemed remarkably calm.

'Hermione can't be your friend.' Maisie looked shocked. 'She's Dad's girlfriend.'

'I know.' Celine pulled at the elastic straps to release the canoe.

'You knew?' Hermione said.

'I've known for some time,' Celine said. 'Maud, can you take the little ones to unpack the food parcel, please?'

'Sure.' Maud shuffled off in the new pink Converse All Stars Harriet had bought her on their shopping trip.

'But . . .' Hermione stammered. 'You still s-spoke to me. We were f-friends.'

'Exactly,' Celine said. 'And I couldn't be sure. I mean, I thought it was a coincidence that first day. We were both with men called Greg. But then the kids came back from your house and Spike called you by your real name. And I put two and two together.'

'But why didn't you say anything?'

'I don't know.' Celine shrugged. 'I wasn't sure how you'd react. I just wanted things to stay the same.' She smiled wryly. 'So I avoided mentioning the kids by name. I even hid the family photos when you and Harriet came to dinner. I lived for our Saturday mornings. I'd been so lonely since Greg left. Why should I give up our friendship?'

'I was lonely too,' Hermione admitted. 'And I still had Greg in *my* life. I guess that says it all really, doesn't it?'

'I don't know,' Celine said. 'We all feel lonely sometimes.'

'I felt as though we had so much in common at first,' Hermione told her. 'I'd lost my parents. My sister was, in essence, lost to me as well. Greg was the first person I'd met who knew what it felt like to lose somebody close to him.'

'Who would that be exactly?'

'His brother,' Hermione said. 'The one who died on the skiddoo.'

'*What?*' Celine looked horrified. 'He told you that?'

'It's not true?'

'Of course it's not,' Celine scoffed. 'The last I

424

heard, Greg's brother was alive and well and living in Wolverhampton. The man's a pathological liar. He'll say anything if he thinks it'll get him a bit of attention.'

'But Greg said he left his wife.' Hermione's lip trembled. 'And you said . . .'

'I chucked him out,' Celine said crisply. 'I told you, the man wouldn't know the truth if it jumped up and bit him on the butt.'

'It wasn't me, though, was it?' Hermione asked.

'Sorry?'

'You said you threw your husband out because you saw him in a bar with a girl. That girl wasn't me. It couldn't have been. I wasn't there. And you'd have known.'

'No, it wasn't you.'

'So who was it?'

'It was his secretary, apparently,' Celine told her. 'Bumble.'

'Bumble?' Hermione said. 'So that's why the kids always called me Bee. They thought I was the same person.'

'They must have done,' Celine said. 'At least, that's what I assumed when I realised who you were. Not that I told them, of course. I'd rather they retained some respect for their father. Spike and Maisie at least. Maud's old enough to think what she likes.'

'So why did he come to me?' Hermione asked her. 'Why didn't he go and live with Bumble?'

'I suppose he thought of her as his bit of stuff,'

Celine said. 'He always liked to differentiate between the woman in the home and the bit on the side. He was like a magpie when it came to anything new and shiny. Pretty pathetic, really. I'm sorry,' she added, noticing Hermione's pale face. 'Perhaps I shouldn't have told you like this.'

'It's OK,' Hermione said.

'Are you sure?' Celine and Harriet echoed.

'Yes.' Hermione was surprised. She didn't even feel that angry. She was more relieved. She wasn't going mad after all. Her instincts had been right.

'What are you going to do?' Celine asked.

'Firstly, I'm going to take the boat out to the cabin. And then I'm going to drive back to Toronto and speak to Josh. It might be too late. But I can try.'

'Should you be driving on your own?' Celine asked her. 'In your condition?'

'Can I make a suggestion?' Harriet said.

'Sure.'

'Why don't we go across to the cabin now? Set up. Get something to eat. The kids must be starving. You can go back to Toronto in the morning. It's getting pretty late.'

On cue, Spike came running back from the Jeep.

'Harry,' he called. 'We got a whole bunch of stuff in the truck. Wait till you see. We got Snickers bars. And burgers. And wieners for a wiener roast. Did you have a wiener roast before? It tastes good if you put cheese in. I always put cheese in. Hey, d'you like Popsicles? Mom says

426

there's a place near here were we can get some. Can we get some?'

Late the following morning, Hermione marched through the sliding doors into the antiseptic foyer of Canon Corporation and headed straight for the lift.

'Hey!' The bouffant-haired receptionist stopped filing her long purple talons. 'You can't go up. Not without a sticker.'

'Bugger the sticker.' Hermione jammed her finger on the button for the third floor, thoroughly enjoying the look on the receptionist's face as the doors slid shut in her face.

She'd timed it perfectly. As she marched into the marketing department, she saw to her delight that Greg appeared to be chairing a meeting in his pretentiously large office. As he swivelled importantly in his chair, Hermione burst in, clutching the big brown envelope she'd brought from home.

'Hermione!' Greg looked shocked. 'What are you doing here? I thought you were at the cabin.'

'I made a special trip,' Hermione said in a sugary voice. 'I missed you.'

'Right.' Greg looked embarrassed. 'Well, I'm kind of in the middle of something right now. But if you give me twenty minutes we could have lunch.'

'No problem.' Hermione held up the envelope and shook it out over the big boardroom-style table in Greg's office, tipping a cascade of brightly coloured magazines all over it. Several people gasped as they took in the contents. A copy of *Slut Slits* had fallen open to reveal a dusky-looking babe, completely naked and positioned on all fours, pulling apart her butt cheeks as wide as they would go.

'I thought you could probably do with some inspiration,' she said, as Greg reddened. 'I brought you these from home.'

Several people sniggered as Greg's colour deepened. He stood up and marched out of his office, taking Hermione with him.

'What the fuck do you think you're doing?'

'I know,' Hermione hissed.

'What?' Greg asked. 'What do you know?'

'I know about Celine,' Hermione said. 'I know she chucked you out because you were shagging your secretary. And I know you're still seeing her. You bought her earrings. I found them.'

'No,' Greg said. 'You've got this wrong. This is your hormones talking.'

'I don't think so,' Hermione said. 'You can get your stuff out of my house before I get back from the cabin. If it's still there when I come home, I'll torch it. *Capisce?*'

'Hey.' Greg held up his hands to shield himself from her anger. 'That's a bit harsh, isn't it?'

'Harsh?' Hermione said. 'You're lucky I haven't lined your office curtains with tiger prawns. And if you think you're having anything to do with this baby when she's born, you've got another think coming. I don't want my daughter growing up with a bitter attitude towards men. I want her to know there are good men in the world. That some men are good and true. Like Josh.' She sneered. 'He was right. You are a waste of space. I should have listened to him a long time ago.'

With that, she marched back into the lift and out of the building.

She sat by the fountain in Nathan Phillips Square, plucking up the courage to ring Josh. Ridiculous, considering he was the person who knew her best in the world. She was nervous. Nervous of things not being OK with them. She needed them to be OK. She needed it desperately. She'd been right. Josh was her soul mate. Her kindred spirit. It didn't matter that they didn't have sex. It wasn't part of the equation. Not any more.

It took Josh just ten minutes to arrive. He came loping over as Hermione was checking her make-up. For some reason, it seemed paramount that she looked her best. It was stupid, really. Josh had seen her cradling the toilet bowl after too many margaritas. He'd seen her the next morning, when the bags under her eyes were big enough to cart a month's worth of clean clothes about in. Why would he care what she looked like?

'Hi,' she said shyly, as he perched on the wall of the fountain beside her. 'Long time no see.'

'You look great.' He nodded at her bump. 'How does it feel.'

'Exciting.' Hermione blushed. 'Scary.'

'I bet.'

'You were right,' Hermione blurted. 'About Greg. I'm sorry.'

'Hey,' Josh said. 'I'm sorry. I didn't want you to get hurt.'

'I know that now,' Hermione said. 'I was stubborn. I wanted me and Greg to work because of the baby. I wanted a family.'

'I would have been your family.'

'I know,' Hermione said. 'I'm sorry. Can you forgive me?'

'Always,' Josh said. 'Can you forgive me?'

'What for?'

'I was jealous,' Josh said.

'Jealous?'

'Of you and Greg.'

'Because of the Bean?'

'No.' Josh shook his head. 'It wasn't just the Bean. I have feelings for you, Hermy One.'

'What do you mean?'

'That's just it.' Josh looked perplexed. 'I don't know. I mean, I fancy men. I know I do. I'm a gay man. But sometimes, I just find myself wanting to . . .'

'What?' Hermione asked.

'I want to do this.'

Josh moved slowly towards her and kissed her, long and hard on the lips. It was a beautiful kiss. A kiss that was pure Josh. A kiss that made her feel loved.

'I'm sorry,' Josh said. 'I've wanted to do that for so long.'

'It was nice,' Hermione said.

'More than nice,' Josh said. 'I want to do it again. But I don't understand it.'

'Maybe you don't have to,' Hermione said. 'Maybe it's just one of those things. Maybe sometimes it's the person you fall in love with and not the sexuality.'

'I do love you, Hermy One,' Josh said. 'You know that, don't you?'

'Yes,' Hermione said happily. 'And I love you.'

'Cool.'

'Josh.'

'Yes?'

'You will come home? When the baby's born?'

'Of course I will.'

'We needn't worry about the sex thing or anything,' Hermione said. 'And we can forget the kiss.'

'OK.'

'When I come back from the cabin,' she said, 'let's go home and just be.'

Josh grinned. 'You're on.'

HARRIET

Afterwards, Harriet would always remember the time at the lake as a week of perfect bliss. The six of them settled easily into a happy routine of swimming and sunbathing around the cabin, which was a model Hansel and Gretel cottage set on the edge of the lake inside a pine forest. The place was paradise. So far removed from her world back in Bath that she soon forgot about Jesse. Here, she wouldn't even know if he'd tried to call. There was no telephone signal anywhere.

She still drove to the nearest village, five kilometres away, every day to call Lizzy. She was getting better. Dan had prescribed her some Valium and she and Conrad were at least on speaking terms again.

Even so, it was so peaceful here that it was hard to feel worried for long. She didn't mind the spartan washing facilities. She didn't even mind the lack of crisp cotton sheets or colour co-ordinated tableware. She'd always loved the countryside. And Proudfoot Lake, as Celine told her it was called, was heaven. Apart from the sound of Spike and

Maisie laughing and splashing as they pushed each other off the jetty, or squealing as their bare feet touched the weeds on the bottom, the only other sounds were the tshatta-tshatta of Maud's headphones and the loons laughing on the lake. In the evenings, they could hear beavers plipping in and out of the reeds at the water's edge or the hiss and sputter of Celine's fire potatoes wrapped in tinfoil. And, apart from the first day, when Hermione insisted that, pregnant or not, she was going to make the six-hour round trip to Toronto, they were all together most of the time.

They spent their days drifting in the boat on the lake. One day, Celine drove them all out to a bigger lake, where they could have water-ski lessons. Maud was thrilled to get up on her first go. Harriet, on the other hand, sat shivering in the shallows, absolutely terrified to take the rope until Hermione waded in fully dressed.

'Hey,' she said softly. 'It's OK. I've got you. You're safe now.'

It reminded Harriet of times gone by, when she'd been too scared to run at the vault at school. Hermione had always been there, silent and steadfast at her side. It made her want to cry.

They did a lot of crying. They cried for their parents. Hermione cried because she was afraid of becoming a mother. Harriet cried about Dan and then about Jesse. Even Celine cried. She wasn't quite sure why, she said. She just felt like it.

On the last night, they sat around the fire toasting marsh-mallows. With the crack of twigs in the background, as squirrels threw things at them from the trees, Spike, his eyes ever wider, told them about the last time they'd come up here from town and Celine had given Maud a driving lesson. Apparently, Maud had backed into a ditch and the car had turned on its side. They had had to go and get help from a man who lived on one of the farms nearby and he'd taken them in his tractor to try and pull the car out.

'There were tomato ketchup chips on the floor,' Maisie interrupted

'I know,' Spike said. *'I'm* telling it.'

'Let him tell it, Maisie,' Celine said softly.

'He went and tried to pull the car out and it got stuck on something and the whole bumper just *came away from the car.'*

His eyes shone like stars.

'He's not very good at stories,' Maisie said. 'Anyway, Spike, you got it wrong. We were staying at Lake Bernard Park that time. Lake Bernard is way better than here,' she explained, for Harriet and Hermione's benefit.

'They just think that because they sell ice cream and chips there,' Celine pointed out.

Harriet slipped away from the group around the fire and went to sit on her own by the water's edge. It was an unbelievably clear night. The sky looked as though a child had just hurled a pot of glitter at it.

She wondered if her parents were up there anywhere, looking down on them.

'Room for a large one?'

Harriet shifted up a little so Hermione could wedge herself between her and a tree stump.

'Do you think they'd be pleased?'

'Who?'

'Mum and Dad,' Hermione said. 'That's who you were thinking about, isn't it?'

'Yes,' Harriet said. 'Silly, really, huh?'

'Not at all. I think about them too. More now the baby's on the way. I was too wrapped up in myself before. Too selfish.'

'They'd be pleased to have a grandchild,' Harriet said.

'Even under the rather dubious circumstances of its conception?' Hermione laughed.

'Of course.' Harriet looked around at the moonlit lake. 'This is such a lovely place. I'm glad you brought me here.'

'I like it too. Although I *am* looking forward to being near a shop again.'

'What will you do now?' Harriet said. 'Stay here?'

'In the cabin?'

'In Toronto,' Harriet said. 'You have nice friends. Celine's lovely.'

'Yes.' Hermione smiled. 'Yes. She is, isn't she? I was thinking, though. I might come home.'

'Home?'

'To Bath.'

'Really?'

'Would you mind?' Hermione said. 'Could we stay with you for a bit?'

'Of course,' Harriet said, delighted. 'I'm so glad you got back in touch,' she said shyly.

'Me too,' Hermione said. 'Oof.'

'What?' Harriet panicked. 'Oh, God. You're not having the baby, are you? Not here.'

'Just a kick,' Hermione said. 'The little one's saying she agrees with us.'

ARTHUR

Arthur Blewitt's last day started off well, considering.

At least, if there was anything different about it, it wasn't anything you might notice. There was no sense of impending disaster. No underlying feeling of doom. Nothing like that at all. So far, the only sign of the massive heart attack that was about to claim his life as he drove to the school in Toronto where he worked as a janitor was the odd blast of acid indigestion, which he thought he'd put paid to with a dose of Pepto Bismol.

The day had started off as usual. Everything had been pleasingly normal. His breakfast, served at the table by the window. It was even the right table cloth. His favourite emerald-green chenille. He liked the way it changed colour, depending on which way he ran his finger across it. Recently, Mother had been using the dark red baize one more. It irked him. So he was glad to see the green one back in its rightful place.

Breakfast had been the same as usual. Eggs over easy, served with a few fried potatoes and a pinch of salt. Just the way he liked it.

He chewed noisily, his lumpy tapioca cheeks bulging with the food as he worked steadily through it. Unbeknown to him, his mother always told her friends that Arthur's cheeks were the reason he'd never had a girlfriend. He'd had terrible acne as a boy. It was a shame for him.

What Mother didn't know was that there had been somebody once. Her name was Gloria and she worked in the café across the road. He'd taken her out a few times, when he was supposed to be out getting fit. Not that he'd told Mother, of course. She would say that Gloria was a brassy name. The girl was probably no better than she should be. A gold digger, no doubt. And then Mother would be cock-a-doodle-doo with I told you sos when it all went wrong.

Still, Gloria had packed him up when he asked her to pay for her cup of tea. She'd said it was the last straw. That there had been any straws at all was news to Arthur. He had never been anything but fair. He always made sure they split everything down the middle. Hot dogs from the stall near the park. Drinks at a bar. A Molson for him and a grapefruit juice for Gloria. He'd never made her pay for anything she hadn't had. Not once. As he watched her walk away, her big bottom wiggling seductively under her bright cotton skirt, he felt a familiar stirring in his loins and thanked the good Lord for the tight cotton underpants he wore. This was neither the time nor the place for an embarrassing erection. He would log the image of Gloria and her glorious bouncy bottom in his mind for when he was alone in the dark with his right hand and a box of Kleenex for company.

This morning, he ate the last of his eggs and put on his spectacles to drive the clapped-out Cadillac that had belonged to his late father the short distance to work. It was the one thing about his job Arthur didn't like. He was a bit afraid of other vehicles. Especially the lorries. And the streetcars, which hurtled along at quite a pace.

As he turned the key in the ignition, the engine wheezed to life and, carefully releasing the hand-brake, Arthur turned nervously into the relentless stream of traffic.

It was as he turned the corner into Madison Avenue that it happened. A jolt of pain shot up his left arm, sending a ring of fire into his chest. He couldn't breathe. Clasping the collar of his brown uniform, he was vaguely aware of the car snaking from side to side but he was powerless – utterly powerless – to do a darned thing about it.

HARRIET

arriet and Celine heard the screech of tyres in the street and ran outside in time to see Arthur Blewitt's geriatric Cadillac hit Hermione from the side, sending her looping through the air. It happened so quickly that Harriet barely had a chance to register that the green-clad figure lying, like a broken swan, in the road was her sister before the street went haywire and everyone rushed to where Arthur's car, bumped and bent in a dozen places, was blaring its horn in the middle of the street.

Celine yelled at Maud to get the kids inside and call 911 as Harriet pushed her way blindly through the rapidly gathering crush of rubber-neckers and doom-seekers to get to her sister. God. Please let her and the baby be all right.

'This guy is dead,' one man, bent over the figure crumpled at the steering wheel of the car, yelled.

'What about the girl?'

Harriet ran to where Hermione was lying in the middle of the road, surrounded by absurdly personal items. Her bag had come open and the asphalt surface of the street was scattered with her things. A lipstick. A pack of chewing gum. Spare underwear.

Her heart twizzled with sympathy and recognition. Hermione had carried a spare pair of knickers around with her ever since, aged six or seven, she'd packed a bag with grapes and seven pairs of Mr Men pants each, and announced that she and Harriet were running away. They had got as far as the lamp post around the corner before Isaac had swung by in the Triumph Herald to tempt them home with the offer of fish, chips and a Wally.

'Is she OK?' A man was clambering through the squash of onlookers. 'I'm a doctor.'

Harriet nodded. Hermione looked absolutely fine. There wasn't a mark on her. No cuts or grazes. Not a scratch.

The ambulance summoned by Maud stopped and two paramedics pushed their way through the crowd.

'What happened?'

'We were just having brunch,' Harriet said blankly.

It had been Hermione's idea to go out for the champagne.

They had all been at Celine's having more doughnuts and coffee for breakfast. Since coming back to Toronto; bronzed and relaxed, Harriet and Hermione had spent a lot of time at Celine's. She had the most amazing garden, filled with scented plants and herbs for cooking. A gracious rosemary hedge ran along the whole of one side. There was thyme, speckled with tiny silver-lilac flowers. Sage.

This morning, as Maisie and Spike chirruped away, quarrelling over who got the apple fritter and who was left with the Boston crème, so that Celine had threatened to throw a cover over the pair of them if they didn't keep quiet, Hermione had raised her glass of orange juice.

'I think we should have a toast.'

'OK,' Celine, Harriet and Maud chorused. 'What are we toasting?'

'Friendship.' Hermione grinned. 'New beginnings.'

'New beginnings,' Harriet said. 'I'll definitely drink to that.'

'You know what?' Hermione put down her juice. 'This doesn't quite cut it, does it? I think we need champagne.'

'Great.' Maud's eyes sparkled. 'Do I get some?'

'You get half a glass!' Celine and Hermione said at exactly the same moment, before dissolving in giggles.

'I might go to the liquor store.' Hermione got to her feet. 'Is one bottle enough, d'you think?'

'Are you sure?' Harriet had asked her. 'We're fine with this. Really. And you shouldn't—'

'Shouldn't, schmouldn't.' Hermione looked down at her tummy. 'The little one's cooked now. Who knows, it might even help her on her way a bit. Come on. Let's live a little. It's only a glass of champagne. It isn't going to kill me, is it?'

Harriet looked to where a smash of broken glass and a froth of bubbles were fizzing, in pointless celebration, all over the road.

She watched, helplessly, as Hermione was strapped onto a stretcher and loaded into the ambulance.

'Can I go with her?'

'You a relative?'

'Yes,' Harriet said desperately. 'I'm her sister.'

The journey to the hospital felt like forever. The ambulance made such a weedy noise compared to those back home. It didn't sound urgent at all. She didn't know if that was a good or a bad thing.

'How is she?' she asked the man leaning over her sister.

He pulled a face.

'What's that supposed to mean?' She flew to his side. 'She's fine. She has to be. I've only just got her back.'

'You just sit down, ma'am,' he said. 'We're doing all we can.'

'But she was fine,' Harriet protested. 'I saw her. There wasn't a scratch on her.'

'We'll be there any minute now.' He smiled at her. 'Then I guess we'll know more.'

'Does this thing go any faster?' Harriet said.

At the hospital, Hermione was whisked straight into the emergency room and Harriet was left with a lurching, sickening feeling in her stomach as she waited for Celine and the others to arrive. Celine had had to call her sister to come and take care of Spike and Maisie because Maud had insisted on coming to the hospital too.

'How is she?' Celine, swiftly followed by a determined-looking Maud, came running through the sliding double doors.

'I don't know.' Harriet pulled helplessly at the cuff of her white hoodie. 'They won't tell me anything. All they'll say is that she's not good. Which can't be right, can it? You saw her. There wasn't even any blood. That has to be good, right?'

'I don't know.' Celine shook her head uselessly. 'I honestly just don't know.'

They sat in the relatives' room for what felt like days. Weeks. Harriet tucked her small, cold hand into Celine's slightly larger, warmer one as the clock ticked. At last, the door opened and a doctor came in, nervously rubbing his hands.

Harriet and Celine both jumped up as though they'd been stung.

'Miss Harker?'

'Yes.' Harriet stepped forward. 'How is she?'

'Miss Harker.' The doctor's face was grave. 'There's no easy way to say this.'

No!

'Your sister has suffered serious head injuries.'

'But she'll be OK,' Harriet said. 'Won't she?'

The doctor cleared his throat. 'There are certain tests we can do to determine cranial activity,' he said. 'But I'm afraid the outlook isn't great. We'd like to operate as soon as possible.'

444

'Operate?' Harriet said numbly. 'What for?'

'There is every indication that the baby is fine.' The doctor checked his watch. 'The little fella's doing OK, considering. But there are certain risks.'

'Risks? What risks?'

'There is a possibility that he may become starved of oxygen if we leave him in there too long. It might be best if we got him out as soon as possible. Would that be OK with you?'

'Why are you asking me?' Harriet said.

'As the next of kin . . .'

Next of kin.

She'd spent the last fifteen years wondering about her next of kin. Now here she was, in a strange hospital in a foreign land, making decisions on her behalf.

It was crazy.

As the clock ticked on, Harriet was completely numb. She was vaguely aware of Josh arriving, his face white and pinched with shock. Afterwards, she thought she could remember Josh and Celine making polite conversation, but she had absolutely no idea what they said to each other, even though they were right there with her. They sounded like the teacher in Charlie Brown cartoons. Wah Wah Wah Waaaaaaaaaah!

Any moment now, she would wake up in her clean white bed in Bath and find this had all been a dream.

After what seemed like an age, Hermione's surgeon came into the waiting room.

'The baby?' Harriet asked.

'He's in the high dependency unit,' the surgeon told her. 'It's just a precaution, seeing as he's pre-term.'

'And Hermione?'

'I'm afraid we've had the results of your sister's tests back.'

'And?'

'It isn't looking good, I'm afraid. There is no sign of cerebral activity.'

'No,' Harriet gasped. 'There must be.'

The surgeon looked grave. 'I'm afraid your sister is brain dead, Miss Harker.'

'Please,' Harriet said. 'She can't be. She wouldn't leave me. Not again. Not now. There must be something you can do.' Harriet sobbed. 'Can you not do the tests again?'

'They will show the same result, Miss Harker.'

'Can I see her?' Harriet stammered.

'Follow me.'

Harriet was taken into a stark room filled with the horrible hiss and suck of the ventilator as it rose and fell. Hermione lay under a sheet on the bed, deathly pale, but still perfect in every way.

'She's still breathing,' Harriet said. 'That's good, right?'

'The machines are keeping her alive, Miss Harker.'

'The machines?'

'She isn't breathing for herself.'

'What does that mean?'

The surgeon scratched his head. He looked upset. 'I'm afraid it means that at some point we will have to ask you for permission to turn off your sister's means of life support.'

'Kill her?' Harriet said. 'No way.'

'You don't have to decide today,' the surgeon said. 'You can take as much time as you need.'

'It doesn't matter how much time I take,' Harriet said. 'The answer's still no. I've only just got her back. I can't let her go now. She promised,' she wailed. 'She promised she wouldn't leave me again.'

'I'm just asking you to think about it.'

'She looks fine.' Harriet looked at her sister, so peaceful on the starched white hospital pillow. 'How do you know she's not going to wake up? She could wake up at any moment. And you're asking me to let her die?'

'She isn't going to wake up.' The surgeon's voice was calm. Patient. 'We've done all the tests. Your sister suffered massive head injuries. There is no brain activity. I'm so sorry. Would you like me to find your friends?'

'Yes,' Harriet said. 'Yes please.'

Celine and Josh floated in like a pair of ghosts. Josh's face looked as though it had been completely leached of blood. Harriet supposed she must look the same.

'I sent Maud home,' Celine said. 'She wasn't dealing with all this. What have they said?'

'They say . . .' Harriet struggled to get the words out. 'They say I have to let her go.'

A terrible, strangled sound rent the air. It was Josh. He'd fallen to his knees and was covering his face and head with his arms as though trying to protect himself from the news. Harriet watched through a veil of misery as Celine squatted down and gathered him into her arms like a mother hen.

'I love her,' Josh said. 'I love her like life itself. I wasted so much time.'

'You did what you thought was right,' Celine told him. 'You gave her space to find out what you already knew. She respected you for that.'

'It's OK,' Harriet said in a flat voice that didn't sound like her at all. 'I won't let them take her away, Josh. I'll just keep saying no till they get it into their thick skulls that we're going to fight this.'

Celine went over to Hermione and, oh so gently, placed the palm of her hand against her forehead.

'It doesn't really look like her,' she said sadly. 'Does it?'

'She'll get better,' Harriet said. 'I might bring some of her make-up in tomorrow. See if we can't brighten her up a bit.'

'I'll bring in her kimono,' Josh said. 'She loves that kimono. That ought to make her feel better.'

'Guys!' Celine said softly.

'We could get some flowers,' Harriet said. 'Roses. Sky blue-pink roses. They were always her favourites.'

'Good idea.'

'Guys,' Celine said. 'Do you think that's really what she'd want?'

'Of course,' Harriet said. 'She loves roses.'

'I mean,' Celine said, 'do you think she'd want us to let her go on living like this?'

'It's a life,' Harriet said staunchly. 'Surely that's better than no life at all.'

'What did you think about?' Celine said. 'All that time, when you were waiting to find Hermione again, how did you think of her?'

Harriet closed her eyes.

'What can you see?'

'I can see Hermione coming down the stairs,' Harriet said slowly. 'She's just got ready for our eighteenth birthday party and she wants to show off her outfit.'

'How does she look?'

'Amazing,' Harriet said.

'What's she doing?'

'She's smiling,' Harriet said. 'Laughing. She knows she looks amazing and she's lapping up all the attention.'

'Do you think she'd like it if she knew she was going to have to spend the last years of her life lying in a hospital bed?' Celine said gently. 'Do you think she'd look that happy if she knew she was going to be fed mush through a tube? Or do you think she'd prefer us to let her go?'

She was right. Harriet knew she was right. Had known it all along. But it seemed preposterous, nonetheless. This morning, Hermione had been

449

laughing and eating with the rest of them in Celine's sunny garden. How could it have come to this so quickly?

Was that what Jesse had meant that time when he talked about fate? Had this always been going to happen? As Hermione selected her maple dip doughnut from the box this morning, had her cards already been marked? Was somebody up there secretly urging her to choose well, because this was going to be the last doughnut she was ever going to eat? Or did it not work like that? Was it all just a great big game of 'Eeeney meeny miney mo' after all?

'I'm not saying you should decide now,' Celine said. 'I'm just saying have a think about what Hermione would want.'

'I know,' Harriet sobbed. 'I just need time.'

Hermione died two days later, at seven o'clock in the evening. A time when, as a teenager, she would have just been getting ready to go out, excitedly putting on make-up as the radio blared in her bedroom. It was a good time for her to go. A time when she'd always been ready for anything, as long as she had her lipstick and cigarettes with her. It had taken Harriet and Josh two days to pluck up the courage to do this. As Josh, Celine and Harriet gathered around the bed, Harriet placed a bunch of sky blue-pink roses on Hermione's chest and took her sister's hands in her own.

'I hope I'm doing the right thing,' she said, her

voice wobbling. 'I can't believe I'm having to do it at all. But I think you'd want me to let you go. I . . .' she heaved. 'I'm so glad we found each other again. It's a privilege to have had you as a sister.' Her voice shook so much she could hardly carry on, but she knew she had to. There wouldn't be any second chances this time.

'And you'll be in my heart wherever I am. You always were. We never left each other. Not really. I hope . . .' She took a deep breath. 'I hope that somewhere up there, someone's putting on a great big party for you.'

She nodded to the nurse, who calmly leaned forward and flipped the switch on the ventilator.

'Bye, Hermione,' she said, as the bleep from the machine stopped. 'I love you.'

TORONTO

Everybody was going to say something at the funeral.

It was Josh's idea. With eyes that were red-rimmed and rheumy with misery, he explained to Harriet that they had decided to do the eulogy between them.

'Is that OK with you?' He gulped. 'I mean. She was my best friend. I would like to . . .'

'Say what you want,' Harriet said blankly. She felt as though none of this was really happening. She'd been walking around in a daze. For some reason, the only person she'd been able to speak to was Dan. She'd called him on the night of Hermione's death. She'd had to. She'd needed to speak to somebody who knew her well. Better than Josh and Celine.

'Harry.' He'd sounded pleased to hear from her. 'How are you getting on over there? What's it like being with your sister again? Lizzy told me all about it. She's back in the land of the living, you'll be pleased to know.'

Harriet winced.

'She and Conrad are talking it through,' he said.

452

'Best thing for them, I reckon. They obviously love each other very much. And he's a reasonable man. He knows she's been through a bad time of it.'

'There was an accident,' Harriet said in a monotone voice.

'An accident?' Dan sounded worried. 'Are you OK?'

'I'm fine,' Harriet said. 'It was Hermione who had the accident.'

'Is she OK?' Dan said. 'No bones broken, I hope.'

'She's dead.'

It was awful at the crematorium. As she, Josh and Celine gathered outside, Harriet's attention was drawn to a notice, pinned on the door. A list of people due to be cremated that day. Hermione's name was third on the list. Eleven hundred hours.

It seemed faintly ridiculous, seeing it in black and white like that. It looked so innocuous. As though it were nothing more than a school roll call or a dentist's appointment schedule. But it wasn't. It was a list of dead people, all waiting to be burned.

It was horrific. It couldn't be real.

'She shouldn't be on there,' Harriet said. 'This is all wrong. Somebody must have made a mistake.'

'Shh.' Celine held out her hand. Harriet took it gratefully. She wasn't sure where she would have been without Celine these past few days. She'd been a rock. A brick. She'd sent Maud and Spike to stay with their father, who had found a new flat to rent in a fairly grotty part of town. It was better that way. She said she didn't want there to be any bad feeling between him and the kids. This way, they would see him as a person who might even be relied on in a time of crisis, as opposed to the useless philanderer he was. And in her own home she looked after Josh and Harriet, making them soup they couldn't eat and turning down beds they wouldn't get a good night's sleep in. But most of all she just listened.

'I'd only just got her back,' Harriet croaked now. 'I'd just found her.'

'I know.'

Hermione's coffin stood on the plinth at the front, swamped with sweet summer flowers. As Harriet clamped her teeth shut to prevent herself from screaming at the unfairness of it all, Josh saw Greg file into a pew on the other side of the room and stiffened.

'Shh.' Celine put a warning hand on his arm. 'You don't want this to be remembered as the day it all kicked off, do you? She wouldn't want that.'

When it was time, Celine, her face working, got up and paid tribute to a friend she hadn't known long but who had touched her in so many ways. She called her funny and gorgeous. Josh told an amusing story about shopping for clothes, which was meant to demonstrate her indomitable zest for life.

Harriet dreaded the moment when she was going to have to get up and add her piece. She shouldn't be having to do this. It wasn't fair. The crematorium was packed to the rafters for her sister and yet she'd never felt more alone. Celine was lovely. And Josh was a gem. But it wasn't Celine and Josh she needed. It was Hermione.

She longed to get home to see Lizzy. She'd called her the day after it had happened. Dan had told her about the accident and she'd phoned in tears. She just wanted to give Harriet a big hug, she said. But she couldn't. She was all the way over in England.

All too soon, it was Harriet's turn to speak. As she stood up and made her way to the microphone, a respectful hush fell on the congregation. She had chosen the poem because it best represented what she wanted to say. A great, achy rush filled her throat and mouth as she started to speak, and the tears glittered behind her eyes. But she held them back long enough to do her sister justice.

'I am standing on a seashore A ship sails in the
    morning breeze and starts for the ocean
She is an object of beauty and I stand watching
    her Till at last she fades on the horizon and
    someone at my side says "She is gone"

Gone! Where?
Gone from my sight – that is all
She is just as large in the masts, hull and spars
    as she was when I saw her

And just as able to bear her load of living
   freight to its destination
The diminished size and total loss of sight is in
   me, not in her

And just at the moment when someone at my
   side says
"She is gone"
There are others who are watching her coming,
   and other voices take up a global shout
"Here she comes"
and that is dying.'

There were tears rolling down her face, smudging
the ink on the paper she'd written the poem out
on. The ink was peacock blue, she realised now
for the first time. The pen had been the first one
that had come to hand as she searched the unbear-
able quiet of Hermione's house for something to
copy it down with.

Afterwards, they went back to the house. Harriet
was reminded of the fish paste sandwiches and tea
Vinegar had laid on for her own parents as she
watched friends and colleagues of the sister she'd
hardly known eat smoked salmon nibbly things
and drink champagne. Josh had insisted on the
champagne. It was the only thing to have, he said,
when they'd made the list for the caterer. Hermione
never went anywhere without it. She would want
to go out to the popping of bubbles. In one way,
it was nice to know her sister had had so many

friends. One woman, a pretty blonde called Sylvie, had come over from London when she'd heard. She'd come over and introduced herself to Harriet, her face streaming with tears. She said nice things about Hermione. Everybody did.

Harriet went over towards the window to take a breather. It was so hot today. Muggy. She needed some air.

'Harriert?'

Harriet turned her head to see a familiar figure leaning against the door frame.

'Dan! What are you doing here?'

'I just thought you might need to see a friendly face.'

Harriet was filled with a rush of gratitude.

'I'm so sorry, Dan.'

'Sorry?' His kind face crinkled with confusion.'Sorry for what?'

'For everything,' Harriet said. 'For not being honest with you. I let you think my sister was dead for all that time.'

'Shh,' Dan said. 'It doesn't matter now.'

'It doesn't?'

'Of course not,' Dan said. 'What matters is that you need your friends around you right now. And I'm here.'

'You're a nice man, Dan,' Harriet said sadly. 'I shouldn't have just let you go like that. I should have fought harder for you.'

'No,' Dan said. 'You shouldn't have.'

'What?'

'We weren't quite right,' Dan said. 'I know that now. We married for all the wrong reasons. We were young.'

'We were happy, though.'

'We were,' Dan said. 'We had some great times. But it's good that we can let it end like this. That way we'll always be in each other's lives.'

'We will be.' Harriet's voice wobbled. 'Won't we?'

'Of course. Actually,' he rubbed his chin, 'there is something you can do for me.'

'Of course,' Harriet said. 'Whatever.'

'You can go outside in the hall and get my stuff,' Dan said. 'I left it out there. I have to go to the loo. It's just one package. Do you mind?'

'Of course not.'

Harriet went into the hall and almost fainted from shock.

'Jesse!'

'Lizzy sends her apologies,' he said. 'She's kind of busy working on her marriage right now. And Joe sends his love and sympathy. He called last night. He's in Mexico, getting up to I don't know what.'

Harriet turned to walk away. After what she'd seen Hermione go through with Greg, she never wanted to let any man get the better of her again.

Jesse grabbed her hand, forcing her to turn round and face him. 'Harriet?'

'What?'

'I'm so sorry. About your sister.'

'Thank you.' Harriet felt her bottom lip tremble.

'It's tragic,' Jesse said. 'You've had so much loss in your life. I wish I could make it better.'

'My sister is dead,' Harriet said dully. 'Nothing can make it any better.'

'Won't you let me be here for you at least?' Jesse's eyes were suspiciously swimmy. 'I thought . . . we were special. We had something. We fitted.'

'So did I,' Harriet told him.

'So why?' Jesse looked confused. 'Why go and not say anything? I got back from work to find a pile of paint cans in the hall. I tried phoning.'

'I know.'

'What did I do wrong, Harry?' Jesse looked very upset. 'Tell me that, at least.'

'You know what you did, Jesse.'

'What?'

'You two-timed me.'

'I *what*?'

'I came to the flat.' Harriet swallowed hard. 'And she was there, Jesse. I saw her with my own eyes.'

'Saw who?'

'Your bit of fluff,' Harriet said. 'Blonde hair. She was wearing your T-shirt.'

Jesse covered his face with his hands.

'So I'm right.' Harriet's heart sank. For a fleeting moment, she'd hoped there might be some other explanation. But there wasn't. Of course there wasn't. Jesse had been sleeping with the girl. He hadn't even bothered to deny it.

'No,' Jesse said. 'You couldn't be more wrong.'

459

'It's disgusting,' Harriet told him. 'She's only about sixteen.'

'Fifteen,' Jesse said. 'And far too old for her age.'

'What?'

'Harriet.' Jesse took her chin between his thumb and forefinger and kissed her nose. 'Delilah is my daughter.'

'You don't have a daughter.'

'I do,' Jesse said. 'We were young, her mother and me. We were stupid. She got pregnant when we were eighteen and was determined to keep the baby whatever. We split up. But I've always tried to see Delilah whenever I can. Which isn't easy. She's a feisty little minx. Lives up to her name.'

'But . . .' Harriet's mouth fell open. 'I asked her if you were together. She let me think . . .'

'Exactly.' Jesse smoothed her hair from her forehead. 'She let you think it. Delilah's going through a difficult time right now. Her mother and step-father have just split up and she's angry. In her eyes, if she can't be happy, she's going to make damn sure nobody else is. Especially not me. It was her with the parrot, you know. I managed to worm that out of her. No wonder she'd been trying to visit me every day since the bloody creature arrived. She'd been phoning every day saying she was bored at home and wanting to come down.'

Harriet remembered the phone call in the bar. The angry female voice she'd assumed was Clare's on the other end of Jesse's mobile.

'So she fed poor Miss Scarlett those pills?'

'No.' Jesse shook his head. 'Thank God. It was some older boy she was trying to impress. The bastard persuaded her to let him send it to my address and she wanted him to like her so she agreed.' He smiled weakly. 'I'll be taking a much firmer line in future, I promise.'

'I'm pleased to hear it.'

'So do we have a future?' Jesse pulled her towards him and peppered the top of her head with kisses. 'Do you think? Are you going to be OK?'

For the first time in days, Harriet felt herself relax. 'I'm getting there.'

Dan went back to England straight after the funeral, where, by all accounts, a sweet little blonde was waiting for him. Harriet was pleased for him. Jesse stayed to help Harriet and Josh sort out Hermione's house. Harriet was spending a lot of time at the hospital with Hermione's baby. He was so small. So vulnerable. And nobody else seemed to bother with him.

The first time, poking her fingers through the glass as she looked at the tiny head, no bigger than a wizened apple and covered in a white fleece bonnet, she'd felt stupidly shy. He might be tiny but his eyes were as deep as pools. It was almost as though he knew her already. She wondered if he could detect that she was an impostor. Not his mother at all.

'This is your Aunt Harriet speaking,' she said

gently. 'And I just want to let you know that everything's going to be OK. Your situation isn't ideal. You've lost your mummy. And your father isn't the best. But nobody's perfect. And he isn't a bad dad. And, of course,' she said shyly, 'you'll always have me. I promise to be a good aunty. You can come and stay with me in England whenever you like.'

It felt silly at first, speaking to this tiny creature with cling film skin. But his big brown eyes were so intelligent. She was sure he could understand some of what she was saying so she kept on. She talked. She sang. She read stories and jingled rattles. After a while, the nurses told her he always seemed calmer after her visits.

One afternoon, as she read to him from *The Tiger Who Came To Tea*, the door opened and somebody peered in.

'Greg'. Harriet felt awkward. They hadn't really been introduced. Not properly.

He looked awful. Really seedy. His hair was stiff with dirt, his eyes were bloodshot and the unpalatable stench of old booze lingered on his breath.

'Celine's taken my kids back.' Greg lurched towards a chair. 'Says I can't cope. Called me a drunk.' He nodded towards Harriet's nephew. 'He's all I've got now.'

Harriet picked up her stuff. Greg was making her feel uncomfortable. It struck her as truly horrible that this man should be responsible for her nephew's welfare. But she didn't know what else to do about it. He was the child's father, wasn't he?

All the same, she dreaded the day when she had to go back to England and leave her darling nephew in Greg's care. It would feel as though she was letting Hermione down.

She was taking the subway train back when she suddenly felt dizzy. The next thing she knew, her legs gave way.

She woke up in bed at Hermione's.

'What happened?'

'You collapsed,' Jesse said. 'On the subway. Gave us all quite a fright. Don't worry,' he said. 'The doctor says it's just flu. And stress. You need to rest.'

'How long have I been asleep?'

Twenty-four hours,' Jesse said. 'Maybe more.'

Harriet struggled to get out of bed.

'Where do you think you're going?'

'I have to go to the hospital. Make sure the baby's OK.'

'You're not going anywhere,' Jesse said. 'Not in this state.'

Harriet tried to climb out of bed but her legs were too cotton woolly to stand.

'Now perhaps you'll believe me,' Jesse said. 'You haven't eaten for days. Please. Let me do all the worrying. Just get some rest. Close your eyes. I'll bring you some soup.'

Harriet drifted in her woozy state for days. Sometimes, her mind consciously wanted to get up and about, but her legs wouldn't let her. Others, she just slept on and on. After what must have been days, she woke up to find that whatever was wrong with her had gone completely. She felt refreshed. For a moment, she was vaguely aware of the pressing need to do something but couldn't quite think what it was. And then her gaze came to rest on the big baby book Hermione had been so proud off, and she was galvanised into action.

The house was empty as she went about the business of dressing herself. She still felt a little wobbly, so she took a cab to the hospital to be on the safe side.

There was somebody in her nephew's room. She could hear voices.

She rushed into the room. Please not Greg. Don't let him be bonding too much with his son. He would try to take him away from her.

'Hi.' Jesse looked up as she came in. 'Feeling better?'

'Jesse! What are you doing here?'

'Taking on the mantle of surrogate uncle, of course.'

'I heard voices.'

Jesse held up the book he had in his hand. '*Danny Champion of the World*,' he said. 'My favourite book. I've read it about a thousand times. I thought it might spur the little chap on a bit.'

'You sweet man,' Harriet said. 'I love you.'

'And I love you,' Jesse said. 'When we get back to normal, I'll show you just how much.'

'There aren't any more secret daughters lurking, are there?' Harriet said. 'I'm not sure I could bear it.'

'No.' Jesse laughed. 'I can promise you that.'

'Everything OK?' A nurse breezed in.

'Fine.' Jesse beamed.

'How is he?' Harriet nodded at the baby.

'Coming on in leaps and bounds.' The nurse picked up the baby. 'He'll be ready to go home soon. Want to change him?'

'Sure.' Harriet held out her arms. 'What do I do?'

'It'll come naturally.' The nurse laughed. 'Here.'

Harriet placed the tiny baby down on a fluffy white towel, her heart turning over as he kicked his little legs. She couldn't let him go. Not to Greg. But she didn't know what she could do about it.

'Isn't he delicious?' the nurse said.

'Gorgeous.' Harriet looked at the cloud of dark curls adorning his sweet head. 'Hermione had hair like that when she was born. He's dark,' she said, pleased. 'Like her.'

'What's that?' Jesse asked. 'On his bottom?'

'We call it Mongolian blue spot,' the nurse said. 'It's nothing to worry about. But it's on his notes. It can sometimes look like a bruise, so we have to record it. It's quite common in darker-skinned babies.'

'Darker-skinned?' Harriet said.

'That's right.' The nurse beamed. 'Lots of Asian and black babies have it. It'll be the Afro-Caribbean in him. I really wouldn't worry.'

'Afro-Caribbean?' Harriet said quickly. 'Are you sure?'

'Definitely.' The nurse checked the baby's notes.

'So . . .' Harriet said slowly. 'So you're saying this baby's father isn't white.'

'No,' the nurse said. 'Not if the mother was.'

'You're sure,' Harriet said. 'You're absolutely sure?'

'One hundred per cent!' The nurse looked at her. 'I take it that's good news?'

Harriet beamed at her.

'The best,' she said. 'The absolute best.'

The meeting with Hermione's solicitors took so long that Harriet, still wiped out from her illness and exhausted from days of deciding exactly what, from her sister's enormous collection of clutter, should be kept, what should go to charity and what should be thrown away, almost fell asleep. Not expecting to be left anything, and knowing that Hermione's house was rented, which meant at least that nobody would have to go to the bother of selling it, she leant her head back against Jesse's chest as they stood in the dark green room listening to the small egg-headed man read out the last will and testament of Hermione Harker. To be honest, most of it went over her head. The solicitor's voice had a peculiar narcotic quality to it. So she was quite surprised when Jesse shook her out of her daze.

'Did you want to take it now?' The solicitor was looking at Harriet.

'Me?'

'Yes,' the man said drily, wiping big blobs of sweat from his forehead. He raised his voice to the clerk, sitting by the door of his office. 'The child is outside, I believe.'

'Correct.'

The door opened and Celine came in, clutching a tightly swaddled bundle.

'This is Theo.' She handed him to Harriet.

'Theo?' Harriet traced the outline of his silk-soft cheek with her little finger.

'It means A Gift from God,' Celine told her. 'That's what Hermione wanted him called if he was a boy. It said so in the will.'

'What?'

'You heard what the solicitor said, didn't you?' Jesse said.

'No,' Harriet admitted. 'I was asleep.'

'She appointed you the baby's guardian,' Celine said.

'When?'

'A month ago, apparently,' Celine said. 'She must have done it while we were at the lake. She went to Toronto that day, didn't she? She changed her will so that if anything happened to her, the baby would be looked after by you.'

A tear oozed from under Harriet's eyelid. 'She really did that?'

'It seems so.' Celine looked at the baby. 'So he wasn't Greg's all along, eh? Who'd have thought it? What a dark horse.'

'She always was.' Harriet laughed. 'You should read her diary. Do you think she knew? That he wasn't Greg's, I mean?'

'No,' Celine said. 'She might have been a bit haphazard. But she wasn't a liar.'

Harriet gazed lovingly at her new responsibility. 'What about you, Josh? You wanted to be the baby's dad.'

'Actually,' Josh looked sheepish, 'I'd have been pretty crap, all things considered. And Bernie and I are thinking of doing some travelling. But I'd like to visit,' he added.

'I'll second that.' Celine nodded. 'You can expect us all in Bath very soon.'

Harriet looked at the solicitor. 'What happens if I say no?'

'Difficult to say.' The solicitor cleared his throat. 'Attempts will be made to find the child's father. Failing that, he will go into care.'

'You're not saying no?' Jesse looked shocked.

'Of course not,' Harriet said. 'I'm just scared. How will I know if I'm doing it right?'

'You'll just know,' Celine said. 'Take it from me. I've had three. And mine turned out OK, didn't they? Even with the slight handicap of having Greg in their lives for the most part.'

'But what will I tell him?' Harriet said. 'How will I make sure he knows who his mother was? I'd only just found her.' She wiped a tear from her cheek with her cuff. 'I didn't have time to get to know her. How will I keep her alive for him?'

Jesse took her head in his hands and looked her straight in the eye.

'She'll be there whenever you sing to him,' he said. 'And she'll be there when you bath him and put him to bed. She'll be there when you read to him last thing at night. Because you knew her better than you think. She was a part of you. She'll always be there somewhere.'

Still holding the baby, Harriet turned to look at him. 'Do you honestly believe that?'

'Yes,' Jesse said. 'I honestly do.'

'Vol-au-vents.' Lizzy wafted a tray of volcanic ash under Harriet's nose. 'Cremated vol-au-vents. Want one?'

'No thanks.' Harriet looked towards the rug by the French windows as the door opened and Jemima, Lucy and Oscar came tearing into the kitchen and started bouncing like three incorrigible Tiggers. 'What time is everyone arriving?'

'Four,' Lizzy said decisively. 'Which means we'd better get a move on. I still haven't iced the cake.'

'You made Theo's christening cake?'

'Sure,' Lizzy said, as Conrad groaned. 'Why not?'

Happily, things between Lizzy and Conrad were back to normal. He'd accepted her affair. Told her he loved her too much to let her go. Slowly but surely, they had moved on. Conrad was working less, which meant that he and Lizzy got to spend more time together. Crack Nanny, now fully rehabilitated, had moved in, so that Lizzy felt more like a woman and less like a milk cow. And the kids were thriving.

Lizzy nodded towards the rug on the floor, where Theo was giggling as Jesse played 'This Little Piggy' with his toes.

'How are you two doing?' she asked.

'We're taking it one day at a time.' Harriet smiled.

'Jesse's a nice man.'

'I know. He never complains. Theo had him up till gone four last night. God.' She covered her face with her hands. 'I promised myself I wasn't going to do that.'

'What?'

'Discuss sleeping times like an obsessive parent.'

'But you're happy,' Lizzy said. 'With Jesse.'

'Very,' Harriet said. 'Although we're taking it slowly. We've all been through a lot. And Delilah's got her exams coming up. We just want to make things as normal as possible.'

'When's Celine coming?'

'Next week,' Harriet told her. 'She's bringing all the kids. They can't wait to see England. Though Spike is apparently concerned about the food. He's filled his case with O Henry bars.'

'I can't wait to meet them.'

'You'll love them,' Harriet said.

'I'm sure I will.'

'Dan's new girlfriend had the baby,' Harriet remembered. 'Did I tell you?'

'She did?' Lizzy was delighted.

'A girl,' Harriet said. 'Dan called. He's over the moon.'

'And you're cool with that?'

Harriet looked at Jesse, playing on the rug with Theo as Lizzy's children clambered all over him.

'Yes.' She smiled, as the jangling of Lizzy's doorbell heralded the arrival of Theo's christening guests. 'We're cool.'